THE BODLEY HEAD

SAKI

D1627672

The following is a complete list of the books in which
Saki's works were first published in volume form.

THE BODLEY HEAD

SAKI

SELECTED AND INTRODUCED BY

J. W. LAMBERT

SHORT STORIES

THE UNBEARABLE BASSINGTON

BOOK CLUB ASSOCIATES
LONDON

CONTENTS

INTRODUCTION

THERE IS no mystery about the continued popularity of Saki's stories. They make us laugh, they up-end respectability, they provide, in broad terms, unflagging entertainment. The deftness of their wit, the ingenuity of their anecdotes, are as effective as ever. The satire is still relevant, although its context was the luxurious, not to say bloated, world of upper-middle-class Edwardian England.

Puzzles there are, though, about both the man and his work. His stories are gobbled with simple pleasure by many who would have been his natural targets; but more sophisticated minds become aware, even as they relish his evident virtues, of some unease in their appreciation. A minor reason is perhaps Saki's adherence to standards of conduct, of courage, endurance, and loyalty, which can hardly be faulted, but which are felt to be expressed in discredited terms—sentimentally, in fact. More important, behind the artist's showing-up of blind materialism and dimness of spirit loom other, more disturbing qualities: ruthlessness tipping over into cruelty, a purely destructive rage, a remarkable limitation of sympathy, a preoccupation with revenge.

These are attributes familiar enough in serious modern writing, or serious writing of any period for that matter, but disconcerting in one who is read primarily as a humorist. They give Saki a complexity which would not necessarily be of interest for its own sake; but which becomes so because its pressures made him, in advance of his time, into a one-man bridge between the Victorian world (of, for example, W. S. Gilbert) and the nervous vivacity of the post-war world (of, say, Noel Coward) which he did not live to see.

Hector Hugh Munro was born in Akyab, Burma, on December 18, 1870. His family, said to have been proud of its Scottish blood (though he himself seems never

to have shown any particular interest in it), had long
Anglo-Indian military connections. And family pride, I
suppose, can hardly have overlooked an appalling incident
which occurred in India in 1792, to the only son of General
Hector Munro. It was recorded by an eye-witness in
The Gentleman's Magazine of July 1793:

To describe the awful, horrid, and lamentable
accident I have been an eye-witness of, is impossible.
Yesterday morning Mr Downey, of the Company's
troops, Lieut. Pyefinch, poor Mr Munro and myself,
went on shore on Saugur Island to shoot deer. We
saw innumerable tracks of tigers and deer, but still
we were induced to pursue our sport, and did the
whole day. About halfpast three we sat down on the
edge of the jungle, to eat some cold meat sent us
from the ship, and had just commenced our meal,
when Mr Pyefinch and a black servant told us there
was a fine deer within six yards of us. Mr Downey
and myself immediately jumped up to take our guns;
mine was the nearest, and I had just laid hold of it
when I heard a roar, like thunder, and saw an immense royal tiger spring on the unfortunate Munro,
who was sitting down. In a moment his head was
in the beast's mouth, and he rushed into the jungle
with him with as much ease as I could lift a kitten,
tearing him through the thickest bushes and trees,
everything yielding to his monstrous strength. The
agonies of horror, regret, and, I must say, fear (for
there were two tigers, male and female) rushed on
me at once. The only effort I could make was to fire
at him, though the poor youth was still in his mouth.
I relied partly on Providence, partly on my own aim,
and fired a musket. I saw the tiger stagger and agitated (*sic*), and cried out so immediately. Mr Downey
then fired two shots, and I one more. We retired from
the jungle, and, a few minutes after, Mr Munro came
up to us, all over blood, and fell. We took him on our

backs to the boat, and got every medical assistance for him from the *Valentine* East India-man, which lay at anchor near the island, but in vain. He lived 24 hours in the extreme of torture; his head and skull were torn, and broke to pieces, and he was wounded by the claws all over his neck and shoulders; but it was better to take him away, though irrecoverable, than leave him to be devoured limb by limb. We have just read the funeral service over the body, and committed it to the deep. He was an amiable and promising youth.

Saki himself, whose stories abound with animals despatching mere human beings, could hardly have improved on this graphic narrative. The misadventure caught the public fancy in England; it was reproduced in Staffordshire chimney ornaments: 'The Death of Munrow,' showing the victim prone, his head in the jaws of an immense tiger, was for decades a popular adornment of many a cottage hearth. However appalling the state of the poor, no doubt they felt that at least they would be spared that fate; or possibly they all unknowing equated the tiger with the rich and powerful, themselves with its helpless victim; or, more likely still, like Saki himself for that matter, retained a juvenile taste for the gruesome.

Saki's father had as a subaltern taken part in the siege of Lucknow; later he married an Admiral's daughter, became a Major in the Bengal Staff Corps and in due course Inspector-General of the Burma Police, retiring in the rank of Colonel. He was remarkably handsome, and his manner was courtly; he could and did kiss a woman's hand with no little distinction. After middle age his complexion was fresh, his hair and moustaches white, his manner gentle, quiet, and smiling. He smoked cheroots all day, but by way of making up for this had, on his retirement to England, all three sash windows in his bedroom nailed open as wide as possible. His wife had died soon after Hector, the youngest of their three children, was born; and thus, before he was two years old, the future Saki was sent back to England with his brother and sister.

Their father had taken a house, Broadgate Villa, in the village of Pilton, near Barnstaple, North Devon. In it lived his mother, his two sisters, and the three children. The house, Saki's sister* has recalled

> was too dark, verandas kept much of the sunlight out, the flower and vegetable gardens were surrounded by high walls and a hedge, and on rainy days we were kept indoors.
>
> Also fresh air was feared, especially in winter; we slept in rooms with windows shut and shuttered, with only the door open on to the landing to admit stale air. All hygienic ideas were to Aunt Augusta, The Autocrat, 'choc rot,' a word of her own invention.
>
> Then we should have had more country walks than we ever got, there were lovely fields and woods quite handy, but Aunt Augusta wanted shops and gossip—also she was afraid of cows.
>
> Fortunately, there were the three of us, and we lived a life of our own, in which the grown-ups had no part, and to which we admitted only animals and a favourite uncle, Wellesley, who stayed with us about once a year. . . .
>
> Our grandmother, a gentle, dignified old lady, was entirely overruled by her turbulent daughters, who hated each other with a ferocity and intensity worthy of a bigger cause. How it was they were not consumed by the strength of their feelings I don't know. I once asked a friend of the family what had started the antagonism.
>
> 'Jealousy,' she said, 'when your Aunt Tom, who was fifteen years older than Augusta, returned from

* This unhappy woman grew to be so fiercely possessive, first of her brother, then of his memory, that having written her own fragmentary memoir she refused access to, and subsequently destroyed, all Saki's papers.

a long visit to Scotland, where she had been much admired, and spoilt, and found the little sister growing up, also pretty and admired, she became intensely jealous of her—from that time they have always quarrelled.'

Aunt Tom was the most extraordinary woman I have ever known—perhaps a reincarnation of Catherine of Russia. What she meant to know or do, that she did. She had no scruples, never saw when she was hurting people's feelings, was possessed of boundless energy and had not a day's real illness until she was seventy-six.

Her religious convictions would fit into any religion ever invented. She took us regularly to Pilton Church on Sunday mornings. For a long time I was struck by her familiarity with the Psalms, which she apparently repeated without looking at her book, but one day I discovered she was merely murmuring, without saying a word at all, and had put on her long-distance glasses in order to take good stock of the congregation and its clothes. A walk back after church with various neighbours provided material for a dramatic account to Granny (not that she was interested) of the doings of the neighbourhood. Whatever Aunt Tom did was dramatic, and whatever story she repeated, she embroidered. No use to try to get to the end before she intended you should. Without any sense of humour whatever, she was the funniest story-teller I've ever met. She was a colossal humbug, and never knew it.

The other aunt, Augusta, is the one who, more or less, is depicted in *Sredni Vashtar* (*Chronicles of Clovis*). She was the autocrat of Broadgate—a woman of ungovernable temper, of fierce likes and dislikes, imperious, a moral coward, possessing no brains worth speaking of, and a primitive disposition. Naturally the last person who should have been in charge of children.

But the character of the aunt in *The Lumber Room* is Aunt Augusta to the life. 'It was her habit, whenever one of the children fell from grace, to improvise something of a festival nature from which the offender would be rigorously debarred; if all the children sinned collectively they were suddenly informed of a circus in a neighbouring town, a circus of unrivalled merit and uncounted elephants, to which, but for their depravity, they would have been taken that very day.... She was a woman of few ideas, with immense powers of concentration.... Tea that evening was partaken of in a fearsome silence.'

Well do I remember those 'fearsome silences!' Nothing could be said, because it was certain to sound silly, in the vast gloom. With Aunt Tom alone we should have fared much better—she adored Hector as long as he kept off the flower-beds and out of the kitchen garden—but as we could not obey both aunts (I believe each gave us orders which she knew were contrary to those issued by the other), we found it better for ourselves, in the end, to obey Aunt Augusta.

Our best time was during some pitched battle in their internecine warfare, 'with Aunt calling to Aunt like mastodons bellowing across primeval swamps';* we lived our little lives, criticized our 'elders and betters' and rejoiced exceedingly when Aunt Augusta went to bed for a whole day with a headache.

This gave us more scope, and we became more venturesome—Hector always the most daring—even exploring the top story because it was forbidden ground, and contained a mysterious room, the original of *The Lumber Room* in *Beasts and Super-Beasts*.

* P. G. Wodehouse.

Aunt Augusta's religion was not elastic; it was definite and High Church and took her into Barnstaple on Sunday evenings. Neither aunt permitted her religion to come between her and her ruling passion, which was to outwit the other. What they squabbled about never seemed to be of much importance. If Aunt Tom came back from Barnstaple market bearing reports of poultry she had bought at 2s. 6d., Aunt Augusta would know no peace until she had seen a far fatter bird at 2s. 4d. and announced it.

Then a row began—more or less intense, according to the length of time that had elapsed since the last one. Fighting probably relieved their tremendous energy. They never swore, so we heard no bad words. One good effect the quarrelling certainly had on us —it looked so ugly, we never copied them—never in our lives have we three had a row.

The aunts' outside interests lay in politics and the gossip of Pilton. Gardening kept Aunt Tom more or less sane, and making yards of useless embroidery had a soothing influence on Aunt Augusta. From morning to night, whether the jobbing gardener were there or not, Aunt Tom would be busy and dirty. Both Aunts were exceedingly loyal to their friends, who, in their eyes, could do no wrong, and very generous to the poor.

As far as circumstances go, the Munro children were clearly no worse off than many Victorian young. A sense of claustrophobia, private lives, and war against adults sounds through so many accounts of late Victorian childhood; it is astonishing that any of those generations, among the middle and upper classes, should ever have approached any sort of maturity. But what they lost in balance of personality (and who are we of a later, more enlightened age, to boast of that?) they made up in vigour.

Young Hector, though never robust, was a most active child. Sometimes his activity took on a prophetic tinge:

> My earliest recollection of my younger brother was in the nursery at home, where, with my elder brother, Charlie, we had been left alone. Hector seized the long-handled hearth-brush, plunged it into the fire, and chased Charlie and me round the table, shouting 'I'm God, and I'm going to destroy the world.'

Later, he found the pen an acceptable substitute for the cleansing fire. In these years, though, he showed no particular urge to write, but concentrated on drawing. He drew mostly the animals in their lives, and notably the many pets they were allowed to keep—and drew them, oddly, always from memory: already, no doubt, he was well set in a lifelong addiction to active response but spiritual withdrawal. When he did draw other subjects, they were also pointers to his state of mind. A bunch of yokels, hymn-books in hand, illustrate the legend 'Missionary Sunday—"Oh we whose lives are lighted, With wisdom from on high." ' Golfing terms were depicted in a series of drawings which display players being attacked by bison. A limerick

> There was a young girl called O'Brien
> Who sang Sunday-school hymns to a lion,
>   Of this lady there's some
>   In the lion's tum-tum
> And the rest is an angel in Zion

evoked a strikingly unattractive young woman and an exceptionally self-satisfied lion, before and after. The story of Elisha and the Mocking Children also prompted two spirited drawings and a characteristic verse:

> Two bears came forth from their cubless den—
> Their cubless den, for their cubs were robbed—
> And hunted about in search of men
> Till they came to the spot where the Prophet was mobbed.

For men must hunt, tho' bears will fret,
And a cub will provide a good price as a pet
And money is always consoling . . .
Thirty-two corpses lay stretched on the sward,
Thirty-two corpses, or possibly more,
For the bears were too busy their bag to record
And the Saint didn't stay to attend to the score.

Hector is said to have been a keen—and Conservative—politician from the age of seven, and history soon drew his imagination—in a manner foreseeing the 'Schartz-Metterklume Method,' put to good use in one of his best-known stories, and described by his sister:

'You must take the Roundheads' part,' he said to me.

'But I would rather be Royalist,' I objected.

'We can't both be Royalists, so you must be Roundhead.'

(The odd thing is that, from being forced into it, I have remained Roundhead ever since.) So we began the period of the Civil Wars with great delight—it soon became exciting—Hector would gloat over a victory of his side, even rising up in his chair to hurl abuse at the Roundheads, which naturally I wouldn't stand, so I abused back; the governess, being a fool, at last stopped the concerted history lesson, but she couldn't stop us; we only waited until she was off, got down the histories and took the battles at a gallop, going through all the gamut of emotions from depression to exultation, according to the fortune of war. History then and ever afterwards became his favourite study, and as he had a wonderful memory his knowledge of European history from its beginning was remarkable.

Natural history, as well, became a passion—notably in the form of birds-nesting: his collection of eggs was later established in Barnstaple Museum. And he fought interminable battles with toy soldiers.

Nothing here speaks at all obviously of the tensions of this particular childhood. But when he was nine he suffered an attack of what was hazily described as 'brain-fever'—and was most devotedly nursed by both warring aunts. Once recovered, he seemed stronger than before; strong enough to follow his elder brother to a preparatory school at Exmouth—but not on to Charterhouse; for Hector, at the late age of fifteen, began two years at Bedford Grammar School. His sister, the only source of information about these years, states that at both these establishments he was happy, whatever that means.

A significant change in the lives of all the children, but especially of Hector and his sister, came with their father's retirement. Previously he had appeared in their lives, a genial magician from the East, once every four years. Now he devoted himself to them, and above all removed them from the shadow of the Aunts. In Saki's stories frightful fates befell these luckless dames, harvested from many a savage juvenile daydream. In fact, however, they had already begun to shrink in stature as the children grew older, and both were afterwards treated with tolerant affection—as witness a letter written by Hector to his sister a few years later:

> Travelling with Aunt Tom is more exciting than motor-carring. We had four changes and on each occasion she expected the railway company to bring our trunks round on a tray to show that they really had them on the train. Every 10 minutes or so she was prophetically certain that her trunk, containing among other things 'poor mother's lace,' would never arrive at Edinburgh. There are times when I almost wish Aunt Tom had never had a mother. Nothing but a merciful sense of humour brought me through that intermittent unstayable outpour of bemoaning. And at Edinburgh, sure enough, her trunk was missing!

It was in vain that the guard assured her that it would come on in the next train, half-an-hour later; she denounced the vile populace of Bristol and Crewe, who had broken open her box and were even then wearing the maternal lace. I said no one wore lace at 8 o'clock in the morning and persuaded her to get some breakfast in the refreshment-room while we waited for the alleged train. Then a worse thing befell—no baps! There were lovely French rolls but she demanded of the terrified waiter if he thought we had come to Edinburgh to eat bread!

In the midst of our bapless breakfast I went out and lit upon her trunk and got a wee bit laddie to carry it in and lay it at her feet. Aunt Tom received it with faint interest and complained of the absence of baps.

Then we spent a happy hour driving from one hostelry to another in search of rooms, Aunt Tom reiterating the existence of a Writer to the Signet who went away and let his rooms 30 years ago, and ought to be doing it still. 'Anyhow,' she said, 'we are seeing Edinburgh,' much as Moses might have informed the companions of his 40 years' wanderings that they were seeing Asia. Then we came here, and she took rooms after scolding the manageress, servants and entire establishment nearly out of their senses because everything was not to her liking. I hurriedly explained to everyone that my aunt was tired and upset after a long journey, and disappointed at not getting the rooms she had expected; after I had comforted two chambermaids and the boots, who were crying quietly in corners, and coaxed the hotel kitten out of the waste-paper basket, I went to get a shave and a wash—when I came back Aunt Tom was beaming on the whole establishment and saying she should recommend the hotel to all her friends. 'You can easily manage these people,' she remarked at lunch, 'if you only know the way to their

hearts.' She told the manageress that I was fright-
fully particular. I believe we are to be there till
Tuesday morning, and then go into rooms; the hotel
people have earnestly recommended a lot to us.

Aunt Tom really is marvellous; after 16 hours in
the train without a wink of sleep, and an hour spent
in hunting for rooms, her only desire is to go out
and see the shops. She says it was a remarkably comfortable journey; personally I have never known such
an exhausting experience.

The children were indeed almost grown-up when their
father returned from India for good, and took over their
further education. First he removed them to another
house, then took them on a series of prolonged visits to
the Continent. At Etretat in Normandy the trio, so long
immured in one corner of North Devon, took at once to
the cosmopolitan high jinks of the resort. Among the
other young people there were some Russians, providing
the first known link (perhaps even the stimulus) with a
country which was to attract Hector throughout his
life. Next they went to Dresden, and played practical
jokes on the girls' school which occupied the floor below
their *pension*; then on to Potsdam and Berlin, keeping a
score, with typical Munro ferocity, of the number of
paintings of St Sebastian, arrow-pierced, in each art gallery
they visited. Nuremberg particularly delighted Hector's
sharp response to the medieval. In Prague he cut a hair
from the tail of Wallenstein's charger, and leaned out,
while their father hung on to him, to see how far the
defenestrated councillors had to fall.

Davos was to become, in the next few years, almost a
second home to the family; and there, as Ethel Munro
proudly asserts, 'We let ourselves go! My father was soon
nicknamed "the Hen that hatched out ducklings." ' In
short, between sketching, tennis, riding, amateur theatricals and natural history, practical joke followed practical
joke (Hector sent out, for example, scores of invitations to

a non-existent party at a notoriously stuffy hotel). The staid inhabitants of many respectable establishments were ruthlessly mocked; Hector, in fact, was living out Saki's stories before writing them. He was also visiting the poet and critic John Addington Symonds, who lived in Davos. 'He and Hector played chess together, and found,' his sister blandly observes, 'they had a taste for heraldry in common.'

This agreeable life, in Davos and in North Devon, continued for some years. Not until he was twenty-three did the question of Hector's occupation rear its ugly head in any acute form. When it did, a solution was found which as it turned out could hardly have been less suitable. What to and fro of discussion preceded the move we cannot know. Hector and his father were, and remained until the latter's death in 1907, on excellent terms; yet when in June 1893 Hector set out to join the Military Police in Burma, he unquestionably felt that he was suffering a kind of banishment. A passage from *The Unbearable Bassington*, describing Comus Bassington's feelings in Africa, he acknowledged as autobiographical: that in which the exile, drowned in a feverish lassitude, first reads a bad novel which all the same recalls the sights and sounds of home, then watches a group of native children joyfully at play: 'Those wild young human kittens represented the joy of life; he was the outsider, the lonely alien.'

He made the best of things, was delighted by animal and bird life, reproached his sister for failing to see *A Woman of No Importance* and *The Second Mrs Tanqueray* ('The plays of the season; what would I not give to be able to see them!'), and sent her glimpses of a conscientious young officer at work:

For the last three days I have been at this place (can't remember the name, but it's six miles from Mandalay) where a high festival is being held in honour of two local deities of great repute, called the Nats. Their history is briefly this: they were two brothers who were ordered by the king to build a temple here, which they did, but omitted two bricks, for which reason the king killed them, in the impulsive way these Eastern monarchs have. After they were dead they seemed to think they had gone rather cheap and they made themselves so unpleasant about it that the king gave them permission to become deities, and built them a temple, and here they are, don't you know. Just that. The original temple with the vacant places for the missing bricks is still here; this is not an orthodox Buddhist belief but the Nats are held in great esteem in Upper Burma and parts of China, and this show is held here every year in their honour. The whole thing is so new to me that I will describe it at some length. Of course I had to come here as the presence of a European officer is necessary to keep order, and twenty-five police had to be drafted here. No martyr ever suffered so much on account of religion as I have. When I arrived the Nats were being escorted to the river to bathe, accompanied by unearthly music which sent the pony I was riding spinning round like a weathercock in a whirlwind. Then I came to where the chief show is held and to my horror I found a solitary chair had been placed on an elevated platform for my especial use, to which I was conducted with great ceremony; I am not sure the orchestra did not try to strike up the National Anthem. I inquired wildly for Carey, but was told he was with his wife somewhere. I was in terror lest they might expect a speech, and how could I get up and tell this people, replete with the learning of centuries of Eastern civilization, 'this animal will eat rice'? Fortunately the sparring commenced at once and was very absorbing to watch; two men fight with hands and legs and go for each other like cats, the one who draws blood first wins. I was quite disappointed to see them stop as soon as one was scratched. I had hoped (such is our fallen nature) that they would fight to the death and was trying hurriedly to remember whether you turned your thumbs up or down for mercy. Some of the encounters were very exciting, but I had to preserve a calm dignity befitting the representative of Great Britain and Ireland, besides which my chair was in rather a risky position and required careful sitting. Noblesse oblige. Then Carey came and told me that he had got quarters in the monastery grounds . . . and had got me a house adjoining the show-place. Not only does it adjoin the building, but it forms part of it and opens on to the arena! The hours of performance are from 10 a.m. to 3 p.m., and from 8 p.m. to 6 a.m. There are two bands. During performances my dining-room is a sort of dress-circle, so I have to get my meals when I can. As to sleep, it's not kept on the premises, while the heat is so great that you could boil an egg on an iceberg. There are also smells. The acting is not up to much but the audience are evidently charmed with it. I go to bed at ten, finding two hours quite enough, but when I get up at 5.30 the audience are applauding as vigorously as ever. Then I am worried to death by princesses; some of the native magistrates' wives are relatives of the ex-king and fancy themselves accordingly. One old lady, who carries enough jewels for twenty ordinary princesses, takes an annoying interest in me and is always pressing me to partake of various fruits at all hours of the day. She asked me, through Mrs. Carey, how old I was, and then told me I was too tall for my age, obligingly showing me the height I ought to be. It reminded me of another royal lady's dictum, 'All persons above a mile high to leave the Court.' I told her that in this damp climate one must allow something for shrinkage, and she did not press the matter.

It is no sinecure to keep order with this huge
mob of mixed nationalities, and I shall be glad when
it is all over.

Conscientiousness is not enough. Having had seven
fevers in thirteen months, Hector was invalided home; and
proved, on arrival in London, to be so ill that a nurse
had to be engaged to look after him before he could
travel down to Devon. Once there he recovered quickly.
His love of animals was this time exercised not only on
more pets, and on long walks with his sister, but in the
hunting-field. He soon bought a horse, and nostalgically
recalled the pleasures of the sport in *When William Came*,
written nearly twenty years later:

Slowly, with a sensuous lingering over detail, his
imagination carried him down to a small, sleepy, yet
withal pleasantly bustling market town, and placed
him unerringly in a wide straw-littered yard, half-full
of men and a quarter full of horses, with a bob-tailed
sheep-dog or two trying not to get in everybody's
way, but insisting on being in the thick of things.
The horses gradually detached themselves from the
crowd of unimportant men and came one by one into
momentary prominence, to be discussed and ap-
praised for their good points and bad points, and
finally to be bid for....
.... The dry warm scent of the stable, the nip of
the morning air, the pleasant squelch-squelch of the
saddle leather, the moist earthy fragrance of the
autumn woods and wet fallows, the cold white mists
of winter days, the whimper of hounds and the hot
restless pushing of the pack through ditch and hedgerow and undergrowth, the birds that flew up and
clucked and chattered as you passed, the hearty
greeting and pleasant gossip in farmhouse kitchens
and market-day bar-parlours—all these remembered
delights of the chase marshalled themselves in the

brain, and made a cumulative appeal that came with special intensity to a man who was a little tired of his wanderings, more than a little drawn away from the jarring centres of life. . . .

Now, the family lived at Westward Ho! (odd that the boys should not, like Kipling a little earlier, have been sent to school there). With his father, his sister, a fox terrier, some Persian cats and a jackdaw, Hector stayed for two years, hunting in the winter, swimming in the summer ('wherever water was, he was not happy unless he was in it'). And then, with an apparently inconsequential suddenness as strange as his departure for Burma, left for London, 'to earn his living by writing.'

He took rooms in Mortimer Street, and, again in an apparently quite inconsequential manner, set about writing a history, *The Rise of the Russian Empire*. He worked from secondary sources, but his list of 'works consulted' suggest that somehow, somewhere, he had already learned Russian, as well as the German and French in which he was fluent. Taking the story from the dawn of history to the establishment of the Romanovs early in the seventeenth century, the book was finished in 1899, when its author, still known as Hector H. Munro, was twenty-nine. It was not particularly well received; bias against the rôle of the Church, if not against Christianity in general, was thought to be ominously allied to an irrepressible levity. And so it is. Nevertheless the young historian disentangles a pretty clear pattern out of an appallingly tangled and bloody skein of events and characters. His style varies between the neo-Gibbonian and the Stracheyan, but seldom flags as it chronicles the bloody sweeps of Poles and Muscovites, Mongols, Tartars, and Cossacks across the desolate, and frequently desolated, marshes and steppes, where peasants cringed and prayed, tyrant after tyrant slaughtered and was slain, traitors in droves sped thriftily from camp to camp. The irrational force and gigantic scale of this drift towards nationhood evidently captured his imagination, without subduing his sceptical fancy.

No respectable historian, to be sure, would allow himself to refer, in speaking of some ravaged patriarch, to 'the excesses of a stormy and well-spent youth.' A disrespectful note unquestionably sounds in this passage:

> In other quarters the zeal and activity of the Roman Church brought her into contact with Russian 'spheres of influence,' to use a modern term. Albrecht, Bishop of the new Livlandish see of Riga, had instituted in that district the Order of the Warriors of Christ, or Sword Brethren, whose mission was to convert the pagan Livlanders by fire, and steel, and thong to the worship of Jesus, and teach them the lesson of peace on earth and goodwill towards men with which His name was associated.

Later, too, this inflection becomes even more hostile:

> In the deserts of Astrakhan, Kotian, the old Polovtzi Khan, had been defeated by the Mongols, and fled, he and his, along the wild steppe country till he came to the Karpathian range and sought refuge in the Hungarian kingdom. Russia no longer offered a safe retreat. Swiftly and remorselessly the death-dealing Horde bore down on the middle provinces, and throughout the length and breadth of the land bishops and priests and people knelt in agonized supplication to their all-powerful God to deliver them from their savage enemies. From cathedral, church, and roadside shrine wails the pitiful litany, 'Save us from the infidels!' Call Him louder. Perchance He sleepeth.
>
> Tchernigov and Péréyaslavl experienced the common fate, the general ruin; town and country alike suffered the affliction of fire and sword and rapine. Shuddering villagers, lying awake around their flickering hearths at night, would hear the uneasy bark-

ing of their watch-dogs, scenting or seeing something not yet palpable to human senses; and later the house-pigeons would fly far and wildly over a landscape lit up by a glow that was not the dawn.

Nor do other branches of the Christian communion escape his lash:

The winter of 1502–3 found matters in much the same state as they had been twelve months earlier. The Grand Prince's troops had been obliged to raise the siege of Smolensk, but they still retained the lands they had seized at the commencement of the war, still held their own in the Baltic districts. A candidate for the blessings traditionally allotted to the peacemaker now appeared in the person of the Pontiff, who sought to bring about an accommodation between the contending sovereigns. The splendid profligate who occupied the throne of St Peter was not actuated by a constitutional or professional abhorrence of bloodshed—under his pontificate The Eternal City had been a shambles rather than a sheepfold,—but for the present the smiting of the Infidel seemed to him more urgent than the harrying of the Orthodox, especially as the Orthodox seemed well able to retaliate. With an uncrushed and un-appeased enemy on their flank, it was clearly impossible for the kings of Hungary and Poland and the Teutonic Order to join in the crusade by which the Borgia fondly hoped to sweep the Ottoman from Europe. Hence the apparition of this very soiled dove masquerading with an olive branch in its crimson beak.

At times, too, his prose acquires a graphic impetus which looks ahead to the exhilarating surge of Patrick Leigh Fermor:

With intervals of exhaustion, the war of the brothers dragged on for many years, kept alive, now

by intrigues at the Mongol Courts, now by raid and
rapine in the lands of Souzdal and Péréyaslavl. But
out of this seething incoherent dust-storm rises one
tangible fact, the independence of the province of
Tver; born of anarchy, this little principality shall
contribute its quota to the red page of Russian history ere it sinks back into obscurity. Under its young
Prince, Mikhail Yaroslavitch, it has taken advantage
of the weakness and embarrassments of Dimitri to
secure for itself a separate existence, and to impair
the solidity of the grand province. The Novgoro-
dians, but languidly attached to the interests of the
rival princes, started a domestic war of their own,
one of those vigorous, exuberant burgh-strifes peculiar to the free cities of Northern Europe in the
Middle Ages—a strife in which the whole population took part, from the Archbishop, posadnik, and
boyarins, down to the 'youngest people'; a strife
which has been handed down blurred and sketchy,
devoid of meaning and purpose, if it ever had any,
but still instinct with life and movement. Wild
crowds skirling through narrow streets, hunting the
posadnik into the protection of the Archbishop, hammering on the closed door of the sanctuary, the
Cathedral of S. Sofia; tumultuous gatherings in the
great square, angry dooming of citizens, hurlings of
struggling victims from the bridge into the Volkhov;
and above all these scenes of disorder, the great bell
of Yaroslav clanging and dinning, like some evil spirit
of unrest prisoned in its owl-tower.

And in the chapter devoted to Ivan the Terrible the
catalogue of horror acquires an ironic dignity which suggests that had he persevered this young enthusiast might
have developed into no mean historian.

But such enterprises were clearly no help when it came
to 'earning his living as a writer'; and young Munro, once
out of the British Museum Reading Room, set about

earning a little money by writing very short short stories for newspapers and magazines. How he fared it is impossible to say; but one of these exercises found itself in print in 1899. A story called 'Dogged' appeared in a periodical called *St Paul's*, accompanied, for no clear reason, by comic drawings of West End life and by photographs of Mdlle Irene Fejer, a 'charming young Roumanian artist, lately at the Alhambra,' and of Mdlle Lionelle Warton, 'a very quaint and clever little dwarf.' The story, which appears over the initials H.H.M., is laboriously facetious but announces several of Saki's favourite themes. Its hero is a dull and meek young man, its anti-hero a spirited dog, by whose means a blameless life is insensibly turned into one of idleness and dissipation, and its exponent exposed as a hypocrite into the bargain.

Yet it was as neither an historian nor a short-story writer that Munro was first to make his mark. Once again the apparently inconsequential took a hand. Not through any London acquaintance, but through friends in distant Devon, he met Francis Carruthers Gould, already established as a political cartoonist; and soon this unshakable young Tory is being taken by Gould to see J. A. Spender, editor of the unshakably Liberal *Westminster Gazette*. 'I have a clear recollection,' says Spender

> of Gould's bringing him to my room at the Office somewhere about the year 1900 and starting then and there on a discussion of articles which the one was to write and the other to illustrate. 'Saki' left most of the talking to Gould, and at the beginning one had to dig hard to get a word out of him. But the word when it came was pungent and original, and in a few minutes I came to the conclusion that Gould was justified in his 'find.' The scheme suggested was that of *The Westminster Alice*—dealing with the South African war and politics in general . . . and I own that I had misgivings about it. Parodies of the famous original had several times been submitted to

me (as I suppose to most editors) and nearly all had
been dismal failures. Such things must either succeed
perfectly or fail lamentably, and to succeed perfectly
meant not merely copying the form but catching the
spirit of the inimitable fantastic original . . .

Of the many political squibs I can remember
none had so immediate and complete a success as
this. It was quoted everywhere, and the whole town
joined in the laugh. The public at this time had long
got over its 'Mafficking' and was thoroughly annoyed
at the mismanagement of the Boer War and its apparently interminable protraction in the guerrilla
stage. But the occasion was not so tragic as to forbid
the play of this delicate raillery.

The ingenuity with which both author and illustrator
manipulate A. J. Balfour as the White Knight, Joseph
Chamberlain as the Red Queen, and so on are wholly
admirable; some of the jokes are quite funny even today;
but satire as leisurely as this needs the salt of topicality.
Its success, however, led to an increased market for
Munro's stories. And it was now that he took the pen-name
'Saki.' It is said, by his sister and by Rothay Reynolds, a
close friend, to have been chosen from one of Fitzgerald's
versions of the Rubaiyat of Omar Khayyam:

Yon rising moon that looks for us again,
How oft hereafter will she wax and wane;
How oft hereafter, rising, look for us!
Through this same Garden—and for *one* in vain!

And when like her, O Saki, you shall pass
Amongst the Guests, star-scattered on the grass,
And in your joyous errand reach the spot
Where I made one—turn down an empty glass.

In Fitzgerald's earlier rendering of the same verses the
name 'Saki' is not mentioned, but the person concerned
is addressed as 'Moon of my Delight who know'st no
Wane.' Why Munro chose to take the name of this middle-

eastern Ganymede we shall probably never know. If he merely plucked a short, easily pronounced name from his memory of a favourite poem, the choice cannot have been wholly at random; and it would be hard to think of any name less obviously suitable than this, with all its hedonistic and elegiac associations, for the mask of a satirist.*

One more series similar to *The Westminster Alice* was written, after Rudyard Kipling; but the law of diminishing returns operated relentlessly as ever, and *Not-So Stories* made little impression. About this time, too, Saki was again seriously ill, this time with double pneumonia; and again, on recovery, was much fitter than he had been before. In 1902 he joined the *Morning Post* and immediately travelled out to cover the current outbreak of war in the Balkans. In 1903 he went out again; this time to Macedonia, Munro for the *Morning Post* in company with H. N. Brailsford for the *Manchester Guardian*. On the way the youthful pair fell in with a distinguished Viennese journalist, an elderly, handsome, bearded man. Munro and Brailsford were both cleanshaven, and at the Turkish frontier a customs officer assumed that they were the sons of their bearded companion, and entered on their passports the interesting item that they were being taken to school in Salonika. The unfortunate Brailsford was some weeks later arrested for running away from his place of education. Munro seems to have been troubled no further.

In the spring of 1904, still as a correspondent of the *Morning Post*, he had moved to Warsaw. His own particular *Drang nach Osten* was well under way, and Eastern Europe was a marvellous playground. 'The American Consul,' he wrote from Warsaw

has a schoolboy nephew staying with him, who goes to swimbath every day with me, and afterwards we

* The Rev. A. Aitken Crawshaw, husband of Saki's niece, offers an alternative explanation: that it is a contracted version of *Sakya Muni*, one of the names of the Buddha, "the enlightened."

play tennis, he, I, Consul and an Irish girl. Poles of
my own age are pleasant enough, but it is impossible
to get them to do anything; on the most scorching
days nothing will induce them to join my amphibious
afternoons in the Vistula; they agree to come, with
every sign of nervous depression, but return presently
beaming to say they have remembered they have got
a cold and it would be dangerous, etc. . . .

P.S.—A 14 year old Polish kid belonging to the
house has constituted himself my valet and carries on
my toilet every day with extreme minuteness, besides
doing most of my shopping. On a hot day I can
thoroughly recommend a syphon of soda-water
turned on between the shoulder blades. . . .

I have got some more coins, old Russian, Polish,
Bohemian, etc., going back to 1300, from a man here
who has an immense collection. I fairly took his
breath away when he started on mediæval history, as
he found I knew rather more about the old lines of
east-European princes than he did, and an Englishman is expected to be profoundly ignorant of such
things.

In the autumn he moved on to St Petersburg, where he
stayed for two congenial years; and the first (by a long
interval) of the Saki books was published in London:
Reginald—fifteen sketches, the monologues of an apparently frivolous young man, a kindergarten Lord Henry
Wotton at large in London; they had had considerable
success in the *Westminster Gazette*.

Though Leningrad was not without its excitements, it
seems a pity that Munro did not stay a little longer. The
events of 1905 might have stirred his conservative yet
destructive dreams as the intermittent clashes of monk-led
deputations and ferocious Cossacks did not. The following passage, admirable in itself, suggests a view of Russia
and the Russians totally blind to the ferment already at
work—a ferment, one would have supposed, to which

Munro's temperament would have rendered him acutely sensitive:

One of the most striking discoveries which one makes in the course of a residence in this country is the all-prevailing inertia of the stalwart and seemingly lusty Russian race, an inertia that appears to be common to all classes, and to spring from no particular accident of circumstance, unless the long Russian winter can be held partly responsible. I have before alluded to the impression of convalescents out for an airing produced by the heavily overcoated, aimlessly lounging soldiers and sailors off duty in the streets of the capital; the officers, in spite of their brilliant and imposing uniforms, do not succeed much better in imparting a tone of dash and vigour to their surroundings.

A young officer stationed in a town drives from his quarters to his club, from his club to his restaurant, back to his club and so forth, and that represents about the sum of his non-professional exertions; by driving it must not be supposed that he climbs into a high dogcart and steers a spirited pony through the streets. If he possesses a private carriage it takes the form of a roomy, well-cushioned brougham or victoria drawn by a pair of heavy, long-maned, flowing-tailed horses and driven by a fat, bearded coachman swathed in thick quilted garments into the semblance of a huge human sack. In this conveyance he takes the air if the weather should be sufficiently tempting. The daily routine of an old lady at Bath with a taste for cards would not be widely different, except that she would perhaps go less often to church and never to parade or café chantant.

Brave, charming, and good-natured as the Russian officer is universally acknowledged to be by those who know him, he has certainly no compelling impulse towards the recreations of saddle and

greensward, and one contrasts wonderingly the unceasing outdoor programme of an Indian military
station under the enervating influence of a tropical
atmosphere. One senior officer, probably not of
Russian stock, may be seen at times taking horse
exercise in the streets of St Petersburg, and I believe
that a letter, addressed to this city, 'to the General
who rides,' would find him without difficulty.

With the younger generation of the military caste
it is the same story. In the spacious grounds attached
to one of the cadet headquarters in St Petersburg one
may find on a late summer evening the youth of the
British and German colonies vigorously engaged in
football practice or in the milder activities of lawn
tennis, while the cadets walk sedately along the
gravel paths or find an outlet for their superfluous
energies in the game of gorodki, somewhat resemb-
ling ninepins.

In civilian walks of life the same stagnation has
universal sway; among peasant agriculturists in the
country districts and among certain classes of towns-
folk there are of course seasons and occasions when
energy is a matter of necessity, but when that com-
pulsion of circumstance is removed or non-existent
the Russian relapses naturally into an atmosphere of
congenial torpidity.

In every Russian town of any size there are thousands or hundreds of well-built, healthy-looking men,
ranging from eighteen years upwards, but mostly in
the prime of early manhood, who occupy the posts
of doorkeepers and yard-keepers, and whose most
laborious functions consist of a little sweeping and
wood-chopping, an occasional errand, and sometimes
escorting an over-drunken wayfarer to his destination. For the rest of the time they sleep, or gossip
by the hour over sweetened concoctions of weak tea,
or play mild baby games with their children or any
friendly dog or kitten that comes their way. And in

their peaked caps, gay shirts, and high Blücher boots, they convey the impression of a sort of Praetorian Guard in undress.

Probably the custom of dressing nearly every male civilian, from small errand-boys to postmen and such minor officials, in high military boots is responsible for many of our earliest notions of the Russians as a stern, truculent warrior breed. An army, it has been said, marches on its stomach; the Russians for several generations have lived on their boots. If an average British boy were put at an early age into such boots he would become a swashbuckling terror to his family and neighbourhood, and in due course would rove abroad and found an Empire, or at any rate die of a tropical disease. A Russian would not feel impelled by the same influence further than the nearest summer garden.

In 1906 the inconsequential stepped in once more. He moved to Paris. Here (having looked for, and found, what his sister describes as an 'original' servant) he is said to have had 'an amusing time' and to have made many friends, before his return to England in 1908. But this Paris period seems to have contributed little or nothing to his work; there is hardly a French character to be found in his stories; and he clearly shared none of the customary British fascination by the Latin lands.

Once settled again in England, he established himself in the Mortimer Street rooms, his sister in a Surrey cottage, and set about writing hard. He was still thought of as a producer of brilliant trifles; but darker forces from the past and from the future were at work on him too; in the considerable output of the next six years strains of savagery and melancholy became more and more evident, though outwardly he preserved the image recorded by Hugh Walpole—'He was to be met with at country houses and London parties, apparently rather cynical, rather idle,

and taking life so gently that he might hardly be said
to be taking it at all.'

A tiny handful of friends recall him with enormous
delight—among them his young cousin Major C. W.
Mercer, better known as Dornford Yates, himself later a
skilful purveyor of romantic comedy:

> I met Hector for the first time when I was fifteen
> or sixteen. My Mother and I were staying with an
> uncle and aunt of mine at their house in Phillimore
> Gardens, Kensington. I rather think he was asked to
> dinner for our sakes: that thereafter he was asked
> for theirs goes without saying, for Hector had beauti-
> ful manners, talked easily and well and possessed
> the precious gift of adaptability. He was then thirty
> or thirty-one—a spare man of average height, brown-
> eyed, clean-shaven, with a ready smile and a most
> intelligent face. His hands were sensitive, and he kept
> them very still. His complexion was sallow. He was
> well-groomed and neat in his attire. Always wore a
> bowler in London. Never careless or untidy in his
> dress. Brilliant satirist as he was, you would never
> have believed this to look at him. In repose, he looked
> his best. In conversation, he had a trick of using
> his mouth and lips too much, to emphasize some
> point.
>
> I never heard him speak sharply to anyone; his
> conversation was always interesting and amusing, but
> seldom displayed the brilliance of his written words.
> He was much liked by Lady St Helier—a widow, old
> enough to have been his mother—and frequently
> visited her at her country house. A very fine Bridge
> player, he would play the game to all hours. From
> time to time I met some of his friends, either in his
> club, The Cocoa Tree, or at one of his parties at
> Soho; but none of them approached him in intellect
> or personality. The women between whom I sat were
> invariably precious and spoke much of 'values,' and

I sometimes think that Hector invited me out of mischief, to enjoy my reactions to such, to my mind, pinchbeck company. His personality stood right out always. But among those of his friends or acquaintances that I met, I cannot remember one man or woman who registered. Some may have been mentally attractive, though, if they were, they concealed their attraction from me; there was not one that was physically attractive among them.

That first evening in Phillimore Gardens, I remember that he said that the ballet, 'Old China,' then running at The Empire, was exceptionally good, and that if my Mother and aunt did not mind visiting a music hall, they would be entranced. Such was his enthusiasm that my uncle declared that he would take seats the next morning. My aunt at once invited Hector to make one of the party, and an evening was fixed. So a few days later he dined with us again and went with us to The Empire. The ballet was exquisite. Mme Adeline Genée was the *première danseuse*. To this day I remember how the curtain rose upon a vast marble mantelpiece upon which there stood three great pieces of Dresden china—a clock in the middle, with a shepherd (life-size) on one side and a shepherdess (life-size) on the other. The clock declared the time to be a few seconds to twelve. Then it struck the hour and, as its notes died, the figures on either side came to life and began to dance. Hector, who had already seen the ballet more than once, sat between my Mother and my aunt, continually indicating to them certain features which they might otherwise have missed.

And yet, Dornford Yates concludes, 'unhappily I seem to remember so little of him. I remember him as very gentle, gay, smiling, but never laughing outright. I never saw or heard him laugh, but a smile was nearly always on his face. I think his personality must have been elusive.'

It must indeed. This successful journalist and writer, habitué of clubs and drawing-rooms and country houses, of the theatre, the ballet and the Café Royal, is almost entirely unremarked in the memoirs of the period; people whom, it would seem, he could hardly have failed to meet frequently seem in fact never to have known him. Yet when he is remembered, it is with remarkable warmth—as, for example, by so acute an observer as H. W. Nevinson:

> One saw the twist of cynicism clearly marked on his face. His aspect of the world was cynical. But the cynicism was humorous and charming, partly assumed as a protective covering to conceal and shelter feeling. . . . To myself his works, like his conversation, have given so many happy moments that when I think with sorrow upon the friends that I lost in the war, his small and twisted face, in expression like a young and humorous bird's, stands among the first that rise before my mind. It stands beside Rupert Brooke's and Edward Thomas's.

His sister once, after his death, let drop—and appeared to regret having let drop—a remark to the effect that there was at one time the possibility of a match between him and a Lady Rosalind Northcote, but that it fell through because he had not enough money (his indifference to money is noted by almost all who knew him). Dornford Yates suggests that he may have put the idea of marriage from him because after their father's death he assumed full responsibility for his difficult, not to say impossible, sister.

Or, as he himself put it of a character in *When William Came*:

> He was a bachelor of the type that is called confirmed, and which might better be labelled consecrated; from his early youth onward to his present age he had never had the faintest flickering intention of marriage. Children and animals he adored, women

and plants he accounted somewhat of a nuisance. A world without women and roses and asparagus would, he admitted, be robbed of much of its charm, but with all their charm these things were tiresome and thorny and capricious, always wanting to climb or creep in places where they were not wanted, and resolutely drooping and fading away when they were desired to flourish. Animals, on the other hand, accepted the world as it was and made the best of it, and children, at least nice children, uncontaminated by grown-up influences, lived in worlds of their own making.

For all their evident differences his dreams and his essential aloofness—and his obviously immense personal charm—are not so very far removed from those of another displaced Victorian: T. E. Lawrence. But gleeful horror rather than disgust both sharpened and blurred the conflict in Saki between idealism and indulgence. He lived in a worldly world, but a basic detachment informs all his best writing as well as what little is known of him as a man: a detachment possibly formed in early childhood as a defence against his sister's emotional cannibalism, and which made it impossible for him to form a close bond with another human being.

And so, in his mid-thirties, established as writer and journalist, he moved through the high Edwardian noon like a jungle-boy in the drawing-room, a jungle-boy nursing a dream of nobler beings than he saw around him. Soon, mockery of idle women and flatulent men was not enough. Into his stories crept more strongly a strain which had always been there: a strain, in more senses than one, of loneliness and disenchantment. The social and professional round continued. He gave a party for Nijinsky, Karsavina, and other Russian dancers on their first visit to England. He had personally made their acquaintance in Russia, and formed the taste for ballet which he was eager to share. Nijinsky was there observed peering under a

table. Asked by Saki's sister what he was looking at, 'C'est
le diable,' he replied. It was in fact an Aberdeen terrier,
a breed of dog new to the dancer, who had been surprised,
he said, not to see more bulldogs: 'In Russia we heard
that every Englishman walks out accompanied by a bull-
dog.' Occasionally, too, Munro could be seen making
one of those gestures of wild hilarity, conspicuously out
of character, which are among the hallmarks of the dis-
tanced man. At his Surrey cottage, in a sunless summer,
he cried one evening 'We will invoke Apollo's aid tonight,
round a bonfire.' And the company danced by firelight,
draped in sheets—the disconcerting result being three
weeks of brilliant sunshine. On one New Year's Eve what
his sister describes as 'hilarious revels' took place in London; 'Hector had thoughtfully provided himself with one
of those toys, new at that time, which imitate a dog growl-
ing.' On another, he 'insisted' on linking hands with a
party of strangers and dancing 'Here we go round the
mulberry bush' in Oxford Circus.

Such determined paganism was most likely a desperate
fling at identification with people at large. But also,
when not writing, visiting, or playing cards, he occupied
himself with the finicky art of 'tapestry painting,' executing
large pictures of subjects such as 'A Boar-hunt in the
Middle Ages,' so that at a casual glance it might appear
to be done in faded threads. His mornings were given to
writing. In a dressing-gown he sat with a writing-pad
propped on a book, and, says his friend and remembrancer
Rothay Reynolds, 'wrote slowly in a very clear hand,
rarely erasing a word or making a correction. His air and
the movement of his hand gave one the impression that
he was drawing and not writing.' And when his morning's
stint was done he would go to lunch at Lyons', before
preparing himself for the *beau monde*.

He did not publish another book until 1910, when
Reginald in Russia appeared. His range and mood had
perceptibly changed in the six years since *Reginald*; only
the title story linked this collection with the modish mono-

logues of the earlier book. Here all the notes in Saki's compass were struck: the purely frivolous, the frivolous-macabre, the rustic-horrific, the supernatural, the cynical, the deeply melancholy, and above all the calling-in of the brute creation to redress the inanity, or worse, of human beings. First, the stories made their mark, in both *Reginald* and *Reginald in Russia*, by their success in epigram and pinpoint flippancy. The field already well cultivated by Oscar Wilde, Anthony Hope, 'John Oliver Hobbes' and the rest was still popular, and Saki could play the game as well as most:

> 'People may say what they like about Christianity; the religious system that produced green Chartreuse can never really die.'
>
> 'To be clever in the afternoon argues that one is dining nowhere in the evening.'
>
> 'She believed in the healthy influence of natural surroundings, not having been in Sicily, where things are different.'
>
> 'Mrs Van Challaby said things about me which in her calmer moments she would have hesitated to spell.'
>
> 'The sort of young man who talks unflaggingly through the thickest soup, and smooths his hair dubiously, as though he thought it might hit back.'
>
> 'I might have been a goldfish in a bowl for all the privacy I got.'

Saki's gifts in this direction being what they were, it is surprising that he did not—especially as he is known to have admired the plays of Wilde and Pinero—turn more wholeheartedly to the stage. His tiny farce, *The Baker's Dozen*, in fact led only to two one-act pieces and one three-act comedy. Both the one-act plays have starkly melodramatic central European settings: one, *The Death-Trap*, is an absurd anecdote about a young prince outfacing, at the point of death, the traitors who surround him; the other, *Karl-Ludwig's Window*, deploys a noble family, a macabre tradition, and—its only point of interest —a romantic dissident young man very nearly failing to live up to his word of honour. The three-act comedy, *The Watched Pot, or The Mistress of Briony*, called for the services of a collaborator, Charles Maude. It was finished just before the outbreak of the first world war, but never produced until the middle of the second, when a few performances, at the Arts Theatre, London, made clear its shortcomings. It had not the humanity to present credible human beings, or the airborne unreality which Wilde achieved in *The Importance of Being Earnest*. It remains a wordy anthology of more or less well-turned jokes:

> (*of a lost husband*) 'For all I know he may have joined the majority, who are powerless to resent these intrusions.'

> 'If servants knew how often the fear of leading them astray by bad example holds us back from desperate wickedness, I'm sure they would ask for double wages.'

> 'So many people who are described as rough diamonds turn out to be merely rough paste.'

> 'I'm walking about practically naked. This suit I've got on was paid for last month, so you may judge how old it is.'

> 'Things lent to you, Réne, are like a hopeless passion, they're never returned.'

Like those of that far weightier decorator of trifles, Henry James, Saki's prose narratives seemed to lean towards the theatre; like James, Saki was all the same unable to catch the dramatic note; and, again as with James, his tales have proved highly successful—notably on television—when put into straight dramatic form by lesser but more theatrically expert hands.

With the publication of *The Chronicles of Clovis* in 1911

he signalized his arrival at a sort of maturity. His range was not enlarged, but these twenty-eight stories had an air of authority about them which was to be maintained in *Beasts and Super-Beasts* (1914), and in the best of the pieces in *The Toys of Peace* (1919), the first of two post-humous volumes. Two stories here, in fact, noticeably did extend his range: 'The Philanthropist and the Happy Cat' is an unexpectedly subtle study of the social and sexual frustrations of a young woman of the prosperous middle class; and 'Morlvera' examines, in terms of children, the dreams and inequities of rich and poor. Neither of these was a topic which can be said to have loomed large in Saki's work; when he did take them up he abandoned much of his flippancy, without tumbling into the senti-mentality which suffused him when he came to deal with subjects in which he was, or wished he was, personally involved. These he largely reserved for treatment in his two full-length prose narratives, *The Unbearable Bassing-ton* (1912) and *When William Came* (1913). 'I can remem-ber very vividly,' Hugh Walpole wrote, 'the shock of sur-prise that *The Unbearable Bassington* gave'; and Saki himself is on record as having laughed at the confusing variety found in reviews of the book, some of which empha-sised its gaiety, others its poignancy. It is no wonder that quick or casual readers were taken aback; they were used to seeing themselves and their friends mocked, but had no reason to expect the story of a quick-witted young man who, far from remaining merely the springboard of satirical high spirits, systematically destroys himself. Small wonder if they prefer not to recognize it as a spiritual self-portrait of the author. But that is what it was.

Circumstantially Saki has covered his tracks well enough. Comus Bassington is yet another in his long line of frivo-lous and unscrupulous young men—Reginald, Rex, René, Cyprian, Bertie, Clovis. Like some of those others, he lives, more or less, as a parasite upon his mother. But here the relationship between mother and son is attempted in much greater detail and depth. Francesca Bassington is as important a figure in the book as her son:

> Her enemies, in their honester moments, would have admitted that she was svelte and knew how to dress, but they would have agreed with her friends in asserting that she had no soul. When one's friends and enemies agree on any particular point they are usually wrong. Francesca herself, if pressed in an unguarded moment to describe her soul, would probably have described her drawing-room. Not that she would have considered that the one had stamped the impress of its character on the other, so that close scrutiny might reveal its outstanding features, and even suggest its hidden places, but because she might have dimly recognized that her drawing-room was her soul.
>
> Francesca was one of those women towards whom Fate appears to have the best intentions and never to carry them into practice. With the advantages put at her disposal she might have been expected to command a more than average share of feminine happiness. So many of the things that make for fretfulness, disappointment and discouragement in a woman's life were removed from her path that she might well have been considered the fortunate Miss Greech, or later, lucky Francesca Bassington. And she was not of the perverse band of those who make a rock-garden of their souls by dragging into them all the stony griefs and unclaimed troubles they can find lying around them. Francesca loved the smooth ways and pleasant places of life; she liked not merely to look on the bright side of things, but to live there and stay there. And the fact that things had, at one time and another, gone badly with her and cheated her of some of her early illusions made her cling the closer to such good fortune as remained to her now that she seemed to have reached a calmer period of her life. To undis-

criminating friends she appeared in the guise of a rather selfish woman, but it was merely the selfishness of one who had seen the happy and unhappy sides of life and wished to enjoy to the utmost what was left to her of the former. The vicissitudes of fortune had not soured her, but they had perhaps narrowed her in the sense of making her concentrate much of her sympathies on things that immediately pleased and amused her, or that recalled and perpetuated the pleasing and successful incidents of other days. And it was her drawing-room in particular that enshrined the memorials or tokens of past and present happiness.

Since Saki himself never had a mother, one might suppose that, setting about depicting a mother-son relationship, he would choose to draw, by way of compensation, a satisfying bond. But his own sense of emptiness was perhaps too strong:

Francesca was, in her own way, fonder of Comus than of any one else in the world, and if he had been browning his skin somewhere east of Suez she would probably have kissed his photograph with genuine fervour every night before going to bed; the appearance of a cholera scare or rumour of native rising in the columns of her daily news-sheet would have caused her a flutter of anxiety, and she would have mentally likened herself to a Spartan mother sacrificing her best-beloved on the altar of State necessities. But with the best-beloved installed under her roof, occupying an unreasonable amount of cubic space, and demanding daily sacrifices instead of providing the raw material for one, her feelings were tinged with irritation rather than affection. She might have forgiven Comus generously for misdeeds of some gravity committed in another continent, but she could never overlook the fact that out of a dish of five plovers' eggs he was certain to take three.

The absent may be always wrong, but they are seldom in a position to be inconsiderate.

Thus a wall of ice had grown up gradually between mother and son, a barrier across which they could hold converse, but which gave a wintry chill even to the sparkle of their lightest words.

In a world of well-furnished houses, green lawns, footmen, bridge tables, and silver tea-sets Comus lives well enough. But, wincing, he throws aways every chance. He may marry an heiress who could love him, and whom he could love—if he were capable of love at all; but he deliberately loses her to Courtenay Youghal, one of those smartish young politicians—icily sketched—who are still with us:

Behind his careful political flippancy and cynicism one might also detect a certain careless sincerity, which would probably in the long run save him from moderate success, and turn him into one of the brilliant failures of his day. Beyond this it was difficult to form an exact appreciation of Courtenay Youghal, and Elaine, who liked to have her impressions distinctly labelled and pigeon-holed, was perpetually scrutinizing the outer surface of his characteristics and utterances, like a baffled art critic vainly searching beneath the varnish and scratches of a doubtfully assigned picture for an enlightening signature. The young man added to her perplexities by his deliberate policy of never trying to show himself in a favourable light even when most anxious to impart a favourable impression. He preferred that people should hunt for his good qualities, and merely took very good care that as far as possible they should never draw blank; even in the matter of selfishness, which was the sheet-anchor of his existence, he contrived to be noted, and justly noted, for doing remarkably unselfish things. As a ruler he would have been reasonably popular; as a husband he would probably be unendurable.

In the end Comus is forced, or allows himself to be forced, towards a post somewhere in Africa, relegation to what used to be so useful a dumping-ground for misfits, the British Empire. And we know that his feelings there were precisely those of the young Munro in Burma; but Comus Bassington, unlike the young Munro, dies in exile; and his mother belatedly discovers the falsity of her scale of values.

The Unbearable Bassington is open to adverse criticism on several counts. Its construction is clumsy, its emotion forced, several of its points made too hard and too explicitly. But then it is in fact a morality. Its villain is a grossly materialistic society, its victim a free spirit who, born and bred to the conventional world, can neither conform nor totally cut himself off. And at its best the novel reaches a fine level of tragi-comic intensity. Two farewell occasions, occurring before Comus leaves for Africa, wonderfully combine the dazzle of social comedy with an undertow of misery—a theatrical first night and a family dinner-party. Both focus the dissatisfaction which lay at the heart of Munro's temperament, if not his personality; and which was to express itself as strongly, though in a quite different form, in his next and only other full-length book, *When William Came*. Here the craft of fiction has given way almost entirely to a series of moralistic episodes. The tone is too often soggily emotional and the book is in no way a satisfactory work of art. Munro was trying, perhaps, to define a set of values, and to explore failures to live up to them. He was himself in the throes of a deep dissatisfaction, and had already spoken of his intention to pull out of cosmopolitan Europe and settle in—of all places—Siberia.

When William Came is set in an England occupied by the Germans. But although it talks of the easy conquest of our unpreparedness (and earned the praise of Lord

Roberts), it is not in fact another of those hortatory fictions (among them Erskine Childers' *The Riddle of the Sands*) published in the twenty years or so before 1914. It is a picture of a society all too easily adapting itself to ignobility. The details of occupied London are presented with adequate imaginative vigour and a frequently savage wit; but the strength of the book lies in its contrast of temperaments. The spirit of resistance is embodied in a remote figure who does not play a large part, though her attitudes are clearly those to which Saki gives his allegiance:

Eleanor, Dowager Lady Greymarten, had for more than half a century been the ruling spirit at Torywood. The affairs of the county had not sufficed for her untiring activities of mind and body; in the wider field of national and Imperial service she had worked and schemed and fought with an energy and a far-sightedness that came probably from the blend of caution and bold restlessness in her Scottish blood. For many educated minds the arena of politics and public life is a weariness of dust and disgust, to others it is a fascinating study, to be watched from the comfortable seat of a spectator. To her it was a home. In her town house or down at Torywood, with her writing-pad on her knee and the telephone at her elbow, or in personal counsel with some trusted colleague or persuasive argument with a halting adherent or half-convinced opponent, she had laboured on behalf of the poor and the ill-equipped, had fought for her idea of the Right, and above all, for the safety and sanity of her Fatherland. Spadework when necessary, and leadership when called for, came alike within the scope of her activities, and not least of her achievements, though perhaps she hardly realized it, was the force of her example, a lone, indomitable fighter calling to the half-caring and the half-discouraged, to the laggard and the slow-moving.

And she stands for a fairy-tale England:

Tall grasses and meadow-weeds stood in deep
shocks, field after field, between the leafy boundaries
of hedge or coppice, thrusting themselves higher and
higher till they touched the low sweeping branches
of the trees that here and there overshadowed them.
Broad streams, bordered with a heavy fringe of reed
and sedge, went winding away into a green distance
where woodland and meadowland seemed indefinitely prolonged; narrow streamlets, lost to view in
the growth that they fostered, disclosed their
presence merely by the water-weed that showed in
a riband of rank verdure threading the mellower
green of the fields. On the stream banks moorhens
walked with jerky confident steps, in the easy bold-
ness of those who had a couple of other elements at
their disposal in an emergency; more timorous partridges raced away from the apparition of the train,
looking all leg and neck, like little forest elves fleeing
from human encounter. And in the distance, over
the tree line, a heron or two flapped with slow
measured wing-beats and an air of being bent on an
immeasurably longer journey than the train that
hurtled so frantically along the rails. Now and then
the meadowland changed itself suddenly into orchard, with close-growing trees already showing the
measure of their coming harvest, and then straw-
yard and farm buildings would slide into view; heavy
dairy cattle, roan and skewbald and dappled, stood
near the gates, drowsily resentful of insect stings,
and bunched-up companies of ducks halted in seeming irresolution between the charms of the horsepond and the alluring neighbourhood of the farm
kitchen. Away by the banks of some rushing mill-
stream, in a setting of copse and cornfield, a village
might be guessed at, just a hint of red roof, grey
wreathed chimney and old church tower as seen

from the windows of the passing train, and over it all brooded a happy, settled calm, like the dreaming murmur of a trout-stream and the faraway cawing of rooks.

It was a land where it seemed as if it must be always summer and generally afternoon, a land where bees hummed among the wild thyme and in the flower-beds of cottage gardens, where the harvest-mice rustled amid the corn and nettles, and the mill-race flowed cool and silent through water-weeds and dark tunnelled sluices, and made soft droning music with the wooden mill-wheel. And the music carried with it the wording of old undying rhymes, and sang of the jolly, uncaring, uncared-for miller, of the farmer who went riding upon his grey mare, of the mouse who lived beneath the merry mill-pin, of the sweet music on yonder green hill and the dancers all in yellow—the songs and fancies of a lingering olden time, when men took life as children take a long summer day, and went to bed at last with a simple trust in something they could not have explained.

This is the England of George Eliot and Thomas Hardy turned over-ripe: the England of the fantasist, of Kenneth Grahame, of Evelyn Waugh (of P. G. Wodehouse, for that matter)—and still, I suspect, for most English people their private image of paradise, whether or not they also seek there standards of aristocratic verve, aplomb, responsibility, courtesy, and chivalry which centuries of high romantic dreaming have set up against the facts of life.

At the centre of *When William Came* stand not the Dowager Lady Greymarten but Murrey Yeovil and his wife Cecily. They are rich; and theirs is a loose-knit marriage. She, like Francesca Bassington, values most her comfortable home and the social London life of which it is the centre. Occupation, as such, by another nation means little or nothing to her; if she can have her comfort, her attendant young men, her fair share of life in society she is content. When the book opens she is enjoying all these things in German-occupied London. Suddenly her husband returns from a long spell of wandering in Russian central Asia. Unlike her, he is appalled by what has happened to his country. Here, again rather surprisingly, Saki brings off a striking picture of a man and a woman who, if love is too strong a word, deeply like and respect one another, and manage to preserve both liking and respect despite the abysmal difference which lies between them (but then, to do this, he must make the relationship —like all his relationships—entirely passionless). Yeovil, however (like the young Munro in Burma) has been fearfully ill in the course of his travels, and near to death. Back in England he bears a double cross. Much as he loathes, by instinct, the existing state of affairs, he finds the will to do anything but accept it ebbing away from him. And, taking himself off (again like the young Saki) for some recuperative hunting, finds himself slipping into friendly terms with the enemy, some of whom at least seem to have noticeably finer qualities than his own or his wife's friends. And Saki leaves him contented and ashamed.

Although *When William Came* ends with a moment of discomfiture for the German Emperor it is not in essence a merely patriotic book; it is rather a study in the decay of moral fibre—and of this, too, it seems likely, Saki accused himself. An attempt to define what values, precisely, this moral fibre should have been put to supporting must break down for want of evidence; but we are made to feel that they are very noble, and I see no particular indication that, as has been suggested, *When William Came* indicated any marked preference for authoritarian regimes; though it is true that this temperamental anarch clearly longed to identify himself with something, to find some sense in the pattern of society which he so relentlessly harried in his fiction.

The approach of war in real earnest allowed him for the moment to resolve his problems in a burst of self-dramatization. In 1914 he had returned to journalism, and was writing parliamentary sketches for a periodical called *Outlook*. His manner was detached and humorously contemptuous, for the most part:

> The member for North Carnarvonshire always gives me the impression of one who in his long-ago youth heard the question-half of a very good riddle, and has spent the remainder of his life in the earnest expectation of hearing some one disclose the answer. Even when such politely wearisome speakers as Reginald McKenna are in possession of the House one can see Mr. William Jones, with a happy smile of strained expectancy on his face, listening intently to every syllable that falls from the orator's lips; one of these days, one feels sure, he will give a wild scream of joy and rush away to apply for the Chiltern Hundreds, with his life's desire at last achieved.

But on Monday, August 3, 1914, he was in the House of Commons when Sir Edward Grey made his statement of Britain's intentions; and he wrote

> Grey's speech, when one looked back at it, was a statesman-like utterance, delivered in excellent manner, dignified and convincing. To sit listening to it, in uncertainty for a long time as to what line of policy it was going to announce, with all the accumulated doubts and suspicions of the previous forty-eight hours heavy on one's mind, was an experience that one would not care to repeat often in a lifetime. Men who read it as it was spelled out jerkily on the tape-machines, letter by letter, told me that the strain of uncertainty was even more cruel; and I can well believe it. When the actual tenor of the speech became clear, and one knew beyond a doubt where we stood, there was only room for one feeling;

the miserable tension of the past two days had been removed, and one discovered that one was slowly recapturing the lost sensation of being in a good temper. Redmond's speech was the dramatic success of the occasion; it obviously isolated the action of the Labour members and the few, but insistent, Radicals who were clamorous against the war, but one hardly realized at the moment with what feelings of dismay and discouragement it would be read in Berlin.

Of the men who rose in melancholy succession to counsel a standing aloof from the war, a desertion of France, a humble submission to the will of Potsdam in the matter of Belgium's neutrality, one wishes to speak fairly. Many of them are men who have gloat-ingly threatened us with class warfare in this country —warfare in which rifles and machineguns should be used to settle industrial disputes; they have seemed to take a ghoulish pleasure in predicting a not-far-distant moment when Britons shall range themselves in organized combat, not against an aggressive foreign enemy, but against their own kith and kin. Never have they been more fluent with these hints and incitements than during the present Session; if a crop of violent armed outbreaks does not spring up one of these days in this country it will not be for lack of sowing of seed. Now these men read us moral lectures on the wickedness of war. One is sometimes assured that every man has at least two sides to his character; so one may charitably assume that an honest Quaker-like detestation of war and bloodshed is really the motive which influences at the present moment some of these men who have harped so assiduously on the idea—one might almost say the ideal—of armed collision between the classes. There are other men in the anti-war party who seemed to be obsessed with the idea of snatching commercial advantages out of the situation, regardless of other considerations which usually influence men of honour. The Triple Entente, after all, is no new thing; even if the nature of its obligations was not clearly defined or well understood, at least it was perfectly well known that there were obligations; it was perfectly well known that the people of the other countries involved in its scope believed that there were obligations—at the very least a sentimental sympathy.

He went straight out and walked with Rothay Reynolds 'at a tremendous pace' to a chop-house in the Strand. Ordering cheese, he was asked by the waiter if he wanted butter, and replied 'peremptorily,' 'Cheese, no butter; there's a war on'—a childish but no doubt satisfying gesture for a man who, passing the age of forty, had earlier lamented 'And I have always looked forward to the romance of a European war.' It seems impossible that such a thing could be said, could ever have been said. But his was no lone voice; in the vast expansion of the nineteenth century doubt dogged confidence, and where intellectual man pressed on, the natural man began to recoil, to feel a sense not of expansion but of contraction, of (one might say) near-hysterical claustrophobia.

Munro, at forty-four well over age, went straight off and enlisted as a trooper in the 2nd King Edward's Horse; observing that, having written *When William Came*, he ought to go half-way to meet him. His friends and family (except his dreadful sister) were dismayed; even Dornford Yates, to whom such a gesture might have been expected to appeal, was shocked by the absurd wastefulness of the situation. In fact, Munro could not stand up to a cavalryman's life, but arranged to be transferred to the 22nd Royal Fusiliers, refusing all suggestions that he should take a commission (in, for example, the Argyll and Sutherland Highlanders: 'I would not accept it, as I should have so much to learn that it would be a case of beginning all over again and I might never see service at all'). And after he had been in the Army for

nine months he was still able to write like this in the
Morning Post:

'I know nothing about war,' a boy of nineteen said
to me two days ago, 'except, of course, that I've heard
of its horrors; yet, somehow, in spite of the horrors,
there seems to be something in it different to anything else in the world, something a little bit finer.'

He spoke wistfully, as one who feared that to him
war would always be an unreal, distant, secondhand
thing, to be read about in special editions, and
peeped at through the medium of cinematograph
shows. He felt that the thing that was a little bit
finer than anything else in the world would never
come into his life.

Nearly every red-blooded human boy has had war,
in some shape or form, for his first love; if his blood
has remained red and he has kept some of his boyish-
ness in after life, that first love will never have been
forgotten. No one could really forget those wonderful leaden cavalry soldiers; the horses were as sleek
and prancing as though they had never left the
parade-ground, and the uniforms were correspondingly spick and span, but the amount of campaigning
and fighting they got through was prodigious. There
are other unforgettable memories for those who had
brothers to play with and fight with, of sieges and
ambushes and pitched encounters, of the slaying of
an entire garrison without quarter, or of chivalrous,
punctilious courtesy to a defeated enemy. Then there
was the slow unfolding of the long romance of actual
war, particularly of European war, ghastly, devastating, heartrending in its effect, and yet somehow
captivating to the imagination. The Thirty Years' War
was one of the most hideously cruel wars ever waged,
but, in conjunction with the subsequent campaigns
of the Great Louis, it throws a glamour over the
scene of the present struggle. The thrill that those

far-off things call forth in us may be ethically indefensible, but it comes in the first place from
something too deep to be driven out; the magic
region of the Low Countries is beckoning to us
again, as it beckoned to our forefathers, who went
campaigning there almost from force of habit.

In November 1915 his dream began to turn into reality.
He went to France with his unit. Rising to the rank of
corporal, and then lance-sergeant, refusing an order to
report as a German speaker, he continued to write occasional sketches (on, for example, 'Birds on the Western
Front') for the *Morning Post* and the *Westminster Gazette*,
and fought off intermittent attacks of malaria. He saw a
good deal of fighting:

> ... We are holding a rather hot part of the line and I
> must say I have enjoyed it better than any we have
> been in. There is not much dug-out accommodation
> so I made my bed (consisting of overcoat and water-
> proof sheet) on the fire-step of the parapet; on Sun-
> day night, while I was on my round looking up the
> sentries, a bomb came into the trench, riddled the
> overcoat and sheet and slightly wounded a man
> sleeping on the other side of the trench. I assumed
> that no 2 bombs would fall exactly in the same spot,
> so remade the bed and had a good sleep ...

In June 1916 he came home on leave, spent in London
with his brother (then Governor of Mountjoy Prison,
Dublin) and sister—who on his return shouted after him,
as he boarded the troop train, 'Kill a good few for me!'
She did, however, notice that he 'showed signs of wear
and tear.' Others have put it less heartily. 'It was evident,'
said Rothay Reynolds, 'that the strain of military life
was telling on him. He was thin and his face was haggard.
But the spiritual change wrought in him by the war was
greater than the physical. He told me he could never
come back to the old life in London. And he wrote asking
me to find out from a person in Russia whether it was

still possible to acquire land in Siberia to till and to hunt, and whether a couple of Yakutsk lads could be got as servants.'

But meanwhile he carried on, winning tributes from all who served with him, until November 14, 1916. Down with malaria, he had struggled back into the trenches in order to take part in an attack (on Beaumont Hamel). Munro's company was 'fanned out' on the left of the advanced line, the troops behind them having been unable to come up because of the condition of the ground (men had sunk in the mud up to their stomachs). In the dark early hours, after a rendezvous in No-Man's-Land, Munro and others were resting, he in a shallow crater, using the lip as a back-rest. He was heard to shout 'Put that bloody cigarette out,' and a moment later was shot through the head.

'When peace comes,' one of Munro's officers had written, 'Saki will give us the most wonderful of all the books about the war.' Perhaps. Yet if it had been honest, it must surely have been more steeped in disillusion even than most of the books that were written about that dreadful conflict. Its hero might have had something in common with Siegfried Sassoon's Sherston in *Memoirs of an Infantry Officer*, as indeed the Englands they supposed themselves to be fighting for had something in common— not least that they were dream-worlds. But could Saki ever have turned his satirical eye—as Sassoon in his poem 'The General,' C. E. Montague in *Disenchantment*, and Evelyn Waugh in his military trilogy *Men at Arms* did after him—upon military disillusion as he had upon the Edwardian scene which so conspicuously failed to live up to his notion of what a civilized world should be like? An idle question, no doubt. Yet by way of answer the suspicion rises that Saki's work was done. Read as an Edwardian, he seems often strikingly modern in tone; imagined as an early post-war writer, he seems absurdly out of date.

The feral and pagan strain in him is one which has, at least for the moment, almost entirely vanished from literature. There is nothing unusual, even today, about preferring animals to human beings; but the lengths to which Saki carried the revenge of the animal kingdom, or the use of the animal kingdom as agents of revenge, is strange indeed. Tiger, elk, hyena, bull, ferret—his private ark resounds with the grunts and snarls of destructive, indeed murderous, brutes: and especially of wolves. These beasts recur in many stories, even the earliest and most frivolous; in, for example, one of Reginald's monologues, in which he describes the play he proposes to write:

> It would commence with wolves worrying something on a lonely waste—you wouldn't see them, of course; but you would hear them snarling and scrunching, and I should arrange to have a wolfy fragrance suggested across the footlights ... The wolves would be a sort of elusive undercurrent in the background that would never be satisfactorily explained.

And so they were, not only through Reginald's drama but through Saki's life. A little later, in 1904, he is writing from Warsaw to his sister:

> Have you thought of getting a wolf instead of a hound? There would be no licence to pay and at first it could feed largely on the smaller Inktons, with biscuits sometimes for a change. You would have to train it to distinguish the small Vernon boys from other edible sorts, or else Cook would be coming with trembling lip nigh upon breakfast-time to say there was no milk in the house.

And in 1915 the wolves are still with him as he writes to his seven-year-old niece: 'Perhaps I may be going out to Servia and may meet some wolves in the forest there, which will be fun.' And, more alarmingly, from the Western Front: 'I think you would enjoy going out at night

to mend the wire entanglements in front of our lines: you
have to creep, creep like a prowling cat, and when the
enemy sends up a flare light, every few minutes, you have
to press yourself flat on the ground and pretend to be a
lump of earth. It reminded me of the times when you
and I were wolves and used to go prowling after fat
farmers' wives.'

Sometimes wolves, sometimes werewolves. Impossible
not to sense, at times, the child who ran round the
nursery crying 'I'm God, and I'm going to destroy the
world' grown into the man whose pointed flippancy barely
masked a deep desire to rend and tear the world which
so betrayed his ideals. His supernatural stories—'Gabriel-
Ernest,' 'The Hounds of Fate,' 'The Music on the Hill'—
should not perhaps, after all, be regarded as merely exercises in a genre. He chose again and again, in the minority
of stories set in the deep countryside, to highlight the
ingrown brooding which he must have found easily enough
in the North Devon of his youth (and could find there
today). And he broke the sullen hush with a panic scream
which must have echoed something in himself.

Transplanted to London, trimmed into the conventions
of the comedy of manners, the feral streak was not submerged. Saki was never a particularly striking satirist of
immediate social issues; his occasional jabs at suffragettes,
advertising, 'the Sherard Blaw school of discursive drama,'
or the Jews (towards whom he felt not the spiteful petu-
lance of, say, Belloc, but rather a sort of bemused curiosity,
not without admiration, as though they were men from
Mars), are no longer interesting. He worked best upon the
perennial absurdities of human nature. He was a moralist
who spoke sometimes through a brilliant image, sometimes
through a well-turned epigram:

> The art of public life consists to a great extent of
> knowing exactly where to stop and going a bit
> further.

Few people talk as brilliantly to impress a friend as they do to depress an enemy.

'Do you suppose we shall all get appropriate punishments in another world for our sins in this?' asked Quentock.

'Not so much for our sins as for our indiscretions; they are the things that do the most harm and cause the greatest trouble.'

He had the loud penetrating voice and prominent penetrating eyes of a man who can do no listening in the ordinary way and whose eyes have to perform the function of listening for him.

He spoke of several duchesses as if he knew them, almost in his more inspired moments as if they knew him.

Her manner of inquiring after a trifling ailment gave one the impression that she was more concerned with the fortunes of the malady than with oneself, and when one got rid of a cold one felt that she almost in his more inspired moments as if they knew

A footman came round the corner with the trained silence that tactfully contrives to make itself felt.

When one's chin begins to lead a double life, one's own opportunities for depravity are insensibly narrowed.

Bondage has this one advantage: it makes a nation merry.

Lady Shalem was a woman of commanding presence, of that type which suggests a consciousness that the command may not necessarily be obeyed.

They kept open house in such an insistently open manner that they created a social draught.

Women with perfect profiles are seldom agreeable.

No one can be an unbeliever nowadays. The Christian Apologists have left one nothing to disbelieve.

The young have aspirations that never come to pass, the old have reminiscences of what never happened. It's only the middle-aged who are really conscious of their limitations.

It is the imperfectly selfish souls that cause themselves and others so many heartburnings. People who make half sacrifices for others always find it is the unfinished half that's being looked at. Naturally they come to regard themselves as unappreciated martyrs.

In spite of everything that proverbs may say, poverty keeps together more homes than it breaks up.

Saki was no Pascal, no Chamfort; but on his level he reached out, from behind his mask and armour, and touched common human experience more widely and more perceptively than Wilde, though with less elegance and less intellectual verve.

Nursing a dream of chivalry, he could not suffer other people. Even the tributes of his friends (except perhaps those in the Army) seem to suggest the charming courtesy which is rooted in indifference. Society was for him a breeding-ground of inanity. When he turns from the attack he becomes a celebrant of loneliness. There is no close human relationship in any of his work, except the twisted skein which binds and cripples Francesca Bassington and her son. There is no physical passion: except in 'The Philanthropist and the Happy Cat' no hint of sex at all. Such marriages as he treats without scorn are companionate:

It was one of the bonds of union and good-fellowship between her husband and herself that each understood and sympathized with the other's tastes without in the least wanting to share them; they went their own ways and were pleased and comradelike when the ways happened to run together for a span, without self-reproach or heart-searching when the ways diverged.

His heroes, children, bright young men, are all essentially solitary spirits, sometimes frivolously seen, sometimes not. The wanderer in the far places of the earth recurs often, appears early—in the story 'Judkin and the Parcels': Judkin, who carried parcels back to his English villa

> ... has known what it was to coax the fret of a thoroughbred, to soothe its toss and sweat as it danced beneath him in the glee and chafe of its pulses and the glory of its thews. He has been in the raw places of the earth, where the desert beasts have whispered their unthinkable psalmody ...

Fifteen years later the author of this embarrassing outburst, twisting and turning in his own private dilemma, had poignantly described the misery of Comus Bassington removed from London to one of those far places, had created Murrey Yeovil, back broken-spirited like Judkin from another, and was himself dreaming of abandoning the civilization he had so dreadfully missed in Burma.

But Saki did not merely laugh that he might not cry. Fascinated by the great world, he turned his adolescent dismay to exhilarating account. Had he survived the war he might have matured; might, for example, have lived to write not a great war book but his own *Animal Farm* before George Orwell (whose life so curiously counterpoints and contrast's with Saki's, a generation later). But his real contribution to a solemn world is his dazzling mischief. We can see now, in a time when black humour is almost a commonplace, the direction of his fantasy. Its comfortable setting and dexterous exposition make it acceptable to all. But it points, with hypnotic glee, towards the fragmentation of established, steady, solid society, the confusion of the bourgeoisie. Not for Saki the plush and mahogany. Not for him, either, the hope in aristocracy and the Roman Catholic Church with which Evelyn Waugh has buttressed a similar revulsion; and still less the desperate clutch at communism with which another middle-class anarch, Brecht, was to ward off the void. Saki sought in romantic patriotism the splendour he could not find in society, in anaesthetizing dreams of battles long ago the gallantry he missed in civilization. He mocked complacency, understood frustration (v. 'The Mappined Life'). He knew all about disillusion: and never better lived up to his own values than in putting it to work with graceful verve.

He wrote too much, true. He remains a minor master, true. But, when pros and cons have been added up, influences dutifully noted; when a suitable docket for the literary card-index game has been prepared—there remains, beyond all his ingenuity as an anecdotalist, beyond his wit, far beyond his skirmishes with human nature, the buoyancy which irradiates all, which broke him out of his self-created prison, and leaves barely a hint of bitterness in our laughter as we watch this well-tailored Ariel at work on the Caliban in ourselves.

In making this selection from Saki's writing I have not attempted to include something of everything. Those who wish to study him closely will do so by way of libraries; the short stories, the single playlet, and *The Unbearable Bassington* have been chosen to provide a cross-section of Saki's work in terms of both quality and entertainment. His parliamentary satires and sketches, his plays, his occasional pieces from the Balkans, Russia, or the Western Front in the first world war do not on the whole qualify in either of these categories. *When William Came* is an apt commentary upon some aspects of the state of England just before 1914, and an even more apt commentary upon Munro's own state of mind; but as a work of art, or as a work of entertainment, it cannot hold its own with the stories—satirical, macabre or plain emotional—represented here.

The relative lack of correspondence, or of biographical material, of any kind (in part the result of his sister's watchdog zeal, in part the echo of his own elusive personality) has been matched by the relative lack of any critical examination. An American scholar, Dr Robert Drake of the University of Texas, has listed what little there is in 'Saki: some problems and a bibliography,' published in *English Fiction in Transition* from Purdue University, Lafayette, Indiana, U.S.A. English men of letters, from Maurice Baring to Graham Greene and V. S. Pritchett, have provided an unfailing flow of appreciation: but Saki has been spared the value-judgments of the new literary establishment, and remains a source of rueful delight.

From

REGINALD

[1904]

REGINALD
AT THE THEATRE

'AFTER ALL,' said the Duchess vaguely, 'there are certain things you can't get away from. Right and wrong, good conduct and moral rectitude, have certain well-defined limits.'

'So, for the matter of that,' replied Reginald, 'has the Russian Empire. The trouble is that the limits are not always in the same place.'

Reginald and the Duchess regarded each other with mutual distrust, tempered by a scientific interest. Reginald considered that the Duchess had much to learn; in particular, not to hurry out of the Carlton as though afraid of losing one's last 'bus. A woman, he said, who is careless of disappearances is capable of leaving town before Goodwood, and dying at the wrong moment of an unfashionable disease.

The Duchess thought that Reginald did not exceed the ethical standard which circumstances demanded.

'Of course,' she resumed combatively, 'it's the prevailing fashion to believe in perpetual change and mutability, and all that sort of thing, and to say we are all merely an improved form of primeval ape—of course you subscribe to that doctrine?'

'I think it decidedly premature; in most people I know the process is far from complete.'

'And equally of course you are quite irreligious?'

'Oh, by no means. The fashion just now is a Roman Catholic frame of mind with an Agnostic conscience: you get the medieval picturesqueness of the one with the modern conveniences of the other.'

The Duchess suppressed a sniff. She was one of those people who regard the Church of England with patronizing affection, as if it were something that had grown up in their kitchen garden.

'But there are other things,' she continued, 'which I suppose are to a certain extent sacred even to you. Patriotism, for instance, and Empire, and Imperial responsibility, and blood-is-thicker-than-water, and all that sort of thing.'

Reginald waited for a couple of minutes before replying, while the Lord of Rimini temporarily monopolized the acoustic possibilities of the theatre.

'That is the worst of a tragedy,' he observed, 'one can't always hear oneself talk. Of course I accept the Imperial idea and the responsibility. After all, I would just as soon think in Continents as anywhere else. And some day, when the season is over, and we have the time, you shall explain to me the exact blood-brotherhood and all that sort of thing that exists between a French Canadian and a mild Hindoo and a Yorkshireman, for instance.'

'Oh, well, "dominion over palm and pine," you know,' quoted the Duchess hopefully; 'of course we mustn't forget that we're all part of the great Anglo-Saxon Empire.'

'Which for its part is rapidly becoming a suburb of Jerusalem. A very pleasant suburb, I admit, and quite a charming Jerusalem. But still a suburb.'

'Really, to be told one's living in a suburb when one is conscious of spreading the benefits of civilization all over the world! Philanthropy—I suppose you will say *that* is a comfortable delusion; and yet even you must admit that whenever want or misery or starvation is known to exist, however distant or difficult of access, we instantly organize relief on the most generous scale, and distribute it, if need be, to the uttermost ends of the earth.'

The Duchess paused, with a sense of ultimate triumph. She had made the same observation at a drawing-room meeting, and it had been extremely well received.

'I wonder,' said Reginald, 'if you have ever walked down the Embankment on a winter night?'

'Gracious, no, child! Why do you ask?'

'I didn't; I only wondered. And even your philanthropy, practised in a world where everything is based on competition, must have a debit as well as a credit account. The young ravens cry for food.'

'And are fed.'

'Exactly. Which presupposes that something else is fed upon.'

'Oh, you're simply exasperating. You've been reading Nietzsche till you haven't got any sense of moral proportion left. May I ask if you are governed by *any* laws of conduct whatever?'

'There are certain fixed rules that one observes for one's own comfort. For instance, never be flippantly rude to any inoffensive, grey-bearded stranger that you may meet in pine forests or hotel smoking-rooms on the Continent. It always turns out to be the King of Sweden.'

'The restraint must be dreadfully irksome to you. When I was younger, boys of your age used to be nice and innocent.'

'Now we are only nice. One must specialize in these days. Which reminds me of the man I read of in some sacred book who was given a choice of what he most desired. And because he didn't ask for titles and honours and dignities, but only for immense wealth, these other things came to him also.'

'I am sure you didn't read about him in any sacred book.'

'Yes; I fancy you will find him in Debrett.'

REGINALD ON WORRIES

I HAVE (said Reginald) an aunt who worries. She's not really an aunt—a sort of amateur one, and they aren't really worries. She is a social success, and has no domestic tragedies worth speaking of, so she adopts any decorative sorrows that are going, myself included. In that way she's the antithesis, or whatever you call it, to those sweet, uncomplaining women one knows who have seen trouble, and worn blinkers ever since. Of course, one just loves them for it, but I must confess they make me uncomfy; they remind one so of a duck that goes flapping about with forced cheerfulness long after its head's been cut off. Ducks have *no* repose. Now, my aunt has a shade of hair that suits her, and a cook who quarrels with the other servants, which is always a hopeful sign, and a conscience that's absentee for about eleven months of the year, and only turns up at Lent to annoy her husband's people, who are considerably lower than the angels, so to speak: with all these natural advantages—she says her particular tint of bronze is a natural advantage, and there can be no two opinions as to the advantage—of course she has to send out for her afflictions, like those restaurants where they haven't got a licence. The system has this advantage, that you can fit your unhappiness in with your other engagements, whereas real worries have a way of arriving at mealtimes, and when you're dressing, or other solemn moments. I knew a canary once that had been trying for months and years to hatch out a family, and every one looked upon it as a blameless infatuation, like the sale of Delagoa Bay, which would be an annual loss to the Press agencies if it ever came to pass; and one day the bird really did bring it off, in the middle of family prayers. I say the middle, but it was also the end: you can't go on being thankful for daily bread when you are wondering what on earth very new canaries expect to be fed on.

At present she's rather in a Balkan state of mind about the treatment of the Jews in Roumania. Personally, I think the Jews have estimable qualities; they're so kind to their poor—and to our rich. I daresay in Roumania the cost of living beyond one's income isn't so great. Over here the trouble is that so many people who have money to throw about seem to have such vague ideas where to throw it. That fund, for instance, to relieve the victims of sudden disasters—what is a sudden disaster? There's Marion Mulciber, who *would* think she could play bridge, just as she would think she could ride down a hill on a bicycle; on that occasion she went to a hospital, now she's gone into a Sisterhood—lost all she had, you know, and gave the rest to Heaven. Still, you can't call it a sudden calamity; *that* occurred when poor dear Marion was born. The doctors said at the time that she couldn't live more than a fortnight, and she's been trying ever since to see if she could. Women aren't so opinionated.

And then there's the Education Question—not that I can see that there's anything to worry about in that direction. To my mind, education is an absurdly overrated affair. At least, one never took it very seriously at school, where everything was done to bring it prominently under one's notice. Anything that is worth knowing one practically teaches oneself, and the rest obtrudes itself sooner or later. The reason one's elders know so comparatively little is because they have to unlearn so much that they acquired by way of education before we were born. Of course I'm a believer in Nature-study; as I said to Lady Beauwhistle, if you want a lesson in elaborate artificiality, just watch the studied unconcern of a Persian cat entering a crowded salon, and then go and practise it for a fortnight. The Beauwhistles weren't born in the Purple, you know, but they're getting there on the instalment system—so much down, and the rest when you feel like it. They have kind hearts, and they never forget birthdays. I forget what he was, something in the City, where the patriotism comes from; and she—oh, well, her frocks are built in Paris, but she wears them with a strong English accent. So public-spirited of her. I think she must have been very strictly brought up, she's so desperately anxious to do the wrong thing correctly. Not that it really matters nowadays, as I told her: I know some perfectly virtuous people who are received everywhere.

REGINALD

ON HOUSE-PARTIES

THE DRAWBACK is, one never really *knows* one's
hosts and hostesses. One gets to know their fox-terriers and
their chrysanthemums, and whether the story about the
go-cart can be turned loose in the drawing-room, or must
be told privately to each member of the party, for fear of
shocking public opinion; but one's host and hostess are a
sort of human hinterland that one never has the time to
explore.

There was a fellow I stayed with once in Warwickshire
who farmed his own land, but was otherwise quite steady.
Should never have suspected him of having a soul, yet not
very long afterwards he eloped with a lion-tamer's widow
and set up as a golf-instructor somewhere on the Persian
Gulf; dreadfully immoral, of course, because he was only
an indifferent player, but still, it showed imagination. His
wife was really to be pitied, because he had been the only
person in the house who understood how to manage the
cook's temper, and now she has to put 'D.V.' on her dinner
invitations. Still, that's better than a domestic scandal; a
woman who leaves her cook never wholly recovers her
position in Society.

I suppose the same thing holds good with the hosts; they
seldom have more than a superficial acquaintance with
their guests, and so often just when they do get to know
you a bit better, they leave off knowing you altogether.
There was *rather* a breath of winter in the air when I
left those Dorsetshire people. You see, they had asked
me down to shoot, and I'm not particularly immense at
that sort of thing. There's such a deadly sameness about
partridges; when you've missed one, you've missed the
lot—at least, that's been my experience. And they tried to
rag me in the smoking-room about not being able to hit a
bird at five yards, a sort of bovine ragging that suggested

cows buzzing round a gadfly and thinking they were teasing it. So I got up the next morning at early dawn— I know it was dawn, because there were lark-noises in the sky, and the grass looked as if it had been left out all night—and hunted up the most conspicuous thing in the bird line that I could find, and measured the distance, as nearly as it would let me, and shot away all I knew. They said afterwards that it was a tame bird; that's simply *silly*, because it was awfully wild at the first few shots. Afterwards it quieted down a bit, and when its legs had stopped waving farewells to the landscape I got a gardener-boy to drag it into the hall, where everybody must see it on their way to the breakfast-room. I breakfasted upstairs myself. I gathered afterwards that the meal was tinged with a very unchristian spirit. I suppose it's unlucky to bring peacock's feathers into a house; anyway, there was a blue-pencilly look in my hostess's eye when I took my departure.

Some hostesses, of course, will forgive anything, even unto pavonicide (is there such a word?), as long as one is nice-looking and sufficiently unusual to counterbalance some of the others; and there *are* others—the girl, for instance, who reads Meredith, and appears at meals with unnatural punctuality in a frock that's made at home and repented at leisure. She eventually finds her way to India and gets married, and comes home to admire the Royal Academy, and to imagine that an indifferent prawn curry is for ever an effective substitute for all that we have been taught to believe is luncheon. It's then that she is really dangerous; but at her worst she is never quite so bad as the woman who fires *Exchange and Mart* questions at you without the least provocation. Imagine the other day, just when I was doing my best to understand half the things I was saying, being asked by one of those seekers after country home truths how many fowls she could keep in a run ten feet by six, or whatever it was! I told her whole crowds, as long as she kept the doors shut, and the idea didn't seem to have struck her before; at least, she brooded over it for the rest of dinner.

Of course, as I say, one never really *knows* one's ground, and one may make mistakes occasionally. But then one's mistakes sometimes turn out assets in the long-run: if we had never bungled away our American colonies we might never have had the boy from the States to teach us how to wear our hair and cut our clothes, and we must get our ideas from somewhere, I suppose. Even the Hooligan was probably invented in China centuries before we thought of him. England must wake up, as the Duke of Devonshire said the other day, wasn't it? Oh, well, it was some one else. Not that I ever indulge in despair about the Future; there always have been men who have gone about despairing of the Future, and when the Future arrives it says nice, superior things about their having acted according to their lights. It is dreadful to think that other people's grandchildren may one day rise up and call one amiable.

There are moments when one sympathizes with Herod.

REGINALD

ON BESETTING SINS

THE WOMAN WHO TOLD THE TRUTH

THERE WAS once (said Reginald) a woman who told the truth. Not all at once, of course, but the habit grew upon her gradually, like lichen on an apparently healthy tree. She had no children—otherwise it might have been different. It began with little things, for no particular reason except that her life was a rather empty one, and it is so easy to slip into the habit of telling the truth in little matters. And then it became difficult to draw the line at more important things, until at last she took to telling the truth about her age; she said she was forty-two and five months—by that time, you see, she was veracious even to months. It may have been pleasing to the angels, but her elder sister was not gratified. On the Woman's birthday, instead of the opera-tickets which she had hoped for, her sister gave her a view of Jerusalem from the Mount of Olives, which is not quite the same thing. The revenge of an elder sister may be long in coming, but, like a South-Eastern express, it arrives in its own good time.

The friends of the Woman tried to dissuade her from over-indulgence in the practice, but she said she was wedded to the truth; whereupon it was remarked that it was scarcely logical to be so much together in public. (No really provident woman lunches regularly with her husband if she wishes to burst upon him as a revelation at dinner. He must have time to forget; an afternoon is not enough.) And after a while her friends began to thin out in patches. Her passion for the truth was not compatible with a large visiting-list. For instance, she told Miriam Klopstock *exactly* how she looked at the Ilexes' ball. Certainly Miriam had asked for her candid opinion, but the Woman prayed in church every Sunday for peace in our time, and it was not consistent.

It was unfortunate, every one agreed, that she had no family; with a child or two in the house, there is an unconscious check upon too free an indulgence in the truth. Children are given us to discourage our better emotions. That is why the stage, with all its efforts, can never be as artificial as life; even in an Ibsen drama one must reveal to the audience things that one would suppress before the children or servants.

Fate may have ordained the truth-telling from the commencement and should justly bear some of the blame; but in having no children the Woman was guilty, at least, of contributory negligence.

Little by little she felt she was becoming a slave to what had once been merely an idle propensity; and one day she knew. Every woman tells ninety per cent. of the truth to her dressmaker; the other ten per cent. is the irreducible minimum of deception beyond which no self-respecting client trespasses. Madame Draga's establishment was a meeting-ground for naked truths and overdressed fictions, and it was here, the Woman felt, that she might make a final effort to recall the artless mendacity of past days. Madame herself was in an inspiring mood, with the air of a sphinx who knew all things and preferred to forget most of them. As a War Minister she might have been celebrated, but she was content to be merely rich.

'If I take it in here, and—Miss Howard, one moment, if you please—and there, and round like this—so—I really think you will find it quite easy.'

The Woman hesitated; it seemed to require such a small effort to simply acquiesce in Madame's views. But habit had become too strong. 'I'm afraid,' she faltered, 'it's just the least little bit in the world too——'

And by that least little bit she measured the deeps and eternities of her thraldom to fact. Madame was not best pleased at being contradicted on a professional matter, and when Madame lost her temper you usually found it afterwards in the bill.

And at last the dreadful thing came, as the Woman had foreseen all along that it must; it was one of those paltry little truths with which she harried her waking hours. On a raw Wednesday morning, in a few ill-chosen words, she told the cook that she drank. She remembered the scene afterwards as vividly as though it had been painted in her mind by Abbey. The cook was a good cook, as cooks go; and as cooks go she went.

Miriam Klopstock came to lunch the next day. Women and elephants never forget an injury.

From

REGINALD

IN RUSSIA

[1910]

REGINALD IN RUSSIA

REGINALD SAT in a corner of the Princess's salon and tried to forgive the furniture, which started out with an obvious intention of being Louise Quinze, but relapsed at frequent intervals into Wilhelm II.

He classified the Princess with that distinct type of woman that looks as if it habitually went out to feed hens in the rain.

Her name was Olga; she kept what she hoped and believed to be a fox-terrier, and professed what she thought were Socialist opinions. It is not necessary to be called Olga if you are a Russian Princess; in fact, Reginald knew quite a number who were called Vera; but the fox-terrier and the Socialism are essential.

'The Countess Lomshen keeps a bull-dog,' said the Princess suddenly. 'In England is it more chic to have a bull-dog than a fox-terrier?'

Reginald threw his mind back over the canine fashions of the last ten years and gave an evasive answer.

'Do you think her handsome, the Countess Lomshen?' asked the Princess.

Reginald thought the Countess's complexion suggested an exclusive diet of macaroons and pale sherry. He said so.

'But that cannot be possible,' said the Princess triumphantly; 'I've seen her eating fish-soup at Donon's.'

The Princess always defended a friend's complexion if it was really bad. With her, as with a great many of her sex, charity began at homeliness and did not generally progress much farther.

Reginald withdrew his macaroon and sherry theory, and became interested in a case of miniatures.

'That?' said the Princess; 'that is the old Princess Lorikoff. She lived in Millionaya Street, near the Winter Palace, and was one of the Court ladies of the Old Russian school. Her knowledge of people and events was extremely limited; but she used to patronize every one who came in contact with her. There was a story that when she died and left the Millionaya for Heaven she addressed St Peter in her formal staccato French: "Je suis la Princess Lor-i-koff. Il me donne grand plaisir à faire votre connaissance. Je vous en prie me présenter au Bon Dieu." St Peter made the desired introduction, and the Princess addressed le Bon Dieu: "Je suis la Princesse Lor-i-koff. Il me donne grand plaisir à faire votre connaissance. On a souvent parlé de vous á l'église de la rue Million." '

'Only the old and the clergy of Established churches know how to be flippant gracefully,' commented Reginald; 'which reminds me that in the Anglican Church in a certain foreign capital, which shall be nameless, I was present the other day when one of the junior chaplains was preaching in aid of distressed somethings or other, and he brought a really eloquent passage to a close with the remark, "The tears of the afflicted, to what shall I liken them—to diamonds?" The other junior chaplain, who had been dozing out of professional jealousy, awoke with a start and asked hurriedly, "Shall I play to diamonds, partner?" It didn't improve matters when the senior chaplain remarked dreamily, but with painful distinctness, "Double Diamonds." Every one looked at the preacher, half expecting him to redouble, but he contented himself with scoring what points he could under the circumstances.'

'You English are always so frivolous,' said the Princess. 'In Russia we have too many troubles to permit of our being light-hearted.'

Reginald gave a delicate shiver, such as an Italian greyhound might give in contemplating the approach of an ice age of which he personally disapproved, and resigned himself to the inevitable political discussion.

'Nothing that you hear about us in England is true,' was the Princess's hopeful beginning.

'I always refused to learn Russian geography at school,' observed Reginald; 'I was certain some of the names must be wrong.'

'Everything is wrong with our system of government,' continued the Princess placidly. 'The Bureaucrats think only of their pockets, and the people are exploited and plundered in every direction, and everything is mismanaged.'

'With us,' said Reginald, 'a Cabinet usually gets the credit of being depraved and worthless beyond the bounds of human conception by the time it has been in office about four years.'

'But if it is a bad Government you can turn it out at the election,' argued the Princess.

'As far as I remember, we generally do,' said Reginald.

'But here it is dreadful, every one goes to such extremes. In England you never go to extremes.'

'We go to the Albert Hall,' explained Reginald.

'There is always a see-saw with us between repression and violence,' continued the Princess; 'and the pity of it is the people are really not in the least inclined to be anything but peaceable. Nowhere will you find people more good-natured, or family circles where there is more affection.'

'There I agree with you,' said Reginald. 'I know a boy who lives somewhere on the French Quay who is a case in point. His hair curls naturally, especially on Sundays, and he plays bridge well, even for a Russian, which is saying much. I don't think he has any other accomplishments, but his family affection is really of a very high order. When his maternal grandmother died he didn't go as far as to give up bridge altogether but he declared on nothing but black suits for the next three months. That, I think, was really beautiful.'

The Princess was not impressed.

'I think you must be very self-indulgent and live only for amusement,' she said. 'A life of pleasure-seeking and card-playing and dissipation brings only dissatisfaction. You will find that out some day.'

'Oh, I know it turns out that way sometimes,' assented Reginald. 'Forbidden fizz is often the sweetest.'

But the remark was wasted on the Princess, who preferred champagne that had at least a suggestion of dis-
solved barley-sugar.

'I hope you will come and see me again,' she said in a
tone that prevented the hope from becoming too infectious;
adding as a happy after-thought, 'you must come to stay
with us in the country.'

Her particular part of the country was a few hundred
versts the other side of Tamboff, with some fifteen miles of
agrarian disturbance between her and the nearest neighbour. Reginald felt that there is some privacy which should
be sacred from intrusion.

THE RETICENCE OF
LADY ANNE

EGBERT CAME into the large, dimly lit drawing-room
with the air of a man who is not certain whether he is
entering a dovecote or a bomb factory, and is prepared for
either eventuality. The little domestic quarrel over the
luncheon-table had not been fought to a definite finish,
and the question was how far Lady Anne was in a mood to
renew or forgo hostilities. Her pose in the arm-chair by
the tea-table was rather elaborately rigid; in the gloom
of a December afternoon Egbert's pince-nez did not
materially help him to discern the expression of her face.

By way of breaking whatever ice might be floating on
the surface he made a remark about a dim religious light.
He or Lady Anne were accustomed to make that remark
between 4.30 and 6 on winter and late autumn evenings;
it was a part of their married life. There was no recognized
rejoinder to it, and Lady Anne made none.

Don Tarquinio lay astretch on the Persian rug, basking
in the firelight with superb indifference to the possible ill-

humour of Lady Anne. His pedigree was as flawlessly Persian as the rug, and his ruff was coming into the glory of its second winter. The page-boy, who had Renaissance tendencies, had christened him Don Tarquinio. Left to themselves, Egbert and Lady Anne would unfailingly have called him Fluff, but they were not obstinate.

Egbert poured himself out some tea. As the silence gave no sign of breaking on Lady Anne's initiative, he braced himself for another Yermak effort.

'My remark at lunch had a purely academic application,' he announced; 'you seem to put an unnecessarily personal significance into it.'

Lady Anne maintained her defensive barrier of silence. The bullfinch lazily filled in the interval with an air from *Iphigénie en Tauride*. Egbert recognized it immediately, because it was the only air the bullfinch whistled, and he had come to them with the reputation for whistling it. Both Egbert and Lady Anne would have preferred something from *The Yeomen of the Guard*, which was their favourite opera. In matters artistic they had a similarity of taste. They leaned towards the honest and explicit in art, a picture, for instance, that told its own story, with generous assistance from its title. A riderless warhorse with harness in obvious disarray, staggering into a courtyard full of pale swooning women, and marginally noted 'Bad News,' suggested to their minds a distinct interpretation of some military catastrophe. They could see what it was meant to convey, and explain it to friends of duller intelligence.

The silence continued. As a rule Lady Anne's displeasure became articulate and markedly voluble after four minutes of introductory muteness. Egbert seized the milk-jug and poured some of its contents into Don Tarquinio's saucer; as the saucer was already full to the brim an unsightly overflow was the result. Don Tarquinio looked on with a surprised interest that evanesced into elaborate unconsciousness when he was appealed to by Egbert to come and drink up some of the spilt matter. Don Tarquinio was prepared to play many rôles in life, but a vacuum carpet-cleaner was not one of them.

'Don't you think we're being rather foolish?' said Egbert cheerfully.

If Lady Anne thought so she didn't say so.

'I daresay the fault has been partly on my side,' continued Egbert, with evaporating cheerfulness. 'After all, I'm only human, you know. You seem to forget that I'm only human.'

He insisted on the point, as if there had been unfounded suggestions that he was built on Satyr lines, with goat continuations where the human left off.

The bullfinch recommenced its air from *Iphigénie en Tauride*. Egbert began to feel depressed. Lady Anne was not drinking her tea. Perhaps she was feeling unwell. But when Lady Anne felt unwell she was not wont to be reticent on the subject. 'No one knows what I suffer from indigestion' was one of her favourite statements; but the lack of knowledge can only have been caused by defective listening; the amount of information available on the subject would have supplied material for a monograph.

Evidently Lady Anne was not feeling unwell.

Egbert began to think he was being unreasonably dealt with; naturally he began to make concessions.

'I daresay,' he observed, taking as central a position on the hearth-rug as Don Tarquinio could be persuaded to concede him, 'I may have been to blame. I am willing, if I can thereby restore things to a happier standpoint, to undertake to lead a better life.'

He wondered vaguely how it would be possible. Temptations came to him, in middle age, tentatively and without insistence, like a neglected butcher-boy who asks for a Christmas box in February for no more hopeful reason than that he didn't get one in December. He had no more idea of succumbing to them than he had of purchasing the fish-knives and fur boas that ladies are impelled to sacrifice through the medium of advertisement columns during twelve months of the year. Still, there was something impressive in this unasked-for renunciation of possibly latent enormities.

Lady Anne showed no sign of being impressed.

Egbert looked at her nervously through his glasses. To get the worst of an argument with her was no new experience. To get the worst of a monologue was a humiliating novelty.

'I shall go and dress for dinner,' he announced in a voice into which he intended some shade of sternness to creep.

At the door a final access of weakness impelled him to make a further appeal.

'Aren't we being very silly?'

'A fool,' was Don Tarquinio's mental comment as the door closed on Egbert's retreat. Then he lifted his velvet forepaws in the air and leapt lightly on to a bookshelf immediately under the bullfinch's cage. It was the first time he had seemed to notice the bird's existence, but he was carrying out a long-formed theory of action with the precision of mature deliberation. The bullfinch, who had fancied himself something of a despot, depressed himself of a sudden into a third of his normal displacement; then he fell to a helpless wing-beating and shrill cheeping. He had cost twenty-seven shillings without the cage, but Lady Anne made no sign of interfering. She had been dead for two hours.

THE BLOOD-FEUD OF
TOAD-WATER

A WEST-COUNTRY EPIC

THE CRICKS lived at Toad-Water; and in the same lonely upland spot Fate had pitched the home of the Saunderses, and for miles around these two dwellings there was never a neighbour or a chimney or even a bury-ing-ground to bring a sense of cheerful communion or social intercourse. Nothing but fields and spinneys and barns, lanes and waste-lands. Such was Toad-Water; and, even so, Toad-Water had its history.

Thrust away in the benighted hinterland of a scattered market district, it might have been supposed that these two detached items of the Great Human Family would have leaned towards one another in a fellowship begotten of kindred circumstances and a common isolation from the outer world. And perhaps it had been so once, but the way of things had brought it otherwise. Indeed, otherwise. Fate, which had linked the two families in such unavoidable association of habitat, had ordained that the Crick house-hold should nourish and maintain among its earthly pos-sessions sundry head of domestic fowls, while to the Saunderses was given a disposition towards the cultivation of garden crops. Herein lay the material, ready to hand, for the coming of feud and ill-blood. For the grudge be-tween the man of herbs and the man of live stock is no new thing; you will find traces of it in the fourth chapter of Genesis. And one sunny afternoon in late spring-time the feud came—came, as such things mostly do come, with seeming aimlessness and triviality. One of the Crick hens, in obedience to the nomadic instincts of her kind, wearied of her legitimate scratching grounds, and flew over the low wall that divided the holdings of the neighbours. And there, on the yonder side, with a hurried consciousness that her time and opportunities might be limited, the misguided bird scratched and scraped and beaked and delved in the soft yielding bed that had been prepared for the solace and well-being of a colony of seedling onions. Little showers of earth-mould and root-fibres went spraying before the hen and behind her, and every minute the area of her operations widened. The onions suffered considerably. Mrs Saunders, sauntering at this luckless moment down the garden path, in order to fill her soul with reproaches at the iniquity of the weeds, which grew faster than she or

THE BLOOD-FEUD OF TOAD-WATER

her good man cared to remove them, stopped in mute
discomfiture before the presence of a more magnificent
grievance. And then, in the hour of her calamity, she
turned instinctively to the Great Mother, and gathered in
her capacious hands large clods of the hard brown soil
that lay at her feet. With a terrible sincerity of purpose,
though with a contemptible inadequacy of aim, she rained
her earth bolts at the marauder, and the bursting pellets
called forth a flood of cackling protest and panic from the
hastily departing fowl. Calmness under misfortune is not
an attribute of either hen-folk or womenkind, and while
Mrs Saunders declaimed over her onion bed such portions
of the slang dictionary as are permitted by the Noncon-
formist conscience to be said or sung, the Vasco da Gama
fowl was waking the echoes of Toad-Water with crescendo
bursts of throat music which compelled attention to her
griefs. Mrs Crick had a long family, and was therefore
licensed, in the eyes of her world, to have a short temper,
and when some of her ubiquitous offspring had informed
her, with the authority of eye-witnesses, that her neighbour had so far forgotten herself as to heave stones at her
hen—her best hen, the best layer in the countryside—her
thoughts clothed themselves in language 'unbecoming to a
Christian woman'—so at least said Mrs Saunders, to whom
most of the language was applied. Nor was she, on her
part, surprised at Mrs Crick's conduct in letting her hens
stray into other body's gardens, and then abusing of
them, seeing as how she remembered things against Mrs
Crick—and the latter simultaneously had recollections
of lurking episodes in the past of Susan Saunders that
were nothing to her credit. 'Fond memory, when all things
fade we fly to thee,' and in the paling light of an April
afternoon the two women confronted each other from
their respective sides of the party wall, recalling with shuddering breath the blots and blemishes of their neighbour's
family record. There was that aunt of Mrs Crick's who
had died a pauper in Exeter workhouse—every one knew
that Mrs Saunders' uncle on her mother's side drank him-

self to death—then there was that Bristol cousin of Mrs Crick's! From the shrill triumph with which his name was dragged in, his crime must have been pilfering from a cathedral at least, but as both remembrancers were speaking at once it was difficult to distinguish his infamy from the scandal which beclouded the memory of Mrs Saunders' brother's wife's mother—who may have been a regicide, and was certainly not a nice person as Mrs Crick painted her. And then, with an air of accumulating and irresistible conviction, each belligerent informed the other that she was no lady—after which they withdrew in a great silence, feeling that nothing further remained to be said. The chaffinches clinked in the apple trees and the bees droned round the berberis bushes, and the waning sunlight slanted pleasantly across the garden plots, but between the neighbour households had sprung up a barrier of hate, permeating and permanent.

The male heads of the families were necessarily drawn into the quarrel, and the children on either side were forbidden to have anything to do with the unhallowed offspring of the other party. As they had to travel a good three miles along the same road to school every day, this was awkward, but such things have to be. Thus all communication between the households was sundered. Except the cats. Much as Mrs Saunders might deplore it, rumour persistently pointed to the Crick he-cat as the presumable father of sundry kittens of which the Saunders she-cat was indisputably the mother. Mrs Saunders drowned the kittens, but the disgrace remained.

Summer succeeded spring, and winter summer, but the feud outlasted the waning seasons. Once, indeed, it seemed as though the healing influences of religion might restore to Toad-Water its erstwhile peace; the hostile families found themselves side by side in the soul-kindling atmosphere of a Revival Tea, where hymns were blended with a beverage that came of tea-leaves and hot water and took after the latter parent, and where ghostly counsel was tempered by garnishings of solidly fashioned buns—and here, wrought up by the environment of festive piety, Mrs Saunders so far unbent as to remark guardedly to Mrs Crick that the evening had been a fine one. Mrs Crick, under the influence of her ninth cup of tea and her fourth hymn, ventured on the hope that it might continue fine, but a maladroit allusion on the part of the Saunders good man to the backwardness of garden crops brought the Feud stalking forth from its corner with all its old bitterness. Mrs Saunders joined heartily in the singing of the final hymn, which told of peace and joy and archangels and golden glories; but her thoughts were dwelling on the pauper aunt of Exeter.

Years have rolled away, and some of the actors in this wayside drama have passed into the Unknown; other onions have arisen, have flourished, have gone their way, and the offending hen has long since expiated her misdeeds and lain with trussed feet and look of ineffable peace under the arched roof of Barnstaple market.

But the Blood-feud of Toad-Water survives to this day.

JUDKIN OF THE PARCELS

A FIGURE in an indefinite tweed suit, carrying brown-paper parcels. That is what we met suddenly, at the bend of a muddy Dorsetshire lane, and the roan mare stared and obviously thought of a curtsey. The mare is road-shy, with intervals of stolidity, and there is no telling what she will pass and what she won't. We call her Redford. That was my first meeting with Judkin, and the next time the circumstances were the same; the same muddy lane, the same rather apologetic figure in the tweed suit, the same—or very similar—parcels. Only this time the roan looked straight in front of her.

Whether I asked the groom or whether he advanced the information, I forget; but someway I gradually reconstructed the life-history of this trudger of the lanes. It was much the same, no doubt, as that of many others who are from time to time pointed out to one as having been aforetime in crack cavalry regiments and noted performers in the saddle; men who have breathed into their lungs the wonder of the East, have romped through life as through a cotillon, have had a thrust perhaps at the Viceroy's Cup, and done fantastic horse-fleshy things around the Gulf of Aden. And then a golden stream has dried up, the sunlight has faded suddenly out of things, and the gods have nodded 'Go.' And they have not gone. They have turned instead to the muddy lanes and cheap villas and the marked-down ills of life, to watch pear trees growing and to encourage hens for their eggs. And Judkin was even as these others; the wine had been suddenly spilt from his cup of life, and he had stayed to suck at the dregs which the wise throw away. In the days of his scorn for most things he would have stared the roan mare and her turnout out of all pretension to smartness, as he would have frozen a cheap claret behind its cork, or a plain woman behind her veil; and now he was walking stoically through the mud, in a tweed suit that would eventually go on to the gardener's boy, and would perhaps fit him. The dear gods, who know the end before the beginning, were perhaps growing a gardener's boy somewhere to fit the garments, and Judkin was only a caretaker, inhabiting a portion of them. That is what I like to think, and I am probably wrong. And Judkin, whose clothes had been to him once more than a religion, scarcely less sacred than a family quarrel, would carry those parcels back to his villa and to the wife who awaited him and them—a wife who may, for all we know to the contrary, have had a figure once, and perhaps has yet a heart of gold—of nine-carat gold, let us say at the least—but assuredly a soul of tape. And he that has fetched and carried will explain how it had fared with him in his dealings, and if he has brought the wrong sort of sugar or thread he will wheedle away the displeasure from that leaden face as a pastrycook girl will drive bluebottles off a stale bun. And that man has known what it was to coax the fret of a thoroughbred, to soothe its toss and sweat as it danced beneath him in the glee and chafe of its pulses and the glory of its thews. He has been in the raw places of the earth, where the desert beasts have whimpered their unthinkable psalmody, and their eyes have shone back the reflex of the midnight stars —and he can immerse himself in the tending of an incubator. It is horrible and wrong, and yet when I have met him in the lanes his face has worn a look of tedious cheerfulness that might pass for happiness. Has Judkin of the Parcels found something in the lees of life that I have missed in going to and fro over many waters? Is there more wisdom in his perverseness than in the madness of the wise? The dear gods know.

I don't think I saw Judkin more than three times all told, and always the lane was our point of contact; but as the roan mare was taking me to the station one heavy, cloud-smeared day, I passed a dull-looking villa that the groom, or instinct, told me was Judkin's home. From beyond a hedge of ragged elder-bushes could be heard the thud, thud of a spade, with an occasional clink and pause, as if some one had picked out a stone and thrown it to a distance, and I knew that *he* was doing nameless things to the roots of a pear tree. Near by him, I felt sure, would be lying a large and late vegetable marrow, and its largeness and lateness would be a theme of conversation at luncheon. It would be suggested that it should grace the harvest thanksgiving service; the harvest having been so generally unsatisfactory, it would be unfair to let the farmers supply all the material for rejoicing.

And while I was speeding townwards along the rails Judkin would be plodding his way to the vicarage bearing a vegetable marrow and a basketful of dahlias. The basket to be returned.

GABRIEL-ERNEST

'THERE IS a wild beast in your woods,' said the artist
Cunningham, as he was being driven to the station. It
was the only remark he had made during the drive, but as
Van Cheele had talked incessantly his companion's silence
had not been noticeable.

'A stray fox or two and some resident weasels. Nothing
more formidable,' said Van Cheele. The artist said nothing.

'What did you mean about a wild beast?' said Van
Cheele later, when they were on the platform.

'Nothing. My imagination. Here is the train,' said
Cunningham.

That afternoon Van Cheele went for one of his frequent
rambles through his woodland property. He had a stuffed
bittern in his study, and knew the names of quite a number of wild flowers, so his aunt had possibly some justification in describing him as a great naturalist. At any
rate, he was a great walker. It was his custom to take
mental notes of everything he saw during his walks, not so
much for the purpose of assisting contemporary science as
to provide topics for conversation afterwards. When the
bluebells began to show themselves in flower he made a
point of informing every one of the fact; the season of the
year might have warned his hearers of the likelihood of
such an occurrence, but at least they felt that he was being
absolutely frank with them.

What Van Cheele saw on this particular afternoon was,
however, something far removed from his ordinary range
of experience. On a shelf of smooth stone overhanging a
deep pool in the hollow of an oak coppice a boy of about
sixteen lay asprawl, drying his wet brown limbs luxuriously
in the sun. His wet hair, parted by a recent dive, lay close
to his head, and his light-brown eyes, so light that there
was an almost tigerish gleam in them, were turned towards
Van Cheele with a certain lazy watchfulness. It was an
unexpected apparition, and Van Cheele found himself

engaged in the novel process of thinking before he spoke. Where on earth could this wild-looking boy hail from? The miller's wife had lost a child some two months ago, supposed to have been swept away by the mill-race, but that had been a mere baby, not a half-grown lad.

'What are you doing there?' he demanded.

'Obviously, sunning myself,' replied the boy.

'Where do you live?'

'Here, in these woods.'

'You can't live in the woods,' said Van Cheele.

'They are very nice woods,' said the boy, with a touch of patronage in his voice.

'But where do you sleep at night?'

'I don't sleep at night; that's my busiest time.'

Van Cheele began to have an irritated feeling that he was grappling with a problem that was eluding him.

'What do you feed on?' he asked.

'Flesh,' said the boy, and he pronounced the word with slow relish, as though he were tasting it.

'Flesh! What flesh?'

'Since it interests you, rabbits, wild-fowl, hares, poultry, lambs in their season, children when I can get any; they're usually too well locked in at night, when I do most of my hunting. It's quite two months since I tasted child-flesh.'

Ignoring the chaffing nature of the last remark, Van Cheele tried to draw the boy on the subject of possible poaching operations.

'You're talking rather through your hat when you speak of feeding on hares.' (Considering the nature of the boy's toilet, the simile was hardly an apt one.) 'Our hillside hares aren't easily caught.'

'At night I hunt on four feet,' was the somewhat cryptic response.

'I suppose you mean that you hunt with a dog?' hazarded Van Cheele.

The boy rolled slowly over on to his back, and laughed

a weird low laugh, that was pleasantly like a chuckle and
disagreeably like a snarl.

'I don't fancy any dog would be very anxious for my
company, especially at night.'

Van Cheele began to feel that there was something
positively uncanny about the strange-eyed, strange-tongued
youngster.

'I can't have you staying in these woods,' he declared
authoritatively.

'I fancy you'd rather have me here than in your house,'
said the boy.

The prospect of this wild, nude animal in Van Cheele's
primly ordered house was certainly an alarming one.

'If you don't go I shall have to make you,' said Van
Cheele.

The boy turned like a flash, plunged into the pool, and
in a moment had flung his wet and glistening body half-
way up the bank where Van Cheele was standing. In an
otter the movement would not have been remarkable; in a
boy Van Cheele found it sufficiently startling. His foot
slipped as he made an involuntary backward movement,
and he found himself almost prostrate on the slippery
weed-grown bank, with those tigerish yellow eyes not very
far from his own. Almost instinctively he half-raised his
hand to his throat. The boy laughed again, a laugh in
which the snarl had nearly driven out the chuckle, and
then, with another of his astonishing lightning movements,
plunged out of view into a yielding tangle of weed and
fern.

'What an extraordinary wild animal!' said Van Cheele as
he picked himself up. And then he recalled Cunningham's
remark, 'There is a wild beast in your woods.'

Walking slowly homeward, Van Cheele began to turn
over in his mind various local occurrences which might be
traceable to the existence of this astonishing young savage.

Something had been thinning the game in the woods
lately, poultry had been missing from the farms, hares were
growing unaccountably scarcer, and complaints had

reached him of lambs being carried off bodily from the hills. Was it possible that this wild boy was really hunting the countryside in company with some clever poacher dog? He had spoken of hunting 'four-footed' by night, but then, again, he had hinted strangely at no dog caring to come near him, 'especially at night.' It was certainly puzzling. And then, as Van Cheele ran his mind over the various depredations that had been committed during the last month or two, he came suddenly to a dead stop, alike in his walk and his speculations. The child missing from the mill two months ago—the accepted theory was that it had tumbled into the mill-race and been swept away; but the mother had always declared she had heard a shriek on the hill side of the house, in the opposite direction from the water. It was unthinkable, of course, but he wished that the boy had not made that uncanny remark about child-flesh eaten two months ago. Such dreadful things should not be said even in fun.

Van Cheele, contrary to his usual wont, did not feel disposed to be communicative about his discovery in the wood. His position as a parish councillor and justice of the peace seemed somehow compromised by the fact that he was harbouring a personality of such doubtful repute on his property; there was even a possibility that a heavy bill of damages for raided lambs and poultry might be laid at his door. At dinner that night he was quite unusually silent.

'Where's your voice gone to?' said his aunt. 'One would think you had seen a wolf.'

Van Cheele, who was not familiar with the old saying, thought the remark rather foolish; if he *had* seen a wolf on his property his tongue would have been extraordinarily busy with the subject.

At breakfast next morning Van Cheele was conscious that his feeling of uneasiness regarding yesterday's episode had not wholly disappeared, and he resolved to go by train to the neighbouring cathedral town, hunt up Cunningham, and learn from him what he had really seen that had prompted the remark about a wild beast in the woods. With this resolution taken, his usual cheerfulness partially returned, and he hummed a bright little melody as he sauntered to the morning-room for his customary cigarette. As he entered the room the melody made way abruptly for a pious invocation. Gracefully asprawl on the ottoman, in an attitude of almost exaggerated repose, was the boy of the woods. He was drier than when Van Cheele had last seen him, but no other alteration was noticeable in his toilet.

'How dare you come here?' asked Van Cheele furiously.

'You told me I was not to stay in the woods,' said the boy calmly.

'But not to come here. Supposing my aunt should see you!'

And with a view to minimizing that catastrophe Van Cheele hastily obscured as much of his unwelcome guest as possible under the folds of a *Morning Post*. At that moment his aunt entered the room.

'This is a poor boy who has lost his way—and lost his memory. He doesn't know who he is or where he comes from,' explained Van Cheele desperately, glancing apprehensively at the waif's face to see whether he was going to add inconvenient candour to his other savage propensities.

Miss Van Cheele was enormously interested.

'Perhaps his underlinen is marked,' she suggested.

'He seems to have lost most of that, too,' said Van Cheele, making frantic little grabs at the *Morning Post* to keep it in its place.

A naked homeless child appealed to Miss Van Cheele as warmly as a stray kitten or derelict puppy would have done.

'We must do all we can for him,' she decided, and in a very short time a messenger, dispatched to the rectory, where a page-boy was kept, had returned with a suit of pantry clothes, and the necessary accessories of shirt, shoes, collar, etc. Clothed, clean, and groomed, the boy lost none of his uncanniness in Van Cheele's eyes, but his aunt found him sweet.

'We must call him something till we know who he really is,' she said. 'Gabriel-Ernest, I think; those are nice suitable names.'

Van Cheele agreed, but he privately doubted whether they were being grafted on to a nice suitable child. His misgivings were not diminished by the fact that his staid and elderly spaniel had bolted out of the house at the first incoming of the boy, and now obstinately remained shivering and yapping at the farther end of the orchard, while the canary, usually as vocally industrious as Van Cheele himself, had put itself on an allowance of frightened cheeps. More than ever he was resolved to consult Cunningham without loss of time.

As he drove off to the station his aunt was arranging that Gabriel-Ernest should help her to entertain the infant members of her Sunday-school class at tea that afternoon.

Cunningham was not at first disposed to be communicative.

'My mother died of some brain trouble,' he explained, 'so you will understand why I am averse to dwelling on anything of an impossibly fantastic nature that I may see or think that I have seen.'

'But what *did* you see?' persisted Van Cheele.

'What I thought I saw was something so extraordinary that no really sane man could dignify it with the credit of having actually happened. I was standing, the last evening I was with you, half-hidden in the hedgegrowth by the orchard gate, watching the dying glow of the sunset. Suddenly I became aware of a naked boy, a bather from some neighbouring pool, I took him to be, who was standing out on the bare hillside also watching the sunset. His pose was so suggestive of some wild faun of Pagan myth that I instantly wanted to engage him as a model, and in another moment I think I should have hailed him. But just then the sun dipped out of view, and all the orange and pink slid out of the landscape, leaving it cold and grey. And at the same moment an astounding thing happened—the boy vanished too!'

'What! vanished away into nothing?' asked Van Cheele excitedly.

'No; that is the dreadful part of it,' answered the artist; 'on the open hillside where the boy had been standing a second ago, stood a large wolf, blackish in colour, with gleaming fangs and cruel, yellow eyes. You may think——'

But Van Cheele did not stop for anything as futile as thought. Already he was tearing at top speed towards the station. He dismissed the idea of a telegram. 'Gabriel-Ernest is a werewolf' was a hopelessly inadequate effort at conveying the situation, and his aunt would think it was a code message to which he had omitted to give her the key. His one hope was that he might reach home before sundown. The cab which he chartered at the other end of the railway journey bore him with what seemed exasperating slowness along the country roads, which were pink and mauve with the flush of the sinking sun. His aunt was putting away some unfinished jams and cake when he arrived.

'Where is Gabriel-Ernest?' he almost screamed.

'He is taking the little Toop child home,' said his aunt. 'It was getting so late, I thought it wasn't safe to let it go back alone. What a lovely sunset, isn't it?'

But Van Cheele, although not oblivious of the glow in the western sky, did not stay to discuss its beauties. At a speed for which he was scarcely geared he raced along the narrow lane that led to the home of the Toops. On one side ran the swift current of the mill-stream, on the other rose the stretch of bare hillside. A dwindling rim of red sun showed still on the skyline, and the next turning must bring him in view of the ill-assorted couple he was pursuing. Then the colour went suddenly out of things, and a grey light settled itself with a quick shiver over the landscape. Van Cheele heard a shrill wail of fear, and stopped running.

Nothing was ever seen again of the Toop child or Gabriel-Ernest, but the latter's discarded garments were found lying in the road, so it was assumed that the child had fallen into the water, and that the boy had stripped and jumped in, in a vain endeavour to save it. Van Cheele and some workmen who were near by at the time testified to having heard a child scream loudly just near the spot where the clothes were found. Mrs. Toop, who had eleven other children, was decently resigned to her bereavement, but Miss Van Cheele sincerely mourned her lost foundling. It was on her initiative that a memorial brass was put up in the parish church to 'Gabriel-Ernest, an unknown boy, who bravely sacrificed his life for another.'

Van Cheele gave way to his aunt in most things, but he flatly refused to subscribe to the Gabriel-Ernest memorial.

CROSS CURRENTS

VANESSA PENNINGTON had a husband who was poor, with few extenuating circumstances, and an admirer who, though comfortably rich, was cumbered with a sense of honour. His wealth made him welcome in Vanessa's eyes, but his code of what was right impelled him to go away and forget her, or at the most to think of her in the intervals of doing a great many other things. And although Alaric Clyde loved Vanessa, and thought he should always go on loving her, he gradually and unconsciously allowed himself to be wooed and won by a more alluring mistress; he fancied that his continued shunning of the haunts of men was a self-imposed exile, but his heart was caught in the spell of the Wilderness, and the Wilderness was kind and beautiful to him. When one is young and strong and unfettered the wild earth can be very kind and very beautiful. Witness the legion of men who were once young and unfettered and now eat out their souls in dustbins, because, having erstwhile known and loved the Wilderness, they broke from her thrall and turned aside into beaten paths.

In the high waste places of the world Clyde roamed and hunted and dreamed, death-dealing and gracious as some god of Hellas, moving with his horses and servants and four-footed camp followers from one dwelling ground to another, a welcome guest among wild primitive village folk and nomads, a friend and slayer of the fleet, shy beasts around him. By the shores of misty upland lakes he shot the wild fowl that had winged their way to him across half the old world; beyond Bokhara he watched the wild Aryan horsemen at their gambols; watched, too, in some dim-lit tea-house one of those beautiful uncouth dances that one can never wholly forget; or, making a wide cast down to the valley of the Tigris, swam and rolled in its snow-cooled racing waters. Vanessa, meanwhile, in a Bayswater back street, was making out the weekly laundry list, attending bargain sales, and, in her more adventurous moments, trying new ways of cooking whiting. Occasionally she went to bridge parties, where, if the play was not illuminating, at least one learned a great deal about the private life of some of the Royal and Imperial Houses. Vanessa, in a way, was glad that Clyde had done the proper thing. She had a strong natural bias towards respectability, though she would have preferred to have been respectable in smarter surroundings, where her example would have done more good. To be beyond reproach was one thing, but it would have been nicer to have been nearer to the Park.

And then of a sudden her regard for respectability and Clyde's sense of what was right were thrown on the scrap-heap of unnecessary things. They had been useful and highly important in their time, but the death of Vanessa's husband made them of no immediate moment.

The news of the altered condition of things followed Clyde with leisurely persistence from one place of call to another, and at last ran him to a standstill somewhere in the Orenburg Steppe. He would have found it exceedingly difficult to analyse his feelings on receipt of the tidings. The Fates had unexpectedly (and perhaps just a little officiously) removed an obstacle from his path. He supposed he was overjoyed, but he missed the feeling of elation which he had experienced some four months ago when he had bagged a snow-leopard with a lucky shot after a day's fruitless stalking. Of course he would go back and ask Vanessa to marry him, but he was determined on enforcing a condition: on no account would he desert his newer love. Vanessa would have to agree to come out into the Wilderness with him.

The lady hailed the return of her lover with even more relief than had been occasioned by his departure. The death of John Pennington had left his widow in circumstances which were more straitened than ever, and the Park had receded even from her notepaper, where it had long been retained as a courtesy title on the principle that addresses are given to us to conceal our whereabouts. Certainly she was more independent now than heretofore, but independence, which means so much to many women, was of little account to Vanessa, who came under the heading of the mere female. She made little ado about accepting Clyde's condition, and announced herself ready to follow him to the end of the world; as the world was round she nourished a complacent idea that in the ordinary course of things one would find oneself in the neighbourhood of Hyde Park Corner sooner or later no matter how far afield one wandered.

East of Budapest her complacency began to filter away, and when she saw her husband treating the Black Sea with a familiarity which she had never been able to assume towards the English Channel, misgivings began to crowd in upon her. Adventures which would have presented an amusing and enticing aspect to a better-bred woman aroused in Vanessa only the twin sensations of fright and discomfort. Flies bit her, and she was persuaded that it was only sheer boredom that prevented camels from doing the same. Clyde did his best, and a very good best it was, to infuse something of the banquet into their prolonged desert picnics, but even snow-cooled Heidsieck lost its flavour when you were convinced that the dusky cupbearer who served it with such reverent elegance was only waiting a convenient opportunity to cut your throat. It was useless for Clyde to give Yussuf a character for devotion such as is rarely found in any Western servant. Vanessa was well enough educated to know that all dusky-skinned people take human life as unconcernedly as Bayswater folk take singing lessons.

And with a growing irritation and querulousness on her part came a further disenchantment, born of the inability of husband and wife to find a common ground of interest. The habits and migrations of the sand grouse, the folklore and customs of Tartars and Turkomans, the points of a Cossack pony—there were matters which evoked only a bored indifference in Vanessa. On the other hand, Clyde was not thrilled on being informed that the Queen of Spain detested mauve, or that a certain Royal duchess, for whose tastes he was never likely to be called on to cater, nursed a violent but perfectly respectable passion for beef olives.

Vanessa began to arrive at the conclusion that a husband who added a roving disposition to a settled income was a mixed blessing. It was one thing to go to the end of the world; it was quite another thing to make oneself at home there. Even respectability seemed to lose some of its virtue when one practised it in a tent.

Bored and disillusioned with the drift of her new life, Vanessa was undisguisedly glad when distraction offered itself in the person of Mr Dobrinton, a chance acquaintance whom they had first run against in the primitive hostelry of a benighted Caucasian town. Dobrinton was elaborately British, in deference perhaps to the memory of his mother, who was said to have derived part of her origin from an English governess who had come to Lemberg a long way back in the last century. If you had called him Dobrinski when off his guard he would probably have responded readily enough; holding, no doubt, that the end crowns all, he had taken a slight liberty with the family patronymic. To look at, Mr Dobrinton was not a very attractive specimen of masculine humanity, but in Vanessa's eyes he was a link with that civilization which Clyde seemed so ready to ignore and forgo. He could sing 'Yip-I-Addy' and spoke of several duchesses as if he knew them—in his more inspired moments almost as if they knew him. He even pointed out blemishes in the cuisine or cellar departments of some of the more august London restaurants, a species of Higher Criticism which was listened to by Vanessa in awe-stricken admiration. And, above all, he sympathized, at first discreetly, afterwards with more latitude, with her fretful discontent at Clyde's nomadic instincts. Business connected with oil-wells had brought Dobrinton to the neighbourhood of Baku; the pleasure of appealing to an appreciative female audience induced him to deflect his return journey so as to coincide a good deal with his new acquaintances' line of march. And while Clyde trafficked with Persian horse-dealers or hunted the wild grey pigs in their lairs and added to his notes on Central Asian game-fowl, Dobrinton and the lady discussed the ethics of desert respectability from points of view that showed a daily tendency to converge. And one evening Clyde dined alone, reading between the courses a long letter from Vanessa, justifying her action in flitting to more civilized lands with a more congenial companion.

It was distinctly evil luck for Vanessa, who really was thoroughly respectable at heart, that she and her lover should run into the hands of Kurdish brigands on the first day of their flight. To be mewed up in a squalid Kurdish village in close companionship with a man who was only your husband by adoption, and to have the attention of all Europe drawn to your plight, was about the least respectable thing that could happen. And there were international complications, which made things worse. 'English lady and her husband, of foreign nationality, held by Kurdish brigands who demand ransom' had been the report of the nearest Consul. Although Dobrinton was British at heart, the other portions of him belonged to the Habsburgs, and though the Habsburgs took no great pride or pleasure in this particular unit of their wide and varied possessions, and would gladly have exchanged him for some interesting bird or mammal for the Schoenbrunn Park, the code of international dignity demanded that they should display a decent solicitude for his restoration. And while the Foreign Offices of the two countries were taking the usual steps to secure the release of their respective subjects a further horrible complication ensued. Clyde, following on the track of the fugitives, not with any special desire to overtake them, but with a dim feeling that it was expected of him, fell into the hands of the same community of brigands. Diplomacy, while anxious to do its best for a lady in misfortune, showed signs of becoming restive at this expansion of its task; as a frivolous young gentleman in Downing Street remarked, 'Any husband of Mrs Dobrinton's we shall be glad to extricate, but let us know how many there are of them.' For a woman who valued respectability Vanessa really had no luck.

Meanwhile the situation of the captives was not free from embarrassment. When Clyde explained to the Kurdish headmen the nature of his relationship with the runaway couple they were gravely sympathetic, but vetoed any idea of summary vengeance, since the Habsburgs would be sure to insist on the delivery of Dobrinton alive, and in a reasonably undamaged condition. They did not object to Clyde administrating a beating to his rival for half an hour every Monday and Thursday, but Dobrinton turned such a sickly green when he heard of this arrangement that the chief was obliged to withdraw the concession.

And so, in the cramped quarters of a mountain hut, the ill-assorted trio watched the insufferable hours crawl slowly by. Dobrinton was too frightened to be conversational, Vanessa was too mortified to open her lips, and Clyde was moodily silent. The little Lemberg *négociant* plucked up heart once to give a quavering rendering of 'Yip-I-Addy,' but when he reached the statement 'home was never like this' Vanessa tearfully begged him to stop. And silence fastened itself with growing insistence on the three captives who were so tragically herded together; thrice a day they drew near to one another to swallow the meal that had been prepared for them, like desert beasts meeting in mute suspended hostility at the drinking-pool, and then drew back to resume the vigil of waiting.

Clyde was less carefully watched than the others. 'Jealousy will keep him to the woman's side,' thought his Kurdish captors. They did not know that his wilder, truer love was calling to him with a hundred voices from beyond the village bounds. And one evening, finding that he was not getting the attention to which he was entitled, Clyde slipped away down the mountain side and resumed his study of Central Asian game-fowl. The remaining captives were guarded henceforth with greater rigour, but Dobrinton at any rate scarcely regretted Clyde's departure.

The long arm, or perhaps one might better say the long purse, of diplomacy at last effected the release of the prisoners, but the Habsburgs were never to enjoy the guerdon of their outlay. On the quay of the little Black Sea port, where the rescued pair came once more into contact with civilization, Dobrinton was bitten by a dog which was assumed to be mad, though it may only have been indiscriminating. The victim did not wait for symptoms of rabies to declare themselves, but died forthwith of fright, and Vanessa made the homeward journey alone, conscious somehow of a sense of slightly restored respectability. Clyde, in the intervals of correcting the proofs of his book on the game-fowl of Central Asia, found time to press a divorce suit through the Courts, and as soon as possible hied him away to the congenial solitudes of the Gobi Desert to collect material for a work on the fauna of that region. Vanessa, by virtue perhaps of her earlier intimacy with the cooking rites of the whiting,

obtained a place on the kitchen staff of a West End Club.
It was not brilliant, but at least it was within two minutes
of the Park.

THE BAKER'S DOZEN

Characters:

MAJOR RICHARD DUMBARTON
MRS CAREWE
MRS PALY-PAGET

Scene: Deck of eastward-bound steamer. Major Dumbarton seated on deck-chair, another chair by his side, with the
name 'Mrs Carewe' painted on it, a third near by.

*Enter, R., Mrs Carewe, seats herself leisurely in her deck-
chair, the Major affecting to ignore her presence.*

MAJOR [*turning suddenly*]: Emily! After all these years!
This is fate!

EM.: Fate! Nothing of the sort; it's only me. You men
are always such fatalists. I deferred my departure three
whole weeks, in order to come out in the same boat that
I saw you were travelling by. I bribed the steward to
put our chairs side by side in an unfrequented corner,
and I took enormous pains to be looking particularly
attractive this morning, and then you say, 'This is fate.'
I *am* looking particularly attractive, am I not?

MAJ.: More than ever. Time has only added a ripeness to
your charms.

EM.: I knew you'd put it exactly in those words. The
phraseology of love-making is awfully limited, isn't it?
After all, the chief charm is in the fact of being made
love to. You *are* making love to me, aren't you?

MAJ.: Emily dearest, I had already begun making advances,
even before you sat down here. I also bribed the steward
to put our seats together in a secluded corner. 'You may

consider it done, sir,' was his reply. That was immediately after breakfast.

EM.: How like a man to have his breakfast first. I attended to the seat business as soon as I left my cabin.

MAJ.: Don't be unreasonable. It was only at breakfast that I discovered your blessed presence on the boat. I paid violent and unusual attention to a flapper all through the meal in order to make you jealous. She's probably in her cabin writing reams about me to a fellow-flapper at this very moment.

EM.: You needn't have taken all that trouble to make me jealous, Dickie. You did that years ago, when you married another woman.

MAJ.: Well, you had gone and married another man—a widower, too, at that.

EM.: Well, there's no particular harm in marrying a widower, I suppose. I'm ready to do it again, if I meet a really nice one.

MAJ.: Look here, Emily, it's not fair to go at that rate. You're a lap ahead of me the whole time. It's my place to propose to you; all you've got to do is to say 'Yes.'

EM.: Well, I've practically said it already, so we needn't dawdle over that part.

MAJ.: Oh, well——

They look at each other, then suddenly embrace with considerable energy.

MAJ.: We dead-heated it that time. [*Suddenly jumping to his feet*] Oh, d—— I'd forgotten!

EM.: Forgotten what?

MAJ.: The children. I ought to have told you. Do you mind children?

EM.: Not in moderate quantities. How many have you got?

MAJ. [*counting hurriedly on his fingers*]: Five.

EM.: Five!

MAJ. [*anxiously*]: Is that too many?

EM.: It's rather a number. The worst of it is, I've some myself.

MAJ.: Many?

EM.: Eight.

MAJ.: Eight in six years! Oh, Emily!

EM.: Only four were my own. The other four were by my husband's first marriage. Still, that practically makes eight.

MAJ.: And eight and five make thirteen. We can't start our married life with thirteen children; it would be most unlucky. [*Walks up and down in agitation.*] Some way must be found out of this. If we could only bring them down to twelve. Thirteen is so horribly unlucky.

EM.: Isn't there some way by which we could part with one or two? Don't the French want more children? I've often seen articles about it in the *Figaro*.

MAJ.: I fancy they want French children. Mine don't even speak French.

EM.: There's always a chance that one of them might turn out depraved and vicious, and then you could disown him. I've heard of that being done.

MAJ.: But, good gracious, you've got to educate him first. You can't expect a boy to be vicious till he's been to a good school.

EM.: Why couldn't he be naturally depraved? Lots of boys are.

MAJ.: Only when they inherit it from depraved parents. You don't suppose there's any depravity in me, do you?

EM.: It sometimes skips a generation, you know. Weren't any of your family bad?

MAJ.: There was an aunt who was never spoken of.

EM.: There you are!

MAJ.: But one can't build too much on that. In mid-Victorian days they labelled all sorts of things as unspeakable that we should speak about quite tolerantly. I daresay this particular aunt had only married a Unitarian, or rode to hounds on both sides of her horse, or something of that sort. Anyhow, we can't wait indefinitely for one of the children to take after a doubtfully depraved great-aunt. Something else must be thought of.

EM.: Don't people ever adopt children from other families?

MAJ.: I've heard of it being done by childless couples, and those sort of people——

EM.: Hush! Some one's coming. Who is it?

MAJ.: Mrs Paly-Paget.

EM.: The very person!

MAJ.: What, to adopt a child? Hasn't she got any?

EM.: Only one miserable hen-baby.

MAJ.: Let's sound her on the subject.

Enter Mrs Paly-Paget, R.

Ah, good morning, Mrs Paly-Paget. I was just wondering at breakfast where did we meet last?

MRS P.-P.: At the Criterion, wasn't it? [*Drops into vacant chair.*]

MAJ.: At the Criterion, of course.

MRS P.-P.: I was dining with Lord and Lady Slugford. Charming people, but so mean. They took us afterwards to the Velodrome, to see some dancer interpreting Mendelssohn's 'songs without clothes.' We were all packed up in a little box near the roof, and you may imagine how hot it was. It was like a Turkish bath. And, of course, one couldn't see anything.

MAJ.: Then it was not like a Turkish bath.

MRS P.-P.: Major!

EM.: We were just talking of you when you joined us.

MRS P.-P.: Really! Nothing very dreadful, I hope.

EM.: Oh, dear, no! It's too early on the voyage for that sort of thing. We were feeling rather sorry for you.

MRS P.-P.: Sorry for me? Whatever for?

MAJ.: Your childless hearth and all that, you know. No little pattering feet.

MRS P.-P.: Major! How dare you? I've got my little girl, I suppose you know. Her feet can patter as well as other children's.

MAJ.: Only one pair of feet.

MRS P.-P.: Certainly. My child isn't a centipede. Considering the way they move us about in those horrid jungle stations, without a decent bungalow to set one's foot in, I consider I've got a heartless child, rather than a childless hearth. Thank you for your sympathy all the same. I daresay it was well meant. Impertinence often is.

EM.: Dear Mrs Paly-Paget, we were only feeling sorry for your sweet little girl when she grows older, you know. No little brothers and sisters to play with.

MRS P.-P.: Mrs Carewe, this conversation strikes me as being indelicate, to say the least of it. I've only been married two and a half years, and my family is naturally a small one.

MAJ.: Isn't it rather an exaggeration to talk of one little female child as a family? A family suggests numbers.

MRS P.-P.: Really, Major, your language is extraordinary. I daresay I've only got a little female child, as you call it, at present——

MAJ.: Oh, it won't change into a boy later on, if that's what you're counting on. Take our word for it; we've had so much more experience in these affairs than you have. Once a female, always a female. Nature is not infallible, but she always abides by her mistakes.

MRS P.-P. [*rising*]: Major Dumbarton, these boats are uncomfortably small, but I trust we shall find ample accommodation for avoiding each other's society during the rest of the voyage. The same wish applies to you, Mrs Carewe.

Exit Mrs Paly-Paget, L.

MAJ.: What an unnatural mother! [*Sinks into chair.*]

EM.: I wouldn't trust a child with any one who had a temper like hers. Oh, Dickie, why did you go and have such a large family? You always said you wanted me to be the mother of your children.

MAJ.: I wasn't going to wait while you were founding and fostering dynasties in other directions. Why you couldn't be content to have children of your own, without collecting them like batches of postage stamps, I can't think. The idea of marrying a man with four children!

EM.: Well, you're asking me to marry one with five.

MAJ.: Five! [*Springing to his feet.*] Did I say five?

EM.: You certainly said five.

MAJ.: Oh, Emily, supposing I've miscounted them! Listen now, keep count with me. Richard—that's after me, of course.

EM.: One.

MAJ.: Albert-Victor—that must have been in Coronation year.

EM.: Two!

MAJ.: Maud. She's called after——

EM.: Never mind who she's called after. Three!

MAJ.: And Gerald.

EM.: Four!

MAJ.: That's the lot.

EM.: Are you sure?

MAJ.: I swear that's the lot. I must have counted Albert-Victor as two.

EM.: Richard!

MAJ.: Emily!

They embrace.

THE MOUSE

THEODORIC VOLER had been brought up, from infancy to the confines of middle age, by a fond mother whose chief solicitude had been to keep him screened from what she called the coarser realities of life. When she died she left Theodoric alone in a world that was as real as ever, and a good deal coarser than he considered it had any need to be. To a man of his temperament and upbringing even a simple railway journey was crammed with petty annoyances and minor discords, and as he settled himself down in a second-class compartment one September morning he was conscious of ruffled feelings and general mental discomposure. He had been staying at a country vicarage, the inmates of which had been certainly neither brutal nor bacchanalian, but their supervision of the domestic establishment had been of that lax order which invites disaster. The pony carriage that was to take him to the station had never been properly ordered, and when the moment for his departure drew near the handy-man who should have produced the required article was nowhere to be found. In this emergency Theodoric, to his mute but very intense disgust, found himself obliged to collaborate with the vicar's daughter in the task of harnessing the pony, which necessitated groping about in an ill-lighted outhouse called a stable, and smelling very like one—except in patches where it smelt of mice. Without being actually afraid of mice, Theodoric classed them among the coarser incidents of life, and considered that Providence, with a little exercise of moral courage, might long ago have recognized that they were not indispensable, and have withdrawn them from circulation. As the train glided out of the station Theodoric's nervous imagination accused himself of exhaling a weak odour of stableyard, and possibly of displaying a mouldy straw or two on his usually well-brushed garments. Fortunately the only other occupant of the compartment, a lady of about the same age as himself, seemed inclined for slumber rather than scrutiny; the train was not due to stop till the terminus was reached, in about an hour's time, and the carriage was of the old-fashioned sort, that held no communication with a corridor, therefore no further travelling companions were likely to intrude on Theodoric's semi-privacy. And yet the train had scarcely attained its normal speed before he became reluctantly but vividly aware that he was not alone with the slumbering lady; he was not even alone in his own clothes. A warm, creeping movement over his flesh betrayed the unwelcome and highly resented presence, unseen but poignant, of a strayed mouse, that had evidently dashed into its present retreat during the episode of the pony harnessing. Furtive stamps and shakes and wildly

directed pinches failed to dislodge the intruder, whose
motto, indeed, seemed to be Excelsior; and the lawful
occupant of the clothes lay back against the cushions and
endeavoured rapidly to evolve some means for putting an
end to the dual ownership. It was unthinkable that he
should continue for the space of a whole hour in the
horrible position of a Rowton House for vagrant mice
(already his imagination had at least doubled the numbers
of the alien invasion). On the other hand, nothing less
drastic than partial disrobing would ease him of his tor-
mentor, and to undress in the presence of a lady, even for
so laudable a purpose, was an idea that made his eartips
tingle in a blush of abject shame. He had never been able
to bring himself even to the mild exposure of open-work
socks in the presence of the fair sex. And yet—the lady
in this case was to all appearances soundly and securely
asleep; the mouse, on the other hand, seemed to be trying
to crowd a Wanderjahr into a few strenuous minutes. If
there is any truth in the theory of transmigration, this
particular mouse must certainly have been in a former state
a member of the Alpine Club. Sometimes in its eagerness
it lost its footing and slipped for half an inch or so; and
then, in fright, or more probably temper, it bit. Theodoric
was goaded into the most audacious undertaking of his
life. Crimsoning to the hue of a beetroot and keeping an
agonized watch on his slumbering fellow-traveller, he
swiftly and noiselessly secured the ends of his railway-rug
to the racks on either side of the carriage, so that a substantial curtain hung athwart the compartment. In the
narrow dressing-room that he had thus improvised he
proceeded with violent haste to extricate himself partially
and the mouse entirely from the surrounding casings of
tweed and half-wool. As the unravelled mouse gave a wild
leap to the floor, the rug, slipping its fastening at either
end, also came down with a heart-curdling flop, and almost
simultaneously the awakened sleeper opened her eyes. With
a movement almost quicker than the mouse's, Theodoric
pounced on the rug, and hauled its ample folds chin-high

over his dismantled person as he collapsed into the further corner of the carriage. The blood raced and beat in the veins of his neck and forehead, while he waited dumbly for the communication-cord to be pulled. The lady, however, contented herself with a silent stare at her strangely muffled companion. How much had she seen, Theodoric queried to himself, and in any case what on earth must she think of his present posture?

'I think I have caught a chill,' he ventured desperately.

'Really, I'm sorry,' she replied. 'I was just going to ask you if you would open this window.'

'I fancy it's malaria,' he added, his teeth chattering slightly, as much from fright as from a desire to support his theory.

'I've got some brandy in my hold-all, if you'll kindly reach it down for me,' said his companion.

'Not for worlds—I mean, I never take anything for it,' he assured her earnestly.

'I suppose you caught it in the Tropics?'

Theodoric, whose acquaintance with the Tropics was limited to an annual present of a chest of tea from an uncle in Ceylon, felt that even the malaria was slipping from him. Would it be possible, he wondered, to disclose the real state of affairs to her in small instalments?

'Are you afraid of mice?' he ventured, growing, if possible, more scarlet in the face.

'Not unless they came in quantities, like those that ate up Bishop Hatto. Why do you ask?'

'I had one crawling inside my clothes just now,' said Theodoric in a voice that hardly seemed his own. 'It was a most awkward situation.'

'It must have been, if you wear your clothes at all tight,' she observed; 'but mice have strange ideas of comfort.'

'I had to get rid of it while you were asleep,' he continued; then, with a gulp, he added, 'it was getting rid of it that brought me to—to this.'

'Surely leaving off one small mouse wouldn't bring on a chill,' she exclaimed, with a levity that Theodoric accounted abominable.

Evidently she had detected something of his predicament, and was enjoying his confusion. All the blood in his body seemed to have mobilized in one concentrated blush, and an agony of abasement, worse than a myriad mice, crept up and down over his soul. And then, as reflection began to assert itself, sheer terror took the place of humiliation. With every minute that passed the train was rushing nearer to the crowded and bustling terminus where dozens of prying eyes would be exchanged for the one paralysing pair that watched him from the further corner of the carriage. There was one slender despairing chance, which the next few minutes must decide. His fellow-traveller might relapse into a blessed slumber. But as the minutes throbbed by, that chance ebbed away. The furtive glance which Theodoric stole at her from time to time disclosed only an unwinking wakefulness.

'I think we must be getting near now,' she presently observed.

Theodoric had already noted with growing terror the recurring stacks of small, ugly dwellings that heralded the journey's end. The words acted as a signal. Like a hunted beast breaking cover and dashing madly towards some other haven of momentary safety he threw aside his rug, and struggled frantically into his dishevelled garments. He was conscious of dull suburban stations racing past the window, of a choking, hammering sensation in his throat and heart, and of an icy silence in that corner towards which he dared not look. Then as he sank back in his seat, clothed and almost delirious, the train slowed down to a final crawl, and the woman spoke.

'Would you be so kind,' she asked, 'as to get me a porter to put me into a cab? It's a shame to trouble you when you're feeling unwell, but being blind makes one so helpless at a railway station.'

From

THE CHRONICLES
OF CLOVIS

[1911]

TOBERMORY

IT WAS a chill, rain-washed afternoon of a late August day, that indefinite season when partridges are still in security or cold storage, and there is nothing to hunt—unless one is bounded on the north by the Bristol Channel, in which case one may lawfully gallop after fat red stags. Lady Blemley's house-party was not bounded on the north by the Bristol Channel, hence there was a full gathering of her guests round the tea-table on this particular afternoon. And, in spite of the blankness of the season and the triteness of the occasion, there was no trace in the company of that fatigued restlessness which means a dread of the pianola and a subdued hankering for auction bridge. The undisguised open-mouthed attention of the entire party was fixed on the homely negative personality of Mr Cornelius Appin. Of all her guests, he was the one who had come to Lady Blemley with the vaguest reputation. Some one had said he was 'clever,' and he had got his invitation in the moderate expectation, on the part of his hostess, that some portion at least of his cleverness would be contributed to the general entertainment. Until tea-time that day she had been unable to discover in what direction, if any, his cleverness lay. He was neither a wit nor a croquet champion, a hypnotic force nor a begetter of amateur theatricals. Neither did his exterior suggest the sort of man in whom women are willing to pardon a generous measure of mental deficiency. He had subsided into mere Mr Appin, and the Cornelius seemed a piece of transparent baptismal bluff. And now he was claiming to have launched on the world a discovery beside which the invention of gunpowder, of the printing-press, and of steam locomotion were inconsiderable trifles. Science had made bewildering strides in many directions during recent decades, but this thing seemed to belong to the domain of miracle rather than to scientific achievement.

'And do you really ask us to believe,' Sir Wilfrid was saying, 'that you have discovered a means for instructing animals in the art of human speech, and that dear old Tobermory has proved your first successful pupil?'

'It is a problem at which I have worked for the last seventeen years,' said Mr Appin, 'but only during the last eight or nine months have I been rewarded with glimmerings of success. Of course I have experimented with thousands of animals, but latterly only with cats, those wonderful creatures which have assimilated themselves so marvellously with our civilization while retaining all their highly developed feral instincts. Here and there among cats one comes across an outstanding superior intellect, just as one does among the ruck of human beings, and when I made the acquaintance of Tobermory a week ago I saw at once that I was in contact with a "Beyond-cat" of extraordinary intelligence. I had gone far along the road to success in recent experiments; with Tobermory, as you call him, I have reached the goal.'

Mr Appin concluded his remarkable statement in a voice which he strove to divest of a triumphant inflection. No one said 'Rats,' though Clovis's lips moved in a monosyllabic contortion, which probably invoked those rodents of disbelief.

'And do you mean to say,' asked Miss Resker, after a slight pause, 'that you have taught Tobermory to say and understand easy sentences of one syllable?'

'My dear Miss Resker,' said the wonder-worker patiently, 'one teaches little children and savages and backward adults in that piecemeal fashion; when one has once solved the problem of making a beginning with an animal of highly developed intelligence one has no need for those halting methods. Tobermory can speak our language with perfect correctness.'

This time Clovis very distinctly said, 'Beyond-rats!' Sir Wilfrid was more polite, but equally sceptical.

'Hadn't we better have the cat in and judge for ourselves?' suggested Lady Blemley.

Sir Wilfrid went in search of the animal, and the company settled themselves down to the languid expectation of witnessing some more or less adroit drawing-room ventriloquism.

In a minute Sir Wilfrid was back in the room, his face white beneath its tan and his eyes dilated with excitement.

'By Gad, it's true!'

His agitation was unmistakably genuine, and his hearers started forward in a thrill of awakened interest.

Collapsing into an arm-chair he continued breathlessly: 'I found him dozing in the smoking-room, and called out to him to come for his tea. He blinked at me in his usual way, and I said, "Come on, Toby; don't keep us waiting"; and, by Gad! he drawled out in a most horribly natural voice that he'd come when he dashed well pleased! I nearly jumped out of my skin!'

Appin had preached to absolutely incredulous hearers; Sir Wilfrid's statement carried instant conviction. A Babel-like chorus of startled exclamation arose, amid which the scientist sat mutely enjoying the first fruit of his stupendous discovery.

In the midst of the clamour Tobermory entered the room and made his way with velvet tread and studied unconcern across to the group seated round the tea-table.

A sudden hush of awkwardness and constraint fell on the company. Somehow there seemed an element of embarrassment in addressing on equal terms a domestic cat of acknowledged mental ability.

'Will you have some milk, Tobermory?' asked Lady Blemley in a rather strained voice.

'I don't mind if I do,' was the response, couched in a tone of even indifference. A shiver of suppressed excitement went through the listeners, and Lady Blemley might be excused for pouring out the saucerful of milk rather unsteadily.

'I'm afraid I've spilt a good deal of it,' she said apologetically.

'After all, it's not my Axminster,' was Tobermory's rejoinder.

Another silence fell on the group, and then Miss Resker, in her best district-visitor manner, asked if the human language had been difficult to learn. Tobermory looked squarely at her for a moment and then fixed his gaze serenely on the middle distance. It was obvious that boring questions lay outside his scheme of life.

'What do you think of human intelligence?' asked Mavis Pellington lamely.

'Of whose intelligence in particular?' asked Tobermory coldly.

'Oh, well, mine for instance,' said Mavis, with a feeble laugh.

'You put me in an embarrassing position,' said Tobermory, whose tone and attitude certainly did not suggest a shred of embarrassment. 'When your inclusion in this house-party was suggested Sir Wilfrid protested that you were the most brainless woman of his acquaintance, and that there was a wide distinction between hospitality and the care of the feeble-minded. Lady Blemley replied that your lack of brain-power was the precise quality which had earned you your invitation, as you were the only person she could think of who might be idiotic enough to buy their old car. You know, the one they call "The Envy of Sisyphus," because it goes quite nicely up-hill if you push it.'

Lady Blemley's protestations would have had greater effect if she had not casually suggested to Mavis only that morning that the car in question would be just the thing for her down at her Devonshire home.

Major Barfield plunged in heavily to effect a diversion.

'How about your carryings-on with the tortoise-shell puss up at the stables, eh?'

The moment he had said it every one realized the blunder.

'One does not usually discuss these matters in public,' said Tobermory frigidly. 'From a slight observation of your ways since you've been in this house I should imagine you'd find it inconvenient if I were to shift the conversation on to your own little affairs.'

The panic which ensued was not confined to the Major.

'Would you like to go and see if cook has got your dinner ready?' suggested Lady Blemley hurriedly, affecting to ignore the fact that it wanted at least two hours to Tobermory's dinner-time.

'Thanks,' said Tobermory, 'not quite so soon after my tea. I don't want to die of indigestion.'

'Cats have nine lives, you know,' said Sir Wilfrid heartily.

'Possibly,' answered Tobermory; 'but only one liver.'

'Adelaide!' said Mrs Cornett, 'do you mean to encourage that cat to go out and gossip about us in the servants' hall?'

The panic had indeed become general. A narrow ornamental balustrade ran in front of most of the bedroom windows at the Towers, and it was recalled with dismay that this had formed a favourite promenade for Tobermory at all hours, whence he could watch the pigeons—and heaven knew what else besides. If he intended to become reminiscent in his present outspoken strain the effect would be something more than disconcerting. Mrs Cornett, who spent much time at her toilet table, and whose complexion was reputed to be of a nomadic though punctual disposition, looked as ill at ease as the Major. Miss Scrawen, who wrote fiercely sensuous poetry and led a blameless life, merely displayed irritation; if you are methodical and virtuous in private you don't necessarily want every one to know it. Bertie van Tahn, who was so depraved at seventeen that he had long ago given up trying to be any worse, turned a dull shade of gardenia white, but he did not commit the error of dashing out of the room like Odo Finsberry, a young gentleman who was understood to be reading for the Church and who was possibly disturbed at the thought of scandals he might hear concerning other people. Clovis had the presence of mind to maintain a composed exterior; privately he was calculating how long it would take to procure a box of fancy mice through the agency of the *Exchange and Mart* as a species of hush-money.

Even in a delicate situation like the present, Agnes Resker could not endure to remain too long in the background.

'Why did I ever come down here?' she asked dramatically.

Tobermory immediately accepted the opening.

'Judging by what you said to Mrs Cornett on the croquet-lawn yesterday, you were out for food. You described the Blemleys as the dullest people to stay with that you knew, but said they were clever enough to employ a first-rate cook; otherwise they'd find it difficult to get any one to come down a second time.'

'There's not a word of truth in it! I appeal to Mrs Cornett——' exclaimed the discomfited Agnes.

'Mrs Cornett repeated your remark afterwards to Bertie van Tahn,' continued Tobermory, 'and said, "That woman is a regular Hunger Marcher; she'd go anywhere for four square meals a day," and Bertie van Tahn said——'

At this point the chronicle mercifully ceased. Tobermory had caught a glimpse of the big yellow Tom from the Rectory working his way through the shrubbery towards the stable wing. In a flash he had vanished through the open French window.

With the disappearance of his too brilliant pupil Cornelius Appin found himself beset by a hurricane of bitter upbraiding, anxious inquiry, and frightened entreaty. The responsibility for the situation lay with him, and he must prevent matters from becoming worse. Could Tobermory impart his dangerous gift to other cats? was the first question he had to answer. It was possible, he replied, that he might have initiated his intimate friend the stable puss into his new accomplishment, but it was unlikely that his teaching could have taken a wider range as yet.

'Then,' said Mrs Cornett, 'Tobermory may be a valuable cat and a great pet; but I'm sure you'll agree,

Adelaide, that both he and the stable cat must be done away with without delay.'

'You don't suppose I've enjoyed the last quarter of an hour, do you?' said Lady Blemley bitterly. 'My husband and I are very fond of Tobermory—at least, we were before this horrible accomplishment was infused into him; but now, of course, the only thing is to have him destroyed as soon as possible.'

'We can put some strychnine in the scraps he always gets at dinner-time,' said Sir Wilfrid, 'and I will go and drown the stable cat myself. The coachman will be very sore at losing his pet, but I'll say a very catching form of mange has broken out in both cats and we're afraid of it spreading to the kennels.'

'But my great discovery!' expostulated Mr Appin; 'after all my years of research and experiment——'

'You can go and experiment on the short-horns at the farm, who are under proper control,' said Mrs Cornett, 'or the elephants at the Zoological Gardens. They're said to be highly intelligent, and they have this recommendation, that they don't come creeping about our bedrooms and under chairs, and so forth.'

An archangel ecstatically proclaiming the Millennium, and then finding that it clashed unpardonably with Henley and would have to be indefinitely postponed, could hardly have felt more crestfallen than Cornelius Appin at the reception of his wonderful achievement. Public opinion, however, was against him—in fact, had the general voice been consulted on the subject it is probable that a strong minority vote would have been in favour of including him in the strychnine diet.

Defective train arrangements and a nervous desire to see matters brought to a finish prevented an immediate dispersal of the party, but dinner that evening was not a social success. Sir Wilfrid had had rather a trying time with the stable cat and subsequently with the coachman. Agnes Resker ostentatiously limited her repast to a morsel of dry toast, which she bit as though it were a personal enemy; while Mavis Pellington maintained a vindictive silence throughout the meal. Lady Blemley kept up a flow of what she hoped was conversation, but her attention was fixed on the doorway. A plateful of carefully dosed fish scraps was in readiness on the sideboard, but sweets and savoury and dessert went their way, and no Tobermory appeared either in the dining-room or kitchen.

The sepulchral dinner was cheerful compared with the subsequent vigil in the smoking-room. Eating and drinking had at least supplied a distraction and cloak to the prevailing embarrassment. Bridge was out of the question in the general tension of nerves and tempers, and after Odo Finsberry had given a lugubrious rendering of 'Mélisande in the Wood' to a frigid audience, music was tacitly avoided. At eleven the servants went to bed, announcing that the small window in the pantry had been left open as usual for Tobermory's private use. The guests read steadily through the current batch of magazines, and fell back gradually on the 'Badminton Library' and bound volumes of *Punch*. Lady Blemley made periodic visits to the pantry, returning each time with an expression of listless depression which forestalled questioning.

At two o'clock Clovis broke the dominating silence.

'He won't turn up tonight. He's probably in the local newspaper office at the present moment, dictating the first instalment of his reminiscences. Lady What's-her-name's book won't be in it. It will be the event of the day.'

Having made this contribution to the general cheerfulness, Clovis went to bed. At long intervals the various members of the house-party followed his example.

The servants taking round the early tea made a uniform announcement in reply to a uniform question. Tobermory had not returned.

Breakfast was, if anything, a more unpleasant function than dinner had been, but before its conclusion the situation was relieved. Tobermory's corpse was brought in from the shrubbery, where a gardener had just discovered it. From the bites on his throat and the yellow fur which coated his claws it was evident that he had fallen in unequal combat with the big Tom from the Rectory.

By midday most of the guests had quitted the Towers, and after lunch Lady Blemley had sufficiently recovered her spirits to write an extremely nasty letter to the Rectory about the loss of her valuable pet.

Tobermory had been Appin's one successful pupil, and he was destined to have no successor. A few weeks later an elephant in the Dresden Zoological Garden, which had shown no previous signs of irritability, broke loose and killed an Englishman who had apparently been teasing it. The victim's name was variously reported in the papers as Oppin and Eppelin, but his front name was faithfully rendered Cornelius.

'If he was trying German irregular verbs on the poor beast,' said Clovis, 'he deserved all he got.'

MRS PACKLETIDE'S TIGER

IT WAS Mrs Packletide's pleasure and intention that she should shoot a tiger. Not that the lust to kill had suddenly descended on her, or that she felt that she would leave India safer and more wholesome than she had found it, with one fraction less of wild beast per million of inhabitants. The compelling motive for her sudden deviation towards the footsteps of Nimrod was the fact that Loona Bimberton had recently been carried eleven miles in an aeroplane by an Algerian aviator, and talked of nothing else; only a personally procured tiger-skin and a heavy harvest of Press photographs could successfully counter that sort of thing. Mrs Packletide had already arranged in her mind the lunch she would give at her house in Curzon Street, ostensibly in Loona Bimberton's honour, with a tiger-skin rug occupying most of the foreground and all of the conversation. She had also already designed in her mind the tiger-claw brooch that she was going to give Loona Bimberton on her next birthday. In a world that is supposed to be chiefly swayed by hunger and by love Mrs Packletide was an exception; her movements and motives were largely governed by dislike of Loona Bimberton.

Circumstances proved propitious. Mrs Packletide had offered a thousand rupees for the opportunity of shooting a tiger without overmuch risk or exertion, and it so happened that a neighbouring village could boast of being the favoured rendezvous of an animal of respectable antecedents, which had been driven by the increasing infirmities of age to abandon game-killing and confine its appetite to the smaller domestic animals. The prospect of earning the thousand rupees had stimulated the sporting and commercial instinct of the villagers; children were posted night and day on the outskirts of the local jungle to head the tiger back in the unlikely event of his attempting to roam away to fresh hunting-grounds, and the cheaper kinds of goats were left about with elaborate carelessness to keep him satisfied with his present quarters. The one great anxiety was lest he should die of old age before the date appointed for the memsahib's shoot. Mothers carrying their babies home through the jungle after the day's work in the fields hushed their singing lest they might curtail the restful sleep of the venerable herd-robber.

The great night duly arrived, moonlit and cloudless. A platform had been constructed in a comfortable and conveniently placed tree, and thereon crouched Mrs Packletide and her paid companion, Miss Mebbin. A goat, gifted with a particularly persistent bleat, such as even a partially deaf tiger might be reasonably expected to hear on a still night, was tethered at the correct distance. With an accurately sighted rifle and a thumb-nail pack of patience cards the sportswoman awaited the coming of the quarry.

'I suppose we are in some danger?' said Miss Mebbin.

She was not actually nervous about the wild beast, but

she had a morbid dread of performing an atom more service than she had been paid for.

'Nonsense,' said Mrs Packletide; 'it's a very old tiger. It couldn't spring up here even if it wanted to.'

'If it's an old tiger I think you ought to get it cheaper. A thousand rupees is a lot of money.'

Louisa Mebbin adopted a protective elder-sister attitude towards money in general, irrespective of nationality or denomination. Her energetic intervention had saved many a rouble from dissipating itself in tips in some Moscow hotel, and francs and centimes clung to her instinctively under circumstances which would have driven them head-long from less sympathetic hands. Her speculations as to the market depreciation of tiger remnants were cut short by the appearance on the scene of the animal itself. As soon as it caught sight of the tethered goat it lay flat on the earth, seemingly less from a desire to take advantage of all available cover than for the purpose of snatching a short rest before commencing the grand attack.

'I believe it's ill,' said Louisa Mebbin, loudly in Hindu-stani, for the benefit of the village headman, who was in ambush in a neighbouring tree.

'Hush!' said Mrs Packletide, and at that moment the tiger commenced ambling towards his victim.

'Now, now!' urged Miss Mebbin with some excitement; 'if he doesn't touch the goat we needn't pay for it.' (The bait was an extra.)

The rifle flashed out with a loud report, and the great tawny beast sprang to one side and then rolled over in the stillness of death. In a moment a crowd of excited natives had swarmed on to the scene, and their shouting speedily carried the glad news to the village, where a thumping of tom-toms took up the chorus of triumph. And their triumph and rejoicing found a ready echo in the heart of Mrs Packletide; already that luncheon-party in Curzon Street seemed immeasurably nearer.

It was Louisa Mebbin who drew attention to the fact that the goat was in death-throes from a mortal bullet-wound, while no trace of the rifle's deadly work could be found on the tiger. Evidently the wrong animal had been hit, and the beast of prey had succumbed to heart-failure, caused by the sudden report of the rifle, accelerated by senile decay. Mrs Packletide was pardonably annoyed at the discovery; but, at any rate, she was the possessor of a dead tiger, and the villagers, anxious for their thousand rupees, gladly connived at the fiction that she had shot the beast. And Miss Mebbin was a paid companion. Therefore did Mrs Packletide face the cameras with a light heart, and her pictured fame reached from the pages of the *Texas Weekly Snapshot* to the illustrated Monday supplement of the *Novoe Vremya*. As for Loona Bimberton, she refused to look at an illustrated paper for weeks, and her letter of thanks for the gift of a tiger-claw brooch was a model of repressed emotions. The luncheon-party she declined; there are limits beyond which repressed emotions become dangerous.

From Curzon Street the tiger-skin rug travelled down to the Manor House, and was duly inspected and admired by the county, and it seemed a fitting and appropriate thing when Mrs Packletide went to the County Costume Ball in the character of Diana. She refused to fall in, however, with Clovis's tempting suggestion of a primeval dance party, at which every one should wear the skins of beasts they had recently slain. 'I should be in rather a Baby Bunting condition,' confessed Clovis, 'with a miserable rabbit-skin or two to wrap up in, but then,' he added, with a rather malicious glance at Diana's proportions, 'my figure is quite as good as that Russian dancing boy's.'

'How amused every one would be if they knew what really happened,' said Louisa Mebbin a few days after the ball.

'What do you mean?' asked Mrs Packletide quickly.

'How you shot the goat and frightened the tiger to death,' said Miss Mebbin, with her disagreeably pleasant laugh.

'No one would believe it,' said Mrs Packletide, her face changing colour as rapidly as though it were going through a book of patterns before post-time.

'Loona Bimberton would,' said Miss Mebbin. Mrs Packletide's face settled on an unbecoming shade of greenish white.

'You surely wouldn't give me away?' she asked.

'I've seen a week-end cottage near Dorking that I should rather like to buy,' said Miss Mebbin with seeming irrelevance. 'Six hundred and eighty, freehold. Quite a bargain, only I don't happen to have the money.'

Louisa Mebbin's pretty week-end cottage, christened by her 'Les Fauves,' and gay in summer-time with its garden borders of tiger-lilies, is the wonder and admiration of her friends.

'It is a marvel how Louisa manages to do it,' is the general verdict.

Mrs Packletide indulges in no more big-game shooting.

'The incidental expenses are so heavy,' she confides to inquiring friends.

THE UNREST-CURE

ON THE rack in the railway carriage immediately opposite Clovis was a solidly wrought travelling bag, with a carefully written label, on which was inscribed, 'J. P. Huddle, The Warren, Tilfield, near Slowborough.' Immediately below the rack sat the human embodiment of the label, a solid, sedate individual, sedately dressed, sedately conversational. Even without his conversation (which was addressed to a friend seated by his side, and touched chiefly on such topics as the backwardness of Roman hyacinths and the prevalence of measles at the Rectory), one could have gauged fairly accurately the temperament and mental outlook of the travelling bag's owner. But he seemed unwilling to leave anything to the imagination of a casual observer, and his talk grew presently personal and introspective.

'I don't know how it is,' he told his friend, 'I'm not much over forty, but I seem to have settled down into a deep groove of elderly middle-age. My sister shows the same tendency. We like everything to be exactly in its accustomed place; we like things to happen exactly at their appointed times; we like everything to be usual, orderly, punctual, methodical, to a hair's breadth, to a minute. It distresses and upsets us if it is not so. For instance, to take a very trifling matter, a thrush has built its nest year after year in the catkin-tree on the lawn; this year, for no obvious reason, it is building in the ivy on the garden wall. We have said very little about it, but I think we both feel that the change is unnecessary, and just a little irritating.'

'Perhaps,' said the friend, 'it is a different thrush.'

'We have suspected that,' said J. P. Huddle, 'and I think it gives us even more cause for annoyance. We don't feel that we want a change of thrush at our time of life; and yet, as I have said, we have scarcely reached an age when these things should make themselves seriously felt.'

'What you want,' said the friend, 'is an Unrest-cure.'

'An Unrest-cure? I've never heard of such a thing.'

'You've heard of Rest-cures for people who've broken down under stress of too much worry and strenuous living; well, you're suffering from overmuch repose and placidity, and you need the opposite kind of treatment.'

'But where would one go for such a thing?'

'Well, you might stand as an Orange candidate for Kilkenny, or do a course of district visiting in one of the Apache quarters of Paris, or give lectures in Berlin to prove that most of Wagner's music was written by Gambetta; and there's always the interior of Morocco to travel in. But, to be really effective, the Unrest-cure ought to be tried in the home. How you would do it I haven't the faintest idea.'

It was at this point in the conversation that Clovis became galvanized into alert attention. After all, his two days' visit to an elderly relative at Slowborough did not promise much excitement. Before the train had stopped he had decorated his sinister shirt-cuff with the inscription, 'J. P. Huddle, The Warren, Tilfield, near Slowborough.'

Two mornings later Mr Huddle broke in on his sister's privacy as she sat reading *Country Life* in the morning-room. It was her day and hour and place for reading *Country Life*, and the intrusion was absolutely irregular; but he bore in his hand a telegram, and in that household telegrams were recognized as happening by the hand of God. This particular telegram partook of the nature of a thunderbolt. 'Bishop examining confirmation class in neighbourhood unable stay rectory on account measles invokes your hospitality sending secretary arrange.'

'I scarcely know the Bishop; I've only spoken to him once,' exclaimed J. P. Huddle, with the exculpating air of one who realizes too late the indiscretion of speaking to strange Bishops. Miss Huddle was the first to rally; she disliked thunderbolts as fervently as her brother did, but the womanly instinct in her told her that thunderbolts must be fed.

'We can curry the cold duck,' she said. It was not the appointed day for curry, but the little orange envelope involved a certain departure from rule and custom. Her brother said nothing, but his eyes thanked her for being brave.

'A young gentleman to see you,' announced the parlour-maid.

'The secretary!' murmured the Huddles in unison; they instantly stiffened into a demeanour which proclaimed that, though they held all strangers to be guilty, they were willing to hear anything they might have to say in their defence. The young gentleman, who came into the room with a certain elegant haughtiness, was not at all Huddle's idea of a bishop's secretary; he had not supposed that the episcopal establishment could have afforded such an expensively upholstered article when there were so many other claims on its resources. The face was fleetingly familiar; if he had bestowed more attention on the fellow-traveller sitting opposite him in the railway carriage two days before he might have recognized Clovis in his present visitor.

'You are the Bishop's secretary?' asked Huddle, becoming consciously deferential.

'His confidential secretary,' answered Clovis. 'You may call me Stanislaus; my other name doesn't matter. The Bishop and Colonel Alberti may be here to lunch. I shall be here in any case.'

It sounded rather like the programme of a Royal visit.

'The Bishop is examining a confirmation class in the neighbourhood, isn't he?' asked Miss Huddle.

'Ostensibly,' was the dark reply, followed by a request for a large-scale map of the locality.

Clovis was still immersed in a seemingly profound study of the map when another telegram arrived. It was addressed to 'Prince Stanislaus, care of Huddle, The Warren, etc.' Clovis glanced at the contents and announced: 'The Bishop and Alberti won't be here till late in the afternoon.' Then he returned to his scrutiny of the map.

The luncheon was not a very festive function. The princely secretary ate and drank with fair appetite, but severely discouraged conversation. At the finish of the meal he broke suddenly into a radiant smile, thanked his hostess for a charming repast, and kissed her hand with deferential rapture. Miss Huddle was unable to decide in her mind whether the action savoured of Louis Quatorzian courtliness or the reprehensible Roman attitude towards the Sabine women. It was not her day for having a headache, but she felt that the circumstances excused her, and retired to her room to have as much headache as was possible before the Bishop's arrival. Clovis, having asked the way to the nearest telegraph office, disappeared presently down the carriage drive. Mr. Huddle met him in the hall some two hours later, and asked when the Bishop would arrive.

'He is in the library with Alberti,' was the reply.

'But why wasn't I told? I never knew he had come!' exclaimed Huddle.

'No one knows he is here,' said Clovis; 'the quieter we can keep matters the better. And on no account disturb him in the library. Those are his orders.'

'But what is all this mystery about? And who is Alberti? And isn't the Bishop going to have tea?'

'The Bishop is out for blood, not tea.'

'Blood!' gasped Huddle, who did not find that the thunderbolt improved on acquaintance.

'Tonight is going to be a great night in the history of Christendom,' said Clovis. 'We are going to massacre every Jew in the neighbourhood.'

'To massacre the Jews!' said Huddle indignantly. 'Do you mean to tell me there's a general rising against them?'

'No, it's the Bishop's own idea. He's in there arranging all the details now.'

'But—the Bishop is such a tolerant, humane man.'

'That is precisely what will heighten the effect of his action. The sensation will be enormous.'

That at least Huddle could believe.

'He will be hanged!' he exclaimed with conviction.

'A motor is waiting to carry him to the coast, where a steam yacht is in readiness.'

'But there aren't thirty Jews in the whole neighbourhood,' protested Huddle, whose brain, under the repeated shocks of the day, was operating with the uncertainty of a telegraph wire during earthquake disturbances.

'We have twenty-six on our list,' said Clovis, referring to a bundle of notes. 'We shall be able to deal with them all the more thoroughly.'

'Do you mean to tell me that you are meditating violence against a man like Sir Leon Birberry?' stammered Huddle; 'he's one of the most respected men in the country.'

'He's down on our list,' said Clovis carelessly; 'after all, we've got men we can trust to do our job, so we shan't have to rely on local assistance. And we've got some Boy Scouts helping us as auxiliaries.'

'Boy Scouts!'

'Yes; when they understood there was real killing to be done they were even keener than the men.'

'This thing will be a blot on the Twentieth Century!'

'And your house will be the blotting-pad. Have you realized that half the papers of Europe and the United States will publish pictures of it? By the way, I've sent some photographs of you and your sister, that I found in the library, to the *Matin* and *Die Woche*; I hope you don't mind. Also a sketch of the staircase; most of the killing will probably be done on the staircase.'

The emotions that were surging in J. P. Huddle's brain were almost too intense to be disclosed in speech, but he managed to gasp out: 'There aren't any Jews in this house.'

'Not at present,' said Clovis.

'I shall go to the police,' shouted Huddle with sudden energy.

'In the shrubbery,' said Clovis, 'are posted ten men, who have orders to fire on any one who leaves the house without my signal of permission. Another armed picquet is in ambush near the front gate. The Boy Scouts watch the back premises.'

At this moment the cheerful hoot of a motor-horn was heard from the drive. Huddle rushed to the hall door with the feeling of a man half-awakened from a nightmare, and beheld Sir Leon Birberry, who had driven himself over in his car. 'I got your telegram,' he said; 'what's up?'

Telegram? It seemed to be a day of telegrams.

'Come here at once. Urgent. James Huddle,' was the purport of the message displayed before Huddle's bewildered eyes.

'I see it all!' he exclaimed suddenly in a voice shaken with agitation, and with a look of agony in the direction of the shrubbery he hauled the astonished Birberry into the house. Tea had just been laid in the hall, but the now thoroughly panic-stricken Huddle dragged his protesting guest upstairs, and in a few minutes' time the entire household had been summoned to that region of momentary safety. Clovis alone graced the tea-table with his presence; the fanatics in the library were evidently too immersed in their monstrous machinations to dally with the solace of teacup and hot toast. Once the youth rose, in answer to the summons of the front-door bell, and admitted Mr. Paul Isaacs, shoemaker and parish councillor, who had also received a pressing invitation to The Warren. With an atrocious assumption of courtesy, which a Borgia could hardly have outdone, the secretary escorted this new captive of his net to the head of the stairway, where his involuntary host awaited him.

And then ensued a long ghastly vigil of watching and waiting. Once or twice Clovis left the house to stroll across to the shrubbery, returning always to the library, for the purpose evidently of making a brief report. Once he took in the letters from the evening postman, and brought them to the top of the stairs with punctilious politeness. After his next absence he came half-way up the stairs to make an announcement.

'The Boy Scouts mistook my signal, and have killed the postman. I've had very little practice in this sort of thing, you see. Another time I shall do better.'

The housemaid, who was engaged to be married to the evening postman, gave way to clamorous grief.

'Remember that your mistress has a headache,' said J. P. Huddle. (Miss Huddle's headache was worse.)

Clovis hastened downstairs, and after a short visit to the library returned with another message:

'The Bishop is sorry to hear that Miss Huddle has a headache. He is issuing orders that as far as possible no firearms shall be used near the house; any killing that is necessary on the premises will be done with cold steel. The Bishop does not see why a man should not be a gentleman as well as a Christian.'

That was the last they saw of Clovis; it was nearly seven o'clock, and his elderly relative liked him to dress for dinner. But, though he had left them for ever, the lurking suggestion of his presence haunted the lower regions of the house during the long hours of the wakeful night, and every creak of the stairway, every rustle of wind through the shrubbery, was fraught with horrible meaning. At about seven next morning the gardener's boy and the early postman finally convinced the watchers that the Twentieth Century was still unblotted.

'I don't suppose,' mused Clovis, as an early train bore him townwards, 'that they will be in the least grateful for the Unrest-cure.'

THE JESTING OF
ARLINGTON STRINGHAM

ARLINGTON STRINGHAM made a joke in the House of Commons. It was a thin House, and a very thin joke; something about the Anglo-Saxon race having a great many angles. It is possible that it was unintentional, but a fellow-member, who did not wish it to be supposed that he was asleep because his eyes were shut, laughed. One or two of the papers noted 'a laugh' in brackets, and another, which was notorious for the carelessness of its political news, mentioned 'laughter.' Things often begin in that way.

'Arlington made a joke in the House last night,' said Eleanor Stringham to her mother; 'in all the years we've been married neither of us has made jokes, and I don't like it now. I'm afraid it's the beginning of the rift in the lute.'

'What lute?' said her mother.

'It's a quotation,' said Eleanor.

To say that anything was a quotation was an excellent method, in Eleanor's eyes, for withdrawing it from discussion, just as you could always defend indifferent lamb late in the season by saying 'It's mutton.'

And, of course, Arlington Stringham continued to tread the thorny path of conscious humour into which Fate had beckoned him.

'The country's looking very green, but, after all, that's what it's there for,' he remarked to his wife two days later.

'That's very modern, and I daresay very clever, but I'm afraid it's wasted on me,' she observed coldly. If she had known how much effort it had cost him to make the remark she might have greeted it in a kinder spirit. It is the tragedy of human endeavour that it works so often unseen and unguessed.

Arlington said nothing, not from injured pride, but because he was thinking hard for something to say. Eleanor mistook his silence for an assumption of tolerant superiority, and her anger prompted her to a further gibe.

'You had better tell it to Lady Isobel. I've no doubt she would appreciate it.'

Lady Isobel was seen everywhere with a fawn-coloured collie at a time when every one else kept nothing but Pekinese, and she had once eaten four green apples at an afternoon tea in the Botanical Gardens, so she was widely credited with a rather unpleasant wit. The censorious said she slept in a hammock and understood Yeats's poems, but her family denied both stories.

'The rift is widening to an abyss,' said Eleanor to her mother that afternoon.

'I should not tell that to any one,' remarked her mother, after long reflection.

'Naturally, I should not talk about it very much,' said Eleanor, 'but why shouldn't I mention it to any one?'

'Because you can't have an abyss in a lute. There isn't room.'

Eleanor's outlook on life did not improve as the afternoon wore on. The page-boy had brought from the library *By Mere and Wold* instead of *By Mere Chance*, the book which every one denied having read. The unwelcome substitute appeared to be a collection of nature notes contributed by the author to the pages of some Northern weekly, and when one had been prepared to plunge with disapproving mind into a regrettable chronicle of ill-spent lives it was intensely irritating to read 'the dainty yellow-hammers are now with us, and flaunt their jaundiced livery from every bush and hillock.' Besides, the thing was so obviously untrue; either there must be hardly any bushes or hillocks in those parts or the country must be fearfully overstocked with yellow-hammers. The thing scarcely seemed worth telling such a lie about. And the page-boy stood there, with his sleekly brushed and parted hair, and his air of chaste and callous indifference to the desires and passions of the world. Eleanor hated boys, and she would have liked to have whipped this one long and often. It was perhaps the yearning of a woman who had no children of her own.

She turned at random to another paragraph. 'Lie quietly concealed in the fern and bramble in the gap by the old rowan tree, and you may see, almost every evening during early summer, a pair of lesser whitethroats creeping up and down the nettles and hedge-growth that mask their nesting-place.'

The insufferable monotony of the proposed recreation! Eleanor would not have watched the most brilliant performance at His Majesty's Theatre for a single evening under such uncomfortable circumstances, and to be asked to watch lesser whitethroats creeping up and down a nettle 'almost every evening' during the height of the season struck her as an imputation on her intelligence that was positively offensive. Impatiently she transferred her attention to the dinner menu, which the boy had thoughtfully brought in as an alternative to the more solid literary fare.

'Rabbit curry,' met her eye, and the lines of disapproval deepened on her already puckered brow. The cook was a great believer in the influence of environment, and nourished an obstinate conviction that if you brought rabbit and curry-powder together in one dish a rabbit curry would be the result. And Clovis and the odious Bertie van Tahn were coming to dinner. Surely, thought Eleanor, if Arlington knew how much she had had that day to try her, he would refrain from joke-making.

At dinner that night it was Eleanor herself who mentioned the name of a certain statesman, who may be decently covered under the disguise of X.

'X,' said Arlington Stringham, 'has the soul of a meringue.'

It was a useful remark to have on hand, because it applied equally well to four prominent statesmen of the day, which quadrupled the opportunities for using it.

'Meringues haven't got souls,' said Eleanor's mother.

'It's a mercy that they haven't,' said Clovis; 'they would be always losing them, and people like my aunt would get up missions to meringues, and say it was wonderful how much one could teach them and how much more one could learn from them.'

'What could you learn from a meringue?' asked Eleanor's mother.

'My aunt has been known to learn humility from an ex-Viceroy,' said Clovis.

'I wish cook would learn to make curry, or have the sense to leave it alone,' said Arlington, suddenly and savagely.

Eleanor's face softened. It was like one of his old remarks in the days when there was no abyss between them.

It was during the debate on the Foreign Office vote that Stringham made his great remark that 'the people of Crete unfortunately make more history than they can consume locally.' It was not brilliant, but it came in the middle of a dull speech, and the House was quite pleased with it. Old gentlemen with bad memories said it reminded them of Disraeli.

It was Eleanor's friend, Gertrude Ilpton, who drew her attention to Arlington's newest outbreak. Eleanor in these days avoided the morning papers.

'It's very modern, and I suppose very clever,' she observed.

'Of course it's clever,' said Gertrude; 'all Lady Isobel's sayings are clever, and luckily they bear repeating.'

'Are you sure it's one of her sayings?' asked Eleanor.

'My dear, I've heard her say it dozens of times.'

'So that is where he gets his humour,' said Eleanor slowly, and the hard lines deepened round her mouth.

The death of Eleanor Stringham from an overdose of chloral, occurring at the end of a rather uneventful season, excited a certain amount of unobtrusive speculation. Clovis, who perhaps exaggerated the importance of curry in the home, hinted at domestic sorrow.

And of course Arlington never knew. It was the tragedy of his life that he should miss the fullest effect of his jesting.

SREDNI VASHTAR

CONRADIN WAS ten years old, and the doctor had pronounced his professional opinion that the boy would not live another five years. The doctor was silky and effete, and counted for little, but his opinion was endorsed by Mrs De Ropp, who counted for nearly everything. Mrs De Ropp was Conradin's cousin and guardian, and in his eyes she represented those three-fifths of the world that are necessary and disagreeable and real; the other two-fifths, in perpetual antagonism to the foregoing, were summed up in himself and his imagination. One of these days Conradin supposed he would succumb to the mastering pressure of wearisome necessary things—such as illnesses and coddling restrictions and drawn-out dullness. Without his imagination, which was rampant under the spur of loneliness, he would have succumbed long ago.

Mrs De Ropp would never, in her honestest moments, have confessed to herself that she disliked Conradin, though she might have been dimly aware that thwarting him 'for his good' was a duty which she did not find particularly irksome. Conradin hated her with a desperate sincerity which he was perfectly able to mask. Such few pleasures as he could contrive for himself gained an added relish from the likelihood that they would be displeasing to his guardian, and from the realm of his imagination she was locked out—an unclean thing, which should find no entrance.

In the dull, cheerless garden, overlooked by so many windows that were ready to open with a message not to do this or that, or a reminder that medicines were due, he found little attraction. The few fruit-trees that it contained were set jealously apart from his plucking, as though they were rare specimens of their kind blooming in an arid waste; it would probably have been difficult to find a market-gardener who would have offered ten shillings for their entire yearly produce. In a forgotten corner, however, almost hidden behind a dismal shrubbery, was a disused tool-shed of respectable proportions, and within its walls Conradin found a haven, something that took on the varying aspects of a playroom and a cathedral. He had peopled it with a legion of familiar phantoms, evoked partly from fragments of history and partly from his own brain, but it also boasted two inmates of flesh and blood. In one corner lived a ragged-plumaged Houdan hen, on which the boy lavished an affection that had scarcely another outlet. Further back in the gloom stood a large hutch, divided into two compartments, one of which was fronted with close iron bars. This was the abode of a large polecat-ferret, which a friendly butcher-boy had once smuggled, cage and all, into its present quarters, in exchange for a long-secreted hoard of small silver. Conradin was dreadfully afraid of the lithe, sharp-fanged beast, but it was his most treasured possession. Its very presence in the tool-shed was a secret and fearful joy, to be kept scrupulously from the knowledge of the Woman, as he privately dubbed his cousin. And one day, out of Heaven knows what material, he spun the beast a wonderful name, and from that moment it grew into a god and a religion. The Woman indulged in religion once a week at a church near by, and took Conradin with her, but to him the church service was an alien rite in the House of Rimmon. Every Thursday, in the dim and musty silence of the tool-shed, he worshipped with mystic and elaborate ceremonial before the wooden hutch where dwelt Sredni Vashtar, the great ferret. Red flowers in their season and scarlet berries in the winter-time were offered at his shrine, for he was a god who laid some special stress on the fierce impatient side of things, as opposed to the Woman's religion, which, as far as Conradin could observe, went to great lengths in the contrary direction. And on great festivals powdered nutmeg was strewn in front of his hutch, an important feature of the offering being that the nutmeg had to be stolen. These festivals were of irregular occurrence, and were chiefly appointed to celebrate some passing event. On one occasion, when Mrs De Ropp suffered from acute toothache for three days. Conradin kept up the festival during the entire three days, and almost succeeded in persuading himself that Sredni Vashtar was personally responsible for the toothache. If the malady had lasted for another day the supply of nutmeg would have given out.

The Houdan hen was never drawn into the cult of Sredni Vashtar. Conradin had long ago settled that she was an Anabaptist. He did not pretend to have the remotest knowledge as to what an Anabaptist was, but he privately hoped that it was dashing and not very respectable. Mrs De Ropp was the ground plan on which he based and detested all respectability.

After a while Conradin's absorption in the tool-shed began to attract the notice of his guardian. 'It is not good for him to be pottering down there in all weathers,' she promptly decided, and at breakfast one morning she announced that the Houdan hen had been sold and taken away overnight. With her short-sighted eyes she peered at Conradin, waiting for an outbreak of rage and sorrow, which she was ready to rebuke with a flow of excellent precepts and reasoning. But Conradin said nothing: there was nothing to be said. Something perhaps in his white set face gave her a momentary qualm, for at tea that afternoon there was toast on the table, a delicacy which she usually banned on the ground that it was bad for him; also because the making of it 'gave trouble,' a deadly offence in the middle-class feminine eye.

'I thought you liked toast,' she exclaimed, with an injured air, observing that he did not touch it.

'Sometimes,' said Conradin.

In the shed that evening there was an innovation in the worship of the hutch-god. Conradin had been wont to chant his praises, tonight he asked a boon.

'Do one thing for me, Sredni Vashtar.'

The thing was not specified. As Sredni Vashtar was a god he must be supposed to know. And choking back a sob as he looked at that other empty corner, Conradin went back to the world he so hated.

And every night, in the welcome darkness of his bedroom, and every evening in the dusk of the tool-shed, Conradin's bitter litany went up: 'Do one thing for me, Sredni Vashtar.'

Mrs De Ropp noticed that the visits to the shed did not cease, and one day she made a further journey of inspection.

'What are you keeping in that locked hutch?' she asked.

I believe it's guinea-pigs. I'll have them all cleared
away.'

Conradin shut his lips tight, but the Woman ransacked
his bedroom till she found the carefully hidden key, and
forthwith marched down to the shed to complete her discovery. It was a cold afternoon, and Conradin had been
bidden to keep to the house. From the furthest window of
the dining-room the door of the shed could just be seen
beyond the corner of the shrubbery, and there Conradin
stationed himself. He saw the Woman enter, and then he
imagined her opening the door of the sacred hutch and
peering down with her short-sighted eyes into the thick
straw· bed where his god lay hidden. Perhaps she would
prod at the straw in her clumsy impatience. And Conradin
fervently breathed his prayer for the last time. But he
knew as he prayed that he did not believe. He knew that
the Woman would come out presently with that pursed
smile he loathed so well on her face, and that in an hour
or two the gardener would carry away his wonderful god,
a god no longer, but a simple brown ferret in a hutch.
And he knew that the Woman would triumph always as
she triumphed now, and that he would grow ever more
sickly under her pestering and domineering and superior
wisdom, till one day nothing would matter much more
with him, and the doctor would be proved right. And in
the sting and misery of his defeat, he began to chant loudly
and defiantly the hymn of his threatened idol:

Sredni Vashtar went forth,
His thoughts were red thoughts and his teeth were white.
His enemies called for peace, but he brought them death.
Sredni Vashtar the Beautiful.

And then of a sudden he stopped his chanting and drew
closer to the window-pane. The door of the shed still stood
ajar as it had been left, and the minutes were slipping by.
They were long minutes, but they slipped by nevertheless.
He watched the starlings running and flying in little parties

across the lawn; he counted them over and over again, with one eye always on that swinging door. A sour-faced maid came in to lay the table for tea, and still Conradin stood and waited and watched. Hope had crept by inches into his heart, and now a look of triumph began to blaze in his eyes that had only known the wistful patience of defeat. Under his breath, with a furtive exultation, he began once again the paean of victory and devastation. And presently his eyes were rewarded; out through that doorway came a long, low, yellow-and-brown beast, with eyes a-blink at the waning daylight, and dark wet stains around the fur of jaws and throat. Conradin dropped on his knees. The great polecat-ferret made its way down to a small brook at the foot of the garden, drank for a moment, then crossed a little plank bridge and was lost to sight in the bushes. Such was the passing of Sredni Vashtar.

'Tea is ready,' said the sour-faced maid; 'where is the mistress?'

'She went down to the shed some time ago,' said Conradin.

And while the maid went to summon her mistress to tea, Conradin fished a toasting-fork out of the sideboard drawer and proceeded to toast himself a piece of bread. And during the toasting of it and the buttering of it with much butter and the slow enjoyment of eating it, Conradin listened to the noises and silences which fell in quick spasms beyond the dining-room door. The loud foolish screaming of the maid, the answering chorus of wondering ejaculations from the kitchen region, the scuttering foot-steps and hurried embassies for outside help, and then, after a lull, the scared sobbings and the shuffling tread of those who bore a heavy burden into the house.

'Whoever will break it to the poor child? I couldn't for the life of me!' exclaimed a shrill voice. And while they debated the matter among themselves, Conradin made himself another piece of toast.

THE CHAPLET

A STRANGE stillness hung over the restaurant; it was one of those rare moments when the orchestra was not discoursing the strains of the Ice-cream Sailor waltz.

'Did I ever tell you,' asked Clovis of his friend, 'the tragedy of music at mealtimes?

'It was a gala evening at the Grand Sybaris Hotel, and a special dinner was being served in the Amethyst dining-hall. The Amethyst dining-hall had almost a European reputation, especially with that section of Europe which is historically identified with the Jordan Valley. Its cooking was beyond reproach, and its orchestra was sufficiently highly salaried to be above criticism. Thither came in shoals the intensely musical and the almost intensely musical, who are very many, and in still greater numbers the merely musical, who know how Tschaikowsky's name is pronounced and can recognize several of Chopin's nocturnes if you give them due warning; these eat in the nervous, detached manner of roebuck feeding in the open, and keep anxious ears cocked towards the orchestra for the first hint of a recognizable melody.

' "Ah, yes, *Pagliacci*," they murmur, as the opening strains follow hot upon the soup, and if no contradiction is forthcoming from any better-informed quarter they break forth into subdued humming by way of supplementing the efforts of the musicians. Sometimes the melody starts on level terms with the soup, in which case the banqueters contrive somehow to hum between the spoonfuls; the facial expression of enthusiasts who are punctuating potage St Germain with *Pagliacci* is not beautiful, but it should be seen by those who are bent on observing all sides of life. One cannot discount the unpleasant things of this world merely by looking the other way.

In addition to the aforementioned types the restaurant was patronized by a fair sprinkling of the absolutely non-musical; their presence in the dining-hall could only be explained on the supposition that they had come there to dine.

'The earlier stages of the dinner had worn off. The wine lists had been consulted, by some with the blank embarrassment of a schoolboy suddenly called on to locate a Minor Prophet in the tangled hinterland of the Old Testament, by others with the severe scrutiny which suggests that they have visited most of the higher-priced wines in their own homes and probed their family weaknesses. The diners who chose their wine in the latter fashion always gave their orders in a penetrating voice, with a plentiful garnishing of stage directions. By insisting on having your bottle pointing to the north when the cork is being drawn, or calling the waiter Max, you may induce an impression on your guests which hours of laboured boasting might be powerless to achieve. For this purpose, however, the guests must be chosen as carefully as the wine.

'Standing aside from the revellers in the shadow of a massive pillar was an interested spectator who was assuredly of the feast, and yet not in it. Monsieur Aristide Saucourt was the *chef* of the Grand Sybaris Hotel, and if he had an equal in his profession he had never acknowledged the fact. In his own domain he was a potentate, hedged around with the cold brutality that Genius expects rather than excuses in her children; he never forgave, and those who served him were careful that there should be little to forgive. In the outer world, the world which devoured his creations, he was an influence; how profound or how shallow an influence he never attempted to guess. It is the penalty and the safeguard of genius that it computes itself by troy weight in a world that measures by vulgar hundredweights.

'Once in a way the great man would be seized with a desire to watch the effects of his master-efforts, just as the guiding brain of Krupp's might wish at a supreme moment to intrude into the firing line of an artillery duel. And such an occasion was the present. For the first time in the history of the Grand Sybaris Hotel, he was presenting to its guests the dish which he had brought to that pitch of perfection which almost amounts to scandal. Canetons à la mode d'Amblève. In thin gilt lettering on the creamy white of the menu how little those words conveyed to the bulk of the imperfectly educated diners. And yet how much specialized effort had been lavished, how much carefully treasured lore had been ungarnered, before those six words could be written. In the Department of Deux-Sèvres ducklings had lived peculiar and beautiful lives and died in the odour of satiety to furnish the main theme of the dish; champignons, which even a purist for Saxon English would have hesitated to address as mushrooms, had contributed their languorous atrophied bodies to the garnishing, and a sauce devised in the twilight reign of the Fifteenth Louis had been summoned back from the imperishable past to take its part in the wonderful confection. Thus far had human effort laboured to achieve the desired result; the rest had been left to human genius—the genius of Aristide Saucourt.

'And now the moment had arrived for the serving of the great dish, the dish which world-weary Grand Dukes and market-obsessed money magnates counted among their happiest memories. And at the same moment something else happened. The leader of the highly salaried orchestra placed his violin caressingly against his chin, lowered his eyelids, and floated into a sea of melody.

'"Hark!" said most of the diners, "he is playing 'The Chaplet.'"

'They knew it was "The Chaplet" because they had heard it played at luncheon and afternoon tea, and at supper the night before, and had not had time to forget.

'"Yes, he is playing 'The Chaplet,'" they reassured one another. The general voice was unanimous on the subject. The orchestra had already played it eleven times that day, four times by desire and seven times from force of habit, but the familiar strains were greeted with the rapture due to a revelation. A murmur of much humming rose from half the tables in the room, and some of the more over-wrought listeners laid down knife and fork in order to be able to burst in with loud clappings at the earliest permissible moment.

'And the Canetons à la mode d'Amblève? In stupefied, sickened wonder Aristide watched them grow cold in total neglect, or suffer the almost worse indignity of perfunctory pecking and listless munching while the banqueters lavished their approval and applause on the music-makers. Calves' liver and bacon, with parsley sauce, could hardly have figured more ignominiously in the evening's entertainment. And while the master of culinary art leaned back against the sheltering pillar, choking with a horrible brain-searing rage that could find no outlet for its agony, the orchestra leader was bowing his acknowledgments of the hand-clappings that rose in a storm around him. Turning to his colleagues he nodded the signal for an encore. But before the violin had been lifted anew into position there came from the shadow of the pillar an explosive negative.

' "Noh! Noh! You do not play thot again!"'

'The musician turned in furious astonishment. Had he taken warning from the look in the other man's eyes he might have acted differently. But the admiring plaudits were ringing in his ears, and he snarled out sharply, "That is for me to decide."

' "Noh! You play thot never again," shouted the *chef*, and the next moment he had flung himself violently upon the loathed being who had supplanted him in the world's esteem. A large metal tureen, filled to the brim with steaming soup, had just been placed on a side table in readiness for a late party of diners; before the waiting staff or the guests had time to realize what was happening, Aristide had dragged his struggling victim up to the table and plunged his head deep down into the almost boiling contents of the tureen. At the further end of the room the diners were still spasmodically applauding in view of an encore.

'Whether the leader of the orchestra died from drowning by soup, or from the shock to his professional vanity, or was scalded to death, the doctors were never wholly able to agree. Monsieur Aristide Saucourt, who now lives in complete retirement, always inclined to the drowning theory.'

THE EASTER EGG

IT WAS distinctly hard lines for Lady Barbara, who came of good fighting stock, and was one of the bravest women of her generation, that her son should be so undisguisedly a coward. Whatever good qualities Lester Slaggby may have possessed, and he was in some respects charming, courage could certainly never be imputed to him. As a child he had suffered from childish timidity, as a boy from unboyish funk, and as a youth he had exchanged unreasoning fears for others which were more formidable from the fact of having a carefully-thought-out basis. He was frankly afraid of animals, nervous with firearms, and never crossed the Channel without mentally comparing the numerical proportion of life belts to passengers. On horseback he seemed to require as many hands as a Hindu god, at least four for clutching the reins, and two more for patting the horse soothingly on the neck. Lady Barbara no longer pretended not to see her son's prevailing weakness; with her usual courage she faced the knowledge of it squarely, and, mother-like, loved him none the less.

Continental travel, anywhere away from the great tourist tracks, was a favoured hobby with Lady Barbara, and Lester joined her as often as possible. Eastertide usually found her at Knobaltheim, an upland township in one of those small princedoms that make inconspicuous freckles on the map of Central Europe.

A long-standing acquaintanceship with the reigning

family made her a personage of due importance in the eyes of her old friend the Burgomaster, and she was anxiously consulted by that worthy on the momentous occasion when the Prince made known his intention of coming in person to open a sanatorium outside the town. All the usual items in a programme of welcome, some of them fatuous and commonplace, others quaint and charming, had been arranged for, but the Burgomaster hoped that the resourceful English lady might have something new and tasteful to suggest in the way of loyal greeting. The Prince was known to the outside world, if at all, as an old-fashioned reactionary, combating modern progress, as it were, with a wooden sword; to his own people he was known as a kindly old gentleman with a certain endearing stateliness which had nothing of standoffishness about it. Knobaltheim was anxious to do its best. Lady Barbara discussed the matter with Lester and one or two acquaintances in her little hotel, but ideas were difficult to come by.

'Might I suggest something to the gnädige Frau?' asked a sallow high-cheek-boned lady to whom the English-woman had spoken once or twice, and whom she had set down in her mind as probably a Southern Slav.

'Might I suggest something for the Reception Fest?' she went on, with a certain shy eagerness. 'Our little child here, our baby, we will dress him in little white coat, with small wings, as an Easter angel, and he will carry a large white Easter egg, and inside shall be a basket of plover eggs, of which the Prince is so fond, and he shall give it to his Highness as Easter offering. It is so pretty an idea; we have seen it done once in Styria.'

Lady Barbara looked dubiously at the proposed Easter angel, a fair, wooden-faced child of about four years old. She had noticed it the day before in the hotel, and won-dered rather how such a tow-headed child could belong to such a dark-visaged couple as the woman and her husband; probably, she thought, an adopted baby, espe-cially as the couple were not young.

'Of course Gnädige Frau will escort the little child up to the Prince,' pursued the woman; 'but he will be quite good, and do as he is told.'

'We haf some pluffers' eggs shall come fresh from Wien,' said the husband.

The small child and Lady Barbara seemed equally un-enthusiastic about the pretty idea; Lester was openly dis-couraging, but when the Burgomaster heard of it he was enchanted. The combination of sentiment and plovers' eggs appealed strongly to his Teutonic mind.

On the eventful day the Easter angel, really quite prettily and quaintly dressed, was a centre of kindly interest to the gala crowd marshalled to receive his Highness. The mother was unobtrusive and less fussy than most parents would have been under the circumstances, merely stipulating that she should place the Easter egg herself in the arms that had been carefully schooled how to hold the precious burden. Then Lady Barbara moved forward, the child marching stolidly and with grim determination at her side. It had been promised cakes and sweeties galore if it gave the egg well and truly to the kind old gentleman who was waiting to receive it. Lester had tried to convey to it privately that horrible smackings would attend any failure in its share of the proceedings, but it is doubtful if his German caused more than an immediate distress. Lady Barbara had thoughtfully provided herself with an emer-gency supply of chocolate sweetmeats; children may some-times be time-servers, but they do not encourage long accounts. As they approached nearer to the princely daïs Lady Barbara stood discreetly aside, and the stolid-faced infant walked forward alone, with staggering but stead-fast gait, encouraged by a murmur of elderly approval. Lester, standing in the front row of the onlookers, turned to scan the crowd for the beaming faces of the happy parents. In a side-road which led to the railway station he saw a cab; entering the cab with every appearance of furtive haste were the dark-visaged couple who had been so plausibly eager for the 'pretty idea.' The sharpened instinct of cowardice lit up the situation to him in one swift flash. The blood roared and surged to his head as though thousands of floodgates had been opened in his veins and arteries, and his brain was the common sluice in which all the torrents met. He saw nothing but a blur around him. Then the blood ebbed away in quick waves, till his very heart seemed drained and empty, and he stood nervelessly, helplessly, dumbly watching the child, bearing its accursed burden with slow, relentless steps nearer and nearer to the group that waited sheep-like to receive him. A fascinated curiosity compelled Lester to turn his head towards the fugitives; the cab had started at hot pace in the direction of the station.

The next moment Lester was running, running faster than any of those present had ever seen a man run, and— he was not running away. For that stray fraction of his life some unwonted impulse beset him, some hint of the stock he came from, and he ran unflinchingly towards danger. He stooped and clutched at the Easter egg as one tries to scoop up the ball in Rugby football. What he meant to do with it he had not considered, the thing was to get it. But the child had been promised cakes and sweetmeats if it safely gave the egg into the hands of the kindly old gentleman; it uttered no scream, but it held to its charge with limpet grip. Lester sank to his knees, tugging savagely at the tightly clasped burden, and angry cries rose from the scandalized onlookers. A questioning, threatening ring formed round him, then shrank back in recoil as he shrieked out one hideous word. Lady Barbara heard the word and saw the crowd race away like scattered sheep, saw the Prince forcibly hustled away by his attendants; also she saw her son lying prone in an agony of over-mastering terror, his spasm of daring shattered by the child's unexpected resistance, still clutching frantically, as though for safety, at that white-satin gew-gaw, unable to crawl even from its deadly neighbourhood, able only to scream and scream and scream. In her brain she was dimly conscious of balancing, or striving to balance, the abject

shame which had him now in thrall against the one compelling act of courage which had flung him grandly and
madly on to the point of danger. It was only for the
fraction of a minute that she stood watching the two
entangled figures, the infant with its woodenly obstinate
face and body tense with dogged resistance, and the boy
limp and already nearly dead with a terror that almost
stifled his screams; and over them the long gala streamers
flapping gaily in the sunshine. She never forgot the scene;
but then, it was the last she ever saw.

Lady Barbara carries her scarred face with its sightless
eyes as bravely as ever in the world, but at Eastertide her
friends are careful to keep from her ears any mention of
the children's Easter symbol.

THE MUSIC ON THE HILL

Sylvia Seltoun ate her breakfast in the morning-
room at Yessney with a pleasant sense of ultimate victory,
such as a fervent Ironside might have permitted himself on
the morrow of Worcester fight. She was scarcely pugnacious by temperament, but belonged to that more successful class of fighters who are pugnacious by circumstance.
Fate had willed that her life should be occupied with a
series of small struggles, usually with the odds slightly
against her, and usually she had just managed to come
through winning. And now she felt that she had brought
her hardest and certainly her most important struggle to a
successful issue. To have married Mortimer Seltoun, 'Dead
Mortimer' as his more intimate enemies called him, in the
teeth of the cold hostility of his family, and in spite of his
unaffected indifference to women, was indeed an achievement that had needed some determination and adroitness
to carry through; yesterday she had brought her victory
to its concluding stage by wrenching her husband away

from Town and its group of satellite watering-places and 'settling him down,' in the vocabulary of her kind, in this remote wood-girt manor farm which was his country house.

'You will never get Mortimer to go,' his mother had said carpingly, 'but if he once goes he'll stay; Yessney throws almost as much a spell over him as Town does. One can understand what holds him to Town, but Yessney——' and the dowager had shrugged her shoulders.

There was a sombre almost savage wildness about Yessney that was certainly not likely to appeal to town-bred tastes, and Sylvia, notwithstanding her name, was accustomed to nothing much more sylvan than 'leafy Kensington.' She looked on the country as something excellent and wholesome in its way, which was apt to become troublesome if you encouraged it overmuch. Distrust of town-life had been a new thing with her, born of her marriage with Mortimer, and she had watched with satisfaction the gradual fading of what she called 'the Jermyn-Street-look' in his eyes as the woods and heather of Yessney had closed in on them yesternight. Her will-power and strategy had prevailed; Mortimer would stay.

Outside the morning-room windows was a triangular slope of turf, which the indulgent might call a lawn, and beyond its low hedge of neglected fuchsia bushes a steeper slope of heather and bracken dropped down into cavernous combes overgrown with oak and yew. In its wild open savagery there seemed a stealthy linking of the joy of life with the terror of unseen things. Sylvia smiled complacently as she gazed with a School-of-Art appreciation at the landscape, and then of a sudden she almost shuddered.

'It is very wild,' she said to Mortimer, who had joined her; 'one could almost think that in such a place the worship of Pan had never quite died out.'

'The worship of Pan never has died out,' said Mortimer. 'Other newer gods have drawn aside his votaries from time to time, but he is the Nature-God to whom all must come back at last. He has been called the Father of all the Gods, but most of his children have been stillborn.'

Sylvia was religious in an honest, vaguely devotional kind of way, and did not like to hear her beliefs spoken of as mere aftergrowths, but it was at least something new and hopeful to hear Dead Mortimer speak with such energy and conviction on any subject.

'You don't really believe in Pan?' she asked incredulously.

'I've been a fool in most things,' said Mortimer quietly, 'but I'm not such a fool as not to believe in Pan when I'm down here. And if you're wise you won't disbelieve in him too boastfully while you're in his country.'

It was not until a week later, when Sylvia had exhausted the attractions of the woodland walks round Yessney, that she ventured on a tour of inspection of the farm buildings. A farmyard suggested in her mind a scene of cheerful bustle, with churns and flails and smiling dairymaids, and teams of horses drinking knee-deep in duck-crowded ponds. As she wandered among the gaunt grey buildings of Yessney manor farm her first impression was one of crushing stillness and desolation, as though she had happened on some lone deserted homestead long given over to owls and cobwebs; then came a sense of furtive watchful hostility, the same shadow of unseen things that seemed to lurk in the wooded combes and coppices. From behind heavy doors and shuttered windows came the restless stamp of hoof or rasp of chain halter, and at times a muffled bellow from some stalled beast. From a distant corner a shaggy dog watched her with intent unfriendly eyes; as she drew near it slipped quietly into its kennel, and slipped out again as noiselessly when she had passed by. A few hens, questing for food under a rick, stole away under a gate at her approach. Sylvia felt that if she had come across any human beings in this wilderness of barn and byre they would have fled wraith-like from her gaze. At last, turning a corner quickly, she came upon a living thing that did not fly from her. Astretch in a pool of mud

was an enormous sow, gigantic beyond the town-woman's
wildest computation of swine-flesh, and speedily alert to
resent and if necessary repel the unwonted intrusion. It
was Sylvia's turn to make an unobtrusive retreat. As she
threaded her way past rickyards and cowsheds and long
blank walls, she started suddenly at a strange sound—the
echo of a boy's laughter, golden and equivocal. Jan, the
only boy employed on the farm, a tow-headed, wizen-faced
yokel, was visibly at work on a potato clearing half-way
up the nearest hill-side, and Mortimer, when questioned,
knew of no other probable or possible begetter of the
hidden mockery that had ambushed Sylvia's retreat. The
memory of that untraceable echo was added to her other
impressions of a furtive sinister 'something' that hung
around Yessney.

Of Mortimer she saw very little; farm and woods and
trout-streams seemed to swallow him up from dawn till
dusk. Once, following the direction she had seen him take
in the morning, she came to an open space in a nut copse,
further shut in by huge yew trees, in the centre of which
stood a stone pedestal surmounted by a small bronze
figure of a youthful Pan. It was a beautiful piece of work-
manship, but her attention was chiefly held by the fact
that a newly cut bunch of grapes had been placed as an
offering at its feet. Grapes were none too plentiful at the
manor house, and Sylvia snatched the bunch angrily from
the pedestal. Contemptuous annoyance dominated her
thoughts as she strolled slowly homeward, and then gave
way to a sharp feeling of something that was very near
fright; across a thick tangle of undergrowth a boy's face
was scowling at her, brown and beautiful, with unutterably
evil eyes. It was a lonely pathway, all pathways round
Yessney were lonely for the matter of that, and she sped
forward without waiting to give a closer scrutiny to this
sudden apparition. It was not till she had reached the
house that she discovered that she had dropped the bunch
of grapes in her flight.

'I saw a youth in the wood today,' she told Mortimer that evening, 'brown-faced and rather handsome, but a scoundrel to look at. A gipsy lad, I suppose.'

'A reasonable theory,' said Mortimer, 'only there aren't any gipsies in these parts at present.'

'Then who was he?' asked Sylvia, and as Mortimer appeared to have no theory of his own, she passed on to recount her finding of the votive offering.

'I suppose it was your doing,' she observed; 'it's a harmless piece of lunacy, but people would think you dreadfully silly if they knew of it.'

'Did you meddle with it in any way?' asked Mortimer.

'I—I threw the grapes away. It seemed so silly,' said Sylvia, watching Mortimer's impassive face for a sign of annoyance.

'I don't think you were wise to do that,' he said reflectively. 'I've heard it said that the Wood Gods are rather horrible to those who molest them.'

'Horrible perhaps to those that believe in them, but you see I don't,' retorted Sylvia.

'All the same,' said Mortimer in his even, dispassionate tone, 'I should avoid the woods and orchards if I were you, and give a wide berth to the horned beasts on the farm.'

It was all nonsense, of course, but in that lonely wood-girt spot nonsense seemed able to rear a bastard brood of uneasiness.

'Mortimer,' said Sylvia suddenly, 'I think we will go back to Town some time soon.'

Her victory had not been so complete as she had supposed; it had carried her on to ground that she was already anxious to quit.

'I don't think you will ever go back to Town,' said Mortimer. He seemed to be paraphrasing his mother's prediction as to himself.

Sylvia noted with dissatisfaction and some self-contempt that the course of her next afternoon's ramble took her instinctively clear of the network of woods. As to the horned cattle, Mortimer's warning was scarcely needed.

for she had always regarded them as of doubtful neutrality
at the best; her imagination unsexed the most matronly
dairy cows and turned them into bulls liable to 'see red'
at any moment. The ram who fed in the narrow paddock
below the orchards she had adjudged, after ample and
cautious probation, to be of docile temper; today, however,
she decided to leave his docility untested, for the usually
tranquil beast was roaming with every sign of restlessness
from corner to corner of his meadow. A low, fitful piping,
as of some reedy flute, was coming from the depth of a
neighbouring copse, and there seemed to be some subtle
connection between the animal's restless pacing and the
wild music from the wood. Sylvia turned her steps in an
upward direction and climbed the heather-clad slopes that
stretched in rolling shoulders high above Yessney. She
had left the piping notes behind her, but across the wooded
combes at her feet the wind brought her another kind of
music, the straining bay of hounds in full chase. Yessney
was just on the outskirts of the Devon-and-Somerset
country, and the hunted deer sometimes came that way.
Sylvia could presently see a dark body, breasting hill after
hill, and sinking again and again out of sight as he crossed
the combes, while behind him steadily swelled that relentless chorus, and she grew tense with the excited sympathy
that one feels for any hunted thing in whose capture one
is not directly interested. And at last he broke through the
outermost line of oak scrub and fern and stood panting
in the open, a fat September stag carrying a well-furnished
head. His obvious course was to drop down to the brown
pools of Undercombe, and thence make his way towards
the red deer's favoured sanctuary, the sea. To Sylvia's
surprise, however, he turned his head to the upland slope
and came lumbering resolutely onward over the heather.
'It will be dreadful,' she thought, 'the hounds will pull him
down under my very eyes.' But the music of the pack
seemed to have died away for a moment, and in its place
she heard again that wild piping, which rose now on this
side, now on that, as though urging the failing stag to a

final effort. Sylvia stood well aside from his path, half hidden in a thick growth of whortle bushes, and watched him swing stiffly upward, his flanks dark with sweat, the coarse hair on his neck showing light by contrast. The pipe music suddenly shrilled around her, seeming to come from the bushes at her very feet, and at the same moment the great beast slewed round and bore directly down upon her. In an instant her pity for the hunted animal was changed to wild terror at her own danger; the thick heather roots mocked her scrambling efforts at flight, and she looked frantically downward for a glimpse of oncoming hounds. The huge antler spikes were within a few yards of her, and in a flash of numbing fear she remembered Mortimer's warning, to beware of horned beasts on the farm. And then with a quick throb of joy she saw that she was not alone; a human figure stood a few paces aside, knee-deep in the whortle bushes.

'Drive it off!' she shrieked. But the figure made no answering movement.

The antlers drove straight at her breast, the acrid smell of the hunted animal was in her nostrils, but her eyes were filled with the horror of something she saw other than her oncoming death. And in her ears rang the echo of a boy's laughter, golden and equivocal.

THE PEACE OF
MOWSLE BARTON

CREFTON LOCKYER sat at his ease, an ease alike of body and soul, in the little patch of ground, half-orchard and half-garden, that abutted on the farmyard at Mowsle Barton. After the stress and noise of long years of city life, the repose and peace of the hill-begirt homestead struck on his senses with an almost dramatic intensity.

Time and space seemed to lose their meaning and their abruptness; the minutes slid away into hours, and the meadows and fallows sloped away into middle distance, softly and imperceptibly. Wild weeds of the hedgerow straggled into the flower-garden, and wallflowers and garden bushes made counter-raids into farmyard and lane. Sleepy-looking hens and solemn preoccupied ducks were equally at home in yard, orchard, or roadway; nothing seemed to belong definitely to anywhere; even the gates were not necessarily to be found on their hinges. And over the whole scene brooded the sense of a peace that had almost a quality of magic in it. In the afternoon you felt that it had always been afternoon, and must always remain afternoon; in the twilight you knew that it could never have been anything else but twilight. Crefton Lockyer sat at his ease in the rustic seat beneath an old medlar tree, and decided that here was the life-anchorage that his mind had so fondly pictured and that latterly his tired and jarred senses had so often pined for. He would make a permanent lodging-place among these simple friendly people, gradually increasing the modest comforts with which he would like to surround himself, but falling in as much as possible with their manner of living.

As he slowly matured this resolution in his mind an elderly woman came hobbling with uncertain gait through the orchard. He recognized her as a member of the farm household, the mother or possibly the mother-in-law of Mrs Spurfield, his present landlady, and hastily formulated some pleasant remark to make to her. She forestalled him.

'There's a bit of writing chalked up on the door over yonder. What is it?'

She spoke in a dull impersonal manner, as though the question had been on her lips for years and had best be got rid of. Her eyes, however, looked impatiently over Crefton's head at the door of a small barn which formed the outpost of a straggling line of farm buildings.

'Martha Pillamon is an old witch,' was the announcement that met Crefton's inquiring scrutiny, and he

hesitated a moment before giving the statement wider publicity. For all he knew to the contrary, it might be Martha
herself to whom he was speaking. It was possible that Mrs
Spurfield's maiden name had been Pillamon. And the
gaunt, withered old dame at his side might certainly fulfil
local conditions as to the outward aspect of a witch.

'It's something about some one called Martha Pillamon,'
he explained cautiously.

'What does it say?'

'It's very disrespectful,' said Crefton; 'it says she's a
witch. Such things ought not to be written up.'

'It's true, every word of it,' said his listener with considerable satisfaction, adding as a special descriptive note
of her own, 'the old toad.'

And as she hobbled away through the farmyard she
shrilled out in her cracked voice, 'Martha Pillamon is an
old witch!'

'Did you hear what she said?' mumbled a weak, angry
voice somewhere behind Crefton's shoulder. Turning
hastily, he beheld another old crone, thin and yellow and
wrinkled, and evidently in a high state of displeasure.
Obviously this was Martha Pillamon in person. The
orchard seemed to be a favourite promenade for the aged
women of the neighbourhood.

' 'Tis lies, 'tis sinful lies,' the weak voice went on. ' 'Tis
Betsy Croot is the old witch. She an' her daughter, the
dirty rat. I'll put a spell on 'em, the old nuisances.'

As she limped slowly away her eye caught the chalk
inscription on the barn door.

'What's written up there?' she demanded, wheeling
round on Crefton.

'Vote for Soarker,' he responded, with the craven bold-
ness of the practised peacemaker.

The old woman grunted, and her mutterings and her
faded red shawl lost themselves gradually among the tree-
trunks. Crefton rose presently and made his way towards
the farmhouse. Somehow a good deal of the peace seemed
to have slipped out of the atmosphere.

The cheery bustle of tea-time in the old farm kitchen, which Crefton had found so agreeable on previous afternoons, seemed to have soured today into a certain uneasy melancholy. There was a dull, dragging silence around the board, and the tea itself, when Crefton came to taste it, was a flat, lukewarm concoction that would have driven the spirit of revelry out of a carnival.

'It's no use complaining of the tea,' said Mrs Spurfield hastily, as her guest stared with an air of polite inquiry at his cup. 'The kettle won't boil, that's the truth of it.'

Crefton turned to the hearth, where an unusually fierce fire was banked up under a big black kettle, which sent a thin wreath of steam from its spout, but seemed otherwise to ignore the action of the roaring blaze beneath it.

'It's been there more than an hour, an' boil it won't,' said Mrs Spurfield, adding, by way of complete explanation, 'we're bewitched.'

'It's Martha Pillamon as has done it,' chimed in the old mother; 'I'll be even with the old toad. I'll put a spell on her.'

'It must boil in time,' protested Crefton, ignoring the suggestions of foul influences. 'Perhaps the coal is damp.'

'It won't boil in time for supper, nor for breakfast to-morrow morning, not if you was to keep the fire a-going all night for it,' said Mrs Spurfield. And it didn't. The household subsisted on fried and baked dishes, and a neighbour obligingly brewed tea and sent it across in a moderately warm condition.

'I suppose you'll be leaving us, now that things has turned up uncomfortable,' Mrs Spurfield observed at breakfast; 'there are folks as deserts one as soon as trouble comes.'

Crefton hurriedly disclaimed any immediate change of plans; he observed, however, to himself that the earlier heartiness of manner had in a large measure deserted the household. Suspicious looks, sulky silences, or sharp speeches had become the order of the day. As for the old mother, she sat about the kitchen or the garden all day, murmuring threats and spells against Martha Pillamon. There was something alike terrifying and piteous in the spectacle of these frail old morsels of humanity consecrating their last flickering energies to the task of making each other wretched. Hatred seemed to be the one faculty which had survived in undiminished vigour and intensity where all else was dropping into ordered and symmetrical decay. And the uncanny part of it was that some horrid unwholesome power seemed to be distilled from their spite and their cursings. No amount of sceptical explanation could remove the undoubted fact that neither kettle nor saucepan would come to boiling-point over the hottest fire. Crefton clung as long as possible to the theory of some defect in the coals, but a wood fire gave the same result, and when a small spirit-lamp kettle, which he ordered out by carrier, showed the same obstinate refusal to allow its contents to boil he felt that he had come suddenly into contact with some unguessed-at and very evil aspect of hidden forces. Miles away, down through an opening in the hills, he could catch glimpses of a road where motor-cars sometimes passed, and yet here, so little removed from the arteries of the latest civilization, was a bat-haunted old homestead, where something unmistakably like witchcraft seemed to hold a very practical sway.

Passing out through the farm garden on his way to the lanes beyond, where he hoped to recapture the comfortable sense of peacefulness that was so lacking around house and hearth—especially hearth—Crefton came across the old mother, sitting mumbling to herself in the seat beneath the medlar tree. 'Let un sink as swims, let un sink as swims,' she was repeating over and over again, as a child repeats a half-learned lesson. And now and then she would break off into a shrill laugh, with a note of malice in it that was not pleasant to hear. Crefton was glad when he found himself out of earshot, in the quiet and seclusion of the deep overgrown lanes that seemed to lead away to nowhere; one, narrower and deeper than the rest, attracted his footsteps, and he was almost annoyed when he found

that it really did act as a miniature roadway to a human
dwelling. A forlorn-looking cottage with a scrap of ill-
tended cabbage garden and a few aged apple trees stood at
an angle where a swift-flowing stream widened out for a
space into a decent-sized pond before hurrying away again
through the willows that had checked its course. Crefton
leaned against a tree-trunk and looked across the swirling
eddies of the pond at the humble little homestead opposite
him; the only sign of life came from a small procession
of dingy-looking ducks that marched in single file down
to the water's edge. There is always something rather
taking in the way a duck changes itself in an instant from
a slow, clumsy waddler of the earth to a graceful, buoyant
swimmer of the waters, and Crefton waited with a certain
arrested attention to watch the leader of the file launch
itself on to the surface of the pond. He was aware at the
same time of a curious warning instinct that something
strange and unpleasant was about to happen. The duck
flung itself confidently forward into the water, and rolled
immediately under the surface. Its head appeared for a
moment and went under again, leaving a train of bubbles
in its wake, while wings and legs churned the water in a
helpless swirl of flapping and kicking. The bird was
obviously drowning. Crefton thought at first that it had
caught itself in some weeds, or was being attacked from
below by a pike or water-rat. But no blood floated to the
surface, and the wildly bobbing body made the circuit of
the pond current without hindrance from any entanglement. A second duck had by this time launched itself into
the pond, and a second struggling body rolled and twisted
under the surface. There was something peculiarly piteous
in the sight of the gasping beaks that showed now and
again above the water, as though in terrified protest at this
treachery of a trusted and familiar element. Crefton gazed
with something like horror as a third duck poised itself
on the bank and splashed in, to share the fate of the other
two. He felt almost relieved when the remainder of the
flock, taking tardy alarm from the commotion of the slowly

drowning bodies, drew themselves up with tense out-stretched necks, and sidled away from the scene of danger, quacking a deep note of disquietude as they went. At the same moment Crefton became aware that he was not the only human witness of the scene; a bent and withered old woman, whom he recognized at once as Martha Pillamon, of sinister reputation, had limped down the cottage path to the water's edge, and was gazing fixedly at the grue-some whirligig of dying birds that went in horrible pro-cession round the pool. Presently her voice rang out in a shrill note of quavering rage:

' 'Tis Betsy Croot adone it, the old rat. I'll put a spell on her, see if I don't.'

Crefton slipped quietly away, uncertain whether or no the old woman had noticed his presence. Even before she had proclaimed the guiltiness of Betsy Croot, the latter's muttered incantation 'Let un sink as swims' had flashed uncomfortably across his mind. But it was the final threat of a retaliatory spell which crowded his mind with mis-giving to the exclusion of all other thoughts or fancies. His reasoning powers could no longer afford to dismiss these old-wives' threats as empty bickerings. The house-hold at Mowsle Barton lay under the displeasure of a vindictive old woman who seemed able to materialize her personal spites in a very practical fashion, and there was no saying what form her revenge for three drowned ducks might not take. As a member of the household Crefton might find himself involved in some general and highly disagreeable visitation of Martha Pillamon's wrath. Of course he knew that he was giving way to absurd fancies, but the behaviour of the spirit-lamp kettle and the subse-quent scene at the pond had considerably unnerved him. And the vagueness of his alarm added to its terrors; when once you have taken the Impossible into your calculations its possibilities become practically limitless.

Crefton rose at his usual early hour the next morning, after one of the least restful nights he had spent at the farm. His sharpened senses quickly detected that subtle atmosphere of things-being-not-altogether well that hangs over a stricken household. The cows had been milked, but they stood huddled about in the yard, waiting impatiently to be driven out afield, and the poultry kept up an importunate querulous reminder of deferred feeding-time; the yard pump, which usually made discordant music at frequent intervals during the early morning, was today ominously silent. In the house itself there was a coming and going of scuttering footsteps, a rushing and dying away of hurried voices, and long, uneasy stillnesses. Crefton finished his dressing and made his way to the head of a narrow staircase. He could hear a dull, complaining voice, a voice into which an awed hush had crept, and recognized the speaker as Mrs Spurfield.

'He'll go away, for sure,' the voice was saying; 'there are those as runs away from one as soon as real misfortune shows itself.'

Crefton felt that he probably was one of 'those,' and that there were moments when it was advisable to be true to type.

He crept back to his room, collected and packed his few belongings, placed the money due for his lodgings on a table, and made his way out by a back door into the yard. A mob of poultry surged expectantly towards him; shaking off their interested attentions he hurried along under cover of cow-stall, piggery, and hayricks till he reached the lane at the back of the farm. A few minutes' walk, which only the burden of his portmanteaux restrained from developing into an undisguised run, brought him to a main road, where the early carrier soon overtook him and sped him onward to the neighbouring town. At a bend of the road he caught a last glimpse of the farm; the old gabled roofs and thatched barns, the straggling orchard, and the medlar tree, with its wooden seat, stood out with an almost spectral clearness in the early morning light, and over it all brooded that air of magic possession which Crefton had once mistaken for peace.

The bustle and roar of Paddington Station smote on his ears with a welcome protective greeting.

'Very bad for our nerves, all this rush and hurry,' said a fellow-traveller; 'give me the peace and quiet of the country.'

Crefton mentally surrendered his share of the desired commodity. A crowded, brilliantly over-lighted music-hall, where an exuberant rendering of '1812' was being given by a strenuous orchestra, came nearest to his ideal of a nerve sedative.

THE HOUNDS OF FATE

In the fading light of a close dull autumn afternoon Martin Stoner plodded his way along muddy lanes and rut-seamed cart tracks that led he knew not exactly whither. Somewhere in front of him, he fancied, lay the sea, and towards the sea his footsteps seemed persistently turning; why he was struggling wearily forward to that goal he could scarcely have explained, unless he was possessed by the same instinct that turns a hard-pressed stag cliffward in its last extremity. In his case the hounds of Fate were certainly pressing him with unrelenting insistence; hunger, fatigue, and despairing hopelessness had numbed his brain, and he could scarcely summon sufficient energy to wonder what underlying impulse was driving him onward. Stoner was one of those unfortunate individuals who seem to have tried everything; a natural slothfulness and improvidence had always intervened to blight any chance of even moderate success, and now he was at the end of his tether, and there was nothing more to try. Desperation had not awakened in him any dormant reserve of energy; on the contrary, a mental torpor grew up round the crisis of his fortunes. With the clothes he stood up in, a halfpenny in his pocket, and no single friend or acquain-

tance to turn to, with no prospect either of a bed for the
night or a meal for the morrow, Martin Stoner trudged
stolidly forward, between moist hedgerows and beneath
dripping trees, his mind almost a blank, except that he was
subconsciously aware that somewhere in front of him lay
the sea. Another consciousness obtruded itself now and
then—the knowledge that he was miserably hungry.
Presently he came to a halt by an open gateway that led
into a spacious and rather neglected farm-garden; there
was little sign of life about, and the farmhouse at the
further end of the garden looked chill and inhospitable.
A drizzling rain, however, was setting in, and Stoner
thought that here perhaps he might obtain a few minutes'
shelter and buy a glass of milk with his last remaining
coin. He turned slowly and wearily into the garden and
followed a narrow, flagged path up to a side door. Before
he had time to knock the door opened and a bent, withered-
looking old man stood aside in the doorway as though to
let him pass in.

'Could I come in out of the rain?' Stoner began, but
the old man interrupted him.

'Come in, Master Tom. I knew you would come back
one of these days.'

Stoner lurched across the threshold and stood staring
uncomprehendingly at the other.

'Sit down while I put you out a bit of supper,' said the
old man with quavering eagerness. Stoner's legs gave way
from very weariness, and he sank inertly into the arm-chair
that had been pushed up to him. In another minute he was
devouring the cold meat, cheese, and bread, that had
been placed on the table at his side.

'You'm little changed these four years,' went on the old
man, in a voice that sounded to Stoner as something in
a dream, far away and inconsequent; 'but you'll find us
a deal changed, you will. There's no one about the place
same as when you left; nought but me and your old Aunt.
I'll go and tell her that you'm come; she won't be seeing
you, but she'll let you stay right enough. She always did

say if you was to come back you should stay, but she'd never set eyes on you or speak to you again.'

The old man placed a mug of beer on the table in front of Stoner and then hobbled away down a long passage. The drizzle of rain had changed to a furious lashing downpour, which beat violently against door and windows. The wanderer thought with a shudder of what the sea-shore must look like under this drenching rainfall, with night bearing down on all sides. He finished the food and beer and sat numbly waiting for the return of his strange host. As the minutes ticked by on the grandfather clock in the corner a new hope began to flicker and grow in the young man's mind; it was merely the expansion of his former craving for food and a few minutes' rest into a longing to find a night's shelter under this seemingly hospitable roof. A clattering of footsteps down the passage heralded the old farm servant's return.

'The old missus won't see you, Master Tom, but she says you are to stay. 'Tis right enough, seeing the farm will be yours when she be put under earth. I've had a fire lit in your room, Master Tom, and the maids has put fresh sheets on to the bed. You'll find nought changed up there. Maybe you'm tired and would like to go there now.'

Without a word Martin Stoner rose heavily to his feet and followed his ministering angel along a passage, up a short creaking stair, along another passage, and into a large room lit with a cheerfully blazing fire. There was but little furniture, plain, old-fashioned, and good of its kind; a stuffed squirrel in a case and a wall-calendar of four years ago were about the only symptoms of decora-tion. But Stoner had eyes for little else than the bed, and could scarce wait to tear his clothes off him before rolling in a luxury of weariness into its comfortable depths. The hounds of Fate seemed to have checked for a brief moment.

In the cold light of morning Stoner laughed mirthlessly as he slowly realized the position in which he found him-self. Perhaps he might snatch a bit of breakfast on the strength of his likeness to this other missing ne'er-do-well, and get safely away before any one discovered the fraud that had been thrust on him. In the room downstairs he found the bent old man ready with a dish of bacon and fried eggs for 'Master Tom's' breakfast, while a hard-faced elderly maid brought in a teapot and poured him out a cup of tea. As he sat at the table a small spaniel came up and made friendly advances.

' 'Tis old Bowker's pup,' explained the old man, whom the hard-faced maid had addressed as George. 'She was main fond of you; never seemed the same after you went away to Australee. She died 'bout a year agone. 'Tis her pup.'

Stoner found it difficult to regret her decease; as a witness for identification she would have left something to be desired.

'You'll go for a ride, Master Tom?' was the next start-ling proposition that came from the old man. 'We've a nice little roan cob that goes well in saddle. Old Biddy is getting a bit up in years, though 'er goes well still, but I'll have the little roan saddled and brought round to door.'

'I've got no riding things,' stammered the castaway, almost laughing as he looked down at his one suit of well-worn clothes.

'Master Tom,' said the old man earnestly, almost with an offended air, 'all your things is just as you left them. A bit of airing before the fire an' they'll be all right. 'Twill be a bit of a distraction like, a little riding and wild-fowling now and agen. You'll find the folk around here has hard and bitter minds towards you. They hasn't for-gotten nor forgiven. No one'll come nigh you, so you'd best get what distraction you can with horse and dog. They'm good company, too.'

Old George hobbled away to give his orders, and Stoner, feeling more than ever like one in a dream, went upstairs to inspect 'Master Tom's' wardrobe. A ride was one of the pleasures dearest to his heart, and there was some protection against immediate discovery of his impos-

ture in the thought that none of Tom's aforetime companions were likely to favour him with a close inspection.

As the interloper thrust himself into some tolerably
well-fitting riding cords he wondered vaguely what manner
of misdeed the genuine Tom had committed to set the
whole countryside against him. The thud of quick, eager
hoofs on damp earth cut short his speculations. The roan
cob had been brought up to the side door.

'Talk of beggars on horseback,' thought Stoner to himself, as he trotted rapidly along the muddy lanes where he
had tramped yesterday as a down-at-heel outcast; and then
he flung reflection indolently aside and gave himself up to
the pleasure of a smart canter along the turf-grown side of
a level stretch of road. At an open gateway he checked
his pace to allow two carts to turn into a field. The lads
driving the carts found time to give him a prolonged
stare, and as he passed on he heard an excited voice call
out, ' 'Tis Tom Prike. I knowed him at once; showing
hisself here agen, is he?'

Evidently the likeness which had imposed at close
quarters on a doddering old man was good enough to
mislead younger eyes at a short distance.

In the course of his ride he met with ample evidence to
confirm the statement that local folk had neither forgotten
nor forgiven the bygone crime which had come to him as
a legacy from the absent Tom. Scowling looks, mutterings,
and nudgings greeted him whenever he chanced upon
human beings; 'Bowker's pup,' trotting placidly by his side,
seemed the one element of friendliness in a hostile world.

As he dismounted at the side door he caught a fleeting
glimpse of a gaunt, elderly woman peering at him from
behind the curtain of an upper window. Evidently this
was his aunt by adoption.

Over the ample midday meal that stood in readiness for
him Stoner was able to review the possibilities of his
extraordinary situation. The real Tom, after four years of
absence, might suddenly turn up at the farm, or a letter
might come from him at any moment. Again, in the

character of heir to the farm, the false Tom might be called on to sign documents, which would be an embarrassing predicament. Or a relative might arrive who would not imitate the aunt's attitude of aloofness. All these things would mean ignominious exposure. On the other hand, the alternative was the open sky and the muddy lanes that led down to the sea. The farm offered him, at any rate, a temporary refuge from destitution; farming was one of the many things he had 'tried,' and he would be able to do a certain amount of work in return for the hospitality to which he was so little entitled.

'Will you have cold pork for your supper,' asked the hard-faced maid, as she cleared the table, 'or will you have it hotted up?'

'Hot, with onions,' said Stoner. It was the only time in his life that he had made a rapid decision. And as he gave the order he knew that he meant to stay.

Stoner kept rigidly to those portions of the house which seemed to have been allotted to him by a tacit treaty of delimitation. When he took part in the farm-work it was as one who worked under orders and never initiated them. Old George, the roan cob, and Bowker's pup were his sole companions in a world that was otherwise frostily silent and hostile. Of the mistress of the farm he saw nothing. Once, when he knew she had gone forth to church, he made a furtive visit to the farm parlour in an endeavour to glean some fragmentary knowledge of the young man whose place he had usurped, and whose ill-repute he had fastened on himself. There were many photographs hung on the walls, or stuck in prim frames, but the likeness he sought for was not among them. At last, in an album thrust out of sight, he came across what he wanted. There was a whole series, labelled 'Tom,' a podgy child of three, in a fantastic frock, an awkward boy of about twelve, holding a cricket bat as though he loathed it, a rather good-looking youth of eighteen with very smooth, evenly parted hair, and, finally, a young man with a somewhat surly dare-devil expression. At this last portrait Stoner looked with

particular interest; the likeness to himself was unmistakable.

From the lips of old George, who was garrulous enough
on most subjects, he tried again and again to learn something of the nature of the offence which shut him off as a
creature to be shunned and hated by his fellow-men.

'What do the folk around here say about me?' he asked
one day as they were walking home from an outlying field.

The old man shook his head.

'They be bitter agen you, mortal bitter. Ay, 'tis a sad
business, a sad business.'

And never could he be got to say anything more enlightening.

On a clear frosty evening, a few days before the festival
of Christmas, Stoner stood in a corner of the orchard
which commanded a wide view of the countryside. Here
and there he could see the twinkling dots of lamp or
candle glow which told of human homes where the good-
will and jollity of the season held their sway. Behind him
lay the grim, silent farmhouse, where no one ever laughed,
where even a quarrel would have seemed cheerful. As he
turned to look at the long grey front of the gloom-
shadowed building, a door opened and old George came
hurriedly forth. Stoner heard his adopted name called in
a tone of strained anxiety. Instantly he knew that something untoward had happened, and with a quick revulsion
of outlook his sanctuary became in his eyes a place of
peace and contentment, from which he dreaded to be
driven.

'Master Tom,' said the old man in a hoarse whisper, 'you
must slip away quiet from here for a few days. Michael
Ley is back in the village, an' he swears to shoot you if
he can come across you. He'll do it, too, there's murder
in the look of him. Get away under cover of night, 'tis
only for a week or so, he won't be here longer.'

'But where am I to go?' stammered Stoner, who had
caught the infection of the old man's obvious terror.

'Go right away along the coast to Punchford and keep
hid there. When Michael's safe gone I'll ride the roan over
to the Green Dragon at Punchford; when you see the cob
stabled at the Green Dragon 'tis a sign you may come
back agen.'

'But——' began Stoner hesitatingly.

' 'Tis all right for money,' said the other; 'the old
Missus agrees you'd best do as I say, and she's given me
this.'

The old man produced three sovereigns and some odd
silver.

Stoner felt more of a cheat than ever as he stole away
that night from the back gate of the farm with the old
woman's money in his pocket. Old George and Bowker's
pup stood watching him a silent farewell from the yard.
He could scarcely fancy that he would ever come back,
and he felt a throb of compunction for those two humble
friends who would wait wistfully for his return. Some
day perhaps the real Tom would come back, and there
would be wild wonderment among those simple farm
folks as to the identity of the shadowy guest they had
harboured under their roof. For his own fate he felt no
immediate anxiety; three pounds goes but little way in the
world when there is nothing behind it, but to a man who
has counted his exchequer in pennies it seems a good
starting-point. Fortune had done him a whimsically kind
turn when last he trod these lanes as a hopeless adventurer, and there might yet be a chance of his finding
some work and making a fresh start; as he got further
from the farm his spirits rose higher. There was a sense
of relief in regaining once more his lost identity and
ceasing to be the uneasy ghost of another. He scarcely
bothered to speculate about the implacable enemy who
had dropped from nowhere into his life; since that life was
now behind him one unreal item the more made little
difference. For the first time for many months he began to
hum a careless light-hearted refrain. Then there stepped
out from the shadow of an overhanging oak tree a man

with a gun. There was no need to wonder who he might be; the moonlight falling on his white set face revealed a glare of human hate such as Stoner in the ups and downs of his wanderings had never seen before. He sprang aside in a wild effort to break through the hedge that bordered the lane, but the tough branches held him fast. The hounds of Fate had waited for him in those narrow lanes, and this time they were not to be denied.

THE SECRET SIN
OF SEPTIMUS BROPE

'WHO AND what is Mr. Brope?' demanded the aunt of Clovis suddenly.

Mrs Riversedge, who had been snipping off the heads of defunct roses, and thinking of nothing in particular, sprang hurriedly to mental attention. She was one of those old-fashioned hostesses who consider that one ought to know something about one's guests, and that the something ought to be to their credit.

'I believe he comes from Leighton Buzzard,' she observed by way of preliminary explanation.

'In these days of rapid and convenient travel,' said Clovis, who was dispersing a colony of green-fly with visitations of cigarette smoke, 'to come from Leighton Buzzard does not necessarily denote any great strength of character. It might only mean mere restlessness. Now if he had left it under a cloud, or as a protest against the incurable and heartless frivolity of its inhabitants, that would tell us something about the man and his mission in life.'

'What does he do?' pursued Mrs Troyle magisterially.

'He edits the *Cathedral Monthly*,' said her hostess, 'and he's enormously learned about memorial brasses and transepts and the influence of Byzantine worship on modern liturgy, and all those sort of things. Perhaps he is just a little bit heavy and immersed in one range of subjects, but it takes all sorts to make a good house-party, you know. You don't find him *too* dull, do you?'

'Dullness I could overlook,' said the aunt of Clovis: 'what I cannot forgive is his making love to my maid.'

'My dear Mrs Troyle,' gasped the hostess, 'what an extraordinary idea! I assure you Mr Brope would not dream of doing such a thing.'

'His dreams are a matter of indifference to me; for all I care his slumbers may be one long indiscretion of unsuitable erotic advances, in which the entire servants' hall may be involved. But in his waking hours he shall not make love to my maid. It's no use arguing about it, I'm firm on the point.'

'But you must be mistaken,' persisted Mrs Riversedge; 'Mr Brope would be the last person to do such a thing.'

'He is the first person to do such a thing, as far as my information goes, and if I have any voice in the matter he certainly shall be the last. Of course, I am not referring to respectably-intentioned lovers.'

'I simply cannot think that a man who writes so charmingly and informingly about transepts and Byzantine influences would behave in such an unprincipled manner,' said Mrs Riversedge; 'what evidence have you that he's doing anything of the sort? I don't want to doubt your word, of course, but we mustn't be too ready to condemn him unheard, must we?'

'Whether we condemn him or not, he has certainly not been unheard. He has the room next to my dressing-room, and on two occasions, when I daresay he thought I was absent, I have plainly heard him announcing through the wall, 'I love you, Florrie.' Those partition walls upstairs are very thin; one can almost hear a watch ticking in the next room.'

'Is your maid called Florence?'

'Her name is Florinda.'

'What an extraordinary name to give a maid!'

'I did not give it to her; she arrived in my service already christened.'

'What I mean is,' said Mrs Riversedge, 'that when I get maids with unsuitable names I call them Jane; they soon get used to it.'

'An excellent plan,' said the aunt of Clovis coldly, 'unfortunately I have got used to being called Jane myself. It happens to be my name.'

She cut short Mrs Riversedge's flood of apologies by abruptly remarking:

'The question is not whether I'm to call my maid Florinda, but whether Mr Brope is to be permitted to call her Florrie. I am strongly of opinion that he shall not.'

'He may have been repeating the words of some song,' said Mrs Riversedge hopefully; 'there are lots of those sorts of silly refrains with girls' names,' she continued, turning to Clovis as a possible authority on the subject. ' "You mustn't call me Mary——" '

'I shouldn't think of doing so,' Clovis assured her; 'in the first place, I've always understood that your name was Henrietta; and then I hardly know you well enough to take such a liberty.'

'I mean there's a *song* with that refrain,' hurriedly explained Mrs Riversedge, 'and there's "Rhoda, Rhoda kept a pagoda," and "Maisie is a daisy," and heaps of others. Certainly it doesn't sound like Mr Brope to be singing such songs, but I think we ought to give him the benefit of the doubt.'

'I had already done so,' said Mrs Troyle, 'until further evidence came my way.'

She shut her eyes with the resolute finality of one who enjoys the blessed certainty of being implored to open them again.

'Further evidence!' exclaimed her hostess; 'do tell me!'

'As I was coming upstairs after breakfast Mr Brope was just passing my room. In the most natural way in the world a piece of paper dropped out of a packet that he held in his hand and fluttered to the ground just at my door. I was going to call out to him "You've dropped something," and then for some reason I held back and didn't show myself till he was safely in his room. You see it occurred to me that I was very seldom in my room just at that hour, and that Florinda was almost always there tidying up things about that time. So I picked up that innocent-looking piece of paper.'

Mrs Troyle paused again, with the self-applauding air of one who has detected an asp lurking in an apple-charlotte.

Mrs Riversedge snipped vigorously at the nearest rose bush, incidentally decapitating a Viscountess Folkestone that was just coming into bloom.

'What was on the paper?' she asked.

'Just the words in pencil, "I love you, Florrie," and then underneath, crossed out with a faint line, but perfectly plain to read, "Meet me in the garden by the yew." '

'There *is* a yew tree at the bottom of the garden,' admitted Mrs Riversedge.

'At any rate he appears to be truthful,' commented Clovis.

'To think that a scandal of this sort should be going on under my roof!' said Mrs Riversedge indignantly.

'I wonder why it is that scandal seems so much worse under a roof,' observed Clovis; 'I've always regarded it as a proof of the superior delicacy of the cat tribe that it conducts most of its scandals above the slates.'

'Now I come to think of it,' resumed Mrs Riversedge, 'there are things about Mr Brope that I've never been able to account for. His income, for instance: he only gets two hundred a year as editor of the *Cathedral Monthly*, and I know that his people are quite poor, and he hasn't any private means. Yet he manages to afford a flat somewhere in Westminster, and he goes abroad to Bruges and those sorts of places every year, and always dresses well, and gives quite nice luncheon-parties in the season. You can't do all that on two hundred a year, can you?'

'Does he write for any other papers?' queried Mrs Troyle.

'No, you see he specializes so entirely on liturgy and ecclesiastical architecture that his field is rather restricted. He once tried the *Sporting and Dramatic* with an article on church edifices in famous fox-hunting centres, but it wasn't considered of sufficient general interest to be accepted. No, I don't see how he can support himself in his present style merely by what he writes.'

'Perhaps he sells spurious transepts to American enthusiasts,' suggested Clovis.

'How could you sell a transept?' said Mrs Riversedge; 'such a thing would be impossible.'

'Whatever he may do to eke out his income,' interrupted Mrs Troyle, 'he is certainly not going to fill in his leisure moments by making love to my maid.'

'Of course not,' agreed her hostess; 'that must be put a stop to at once. But I don't quite know what we ought to do.'

'You might put a barbed wire entanglement round the yew tree as a precautionary measure,' said Clovis.

'I don't think that the disagreeable situation that has arisen is improved by flippancy,' said Mrs Riversedge; 'a good maid is a treasure——'

'I am sure I don't know what I should do without Florinda,' admitted Mrs Troyle; 'she understands my hair. I've long ago given up trying to do anything with it myself. I regard one's hair as I regard husbands: as long as one is seen together in public one's private divergences don't matter. Surely that was the luncheon gong.'

Septimus Brope and Clovis had the smoking-room to themselves after lunch. The former seemed restless and preoccupied, the latter quietly observant.

'What is a lorry?' asked Septimus suddenly; 'I don't mean the thing on wheels, of course I know what that is, but isn't there a bird with a name like that, the larger form of a lorikeet?'

'I fancy it's a lory, with one "r," ' said Clovis lazily, 'in which case it's no good to you.'

Septimus Brope stared in some astonishment.

'How do you mean, no good to me?' he asked, with more than a trace of uneasiness in his voice.

'Won't rhyme with Florrie,' exclaimed Clovis briefly.

Septimus sat upright in his chair, with unmistakable alarm on his face.

'How did you find out? I mean, how did you know I was trying to get a rhyme to Florrie?' he asked sharply.

'I didn't know,' said Clovis, 'I only guessed. When you wanted to turn the prosaic lorry of commerce into a feathered poem flitting through the verdure of a tropical forest, I knew you must be working up a sonnet, and Florrie was the only female name that suggested itself as rhyming with lorry.'

Septimus still looked uneasy.

'I believe you know more,' he said.

Clovis laughed quietly, but said nothing.

'How much do you know?' Septimus asked desperately.

'The yew tree in the garden,' said Clovis.

'There! I felt certain I'd dropped it somewhere. But you must have guessed something before. Look here, you have surprised my secret. You won't give me away, will you? It is nothing to be ashamed of, but it wouldn't do for the editor of the *Cathedral Monthly* to go in openly for that sort of thing, would it?'

'Well, I suppose not,' admitted Clovis.

'You see,' continued Septimus, 'I get quite a decent lot of money out of it. I could never live in the style I do on what I get as editor of the *Cathedral Monthly.*'

Clovis was even more startled than Septimus had been earlier in the conversation, but he was better skilled in repressing surprise.

'Do you mean to say you get money out of—Florrie?' he asked.

'Not out of Florrie, as yet,' said Septimus; 'in fact, I

don't mind saying that I'm having a good deal of trouble over Florrie. But there are a lot of others.'

Clovis's cigarette went out.

'This is *very* interesting,' he said slowly. And then, with Septimus Brope's next words, illumination dawned on him.

'There are heaps of others; for instance:

> ' "Cora with the lips of coral,
>   You and I will never quarrel."

That was one of my earliest successes, and it still brings me in royalties. And then there is—"Esmeralda, when I first beheld her," and "Fair Teresa, how I love to please her," both of those have been fairly popular. And there is one rather dreadful one,' continued Septimus, flushing deep carmine, 'which has brought me in more money than any of the others:

> ' "Lively little Lucie
>   With her naughty nez retrousse."

Of course, I loathe the whole lot of them; in fact, I'm rapidly becoming something of a woman-hater under their influence, but I can't afford to disregard the financial aspect of the matter. And at the same time you can understand that my position as an authority on ecclesiastical architecture and liturgical subjects would be weakened, if not altogether ruined, if it once got about that I was the author of "Cora with the lips of coral" and all the rest of them.'

Clovis had recovered sufficiently to ask in a sympathetic, if rather unsteady, voice what was the special trouble with 'Florrie.'

'I can't get her into lyric shape, try as I will,' said Septimus mournfully. 'You see, one has to work in a lot of sentimental, sugary compliment with a catchy rhyme, and a certain amount of personal biography or prophecy. They've all of them got to have a long string of past successes recorded about them, or else you've got to foretell

blissful things about them and yourself in the future. For
instance, there is:

> ' "Dainty little girlie Mavis,
>   She is such a rara avis,
>   All the money I can save is
>   All to be for Mavis mine."

It goes to a sickening namby-pamby waltz tune, and for
months nothing else was sung and hummed in Blackpool
and other popular centres.'

This time Clovis's self-control broke down badly.

'Please excuse me,' he gurgled, 'but I can't help it when
I remember the awful solemnity of that article of yours that
you so kindly read us last night, on the Coptic Church in
its relation to early Christian worship.'

Septimus groaned.

'You see how it would be,' he said; 'as soon as people
knew me to be the author of that miserable sentimental
twaddle, all respect for the serious labours of my life
would be gone. I daresay I know more about memorial
brasses than anyone living, in fact I hope one day to publish a monograph on the subject, but I should be pointed
out everywhere as the man whose ditties were in the
mouths of nigger minstrels along the entire coast-line of
our Island home. Can you wonder that I positively hate
Florrie all the time that I'm trying to grind out sugar-
coated rhapsodies about her?'

'Why not give free play to your emotions and be
brutally abusive? An uncomplimentary refrain would have
an instant success as a novelty if you were sufficiently outspoken.'

'I've never thought of that,' said Septimus, 'and I'm
afraid I couldn't break away from the habit of fulsome
adulation and suddenly change my style.'

'You needn't change your style in the least,' said Clovis;
'merely reverse the sentiment and keep to the inane phraseology of the thing. If you'll do the body of the song I'll
knock off the refrain, which is the thing that principally

matters, I believe. I shall charge half-shares in the royalties, and throw in my silence as to your guilty secret. In the eyes of the world you shall still be the man who has devoted his life to the study of transepts and Byzantine ritual; only sometimes, in the long winter evenings, when the wind howls drearily down the chimney and the rain beats against the windows, I shall think of you as the author of "Cora with the lips of coral." Of course, if in sheer gratitude at my silence you like to take me for a much-needed holiday to the Adriatic or somewhere equally interesting, paying all expenses, I shouldn't dream of refusing.'

Later in the afternoon Clovis found his aunt and Mrs Riversedge indulging in gentle exercise in the Jacobean garden.

'I've spoken to Mr Brope about F.,' he announced.

'How splendid of you! What did he say?' came in a quick chorus from the two ladies.

'He was quite frank and straightforward with me when he saw that I knew his secret,' said Clovis, 'and it seems that his intentions were quite serious, if slightly unsuitable. I tried to show him the impracticability of the course that he was following. He said he wanted to be understood, and he seemed to think that Florinda would excel in that requirement, but I pointed out that there were probably dozens of delicately nurtured, pure-hearted young English girls who would be capable of understanding him, while Florinda was the only person in the world who understood my aunt's hair. That rather weighed with him, for he's not really a selfish animal, if you take him in the right way, and when I appealed to the memory of his happy childish days, spent amid the daisied fields of Leighton Buzzard (I suppose daisies do grow there), he was obviously affected. Anyhow, he gave me his word that he would put Florinda absolutely out of his mind, and he has agreed to go for a short trip abroad as the best distraction for his thoughts. I am going with him as far as Ragusa. If my aunt should wish to give me a really nice scarf-pin (to be chosen by myself), as a small recognition of the very considerable service I have done her, I shouldn't dream of refusing. I'm not one of those who think that because one is abroad one can go about dressed anyhow.'

A few weeks later in Blackpool and places where they sing, the following refrain held undisputed sway:

> 'How you bore me, Florrie,
> With those eyes of vacant blue;
> You'll be very sorry, Florrie,
> If I marry you.
> Though I'm easy-goin', Florrie,
> This I swear is true,
> I'll throw you down a quarry, Florrie,
> If I marry you.'

THE REMOULDING
OF GROBY LINGTON

'A man is known by the company he keeps.'

IN THE morning-room of his sister-in-law's house Groby Lington fidgeted away the passing minutes with the demure restlessness of advanced middle age. About a quarter of an hour would have to elapse before it would be time to say his good-byes and make his way across the village green to the station, with a selected escort of nephews and nieces. He was a good-natured, kindly dispositioned man, and in theory he was delighted to pay periodical visits to the wife and children of his dead brother William; in practice, he infinitely preferred the comfort and seclusion of his own house and garden, and the companionship of his books and his parrot, to these rather meaningless and tiresome incursions into a family circle with which he had little in common. It was not so much the spur of his own

conscience that drove him to make the occasional short
journey by rail to visit his relatives, as an obedient concession to the more insistent but vicarious conscience of his
brother, Colonel John, who was apt to accuse him of
neglecting poor old William's family. Groby usually forgot
or ignored the existence of his neighbour kinsfolk until
such time as he was threatened with a visit from the
Colonel, when he would put matters straight by a hurried
pilgrimage across the few miles of intervening country to
renew his acquaintance with the young people and assume
a kindly if rather forced interest in the well-being of his
sister-in-law. On this occasion he had cut matters so fine
between the timing of his exculpatory visit and the coming
of Colonel John, that he would scarcely be home before
the latter was due to arrive. Anyhow, Groby had got it
over, and six or seven months might decently elapse before
he need again sacrifice his comforts and inclinations on
the altar of family sociability. He was inclined to be distinctly cheerful as he hopped about the room, picking up
first one object, then another, and subjecting each to a
brief bird-like scrutiny.

Presently his cheerful listlessness changed sharply to an
attitude of vexed attention. In a scrap-book of drawings and
caricatures belonging to one of his nephews he had come
across an unkindly clever sketch of himself and his parrot,
solemnly confronting each other in postures of ridiculous
gravity and repose, and bearing a likeness to one another
that the artist had done his utmost to accentuate. After the
first flush of annoyance had passed away, Groby laughed
good-naturedly and admitted to himself the cleverness of
the drawing. Then the feeling of resentment repossessed
him, resentment not against the caricaturist who had
embodied the idea in pen and ink, but against the possible
truth that the idea represented. Was it really the case that
people grew in time to resemble the animals they kept as
pets, and had he unconsciously become more and more like
the comically solemn bird that was his constant companion? Groby was unusually silent as he walked to the

train with his escort of chattering nephews and nieces, and during the short railway journey his mind was more and more possessed with an introspective conviction that he had gradually settled down into a sort of parrot-like existence. What, after all, did his daily routine amount to but a sedate meandering and pecking and perching, in his garden, among his fruit trees, in his wicker chair on the lawn, or by the fireside in his library? And what was the sum total of his conversation with chance-encountered neighbours? 'Quite a spring day, isn't it?' 'It looks as though we should have some rain.' 'Glad to see you about again; you must take care of yourself.' 'How the young folk shoot up, don't they?' Strings of stupid, inevitable perfunctory remarks came to his mind, remarks that were certainly not the mental exchange of human intelligences, but mere empty parrot-talk. One might really just as well salute one's acquaintances with 'Pretty Polly. Puss, puss, miaow!' Groby began to fume against the picture of himself as a foolish feathered fowl which his nephew's sketch had first suggested, and which his own accusing imagination was filling in with such unflattering detail.

'I'll give the beastly bird away,' he said resentfully; though he knew at the same time that he would do no such thing. It would look so absurd after all the years that he had kept the parrot and made much of it suddenly to try and find it a new home.

'Has my brother arrived?' he asked of the stable-boy, who had come with the pony-carriage to meet him.

'Yessir, came down by the two-fifteen. Your parrot's dead.' The boy made the latter announcement with the relish which his class finds in proclaiming a catastrophe.

'My parrot dead?' said Groby. 'What caused its death?'

'The ipe,' said the boy briefly.

'The ipe?' queried Groby. 'Whatever's that?'

'The ipe what the Colonel brought down with him,' came the rather alarming answer.

'Do you mean to say my brother is ill?' asked Groby. 'Is it something infectious?'

'Th' Colonel's so well as ever he was,' said the boy; and as no further explanation was forthcoming Groby had to possess himself in mystified patience till he reached home. His brother was waiting for him at the hall door.

'Have you heard about the parrot?' he asked at once. ' 'Pon my soul I'm awfully sorry. The moment he saw the monkey I'd brought down as a surprise for you he squawked out, "Rats to you, sir!" and the blessed monkey made one spring at him, got him by the neck and whirled him round like a rattle. He was as dead as mutton by the time I'd got him out of the little beggar's paws. Always been such a friendly little beast, the monkey has, should never have thought he'd got it in him to see red like that. Can't tell you how sorry I feel about it, and now of course you'll hate the sight of the monkey.'

'Not at all,' said Groby sincerely. A few hours earlier the tragic end which had befallen his parrot would have presented itself to him as a calamity; now it arrived almost as a polite attention on the part of the Fates.

'The bird was getting old, you know,' he went on, in explanation of his obvious lack of decent regret at the loss of his pet. 'I was really beginning to wonder if it was an unmixed kindness to let him go on living till he succumbed to old age. What a charming little monkey!' he added, when he was introduced to the culprit.

The new-comer was a small, long-tailed monkey from the Western Hemisphere, with a gentle, half-shy, half-trusting manner that instantly captured Groby's confidence; a student of simian character might have seen in the fitful red light in its eyes some indication of the under-lying temper which the parrot had so rashly put to the test with such dramatic consequences for itself. The servants, who had come to regard the defunct bird as a regular member of the household, and one who gave really very little trouble, were scandalized to find his bloodthirsty aggressor installed in his place as an honoured domestic pet.

'A nasty heathen ipe what don't never say nothing sensible and cheerful, same as pore Polly did,' was the unfavourable verdict of the kitchen quarters.

One Sunday morning, some twelve or fourteen months after the visit of Colonel John and the parrot-tragedy, Miss Wepley sat decorously in her pew in the parish church, immediately in front of that occupied by Groby Lington. She was, comparatively speaking, a new-comer in the neighbourhood, and was not personally acquainted with her fellow-worshipper in the seat behind, but for the past two years the Sunday morning service had brought them regularly within each other's sphere of consciousness. Without having paid particular attention to the subject, she could probably have given a correct rendering of the way in which he pronounced certain words occurring in the responses, while he was well aware of the trivial fact that, in addition to her prayer book and handkerchief, a small paper packet of throat lozenges always reposed on the seat beside her. Miss Wepley rarely had recourse to her lozenges, but in case she should be taken with a fit of coughing she wished to have the emergency duly provided for. On this particular Sunday the lozenges occasioned an unusual diversion in the even tenor of her devotions, far more disturbing to her personally than a prolonged attack of coughing would have been. As she rose to take part in the singing of the first hymn, she fancied that she saw the hand of her neighbour, who was alone in the pew behind her, make a furtive downward grab at the packet lying on the seat; on turning sharply round she found that the packet had certainly disappeared, but Mr Lington was to all outward seeming serenely intent on his hymn-book. No amount of interrogatory glaring on the part of the despoiled lady could bring the least shade of conscious guilt to his face.

'Worse was to follow,' as she remarked afterwards to a scandalized audience of friends and acquaintances. 'I had scarcely knelt in prayer when a lozenge, one of *my* lozenges, came whizzing into the pew, just under my nose. I turned round and stared, but Mr Lington had his eyes closed and his lips moving as though engaged in prayer. The moment I resumed my devotions another lozenge came rattling in, and then another. I took no notice for a while, and then turned round suddenly just as the dreadful man was about to flip another one at me. He hastily pretended to be turning over the leaves of his book, but I was not to be taken in that time. He saw that he had been discovered and no more lozenges came. Of course I have changed my pew.'

'No gentleman would have acted in such a disgraceful manner,' said one of her listeners; 'and yet Mr Lington used to be so respected by everybody. He seems to have behaved like a little ill-bred schoolboy.'

'He behaved like a monkey,' said Miss Wepley.

Her unfavourable verdict was echoed in other quarters about the same time. Groby Lington had never been a hero in the eyes of his personal retainers, but he had shared the approval accorded to his defunct parrot as a cheerful, well-dispositioned body, who gave no particular trouble. Of late months, however, this character would hardly have been endorsed by the members of his domestic establishment. The stolid stable-boy, who had first announced to him the tragic end of his feathered pet, was one of the first to give voice to the murmurs of disapproval which became rampant and general in the servants' quarters, and he had fairly substantial grounds for his disaffection. In a burst of hot summer weather he had obtained permission to bathe in a modest-sized pond in the orchard, and thither one afternoon Groby had bent his steps, attracted by loud imprecations of anger mingled with the shriller chattering of monkey-language. He beheld his plump diminutive servitor, clad only in a waistcoat and a pair of socks, storming ineffectually at the monkey, which was seated on a low branch of an apple tree, abstractedly fingering the remainder of the boy's outfit, which he had removed just out of his reach.

'The ipe's been an' took my clothes,' whined the boy, with the passion of his kind for explaining the obvious. His incomplete toilet effect rather embarrassed him, but he hailed the arrival of Groby with relief, as promising moral and material support in his efforts to get back his raided garments. The monkey had ceased its defiant jabbering, and doubtless with a little coaxing from its master it would hand back the plunder.

'If I lift you up,' suggested Groby, 'you will just be able to reach the clothes.'

The boy agreed, and Groby clutched him firmly by the waistcoat, which was about all there was to catch hold of, and lifted him clear of the ground. Then, with a deft swing he sent him crashing into a clump of tall nettles, which closed receptively round him. The victim had not been brought up in a school which teaches one to repress one's emotions—if a fox had attempted to gnaw at his vitals he would have flown to complain to the nearest hunt committee rather than have affected an attitude of stoical indifference. On this occasion the volume of sound which he produced under the stimulus of pain and rage and astonishment was generous and sustained, but above his bellowings he could distinctly hear the triumphant chattering of his enemy in the tree, and a peal of shrill laughter from Groby.

When the boy had finished an improvised St Vitus caracole, which would have brought him fame on the boards of the Coliseum, and which indeed met with ready appreciation and applause from the retreating figure of Groby Lington, he found that the monkey had also discreetly retired, while his clothes were scattered on the grass at the foot of the tree.

'They'm two ipes, that's what they be,' he muttered angrily, and if his judgment was severe, at least he spoke under the sting of considerable provocation.

It was a week or two later that the parlour-maid gave notice, having been terrified almost to tears by an outbreak of sudden temper on the part of the master anent some

underdone cutlets. ' 'E gnashed 'is teeth at me, 'e did reely,'
she informed a sympathetic kitchen audience.

'I'd like to see 'im talk like that to me, I would,' said
the cook defiantly, but her cooking from that moment
showed a marked improvement.

It was seldom that Groby Lington so far detached himself from his accustomed habits as to go and form one of a
house-party, and he was not a little piqued that Mrs Glen-
duff should have stowed him away in the musty old Georgian wing of the house, in the next room, moreover, to
Leonard Spabbink, the eminent pianist.

'He plays Liszt like an angel,' had been the hostess's
enthusiastic testimonial.

'He may play him like a trout for all I care,' had been
Groby's mental comment, 'but I wouldn't mind betting
that he snores. He's just the sort and shape that would.
And if I hear him snoring through those ridiculous thin-
panelled walls, there'll be trouble.'

He did, and there was.

Groby stood it for about two and a quarter minutes, and
then made his way through the corridor into Spabbink's
room. Under Groby's vigorous measures the musician's
flabby, redundant figure sat up in bewildered semi-
consciousness like an ice-cream that has been taught to
beg. Groby prodded him into complete wakefulness, and
then the pettish self-satisfied pianist fairly lost his temper
and slapped his domineering visitant on the hand. In another moment Spabbink was being nearly stifled and very
effectually gagged by a pillow-case tightly bound round
his head, while his plump pyjama'd limbs were hauled
out of bed and smacked, pinched, kicked, and bumped in
a catch-as-catch-can progress across the floor, towards the
flat shallow bath in whose utterly inadequate depths
Groby perseveringly strove to drown him. For a few
moments the room was almost in darkness: Groby's candle
had overturned in an early stage of the scuffle, and its
flicker scarcely reached to the spot where splashings,
smacks, muffled cries, and splutterings, and a chatter of

ape-like rage told of the struggle that was being waged round the shores of the bath. A few instants later the one-sided combat was brightly lit up by the flare of blazing curtains and rapidly kindling panelling.

When the hastily aroused members of the house-party stampeded out on to the lawn, the Georgian wing was well alight and belching forth masses of smoke, but some moments elapsed before Groby appeared with the half-drowned pianist in his arms, having just bethought him of the superior drowning facilities offered by the pond at the bottom of the lawn. The cool night air sobered his rage, and when he found that he was innocently acclaimed as the heroic rescuer of poor Leonard Spabbink, and loudly commended for his presence of mind in tying a wet cloth round his head to protect him from smoke suffocation, he accepted the situation, and subsequently gave a graphic account of his finding the musician asleep with an over-turned candle by his side and the conflagration well started. Spabbink gave *his* version some days later, when he had partially recovered from the shock of his midnight castiga-tion and immersion, but the gentle pitying smiles and evasive comments with which his story was greeted warned him that the public ear was not at his disposal. He refused, however, to attend the ceremonial presentation of the Royal Humane Society's life-saving medal.

It was about this time that Groby's pet monkey fell a victim to the disease which attacks so many of its kind when brought under the influence of a northern climate. Its master appeared to be profoundly affected by its loss, and never quite recovered the level of spirits that he had recently attained. In company with the tortoise, which Colonel John presented to him on his last visit, he potters about his lawn and kitchen garden, with none of his erst-while sprightliness; and his nephews and nieces are fairly well justified in alluding to him as 'Old Uncle Groby.'

From

BEASTS AND
SUPER-BEASTS
[1914]

THE SHE-WOLF

LEONARD BILSITER was one of those people who have failed to find this world attractive or interesting, and who have sought compensation in an 'unseen world' of their own experience or imagination—or invention. Children do that sort of thing successfully, but children are content to convince themselves, and do not vulgarize their beliefs by trying to convince other people. Leonard Bilsiter's beliefs were for 'the few,' that is to say, any one who would listen to him.

His dabblings in the unseen might not have carried him beyond the customary platitudes of the drawing-room visionary if accident had not reinforced his stock-in-trade of mystical lore. In company with a friend, who was interested in a Ural mining concern, he had made a trip across Eastern Europe at a moment when the great Russian railway strike was developing from a threat to a reality; its outbreak caught him on the return journey, somewhere on the further side of Perm, and it was while waiting for a couple of days at a wayside station in a state of suspended locomotion that he made the acquaintance of a dealer in harness and metalware, who profitably whiled away the tedium of the long halt by initiating his English travelling companion in a fragmentary system of folk-lore that he had picked up from Trans-Baikal traders and natives. Leonard returned to his home circle garrulous about his Russian strike experiences, but oppressively reticent about certain dark mysteries, which he alluded to under the resounding title of Siberian Magic. The reticence wore off in a week or two under the influence of an entire lack of general curiosity, and Leonard began to make more detailed allusions to the enormous powers which this new esoteric force, to use his own description of it, conferred on the initiated few who knew how to wield it. His aunt, Cecilia Hoops, who loved sensation perhaps rather better than she loved the truth, gave him as clamorous an advertise-

ment as any one could wish for by retailing an account of
how he had turned a vegetable marrow into a wood-
pigeon before her very eyes. As a manifestation of the
possession of supernatural powers, the story was dis-
counted in some quarters by the respect accorded to Mrs
Hoops' powers of imagination.

However divided opinion might be on the question of
Leonard's status as a wonder-worker or a charlatan, he
certainly arrived at Mary Hampton's house-party with a
reputation for pre-eminence in one or other of those pro-
fessions, and he was not disposed to shun such publicity
as might fall to his share. Esoteric forces and unusual
powers figured largely in whatever conversation he or his
aunt had a share in, and his own performances, past and
potential, were the subject of mysterious hints and dark
avowals.

'I wish you would turn me into a wolf, Mr Bilsiter,'
said his hostess at luncheon the day after his arrival.

'My dear Mary,' said Colonel Hampton, 'I never knew
you had a craving in that direction.'

'A she-wolf, of course,' continued Mrs Hampton; 'it
would be too confusing to change one's sex as well as one's
species at a moment's notice.'

'I don't think one should jest on these subjects,' said
Leonard.

'I'm not jesting. I'm quite serious, I assure you. Only
don't do it today; we have only eight available bridge
players, and it would break up one of our tables. Tomorrow we shall be a larger party. Tomorrow night, after
dinner——'

'In our present imperfect understanding of these hidden
forces I think one should approach them with humbleness
rather than mockery,' observed Leonard, with such severity
that the subject was forthwith dropped.

Clovis Sangrail had sat unusually silent during the discussion on the possibilities of Siberian magic; after lunch
he sidetracked Lord Pabham into the comparative seclusion

of the billiard-room and delivered himself of a searching question.

'Have you such a thing as a she-wolf in your collection of wild animals? A she-wolf of moderately good temper?'

Lord Pabham considered. 'There is Louisa,' he said, 'a rather fine specimen of the timber-wolf. I got her two years ago in exchange for some Arctic foxes. Most of my animals get to be fairly tame before they've been with me very long; I think I can say Louisa has an angelic temper, as she-wolves go. Why do you ask?'

'I was wondering whether you would lend her to me for tomorrow night,' said Clovis, with a careless solicitude of one who borrows a collar stud or a tennis racquet.

'Tomorrow night?'

'Yes, wolves are nocturnal animals, so the late hours won't hurt her,' said Clovis, with the air of one who has taken everything into consideration; 'one of your men could bring her over from Pabham Park after dusk, and with a little help he ought to be able to smuggle her into the conservatory at the same moment that Mary Hampton makes an unobtrusive exit.'

Lord Pabham stared at Clovis for a moment in pardonable bewilderment; then his face broke into a wrinkled network of laughter.

'Oh, that's your game, is it? You are going to do a little Siberian magic on your own account. And is Mrs Hampton willing to be a fellow-conspirator?'

'Mary is pledged to see me through with it, if you will guarantee Louisa's temper.'

'I'll answer for Louisa,' said Lord Pabham.

By the following day the house-party had swollen to larger proportions, and Bilsiter's instinct for self-advertisement expanded duly under the stimulant of an increased audience. At dinner that evening he held forth at length on the subject of unseen forces and untested powers, and his flow of impressive eloquence continued unabated while coffee was being served in the drawing-room preparatory to a general migration to the card-room. His aunt ensured a respectful hearing for his utterances, but her sensation-loving soul hankered after something more dramatic than mere vocal demonstration.

'Won't you do something to *convince* them of your powers, Leonard?' she pleaded. 'Change something into another shape. He can, you know, if he only chooses to,' she informed the company.

'Oh, do,' said Mavis Pellington earnestly, and her request was echoed by nearly every one present. Even those who were not open to conviction were perfectly willing to be entertained by an exhibition of amateur conjuring.

Leonard felt that something tangible was expected of him.

'Has any one present,' he asked, 'got a three-penny bit or some small object of no particular value——?'

'You're surely not going to make coins disappear, or something primitive of that sort?' said Clovis contemptuously.

'I think it is very unkind of you not to carry out my suggestion of turning me into a wolf,' said Mary Hampton, as she crossed over to the conservatory to give her macaws their usual tribute from the dessert dishes.

'I have already warned you of the danger of treating these powers in a mocking spirit,' said Leonard solemnly.

'I don't believe you can do it,' laughed Mary provocatively from the conservatory; 'I dare you to do it if you can. I defy you to turn me into a wolf.'

As she said this she was lost to view behind a clump of azaleas.

'Mrs Hampton——' began Leonard with increased solemnity, but he got no further. A breath of chill air seemed to rush across the room, and at the same time the macaws broke forth into ear-splitting screams.

'What on earth is the matter with those confounded birds, Mary?' exclaimed Colonel Hampton; at the same moment an even more piercing scream from Mavis Pellington stampeded the entire company from their seats. In various attitudes of helpless horror or instinctive defence they confronted the evil-looking grey beast that was peering at them from amid a setting of fern and azalea.

Mrs Hoops was the first to recover from the general chaos of fright and bewilderment.

'Leonard!' she screamed shrilly to her nephew, 'turn it back into Mrs Hampton at once! It may fly at us at any moment. Turn it back!'

'I—I don't know how to,' faltered Leonard, who looked more scared and horrified than any one.

'What!' shouted Colonel Hampton, 'you've taken the abominable liberty of turning my wife into a wolf, and now you stand there calmly and say you can't turn her back again!'

To do strict justice to Leonard, calmness was not a distinguishing feature of his attitude at the moment.

'I assure you I didn't turn Mrs Hampton into a wolf; nothing was further from my intentions,' he protested.

'Then where is she, and how came that animal into the conservatory?' demanded the Colonel.

'Of course we must accept your assurance that you didn't turn Mrs Hampton into a wolf,' said Clovis politely, 'but you will agree that appearances are against you.'

'Are we to have all these recriminations with that beast standing there ready to tear us to pieces?' wailed Mavis indignantly.

'Lord Pabham, you know a good deal about wild beasts ——' suggested Colonel Hampton.

'The wild beasts that I have been accustomed to,' said Lord Pabham, 'have come with proper credentials from well-known dealers, or have been bred in my own menagerie. I've never before been confronted with an animal that walks unconcernedly out of an azalea bush, leaving a charming and popular hostess unaccounted for. As far as one can judge from *outward* characteristics,' he continued, 'it has the appearance of a well-grown female of the North American timber-wolf, a variety of the common species *canis lupus.*'

'Oh, never mind its Latin name,' screamed Mavis, as the

beast came a step or two further into the room; 'can't you entice it away with food, and shut it up where it can't do any harm?'

'If it is really Mrs Hampton, who has just had a very good dinner, I don't suppose food will appeal to it very strongly,' said Clovis.

'Leonard,' beseeched Mrs Hoops tearfully, 'even if this is none of your doing, can't you use your great powers to turn this dreadful beast into something harmless before it bites us all—a rabbit or something?'

'I don't suppose Colonel Hampton would care to have his wife turned into a succession of fancy animals as though we were playing a round game with her,' interposed Clovis.

'I absolutely forbid it,' thundered the Colonel.

'Most wolves that I've had anything to do with have been inordinately fond of sugar,' said Lord Pabham; 'if you like I'll try the effect on this one.'

He took a piece of sugar from the saucer of his coffee cup and flung it to the expectant Louisa, who snapped it in mid-air. There was a sigh of relief from the company; a wolf that ate sugar when it might at the least have been employed in tearing macaws to pieces had already shed some of its terrors. The sigh deepened to a gasp of thanksgiving when Lord Pabham decoyed the animal out of the room by a pretended largesse of further sugar. There was an instant rush to the vacated conservatory. There was no trace of Mrs Hampton except the plate containing the macaw's supper.

'The door is locked on the inside!' exclaimed Clovis, who had deftly turned the key as he affected to test it.

Every one turned towards Bilsiter.

'If you haven't turned my wife into a wolf,' said Colonel Hampton, 'will you kindly explain where she has disappeared to, since she obviously could not have gone through a locked door? I will not press you for an explanation of how a North American timber wolf suddenly appeared in the conservatory, but I think I have some right to inquire what has become of Mrs Hampton.'

Bilsiter's reiterated disclaimer was met with a general murmur of impatient disbelief.

'I refuse to stay another hour under this roof,' declared Mavis Pellington.

'If our hostess has really vanished out of human form,' said Mrs Hoops, 'none of the ladies of the party can very well remain. I absolutely decline to be chaperoned by a wolf!'

'It's a she-wolf,' said Clovis soothingly.

The correct etiquette to be observed under the unusual circumstances received no further elucidation. The sudden entry of Mary Hampton deprived the discussion of its immediate interest.

'Some one has mesmerized me,' she exclaimed crossly; 'I found myself in the game larder, of all places, being fed with sugar by Lord Pabham. I hate being mesmerized, and the doctor has forbidden me to touch sugar.'

The situation was explained to her, as far as it permitted of anything that could be called explanation.

'Then you *really* did turn me into a wolf, Mr Bilsiter?' she exclaimed excitedly.

But Leonard had burned the boat in which he might now have embarked on a sea of glory. He could only shake his head feebly.

'It was I who took that liberty,' said Clovis; 'you see, I happen to have lived for a couple of years in North-eastern Russia, and I have more than a tourist's acquaintance with the magic craft of that region. One does not care to speak about these strange powers, but once in a way, when one hears a lot of nonsense being talked about them, one is tempted to show what Siberian magic can accomplish in the hands of some one who really understands it. I yielded to that temptation. May I have some brandy? the effort has left me rather faint.'

If Leonard Bilsiter could at that moment have transformed Clovis into a cockroach and then have stepped on him he would gladly have performed both operations.

LAURA

'You are not really dying, are you?' asked Amanda.

'I have the doctor's permission to live till Tuesday,' said Laura.

'But today is Saturday; this is serious!' gasped Amanda.

'I don't know about it being serious; it is certainly Saturday,' said Laura.

'Death is always serious,' said Amanda.

'I never said I was going to die. I am presumably going to leave off being Laura, but I shall go on being something. An animal of some kind, I suppose. You see, when one hasn't been very good in the life one has just lived, one reincarnates in some lower organism. And I haven't been very good, when one comes to think of it. I've been petty and mean and vindictive and all that sort of thing when circumstances have seemed to warrant it.'

'Circumstances never warrant that sort of thing,' said Amanda hastily.

'If you don't mind my saying so,' observed Laura, 'Egbert is a circumstance that would warrant any amount of that sort of thing. You're married to him—that's different; you've sworn to love, honour and endure him: I haven't.'

'I don't see what's wrong with Egbert,' protested Amanda.

'Oh, I dare say the wrongness has been on my part,' admitted Laura dispassionately; 'he has merely been the extenuating circumstance. He made a thin, peevish kind of fuss, for instance, when I took the collie puppies from the farm out for a run the other day.'

'They chased his young broods of speckled Sussex and drove two sitting hens off their nests, besides running all over the flower beds. You know how devoted he is to his poultry and garden.'

'Anyhow, he needn't have gone on about it for the entire evening, and then have said, "Let's say no more about it" just when I was beginning to enjoy the discussion. That's where one of my petty vindictive revenges came in,' added Laura with an unrepentant chuckle; 'I turned the entire family of speckled Sussex into his seedling shed the day after the puppy episode.'

'How could you?' exclaimed Amanda.

'It came quite easy,' said Laura; 'two of the hens pretended to be laying at the time, but I was firm.'

'And we thought it was an accident!'

'You see,' resumed Laura, 'I really *have* some grounds for supposing that my next incarnation will be in a lower organism. I shall be an animal of some kind. On the other hand, I haven't been a bad sort in my way, so I think I may count on being a nice animal, something elegant and lively, with a love of fun. An otter, perhaps.'

'I can't imagine you as an otter,' said Amanda.

'Well, I don't suppose you can imagine me as an angel, if it comes to that,' said Laura.

Amanda was silent. She couldn't.

'Personally I think an otter life would be rather enjoyable,' continued Laura; 'salmon to eat all the year round, and the satisfaction of being able to fetch the trout in their own homes without having to wait for hours till they condescend to rise to the fly you've been dangling before them; and an elegant svelte figure——'

'Think of the otter hounds,' interposed Amanda; 'how dreadful to be hunted and harried and finally worried to death!'

'Rather fun with half the neighbourhood looking on, and anyhow not worse than this Saturday-to-Tuesday business of dying by inches; and then I should go on into something else. If I had been a moderately good otter I suppose I should get back into human shape of some sort; probably something rather primitive—a little brown, unclothed Nubian boy, I should think.'

'I wish you would be serious,' sighed Amanda; 'you really ought to be if you're only going to live till Tuesday.'

As a matter of fact Laura died on Monday.

'So dreadfully upsetting,' Amanda complained to her uncle-in-law, Sir Lulworth Quayne. 'I've asked quite a lot of people down for golf and fishing, and the rhododendrons are just looking their best.'

'Laura always was inconsiderate,' said Sir Lulworth; 'she was born during Goodwood week, with an Ambassador staying in the house who hated babies.'

'She had the maddest kind of ideas,' said Amanda; 'do you know if there was any insanity in her family?'

'Insanity? No, I never heard of any. Her father lives in West Kensington, but I believe he's sane on all other subjects.'

'She had an idea that she was going to be reincarnated as an otter,' said Amanda.

'One meets with those ideas of reincarnation so frequently, even in the West,' said Sir Lulworth, 'that one can hardly set them down as being mad. And Laura was such an unaccountable person in this life that I should not like to lay down definite rules as to what she might be doing in an after state.'

'You think she really might have passed into some animal form?' asked Amanda. She was one of those who shape their opinions rather readily from the standpoint of those around them.

Just then Egbert entered the breakfast-room, wearing an air of bereavement that Laura's demise would have been insufficient, in itself, to account for.

'Four of my speckled Sussex have been killed,' he exclaimed; 'the very four that were to go to the show on Friday. One of them was dragged away and eaten right in the middle of that new carnation bed that I've been to such trouble and expense over. My best flower bed and my best fowls singled out for destruction; it almost seems as if the brute that did the deed had special knowledge how to be as devastating as possible in a short space of time.'

'Was it a fox, do you think?' asked Amanda.

'Sounds more like a polecat,' said Sir Lulworth.

'No,' said Egbert, 'there were marks of webbed feet all

over the place, and we followed the tracks down to the stream at the bottom of the garden; evidently an otter.'

Amanda looked quickly and furtively across at Sir Lulworth.

Egbert was too agitated to eat any breakfast, and went out to superintend the strengthening of the poultry yard defences.

'I think she might at least have waited till the funeral was over,' said Amanda in a scandalized voice.

'It's her own funeral, you know,' said Sir Lulworth; 'it's a nice point in etiquette how far one ought to show respect to one's own mortal remains.'

Disregard for mortuary convention was carried to further lengths next day; during the absence of the family at the funeral ceremony the remaining survivors of the speckled Sussex were massacred. The marauder's line of retreat seemed to have embraced most of the flower beds on the lawn, but the strawberry beds in the lower garden had also suffered.

'I shall get the otter hounds to come here at the earliest possible moment,' said Egbert savagely.

'On no account! You can't dream of such a thing!' exclaimed Amanda. 'I mean, it wouldn't do, so soon after a funeral in the house.'

'It's a case of necessity,' said Egbert; 'once an otter takes to that sort of thing it won't stop.'

'Perhaps it will go elsewhere now that there are no more fowls left,' suggested Amanda.

'One would think you wanted to shield the beast,' said Egbert.

'There's been so little water in the stream lately,' objected Amanda; 'it seems hardly sporting to hunt an animal when it has so little chance of taking refuge anywhere.'

'Good gracious!' fumed Egbert, 'I'm not thinking about sport. I want to have the animal killed as soon as possible.'

Even Amanda's opposition weakened when, during church time on the following Sunday, the otter made its way into the house, raided half a salmon from the larder and worried it into scaly fragments on the Persian rug in Egbert's studio.

'We shall have it hiding under our beds and biting pieces out of our feet before long,' said Egbert, and from what Amanda knew of this particular otter she felt that the possibility was not a remote one.

On the evening preceding the day fixed for the hunt Amanda spent a solitary hour walking by the banks of the stream, making what she imagined to be hound noises. It was charitably supposed by those who overheard her performance that she was practising for farmyard imitations at the forthcoming village entertainment.

It was her friend and neighbour, Aurora Burret, who brought her news of the day's sport.

'Pity you weren't out; we had quite a good day. We found it at once, in the pool just below your garden.'

'Did you—kill?' asked Amanda.

'Rather. A fine she-otter. Your husband got rather badly bitten in trying to 'tail it.' Poor beast, I felt quite sorry for it, it had such a human look in its eyes when it was killed. You'll call me silly, but do you know who the look reminded me of? My dear woman, what is the matter?'

When Amanda had recovered to a certain extent from her attack of nervous prostration Egbert took her to the Nile Valley to recuperate. Change of scenery speedily brought about the desired recovery of health and mental balance. The escapades of an adventurous otter in search of a variation of diet were viewed in their proper light. Amanda's normally placid temperament reasserted itself. Even a hurricane of shouted curses, coming from her husband's dressing-room, in her husband's voice, but hardly in his usual vocabulary, failed to disturb her serenity as she made a leisurely toilet one evening in a Cairo hotel.

'What is the matter? What has happened?' she asked in amused curiosity.

'The little beast has thrown all my clean shirts into the bath! Wait till I catch you, you little——'

'What little beast?' asked Amanda, suppressing a desire to laugh; Egbert's language was so hopelessly inadequate to express his outraged feelings.

'A little beast of a naked brown Nubian boy,' spluttered Egbert.

And now Amanda is seriously ill.

THE BOAR-PIG

'There is a back way on to the lawn,' said Mrs Philidore Stossen to her daughter, 'through a small grass paddock and then through a walled fruit garden full of gooseberry bushes. I went all over the place last year when the family were away. There is a door that opens from the fruit garden into a shrubbery, and once we emerge from there we can mingle with the guests as if we had come in by the ordinary way. It's much safer than going in by the front entrance and running the risk of coming bang up against the hostess; that would be so awkward when she doesn't happen to have invited us.'

'Isn't it a lot of trouble to take for getting admittance to a garden party?'

'To a garden party, yes; to *the* garden party of the season, certainly not. Every one of any consequence in the county, with the exception of ourselves, has been asked to meet the Princess, and it would be far more troublesome to invent explanations as to why we weren't there than to get in by a roundabout way. I stopped Mrs Cuvering in the road yesterday and talked very pointedly about the Princess. If she didn't choose to take the hint and send me an invitation it's not my fault, is it? Here we are: we just cut across the grass and through that little gate into the garden.'

Mrs Stossen and her daughter, suitably arrayed for a county garden party function with an infusion of Almanack de Gotha, sailed through the narrow grass paddock and the ensuing gooseberry garden with the air of state barges making an unofficial progress along a rural trout stream. There was a certain amount of furtive haste mingled with the stateliness of their advance as though hostile search-lights might be turned on them at any moment; and, as a matter of fact, they were not unobserved. Matilda Cuvering, with the alert eyes of thirteen years and the added advantage of an exalted position in the branches of a medlar tree, had enjoyed a good view of the Stossen flanking movement and had foreseen exactly where it would break down in execution.

'They'll find the door locked, and they'll jolly well have to go back the way they came,' she remarked to herself. 'Serves them right for not coming in by the proper entrance. What a pity Tarquin Superbus isn't loose in the paddock. After all, as everyone else is enjoying themselves, I don't see why Tarquin shouldn't have an afternoon out.'

Matilda was of an age when thought is action; she slid down from the branches of the medlar tree, and when she clambered back again, Tarquin, the huge white Yorkshire boar-pig, had exchanged the narrow limits of his sty for the wider range of the grass paddock. The discomfited Stossen expedition, returning in recriminatory but otherwise orderly retreat from the unyielding obstacle of the locked door, came to a sudden halt at the gate dividing the paddock from the gooseberry garden.

'What a villainous-looking animal,' exclaimed Mrs Stossen; 'it wasn't there when we came in.'

'It's there now, anyhow,' said her daughter. 'What on earth are we to do? I wish we had never come.'

The boar-pig had drawn nearer to the gate for a closer inspection of the human intruders, and stood champing his jaws and blinking his small red eyes in a manner that was doubtless intended to be disconcerting, and, as far as the Stossens were concerned, thoroughly achieved that result.

'Shoo! Hish! Hish! Shoo!' cried the ladies in chorus.

'If they think they're going to drive him away by reciting lists of the kings of Israel and Judah they're laying themselves out for disappointment,' observed Matilda from her seat in the medlar tree. As she made the observation aloud Mrs Stossen became for the first time aware of her presence. A moment or two earlier she would have been anything but pleased at the discovery that the garden was not as deserted as it looked, but now she hailed the fact of the child's presence on the scene with absolute relief.

'Little girl, can you find some one to drive away——' she began hopefully.

'*Comment? Comprends pas*,' was the response.

'Oh, are you French? *Êtes vous française?*'

'*Pas du tout. 'Suis anglaise.*'

'Then why not talk English? I want to know if——'

'*Permettez-moi expliquer.* You see, I'm rather under a cloud,' said Matilda. 'I'm staying with my aunt, and I was told I must behave particularly well today, as lots of people were coming for a garden party, and I was told to imitate Claude, that's my young cousin, who never does anything wrong except by accident, and then is always apologetic about it. It seems they thought I ate too much raspberry trifle at lunch, and they said Claude never eats too much raspberry trifle. Well, Claude always goes to sleep for half an hour after lunch, because he's told to, and I waited till he was asleep, and tied his hands and started forcible feeding with a whole bucketful of raspberry trifle that they were keeping for the garden party. Lots of it went on to his sailor-suit and some of it on to the bed, but a good deal went down Claude's throat, and they can't say again that he has never been known to eat too much raspberry trifle. That is why I am not allowed to go to the party, and as an additional punishment I must speak French all the afternoon. I've had to tell you all this in English, as there were words like "forcible feeding" that I didn't know the French for; of course I could have invented them, but if I had said *nourriture obligatoire* you wouldn't have had the least idea what I was talking about. *Mais maintenant, nous parlons français.*'

'Oh, very well, *très bien*,' said Mrs Stossen reluctantly; in moments of flurry such French as she knew was not under very good control. '*Là, à l'autre côté de la porte, est un cochon——*'

'*Un cochon? Ah, le petit charmant!*' exclaimed Matilda with enthusiasm.

'*Mais non, pas du tout petit, et pas tout charmant; un bête féroce——*'

'*Une bête*,' corrected Matilda; 'a pig is masculine as long as you call it a pig, but if you lose your temper with it and call it a ferocious beast it becomes one of us at once. French is a dreadfully unsexing language.'

'For goodness' sake let us talk English then,' said Mrs Stossen. 'Is there any way out of this garden except through the paddock where the pig is?'

'I always go over the wall, by way of the plum tree,' said Matilda.

'Dressed as we are we could hardly do that,' said Mrs Stossen; it was difficult to imagine her doing it in any costume.

'Do you think you could go and get some one who would drive the pig away?' asked Miss Stossen.

'I promised my aunt I would stay here till five o'clock; it's not four yet.'

'I am sure, under the circumstances, your aunt would permit——'

'My conscience would not permit,' said Matilda with cold dignity.

'We can't stay here till five o'clock,' exclaimed Mrs Stossen with growing exasperation.

'Shall I recite to you to make the time pass quicker?' asked Matilda obligingly. ' "Belinda, the little Breadwinner," is considered my best piece, or, perhaps, it ought to be something in French. Henri Quatre's address to his soldiers is the only thing I really know in that language.'

'If you will go and fetch some one to drive that animal

away I will give you something to buy yourself a nice present,' said Mrs Stossen.

Matilda came several inches lower down the medlar tree.

'That is the most practical suggestion you have made yet for getting out of the garden,' she remarked cheerfully; 'Claude and I are collecting money for the Children's Fresh Air Fund, and we are seeing which of us can collect the biggest sum.'

'I shall be very glad to contribute half a crown, very glad indeed,' said Mrs Stossen, digging that coin out of the depths of a receptacle which formed a detached outwork of her toilet.

'Claude is a long way ahead of me at present,' continued Matilda, taking no notice of the suggested offering; 'you see, he's only eleven, and has golden hair, and those are enormous advantages when you're on the collecting job. Only the other day a Russian lady gave him ten shillings. Russians understand the art of giving far better than we do. I expect Claude will net quite twenty-five shillings this afternoon; he'll have the field to himself, and he'll be able to do the pale, fragile, not-long-for-this-world business to perfection after his raspberry trifle experience. Yes, he'll be *quite* two pounds ahead of me by now.'

With much probing and plucking and many regretful murmurs the beleaguered ladies managed to produce seven-and-sixpence between them.

'I am afraid this is all we've got,' said Mrs Stossen.

Matilda showed no sign of coming down either to the earth or to their figure.

'I could not do violence to my conscience for anything less than ten shillings,' she announced stiffly.

Mother and daughter muttered certain remarks under their breath, in which the word 'beast' was prominent, and probably had no reference to Tarquin.

'I find I *have* got another half-crown,' said Mrs Stossen in a shaking voice; 'here you are. Now please fetch some one quickly.'

Matilda slipped down from the tree, took possession of the donation, and proceeded to pick up a handful of over-ripe medlars from the grass at her feet. Then she climbed over the gate and addressed herself affectionately to the boar-pig.

'Come, Tarquin, dear old boy; you know you can't resist medlars when they're rotten and squashy.'

Tarquin couldn't. By dint of throwing the fruit in front of him at judicious intervals Matilda decoyed him back to his sty, while the delivered captives hurried across the paddock.

'Well, I never! The little minx!' exclaimed Mrs Stossen when she was safely on the high road. 'The animal wasn't savage at all, and as for the ten shillings, I don't believe the Fresh Air Fund will see a penny of it!'

There she was unwarrantably harsh in her judgment. If you examine the books of the fund you will find the acknowledgment: 'Collected by Miss Matilda Cuvering, 2s. 6d.'

THE BROGUE

THE HUNTING season had come to an end, and the Mullets had not succeeded in selling the Brogue. There had been a kind of tradition in the family for the past three or four years, a sort of fatalistic hope, that the Brogue would find a purchaser before the hunting was over; but seasons came and went without anything happening to justify such ill-founded optimism. The animal had been named Berserker in the earlier stages of its career; it had been rechristened the Brogue later on, in recognition of the fact that, once acquired, it was extremely difficult to get rid of. The unkinder wits of the neighbourhood had been known to suggest that the first letter of its name was superfluous. The Brogue had been variously described in sale catalogues as a light-weight hunter, a lady's hack, and, more simply, but still with a touch of imagination, as a useful brown gelding, standing 15.1. Toby Mullet had ridden him for four seasons with the West Wessex; you can ride almost any sort of horse with the West Wessex as long as it is an animal that knows the country. The Brogue knew the country intimately, having personally created most of the gaps that were to be met with in banks and hedges for many miles round. His manners and characteristics were not ideal in the hunting field, but he was probably rather safer to ride to hounds than he was as a hack on country roads. According to the Mullet family, he was not really road-shy, but there were one or two objects of dislike that brought on sudden attacks of what Toby called swerving sickness. Motors and cycles he treated with tolerant disregard, but pigs, wheelbarrows, piles of stones by the roadside, perambulators in a village street, gates painted too aggressively white, and sometimes, but not always, the newer kind of beehives, turned him aside from his tracks in vivid imitation of the zigzag course of forked lightning. If a pheasant rose noisily from the other side of a hedgerow the Brogue would spring into the air at the same moment, but this may have been due to a desire to be companionable. The Mullet family contradicted the widely prevalent report that the horse was a confirmed crib-biter.

It was about the third week in May that Mrs Mullet, relict of the late Sylvester Mullet, and mother of Toby and a bunch of daughters, assailed Clovis Sangrail on the outskirts of the village with a breathless catalogue of local happenings.

'You know our new neighbour, Mr Penricarde?' she vociferated; 'awfully rich, owns tin mines in Cornwall, middle-aged and rather quiet. He's taken the Red House on a long lease and spent a lot of money on alterations and improvements. Well, Toby's sold him the Brogue!'

Clovis spent a moment or two in assimilating the astonishing news; then he broke out into unstinted congratulation. If he had belonged to a more emotional race he would probably have kissed Mrs Mullet.

'How wonderful lucky to have pulled it off at last! Now you can buy a decent animal. I've always said that Toby was clever. Ever so many congratulations.'

'Don't congratulate me. It's the most unfortunate thing that could have happened!' said Mrs Mullet dramatically.

Clovis stared at her in amazement.

'Mr Penricarde,' said Mrs Mullet, sinking her voice to what she imagined to be an impressive whisper, though it rather resembled a hoarse, excited squeak, 'Mr Penricarde has just begun to pay attentions to Jessie. Slight at first, but now unmistakable. I was a fool not to have seen it sooner. Yesterday, at the Rectory garden party, he asked her what her favourite flowers were, and she told him carnations, and today a whole stack of carnations has arrived, clove and malmaison and lovely dark red ones, regular exhibition blooms, and a box of chocolates that he must have got on purpose from London. And he's asked her to go round the links with him tomorrow. And now, just at this critical moment, Toby has sold him that animal. It's a calamity!'

'But you've been trying to get the horse off your hands for years,' said Clovis.

'I've got a houseful of daughters,' said Mrs Mullet, 'and I've been trying—well, not to get them off my hands, of course, but a husband or two wouldn't be amiss among the lot of them; there are six of them, you know.'

'I don't know,' said Clovis, 'I've never counted, but I expect you're right as to the number; mothers generally know these things.'

'And now,' continued Mrs Mullet, in her tragic whisper, 'when there's a rich husband-in-prospect imminent on the horizon Toby goes and sells him that miserable animal. It will probably kill him if he tries to ride it; anyway, it will kill any affection he might have felt towards any member of our family. What is to be done? We can't very well ask to have the horse back; you see, we praised it up like anything when we thought there was a chance of his buying it, and said it was just the animal to suit him.'

'Couldn't you steal it out of his stable and send it to grass at some farm miles away?' suggested Clovis. 'Write "Votes for Women" on the stable door, and the thing would pass for a Suffragette outrage. No one who knew the horse could possibly suspect you of wanting to get it back again.'

'Every newspaper in the country would ring with the affair,' said Mrs Mullet; 'can't you imagine the headline, "Valuable Hunter Stolen by Suffragettes"? The police would scour the countryside till they found the animal.'

'Well, Jessie must try and get it back from Penricarde on the plea that it's an old favourite. She can say it was only sold because the stable had to be pulled down under the terms of an old repairing lease, and that now it has been arranged that the stable is to stand for a couple of years longer.'

'It sounds a queer proceeding to ask for a horse back when you've just sold him,' said Mrs Mullet, 'but something must be done, and done at once. The man is not used to horses, and I believe I told him it was as quiet as a lamb. After all, lambs go kicking and twisting about as if they were demented, don't they?'

'The lamb has an entirely unmerited character for sedateness,' agreed Clovis.

Jessie came back from the golf links next day in a state of mingled elation and concern.

'It's all right about the proposal,' she announced, 'he came out with it at the sixth hole. I said I must have time to think it over. I accepted him at the seventh.'

'My dear,' said her mother, 'I think a little more maidenly reserve and hesitation would have been advisable, as you've known him so short a time. You might have waited till the ninth hole.'

'The seventh is a very long hole,' said Jessie; 'besides, the tension was putting us both off our game. By the time we'd got to the ninth hole we'd settled lots of things. The honeymoon is to be spent in Corsica, with perhaps a flying visit to Naples if we feel like it, and a week in London to wind up with. Two of his nieces are to be asked to be bridesmaids, so with our lot there will be seven, which is rather a lucky number. You are to wear your pearl grey, with any amount of Honiton lace jabbed into it. By the way, he's coming over this evening to ask your consent to the whole affair. So far all's well, but about the Brogue it's a different matter. I told him the legend about the stable, and how keen we were about buying the horse back, but he seems equally keen on keeping it. He said he must have horse exercise now that he's living in the country, and he's going to start riding tomorrow. He's ridden a few times in the Row on an animal that was accustomed to carry octogenarians and people undergoing rest cures, and that's about all his experience in the saddle—oh, and he rode a pony once in Norfolk, when he was fifteen and the pony twenty-four; and tomorrow he's going to ride the Brogue! I shall be a widow before I'm married, and I do so want to see what Corsica's like; it looks so silly on the map.'

Clovis was sent for in haste, and the developments of the situation put before him.

'Nobody can ride that animal with any safety,' said Mrs Mullet, 'except Toby, and he knows by long experience what it is going to shy at, and manages to swerve at the same time.'

'I did hint to Mr Penricarde—to Vincent, I should say—that the Brogue didn't like white gates,' said Jessie.

'White gates!' exclaimed Mrs Mullet; 'did you mention what effect a pig has on him? He'll have to pass Lockyer's farm to get to the high road, and there's sure to be a pig or two grunting about in the lane.'

'He's taken rather a dislike to turkeys lately,' said Toby.

'It's obvious that Penricarde mustn't be allowed to go out on that animal,' said Clovis, 'at least not till Jessie has married him, and tired of him. I tell you what: ask him to a picnic tomorrow, starting at an early hour; he's not the sort to go out for a ride before breakfast. The day after

I'll get the rector to drive him over to Crowleigh before lunch, to see the new cottage hospital they're building there. The Brogue will be standing idle in the stable and Toby can offer to exercise it; then it can pick up a stone or something of the sort and go conveniently lame. If you hurry on the wedding a bit the lameness fiction can be kept up till the ceremony is safely over.'

Mrs Mullet belonged to an emotional race, and she kissed Clovis.

It was nobody's fault that the rain came down in torrents the next morning, making a picnic a fantastic impossibility. It was also nobody's fault, but sheer ill-luck, that the weather cleared up sufficiently in the afternoon to tempt Mr Penricarde to make his first essay with the Brogue. They did not get as far as the pigs at Lockyer's farm; the rectory gate was painted a dull unobtrusive green, but it had been white a year or two ago, and the Brogue never forgot that he had been in the habit of making a violent curtsey, a back-pedal and a swerve at this particular point of the road. Subsequently, there being apparently no further call on his services, he broke his way into the rectory orchard, where he found a hen turkey in a coop; later visitors to the orchard found the coop almost intact, but very little left of the turkey.

Mr Penricarde, a little stunned and shaken, and suffering from a bruised knee and some minor damages, good-naturedly ascribed the accident to his own inexperience with horses and country roads, and allowed Jessie to nurse him back into complete recovery and golf-fitness within something less than a week.

In the list of wedding presents which the local newspaper published a fortnight or so later appeared the following item:

'Brown saddle-horse, "The Brogue," bridegroom's gift to the bride.'

'Which shows,' said Toby Mullet, 'that he knew nothing.'

'Or else,' said Clovis, 'that he has a very pleasing wit.'

THE OPEN WINDOW

'MY AUNT will be down presently, Mr Nuttel,' said a very self-possessed young lady of fifteen; 'in the meantime you must try and put up with me.'

Framton Nuttel endeavoured to say the correct something which should duly flatter the niece of the moment without unduly discounting the aunt that was to come. Privately he doubted more than ever whether these formal visits on a succession of total strangers would do much towards helping the nerve cure which he was supposed to be undergoing.

'I know how it will be,' his sister had said when he was preparing to migrate to this rural retreat; 'you will bury yourself down there and not speak to a living soul, and your nerves will be worse than ever from moping. I shall just give you letters of introduction to all the people I know there. Some of them, as far as I can remember, were quite nice.'

Framton wondered whether Mrs Sappleton, the lady to whom he was presenting one of the letters of introduction, came into the nice division.

'Do you know many of the people round here?' asked the niece, when she judged that they had had sufficient silent communion.

'Hardly a soul,' said Framton. 'My sister was staying here, at the rectory, you know, some four years ago, and she gave me letters of introduction to some of the people here.'

He made the last statement in a tone of distinct regret.

'Then you know practically nothing about my aunt?' pursued the self-possessed young lady.

'Only her name and address,' admitted the caller. He was wondering whether Mrs Sappleton was in the married or widowed state. An undefinable something about the room seemed to suggest masculine habitation.

'Her great tragedy happened just three years ago,' said the child; 'that would be since your sister's time.'

'Her tragedy?' asked Framton; somehow in this restful country spot tragedies seemed out of place.

'You may wonder why we keep that window wide open on an October afternoon,' said the niece, indicating a large French window that opened on to a lawn.

'It is quite warm for the time of the year,' said Framton; 'but has that window got anything to do with the tragedy?'

'Out through that window, three years ago to a day, her husband and her two young brothers went off for their day's shooting. They never came back. In crossing the moor to their favourite snipe-shooting ground they were all three engulfed in a treacherous piece of bog. It had been that dreadful wet summer, you know, and places that were safe in other years gave way suddenly without warning. Their bodies were never recovered. That was the dreadful part of it.' Here the child's voice lost its self-possessed note and became falteringly human. 'Poor aunt always thinks that they will come back some day, they and the little brown spaniel that was lost with them, and walk in at that window just as they used to do. That is why the window is kept open every evening till it is quite dusk. Poor dear aunt, she has often told me how they went out, her husband with his white waterproof coat over his arm, and Ronnie, her youngest brother, singing, "Bertie, why do you bound?" as he always did to tease her, because she said it got on her nerves. Do you know, sometimes on still, quiet evenings like this, I almost get a creepy feeling that they will all walk in through that window——'

She broke off with a little shudder. It was a relief to Framton when the aunt bustled into the room with a whirl of apologies for being late in making her appearance.

'I hope Vera has been amusing you?' she said.

'She has been very interesting,' said Framton.

'I hope you don't mind the open window,' said Mrs Sappleton briskly; 'my husband and brothers will be home directly from shooting, and they always come in this way. They've been out for snipe in the marshes today, so they'll make a fine mess over my poor carpets. So like you men-folk, isn't it?'

She rattled on cheerfully about the shooting and the scarcity of birds, and the prospects for duck in the winter. To Framton it was all purely horrible. He made a desperate but only partially successful effort to turn the talk on to a less ghastly topic; he was conscious that his hostess was giving him only a fragment of her attention, and her eyes were constantly straying past him to the open window and the lawn beyond. It was certainly an unfortunate coincidence that he should have paid his visit on this tragic anniversary.

'The doctors agree in ordering me complete rest, an absence of mental excitement, and avoidance of anything in the nature of violent physical exercise,' announced Framton, who laboured under the tolerably widespread delusion that total strangers and chance acquaintances are hungry for the least detail of one's ailments and infirmities, their cause and cure. 'On the matter of diet they are not so much in agreement,' he continued.

'No?' said Mrs Sappleton, in a voice which only replaced a yawn at the last moment. Then she suddenly brightened into alert attention—but not to what Framton was saying.

'Here they are at last!' she cried. 'Just in time for tea, and don't they look as if they were muddy up to the eyes!'

Framton shivered slightly and turned towards the niece with a look intended to convey sympathetic comprehension. The child was staring out through the open window with dazed horror in her eyes. In a chill shock of nameless fear Framton swung round in his seat and looked in the same direction.

In the deepening twilight three figures were walking across the lawn towards the window; they all carried guns under their arms, and one of them was additionally burdened with a white coat hung over his shoulders. A tired brown spaniel kept close at their heels. Noiselessly they neared the house, and then a hoarse young voice chanted out of the dusk: 'I said, Bertie, why do you bound?'

Framton grabbed wildly at his stick and hat; the hall-door, the gravel-drive, and the front gate were dimly noted stages in his headlong retreat. A cyclist coming along the road had to run into the hedge to avoid imminent collision.

'Here we are, my dear,' said the bearer of the white mackintosh, coming in through the window; 'fairly muddy, but most of it's dry. Who was that who bolted out as we came up?'

'A most extraordinary man, a Mr Nuttel,' said Mrs Sappleton; 'could only talk about his illnesses, and dashed off without a word of good-bye or apology when you arrived. One would think he had seen a ghost.'

'I expect it was the spaniel,' said the niece calmly; 'he told me he had a horror of dogs. He was once hunted into a cemetery somewhere on the banks of the Ganges by a pack of pariah dogs, and had to spend the night in a newly dug grave with the creatures snarling and grinning and foaming just above him. Enough to make any one lose their nerve.'

Romance at short notice was her speciality.

THE TREASURE-SHIP

THE GREAT galleon lay in semi-retirement under the sand, weed and water of the northern bay where the fortune of war and weather had long ago ensconced it. Three and a quarter centuries had passed since the day when it had taken the high seas as an important unit of a fighting squadron—precisely which squadron the learned were not agreed. The galleon had brought nothing into the world, but it had, according to tradition and report, taken much out of it. But how much? There again the learned were in disagreement. Some were as generous in their estimate as an income-tax assessor, others applied a species of higher criticism to the submerged treasure chests, and debased their contents to the currency of goblin gold. Of the former school was Lulu, Duchess of Dulverton.

The Duchess was not only a believer in the existence of a sunken treasure of alluring proportions; she also believed that she knew of a method by which the said treasure might be precisely located and cheaply disembedded. An aunt on her mother's side of the family had been Maid of Honour at the Court of Monaco, and had taken a respectful interest in the deep-sea researches in which the Throne of that country, impatient perhaps of its terrestrial restrictions, was wont to immerse itself. It was through the instrumentality of this relative that the Duchess learned of an invention, perfected and very nearly patented by a Monegaskan savant, by means of which the home-life of the Mediterranean sardine might be studied at a depth of many fathoms in a cold white light of more than ballroom brilliancy. Implicated in this invention (and, in the Duchess's eyes, the most attractive part of it) was an electric suction dredge, specially designed for dragging to the surface such objects of interest and value as might be found in the more accessible levels of the ocean-bed. The rights of the invention were to be acquired for a matter of eighteen hundred francs, and the apparatus for a few thousand more. The Duchess of Dulverton was rich, as the world counted wealth; she nursed the hope of being one day rich at her own computation. Companies had been formed and efforts had been made again and again during the course of three centuries to probe for the alleged treasures of the interesting galleon; with the aid of this invention she considered that she might go to work on the wreck privately and independently. After all, one of her ancestors on her mother's side was descended from Medina Sidonia, so she was of opinion that she had as much right to the treasure as any one. She acquired the invention and bought the apparatus.

Among other family ties and encumbrances, Lulu possessed a nephew, Vasco Honiton, a young gentleman who was blessed with a small income and a large circle of relatives, and lived impartially and precariously on both. The name Vasco had been given him possibly in the hope that he might live up to its adventurous tradition, but he limited himself strictly to the home industry of adventurer, preferring to exploit the assured rather than to explore the unknown. Lulu's intercourse with him had been restricted of recent years to the negative processes of being out of town when he called on her, and short of money when he wrote to her. Now, however, she bethought herself of his eminent suitability for the direction of a treasure-seeking experiment; if any one could extract gold from an unpromising situation it would certainly be Vasco—of course, under the necessary safeguards in the way of supervision. Where money was in question Vasco's conscience was liable to fits of obstinate silence.

Somewhere on the west coast of Ireland the Dulverton property included a few acres of shingle, rock, and heather, too barren to support even an agrarian outrage, but embracing a small and fairly deep bay where the lobster yield was good in most seasons. There was a bleak little house on the property, and for those who liked lobsters and solitude, and were able to accept an Irish cook's ideas as to what might be perpetrated in the name of mayonnaise, Innisgluther was a tolerable exile during the summer months. Lulu seldom went there herself, but she lent the house lavishly to friends and relations. She put it now at Vasco's disposal.

'It will be the very place to practise and experiment with the salvage apparatus,' she said; 'the bay is quite deep in places, and you will be able to test everything thoroughly before starting on the treasure hunt.'

In less than three weeks Vasco turned up in town to report progress.

'The apparatus works beautifully,' he informed his aunt; 'the deeper one got the clearer everything grew. We found something in the way of a sunken wreck to operate on, too!'

'A wreck in Innisgluther Bay!' exclaimed Lulu.

'A submerged motor-boat, the *Sub-Rosa*,' said Vasco.

'No! really?' said Lulu; 'poor Billy Yuttley's boat. I remember it went down somewhere off that coast some three years ago. His body was washed ashore at the Point. People said at the time that the boat was capsized intentionally—a case of suicide, you know. People always say that sort of thing when anything tragic happens.'

'In this case they were right,' said Vasco.

'What do you mean?' asked the Duchess hurriedly. 'What makes you think so?'

'I know,' said Vasco simply.

'Know? How can you know? How can any one know? The thing happened three years ago.'

'In a locker of the *Sub-Rosa* I found a water-tight strong-box. It contained papers.' Vasco paused with dramatic effect and searched for a moment in the inner breast-pocket of his coat. He drew out a folded slip of paper. The Duchess snatched at it in almost indecent haste and moved appreciably nearer the fireplace.

'Was this in the *Sub-Rosa's* strong-box?' she asked.

'Oh, no,' said Vasco carelessly, 'that is a list of the well-known people who would be involved in a very disagreeable scandal if the *Sub-Rosa's* papers were made public. I've put you at the head of it, otherwise it follows alphabetical order.'

The Duchess gazed helplessly at the string of names, which seemed for the moment to include nearly every one she knew. As a matter of fact, her own name at the head of the list exercised an almost paralysing effect on her thinking faculties.

'Of course you have destroyed the papers?' she asked, when she had somewhat recovered herself. She was conscious that she made the remark with an entire lack of conviction.

Vasco shook his head.

'But you should have,' said Lulu angrily; 'if, as you say, they are highly compromising——'

'Oh, they are, I assure you of that,' interposed the young man.

'Then you should put them out of harm's way at once. Supposing anything should leak out, think of all these poor unfortunate people who would be involved in the disclosures,' and Lulu tapped the list with an agitated gesture.

'Unfortunate, perhaps, but not poor,' corrected Vasco; 'if you read the list carefully you'll notice that I haven't troubled to include any one whose financial standing isn't above question.'

Lulu glared at her nephew for some moments in silence. Then she asked hoarsely: 'What are you going to do?'

'Nothing—for the remainder of my life,' he answered meaningly. 'A little hunting, perhaps,' he continued, 'and I shall have a villa at Florence. The Villa Sub-Rosa would sound rather quaint and picturesque, don't you think, and quite a lot of people would be able to attach a meaning to the name. And I suppose I must have a hobby; I shall probably collect Raeburns.'

Lulu's relative, who lived at the Court of Monaco, got quite a snappish answer when she wrote recommending some further invention in the realm of marine research.

THE COBWEB

THE FARMHOUSE kitchen probably stood where it did as a matter of accident or haphazard choice; yet its situation might have been planned by a master-strategist in farmhouse architecture. Dairy and poultry-yard, and herb garden, and all the busy places of the farm seemed to lead by easy access into its wide flagged haven, where there was room for everything and where muddy boots left traces that were easily swept away. And yet, for all that it stood so well in the centre of human bustle, its long, latticed window, with the wide window seat, built into an embrasure beyond the huge fireplace, looked out on a wild spreading view of hill and heather and wooded combe. The window nook made almost a little room in itself, quite the pleasantest room in the farm as far as situation and capabilities went. Young Mrs Ladbruk, whose husband had just come into the farm by way of inheritance, cast covetous eyes on this snug corner, and her fingers itched to make it bright and cosy with chintz curtains and bowls of flowers, and a shelf or two of old china. The musty farm parlour, looking out to a prim, cheerless garden imprisoned within high, blank walls, was not a room that lent itself readily either to comfort or decoration.

'When we are more settled I shall work wonders in the way of making the kitchen habitable,' said the young woman to her occasional visitors. There was an unspoken wish in those words, a wish which was unconfessed as well as unspoken. Emma Ladbruk was the mistress of the farm; jointly with her husband she might have her say, and to a certain extent her way, in ordering its affairs. But she was not mistress of the kitchen.

On one of the shelves of an old dresser, in company with chipped sauce-boats, pewter jugs, cheese-graters, and paid bills, rested a worn and ragged Bible, on whose front page was the record, in faded ink, of a baptism dated ninety-four years ago. 'Martha Crale' was the name written on that yellow page. The yellow, wrinkled old dame who hobbled and muttered about the kitchen, looking like a dead autumn leaf which the winter winds still pushed hither and thither, had once been Martha Crale; for seventy odd years she had been Martha Mountjoy. For longer than any one could remember she had pattered to and fro between oven and wash-house and dairy, and out to chicken-run and garden, grumbling and muttering and scolding, but working unceasingly. Emma Ladbruk, of whose coming she took as little notice as she would of a bee wandering in

at a window on a summer's day, used at first to watch her
with a kind of frightened curiosity. She was so old and
so much a part of the place, it was difficult to think of
her exactly as a living thing. Old Shep, the white-nozzled,
stiff-limbed collie, waiting for his time to die, seemed
almost more human than the withered, dried-up old
woman. He had been a riotous, roystering puppy, mad with
the joy of life, when she was already a tottering, hobbling
dame; now he was just a blind, breathing carcase, nothing
more, and she still worked with frail energy, still swept
and baked and washed, fetched and carried. If there were
something in these wise old dogs that did not perish
utterly with death, Emma used to think to herself, what
generations of ghost-dogs there must be out on those
hills, that Martha had reared and fed and tended and
spoken a last good-bye word to in that old kitchen. And
what memories she must have of human generations that
had passed away in her time. It was difficult for any one,
let alone a stranger like Emma, to get her to talk of the
days that had been; her shrill, quavering speech was of
doors that had been left unfastened, pails that had got
mislaid, calves whose feeding-time was overdue, and the
various little faults and lapses that chequer a farmhouse
routine. Now and again, when election time came round,
she would unstore her recollections of the old names
round which the fight had waged in the days gone by.
There had been a Palmerston, that had been a name
down Tiverton way; Tiverton was not a far journey as the
crow flies, but to Martha it was almost a foreign country.
Later there had been Northcotes and Aclands, and many
other newer names that she had forgotten; the names
changed, but it was always Libruls and Toories, Yellows
and Blues. And they always quarrelled and shouted as to
who was right and who was wrong. The one they quarrelled
about most was a fine old gentleman with an angry face
—she had seen his picture on the walls. She had seen
it on the floor too, with a rotten apple squashed over it,
for the farm had changed its politics from time to time.

Martha had never been on one side or the other; none of 'they' had ever done the farm a stroke of good. Such was her sweeping verdict, given with all a peasant's distrust of the outside world.

When the half-frightened curiosity had somewhat faded away, Emma Ladbruk was uncomfortably conscious of another feeling towards the old woman. She was a quaint old tradition, lingering about the place, she was part and parcel of the farm itself, she was something at once pathetic and picturesque—but she was dreadfully in the way. Emma had come to the farm full of plans for little reforms and improvements, in part the result of training in the newest ways and methods, in part the outcome of her own ideas and fancies. Reforms in the kitchen region, if those deaf old ears could have been induced to give them even a hearing, would have met with short shrift and scornful rejection, and the kitchen region spread over the zone of dairy and market business and half the work of the household. Emma, with the latest science of dead-poultry dressing at her fingertips, sat by, an unheeded watcher, while old Martha trussed the chickens for the market-stall as she had trussed them for nearly four-score years—all leg and no breast. And the hundred hints anent effective cleaning and labour-lightening and the things that make for wholesomeness which the young woman was ready to impart or to put into action dropped away into nothingness before that wan, muttering, unheeding presence. Above all, the coveted window corner, that was to be a dainty, cheerful oasis in the gaunt old kitchen, stood now choked and lumbered with a litter of odds and ends that Emma, for all her nominal authority, would not have dared or cared to displace; over them seemed to be spun the protection of something that was like a human cobweb. Decidedly Martha was in the way. It would have been an unworthy meanness to have wished to see the span of that brave old life shortened by a few paltry months, but as the days sped by Emma was conscious that the wish was there, disowned though it might be, lurking at the back of her mind.

She felt the meanness of the wish come over her with a qualm of self-reproach one day when she came into the kitchen and found an unaccustomed state of things in that usually busy quarter. Old Martha was not working. A basket of corn was on the floor by her side, and out in the yard the poultry were beginning to clamour a protest of overdue feeding-time. But Martha sat huddled in a shrunken bunch on the window seat, looking out with her dim old eyes as though she saw something stranger than the autumn landscape.

'Is anything the matter, Martha,' asked the young woman.

' 'Tis death, 'tis death a-coming,' answered the quavering voice; 'I knew 'twere coming. I knew it. 'Tweren't for nothing that old Shep's been howling all morning. An' last night I heard the screech-owl give the death-cry, and there were something white as run across the yard yesterday; 'tweren't a cat nor a stoat, 'twere something. The fowls knew 'twere something; they all drew off to one side. Ay, there's been warnings. I knew it were a-coming.'

The young woman's eyes clouded with pity. The old thing sitting there so white and shrunken had once been a merry, noisy child, playing about in lanes and hay-lofts and farmhouse garrets; that had been eighty odd years ago, and now she was just a frail old body cowering under the approaching chill of the death that was coming at last to take her. It was not probable that much could be done for her, but Emma hastened away to get assistance and counsel. Her husband, she knew, was down at a tree-felling some little distance off, but she might find some other intelligent soul who knew the old woman better than she did. The farm, she soon found out, had that faculty common to farmyards of swallowing up and losing its human population. The poultry followed her in inter-ested fashion, and swine grunted interrogations at her from behind the bars of their sties, but barnyard and rickyard, orchard and stables and dairy, gave no reward to her search. Then, as she retraced her steps towards the kitchen, she came suddenly on her cousin, young Mr. Jim, as every one called him, who divided his time between amateur horse-dealing, rabbit-shooting, and flirting with the farm maids.

'I'm afraid old Martha is dying,' said Emma. Jim was not the sort of person to whom one had to break news gently.

'Nonsense,' he said; 'Martha means to live to a hundred. She told me so, and she'll do it.'

'She may be actually dying at this moment, or it may just be the beginning of the break-up,' persisted Emma, with a feeling of contempt for the slowness and dullness of the young man.

A grin spread over his good-natured features.

'It don't look like it,' he said, nodding towards the yard. Emma turned to catch the meaning of his remark. Old Martha stood in the middle of a mob of poultry scattering handfuls of grain around her. The turkey-cock, with the bronzed sheen of his feathers and the purple-red of his wattles, the gamecock with the glowing metallic lustre of his Eastern plumage, the hens, with their ochres and buffs and umbers and their scarlet combs, and the drakes, with their bottle-green heads, made a medley of rich colour, in the centre of which the old woman looked like a withered stalk standing amid the riotous growth of gaily-hued flowers. But she threw the grain deftly amid the wilderness of beaks, and her quavering voice carried as far as the two people who were watching her. She was still harping on the theme of death coming to the farm.

'I knew 'twere a-coming. There's been signs an' warnings.'

'Who's dead, then, old Mother?' called out the young man.

' 'Tis young Mister Ladbruk,' she shrilled back; 'they've just a-carried his body in. Run out of the way of a tree that

was coming down an' ran hisself on to an iron post. Dead
when they picked un up. Ay, I knew 'twere coming.'

And she turned to fling a handful of barley at a belated
group of guinea-fowl that came racing towards her.

The farm was a family property, and passed to the
rabbit-shooting cousin as the next-of-kin. Emma Ladbruk
drifted out of its history as a bee that had wandered in
at an open window might flit its way out again. On a cold
grey morning she stood waiting with her boxes already
stowed in the farm cart, till the last of the market produce
should be ready, for the train she was to catch was of less
importance than the chickens and butter and eggs that
were to be offered for sale. From where she stood she
could see an angle of the long latticed window that was
to have been cosy with curtains and gay with bowls of
flowers. Into her mind came the thought that for months,
perhaps for years, long after she had been utterly forgotten, a white, unheeding face would be seen peering out
through those latticed panes, and a weak muttering voice
would be heard quavering up and down those flagged
passages. She made her way to a narrow barred casement
that opened into the farm larder. Old Martha was standing
at a table trussing a pair of chickens for the market stall
as she had trussed them for nearly fourscore years.

THE LULL

'I've asked Latimer Springfield to spend Sunday with
us and stop the night,' announced Mrs Durmot at the
breakfast-table.

'I thought he was in the throes of an election,' remarked
her husband.

'Exactly; the poll is on Wednesday, and the poor man
will have worked himself to a shadow by that time.

Imagine what electioneering must be like in this awful soaking rain, going along slushy country roads and speaking to damp audiences in draughty schoolrooms, day after day for a fortnight. He'll have to put in an appearance at some place of worship on Sunday morning, and he can come to us immediately afterwards and have a thorough respite from everything connected with politics. I won't let him even think of them. I've had the picture of Cromwell dissolving the Long Parliament taken down from the staircase, and even the portrait of Lord Rosebery's "Ladas" removed from the smoking-room. And, Vera,' added Mrs Durmot, turning to her sixteen-year-old niece, 'be careful what colour ribbon you wear in your hair; not blue or yellow on any account; those are the rival party colours, and emerald green or orange would be almost as bad, with this Home Rule business to the fore.'

'On state occasions I always wear a black ribbon in my hair,' said Vera with crushing dignity.

Latimer Springfield was a rather cheerless, oldish young man, who went into politics somewhat in the spirit in which other people might go into half mourning. Without being an enthusiast, however, he was a fairly strenuous plodder, and Mrs Durmot had been reasonably near the mark in asserting that he was working at high pressure over this election. The restful lull which his hostess enforced on him was decidedly welcome, and yet the nervous excitement of the contest had too great a hold on him to be totally banished.

'I know he's going to sit up half the night working up points for his final speeches,' said Mrs Durmot regretfully; 'however, we've kept politics at arm's length all the afternoon and evening. More than that we cannot do.'

'That remains to be seen,' said Vera, but she said it to herself.

Latimer had scarcely shut his bedroom door before he was immersed in a sheaf of notes and pamphlets, while a fountain-pen and pocket-book were brought into play for the due marshalling of useful facts and discreet fictions.

He had been at work for perhaps thirty-five minutes, and the house was seemingly consecrated to the healthy slumber of country life, when a stifled squealing and scuffling in the passage was followed by a loud-tap at his door. Before he had time to answer, a much-encumbered Vera burst into the room with the question: 'I say, can I leave these here?'

'These' were a small black pig and a lusty specimen of black-red gamecock.

Latimer was moderately fond of animals, and particularly interested in small livestock rearing from the economic point of view; in fact, one of the pamphlets on which he was at that moment engaged warmly advocated the further development of the pig and poultry industry in our rural districts; but he was pardonably unwilling to share even a commodious bedroom with samples of henroost and sty products.

'Wouldn't they be happier somewhere outside?' he asked, tactfully expressing his own preference in the matter in an apparent solicitude for theirs.

'There is no outside,' said Vera impressively, 'nothing but a waste of dark, swirling waters. The reservoir at Brinkley has burst.'

'I didn't know there was a reservoir at Brinkley,' said Latimer.

'Well, there isn't now, it's jolly well all over the place, and as we stand particularly low we're the centre of an inland sea just at present. You see, the river has overflowed its banks as well.'

'Good gracious! Have any lives been lost?'

'Heaps, I should say. The second housemaid has already identified three bodies that have floated past the billiard-room window as being the young man she's engaged to. Either she's engaged to a large assortment of the population round here or else she's very careless at identification. Of course it may be the same body coming round again and again in a swirl; I hadn't thought of that.'

'But we ought to go out and do rescue work, oughtn't we?' said Latimer, with the instinct of a Parliamentary candidate for getting into the local limelight.

'We can't,' said Vera decidedly, 'we haven't any boats and we're cut off by a raging torrent from any human habitation. My aunt particularly hoped you would keep to your room and not add to the confusion, but she thought it would be so kind of you if you would take in Hartlepool's Wonder, the gamecock, you know, for the night. You see, there are eight other gamecocks, and they fight like furies if they get together, so we're putting one in each bedroom. The fowl-houses are all flooded out, you know. And then I thought perhaps you wouldn't mind taking in this wee piggie; he's rather a little love, but he has a vile temper. He gets that from his mother—not that I like to say things against her when she's lying dead and drowned in her sty, poor thing. What he really wants is a man's firm hand to keep him in order. I'd try and grapple with him myself, only I've got my chow in my room, you know, and he goes for pigs wherever he finds them.'

'Couldn't the pig go in the bathroom?' asked Latimer faintly, wishing he had taken up as determined a stand on the subject of bedroom swine as the chow had.

'The bathroom?' Vera laughed shrilly. 'It'll be full of Boy Scouts till morning if the hot water holds out.'

'Boy Scouts?'

'Yes, thirty of them came to rescue us while the water was only waist-high; then it rose another three feet or so and we had to rescue them. We're giving them hot baths in batches and drying their clothes in the hot-air cupboard, but, of course, drenched clothes don't dry in a minute, and the corridor and staircase are beginning to look like a bit of coast scenery by Tuke. Two of the boys are wearing your Melton overcoat; I hope you don't mind.'

'It's a new overcoat,' said Latimer, with every indication of minding dreadfully.

'You'll take every care of Hartlepool's Wonder, won't you?' said Vera. 'His mother took three firsts at Birmingham, and he was second in the cockerel class last year at Gloucester. He'll probably roost on the rail at the bottom of your bed. I wonder if he'd feel more at home if some of his wives were up here with him? The hens are all in the pantry, and I think I could pick out Hartlepool Helen; she's his favourite.'

Latimer showed a belated firmness on the subject of Hartlepool Helen, and Vera withdrew without pressing the point, having first settled the gamecock on his extemporized perch and taken an affectionate farewell of the pigling. Latimer undressed and got into bed with all due speed, judging that the pig would abate its inquisitorial restlessness once the light was turned out. As a substitute for a cosy, straw-bedded sty the room offered, at first inspection, few attractions, but the disconsolate animal suddenly discovered an appliance in which the most luxuriously contrived piggeries were notably deficient. The sharp edge of the underneath part of the bed was pitched at exactly the right elevation to permit the pigling to scrape himself ecstatically backwards and forwards, with an artistic humping of the back at the crucial moment and an accompanying gurgle of long-drawn delight. The gamecock, who may have fancied that he was being rocked in the branches of a pine-tree, bore the motion with greater fortitude than Latimer was able to command. A series of slaps directed at the pig's body were accepted more as an additional and pleasing irritant than as a criticism of conduct or a hint to desist; evidently something more than a man's firm hand was needed to deal with the case. Latimer slipped out of bed in search of a weapon of dissuasion. There was sufficient light in the room to enable the pig to detect this manœuvre, and the vile temper, inherited from the drowned mother, found full play. Latimer bounded back into bed, and his conqueror, after a few threatening snorts and champings of its jaws, resumed its massage operations with renewed zeal. During the long wakeful hours which ensued Latimer tried to distract his mind from his own immediate troubles by dwelling with decent sympathy on the second housemaid's bereavement, but he found himself more often wondering how many Boy Scouts were sharing his Melton overcoat. The rôle of Saint Martin *malgré lui* was not one which appealed to him.

Towards dawn the pigling fell into a happy slumber, and Latimer might have followed its example, but at about the same time Stupor Hartlepooli gave a rousing crow, clattered down to the floor and forthwith commenced a spirited combat with his reflection in the wardrobe mirror. Remembering that the bird was more or less under his care Latimer performed Hague Tribunal offices by draping a bath-towel over the provocative mirror, but the ensuing peace was local and short-lived. The deflected energies of the gamecock found new outlet in a sudden and sustained attack on the sleeping and temporarily inoffensive pigling, and the duel which followed was desperate and embittered beyond any possibility of effective intervention. The feathered combatant had the advantage of being able, when hard pressed, to take refuge on the bed, and freely availed himself of this circumstance; the pigling never quite succeeded in hurling himself on to the same eminence, but it was not from want of trying.

Neither side could claim any decisive success, and the struggle had been practically fought to a standstill by the time that the maid appeared with the early morning tea.

'Lor, sir,' she exclaimed in undisguised astonishment, 'do you want those animals in your room?'

Want!

The pigling, as though aware that it might have outstayed its welcome, dashed out at the door, and the gamecock followed it at a more dignified pace.

'If Miss Vera's dog sees that pig——!' exclaimed the maid, and hurried off to avert such a catastrophe.

A cold suspicion was stealing over Latimer's mind; he went to the window and drew up the blind. A light, drizzling rain was falling, but there was not the faintest trace of any inundation.

Some half-hour later he met Vera on the way to the breakfast-room.

'I should not like to think of you as a deliberate liar,' he observed coldly, 'but one occasionally has to do things one does not like.'

'At any rate I kept your mind from dwelling on politics all the night,' said Vera.

Which was, of course, perfectly true.

THE UNKINDEST BLOW

THE SEASON of strikes seemed to have run itself to a standstill. Almost every trade and industry and calling in which a dislocation could possibly be engineered had indulged in that luxury. The last and least successful convulsion had been the strike of the World's Union of Zoological Garden attendants, who, pending the settlement of certain demands, refused to minister further to the wants of the animals committed to their charge or to allow any other keepers to take their place. In this case the threat of the Zoological Gardens authorities that if the men 'came out' the animals should come out also had intensified and precipitated the crisis. This imminent prospect of the larger carnivores, to say nothing of rhinoceroses and bull bison, roaming at large and unfed in the heart of London, was not one which permitted of prolonged conferences. The Government of the day, which from its tendency to be a few hours behind the course of events had been nicknamed the Government of the afternoon, was obliged to intervene with promptitude and decision. A strong force of Blue-jackets was despatched to Regent's Park to take over the temporarily abandoned duties of the strikers. Blue-jackets were chosen in preference to land forces, partly on account of the traditional readiness of the British Navy to go anywhere and do anything, partly by reason of the familiarity of the average sailor with monkeys, parrots, and other tropical fauna, but chiefly at the urgent request of the First Lord of the Admiralty, who was keenly desirous of an opportunity for performing some personal act of unobtrusive public service within the province of his department.

'If he insists on feeding the infant jaguar himself, in defiance of its mother's wishes, there may be another by-election in the north,' said one of his colleagues, with a hopeful inflection in his voice. 'By-elections are not very desirable at present, but we must not be selfish.'

As a matter of fact the strike collapsed peacefully without any outside intervention. The majority of the keepers had become so attached to their charges that they returned to work of their own accord.

And then the nation and the newspapers turned with a sense of relief to happier things. It seemed as if a new era of contentment was about to dawn. Everybody had struck who could possibly want a strike or who could possibly be cajoled or bullied into striking, whether they wanted to or not. The lighter and brighter side of life might now claim some attention. And conspicuous among the other topics that sprang into sudden prominence was the pending Falvertoon divorce suit.

The Duke of Falvertoon was one of those human *hors d'œuvres* that stimulate the public appetite for sensation without giving it much to feed on. As a mere child he had been precociously brilliant; he had declined the editorship of the *Anglian Review* at an age when most boys are content to have declined *mensa*, a table, and though he could not claim to have originated the Futurist movement in literature, his 'Letters to a Possible Grandson,' written at the age of fourteen, had attracted considerable notice. In later days his brilliancy had been less conspicuously displayed. During a debate in the House of Lords on affairs in Morocco, at a moment when that country, for the fifth

time in seven years, had brought half Europe to the verge
of war, he had interpolated the remark 'a little Moor and
how much it is,' but in spite of the encouraging reception
accorded to this one political utterance he was never
tempted to a further display in that direction. It began
to be generally understood that he did not intend to supplement his numerous town and country residences by
living overmuch in the public eye.

And then had come the unlooked-for tidings of the imminent proceedings for divorce. And such a divorce! There
were cross-suits and allegations and counter-allegations,
charges of cruelty and desertion, everything in fact that was
necessary to make the case one of the most complicated
and sensational of its kind. And the number of distinguished people involved or cited as witnesses not only
embraced both political parties in the realm and several
Colonial governors, but included an exotic contingent from
France, Hungary, the United States of North America,
and the Grand Duchy of Baden. Hotel accommodation of
the more expensive sort began to experience a strain on its
resources. 'It will be quite like the Durbar without the
elephants,' exclaimed an enthusiastic lady who, to do her
justice, had never seen a Durbar. The general feeling was
one of thankfulness that the last of the strikes had been
got over before the date fixed for the hearing of the great
suit.

As a reaction from the season of gloom and industrial
strife that had just passed away the agencies that purvey
and stage-manage sensations laid themselves out to do
their level best on this momentous occasion. Men who had
made their reputations as special descriptive writers were
mobilized from distant corners of Europe and the further
side of the Atlantic in order to enrich with their pens the
daily printed records of the case; one word-painter, who
specialized in descriptions of how witnesses turn pale
under cross-examination, was summoned hurriedly back
from a famous and prolonged murder trial in Sicily, where

indeed his talents were being decidedly wasted. Thumb-nail artists and expert kodak manipulators were retained at extravagant salaries, and special dress reporters were in high demand. An enterprising Paris firm of costume build-ers presented the defendant Duchess with three special creations, to be worn, marked, learned, and extensively reported at various critical stages of the trial; and as for the cinematograph agents, their industry and persistence was untiring. Films representing the Duke saying good-bye to his favourite canary on the eve of the trial were in readiness weeks before the event was due to take place; other films depicted the Duchess holding imaginary con-sultations with fictitious lawyers or making a light repast off specially advertised vegetarian sandwiches during a supposed luncheon interval. As far as human foresight and human enterprise could go nothing was lacking to make the trial a success.

Two days before the case was down for hearing the advance reporter of an important syndicate obtained an interview with the Duke for the purpose of gleaning some final grains of information concerning his Grace's personal arrangements during the trial.

'I suppose I may say this will be one of the biggest affairs of its kind during the lifetime of a generation,' began the reporter as an excuse for the unsparing minuteness of detail that he was about to make quest for.

'I suppose so—if it comes off,' said the Duke lazily.

'If?' queried the reporter, in a voice that was something between a gasp and a scream.

'The Duchess and I are both thinking of going on strike,' said the Duke.

'Strike!'

The baleful word flashed out in all its old hideous familiarity. Was there to be no end to its recurrence?

'Do you mean,' faltered the reporter, 'that you are con-templating a mutual withdrawal of the charges?'

'Precisely,' said the Duke.

'But think of the arrangements that have been made, the special reporting, the cinematographs, the catering for the distinguished foreign witnesses, the prepared music-hall allusions; think of all the money that has been sunk——'

'Exactly,' said the Duke coldly. 'The Duchess and I have realized that it is we who provide the material out of which this great far-reaching industry has been built up. Widespread employment will be given and enormous profits made during the duration of the case, and we, on whom all the stress and racket falls, will get—what? An unenviable notoriety and the privilege of paying heavy legal expenses whichever way the verdict goes. Hence our decision to strike. We don't wish to be reconciled; we fully realize that it is a grave step to take, but unless we get some reasonable consideration out of this vast stream of wealth and industry that we have called into being we intend coming out of court and staying out. Good afternoon.'

The news of this latest strike spread universal dismay. Its inaccessibility to the ordinary methods of persuasion made it peculiarly formidable. If the Duke and Duchess persisted in being reconciled the Government could hardly be called on to interfere. Public opinion in the shape of social ostracism might be brought to bear on them, but that was as far as coercive measures could go. There was nothing for it but a conference, with powers to propose liberal terms. As it was, several of the foreign witnesses had already departed and others had telegraphed cancelling their hotel arrangements.

The conference, protracted, uncomfortable, and occasionally acrimonious, succeeded at last in arranging for a resumption of litigation, but it was a fruitless victory. The Duke, with a touch of his earlier precocity, died of premature decay, a fortnight before the date fixed for the new trial.

THE ROMANCERS

IT WAS autumn in London, that blessed season between the harshness of winter and the insincerities of summer; a trustful season when one buys bulbs and sees to the registration of one's vote, believing perpetually in spring and a change of Government.

Morton Crosby sat on a bench in a secluded corner of Hyde Park, lazily enjoying a cigarette and watching the slow grazing promenade of a pair of snow-geese, the male looking rather like an albino edition of the russet-hued female. Out of the corner of his eye Crosby also noted with some interest the hesitating hoverings of a human figure, which had passed and repassed his seat two or three times at shortening intervals, like a wary crow about to alight near some possibly edible morsel. Inevitably the figure came to an anchorage on the bench, within easy talking distance of its original occupant. The uncared-for clothes, the aggressive, grizzled beard, and the furtive, evasive eye of the new-comer bespoke the professional cadger, the man who would undergo hours of humiliating tale-spinning and rebuff rather than adventure on half a day's decent work.

For a while the new-comer fixed his eyes straight in front of him in a strenuous, unseeing gaze; then his voice broke out with the insinuating inflection of one who has a story to retail well worth any loiterer's while to listen to.

'It's a strange world,' he said.

As the statement met with no response he altered it to the form of a question.

'I dare say you've found it to be a strange world, mister?'

'As far as I am concerned,' said Crosby, 'the strangeness has worn off in the course of thirty-six years.'

'Ah,' said the greybeard, 'I could tell you things that you'd hardly believe. Marvellous things that have really happened to me.'

'Nowadays there is no demand for marvellous things that have really happened,' said Crosby discouragingly; 'the professional writers of fiction turn these things out so much better. For instance, my neighbours tell me wonderful, incredible things that their Aberdeens and chows and borzois have done; I never listen to them. On the other hand, I have read *The Hound of the Baskervilles* three times.'

The greybeard moved uneasily in his seat; then he opened up new country.

'I take it that you are a professing Christian,' he observed.

'I am a prominent and I think I may say an influential member of the Mussulman community of Eastern Persia,' said Crosby, making an excursion himself into the realms of fiction.

The greybeard was obviously disconcerted at this new check of introductory conversation, but the defeat was only momentary.

'Persia. I should never have taken you for a Persian,' he remarked, with a somewhat aggrieved air.

'I am not,' said Crosby; 'my father was an Afghan.'

'An Afghan!' said the other, smitten into bewildered silence for a moment. Then he recovered himself and renewed his attack.

'Afghanistan. Ah! We've had some wars with that country; now, I dare say, instead of fighting it we might have learned something from it. A very wealthy country, I believe. No real poverty there.'

He raised his voice on the word 'poverty' with a suggestion of intense feeling. Crosby saw the opening and avoided it.

'It possesses, nevertheless, a number of highly talented and ingenious beggars,' he said; 'if I had not spoken so disparagingly of marvellous things that have really happened I would tell you the story of Ibrahim and the eleven camel-loads of blotting-paper. Also I have forgotten exactly how it ended.'

'My own life-story is a curious one,' said the stranger, apparently stifling all desire to hear the history of Ibrahim; 'I was not always as you see me now.'

'We are supposed to undergo complete change in the course of every seven years,' said Crosby, as an explanation of the foregoing announcement.

'I mean I was not always in such distressing circumstances as I am at present,' pursued the stranger doggedly.

'That sounds rather rude,' said Crosby stiffly, 'considering that you are at present talking to a man reputed to be one of the most gifted conversationalists of the Afghan border.'

'I don't mean in that way,' said the greybeard hastily; 'I've been very much interested in your conversation. I was alluding to my unfortunate financial position. You mayn't hardly believe it, but at the present moment I am absolutely without a farthing. Don't see any prospect of getting any money, either, for the next few days. I don't suppose you've ever found yourself in such a position,' he added.

'In the town of Yom,' said Crosby, 'which is in Southern Afghanistan, and which also happens to be my birthplace, there was a Chinese philosopher who used to say that one of the three chief human blessings was to be absolutely without money. I forget what the other two were.'

'Ah, I dare say,' said the stranger, in a tone that betrayed no enthusiasm for the philosopher's memory; 'and did he practise what he preached? That's the test.'

'He lived happily with very little money or resources,' said Crosby.

'Then I expect he had friends who would help him liberally whenever he was in difficulties, such as I am in at present.'

'In Yom,' said Crosby, 'it is not necessary to have friends in order to obtain help. Any citizen of Yom would help a stranger as a matter of course.'

The greybeard was now genuinely interested. The conversation had at last taken a favourable turn.

'If some one, like me, for instance, who was in un-deserved difficulties, asked a citizen of that town you speak of for a small loan to tide over a few days' impe-cuniosity—five shillings, or perhaps a rather larger sum—would it be given to him as a matter of course?'

'There would be a certain preliminary,' said Crosby; 'one would take him to a wine-shop and treat him to a measure of wine, and then after a little high-flown conversation, one would put the desired sum in his hand and wish him good-day. It is a roundabout way of performing a simple transaction, but in the East all ways are roundabout.'

The listener's eyes were glittering.

'Ah,' he exclaimed, with a thin sneer ringing meaningly through his words, 'I suppose you've given up all those generous customs since you left your town. Don't practise them now, I expect.'

'No one who has lived in Yom,' said Crosby fervently, 'and remembers its green hills covered with apricot and almond trees, and the cold water that rushes down like a caress from the upland snows and dashes under the little wooden bridges, no one who remembers these things and treasures the memory of them would ever give up a single one of its unwritten laws and customs. To me they are as binding as though I still lived in that hallowed home of my youth.'

'Then if I was to ask you for a small loan——' began the greybeard fawningly, edging nearer on the seat and hurriedly wondering how large he might safely make his request, 'if I was to ask you for, say——'

'At any other time, certainly,' said Crosby; 'in the months of November and December, however, it is abso-lutely forbidden for any one of our race to give or receive loans or gifts; in fact, one does not willingly speak of them. It is considered unlucky. We will therefore close this discussion.'

'But it is still October!' exclaimed the adventurer with an eager, angry whine, as Crosby rose from his seat; 'wants eight days to the end of the month!'

'The Afghan November began yesterday,' said Crosby severely, and in another moment he was striding across the Park, leaving his recent companion scowling and muttering furiously on the seat.

'I don't believe a word of his story,' he chattered to himself; 'pack of nasty lies from beginning to end. Wish I'd told him so to his face. Calling himself an Afghan.'

The snorts and snarls that escaped from him for the next quarter of an hour went far to support the truth of the old saying that two of a trade never agree.

THE SCHARTZ-METTERKLUME
METHOD

LADY CARLOTTA stepped out on to the platform of the small wayside station and took a turn or two up and down its uninteresting length, to kill time till the train should be pleased to proceed on its way. Then, in the roadway beyond, she saw a horse struggling with a more than ample load, and a carter of the sort that seems to bear a sullen hatred against the animal that helps him to earn a living. Lady Carlotta promptly betook her to the roadway, and put rather a different complexion on the struggle. Certain of her acquaintances were wont to give her plentiful admonition as to the undesirability of interfering on behalf of a distressed animal, such interference being 'none of her business.' Only once had she put the doctrine of non-interference into practice, when one of its most eloquent exponents had been besieged for nearly three hours in a small and extremely uncomfortable may-tree by an angry boar-pig, while Lady Carlotta, on the other side of the fence, had proceeded with the water-colour sketch she was engaged on, and refused to interfere between the boar and his prisoner. It is to be feared that she lost the friendship of the ultimately rescued lady. On this occasion she merely lost the train, which gave way to the first sign of impatience it had shown throughout the journey, and steamed off without her. She bore the desertion with philosophical indifference; her friends and relations were thoroughly well used to the fact of her luggage arriving without her. She wired a vague non-committal message to her destination to say that she was coming on 'by another train.' Before she had time to think what her next move might be, she was confronted by an imposingly attired lady, who seemed to be taking a prolonged mental inventory of her clothes and looks.

'You must be Miss Hope, the governess I've come to meet,' said the apparition, in a tone that admitted of very little argument.

'Very well, if I must I must,' said Lady Carlotta to herself with dangerous meekness.

'I am Mrs Quabarl,' continued the lady; 'and where, pray, is your luggage?'

'It's gone astray,' said the alleged governess, falling in with the excellent rule of life that the absent are always to blame; the luggage had, in point of fact, behaved with perfect correctitude. 'I've just telegraphed about it,' she added, with a nearer approach to truth.

'How provoking,' said Mrs Quabarl; 'these railway companies are so careless. However, my maid can lend you things for the night,' and she led the way to her car.

During the drive to the Quabarl mansion Lady Carlotta was impressively introduced to the nature of the charge that had been thrust upon her; she learned that Claude and Wilfrid were delicate, sensitive young people, that Irene had the artistic temperament highly developed, and that Viola was something or other else of a mould equally commonplace among children of that class and type in the twentieth century.

'I wish them not only to be *taught*,' said Mrs Quabarl, 'but *interested* in what they learn. In their history lessons, for instance, you must try to make them feel that they are being introduced to the life-stories of men and women who really lived, not merely committing a mass of names and dates to memory. French, of course, I shall expect you to talk at mealtimes several days in the week.'

'I shall talk French four days of the week and Russian in the remaining three.'

'Russian? My dear Miss Hope, no one in the house speaks or understands Russian.'

'That will not embarrass me in the least,' said Lady Carlotta coldly.

Mrs Quabarl, to use a colloquial expression, was knocked off her perch. She was one of those imperfectly self-assured individuals who are magnificent and autocratic as long as they are not seriously opposed. The least show of un-expected resistance goes a long way towards rendering them cowed and apologetic. When the new governess failed to express wondering admiration of the large newly pur-chased and expensive car, and lightly alluded to the superior advantages of one or two makes which had just been put on the market, the discomfiture of her patroness became almost abject. Her feelings were those which might have animated a general of ancient warfaring days, on be-holding his heaviest battle-elephant ignominiously driven off the field by slingers and javelin throwers.

At dinner that evening, although reinforced by her husband, who usually duplicated her opinions and lent her moral support generally, Mrs Quabarl regained none of her lost ground. The governess not only helped herself well and truly to wine, but held forth with considerable show of critical knowledge on various vintage matters, concern-ing which the Quabarls were in no wise able to pose as authorities. Previous governesses had limited their con-versation on the wine topic to a respectful and doubtless sincere expression of a preference for water. When this one went as far as to recommend a wine firm in whose hands you could not go very far wrong Mrs Quabarl thought it time to turn the conversation into more usual channels.

'We got very satisfactory references about you from Canon Teep,' she observed; 'a very estimable man, I should think.'

'Drinks like a fish and beats his wife, otherwise a very lovable character,' said the governess imperturbably.

'My *dear* Miss Hope! I trust you are exaggerating,' exclaimed the Quabarls in unison.

'One must in justice admit that there is some provocation,' continued the romancer. 'Mrs Teep is quite the most irritating bridge-player that I have ever sat down with; her leads and declarations would condone a certain amount of brutality in her partner, but to souse her with the contents of the only soda-water syphon in the house on a Sunday afternoon, when one couldn't get another, argues an indifference to the comfort of others which I cannot altogether overlook. You may think me hasty in my judgments, but it was practically on account of the syphon incident that I left.'

'We will talk of this some other time,' said Mrs Quabarl hastily.

'I shall never allude to it again,' said the governess with decision.

Mr Quabarl made a welcome diversion by asking what studies the new instructress proposed to inaugurate on the morrow.

'History to begin with,' she informed him.

'Ah, history,' he observed sagely; 'now in teaching them history you must take care to interest them in what they learn. You must make them feel that they are being introduced to the life-stories of men and women who really lived——'

'I've told her all that,' interposed Mrs Quabarl.

'I teach history on the Schartz-Metterklume method,' said the governess loftily.

'Ah, yes,' said her listeners, thinking it expedient to assume an acquaintance at least with the name.

'What are you children doing out here?' demanded

Mrs Quabarl the next morning, on finding Irene sitting rather glumly at the head of the stairs, while her sister was perched in an attitude of depressed discomfort on the window-seat behind her, with a wolf-skin rug almost covering her.

'We are having a history lesson,' came the unexpected reply. 'I am supposed to be Rome, and Viola up there is the she-wolf; not a real wolf, but the figure of one that the Romans used to set store by—I forget why. Claude and Wilfrid have gone to fetch the shabby women.'

'The shabby women?'

'Yes, they've got to carry them off. They didn't want to, but Miss Hope got one of father's fives-bats and said she'd give them a number nine spanking if they didn't, so they've gone to do it.'

A loud, angry screaming from the direction of the lawn drew Mrs Quabarl thither in hot haste, fearful lest the threatened castigation might even now be in process of infliction. The outcry, however, came principally from the two small daughters of the lodge-keeper, who were being hauled and pushed towards the house by the panting and dishevelled Claude and Wilfrid, whose task was rendered even more arduous by the incessant, if not very effectual, attacks of the captured maidens' small brother. The governess, fives-bat in hand, sat negligently on the stone balustrade, presiding over the scene with the cold impartiality of a Goddess of Battles. A furious and repeated chorus of 'I'll tell muvver' rose from the lodge children, but the lodge-mother, who was hard of hearing, was for the moment immersed in the preoccupation of her washtub. After an apprehensive glance in the direction of the lodge (the good woman was gifted with the highly militant temper which is sometimes the privilege of deafness) Mrs Quabarl flew indignantly to the rescue of the struggling captives.

'Wilfrid! Claude! Let those children go at once. Miss Hope, what on earth is the meaning of this scene?'

'Early Roman history; the Sabine women, don't you know? It's the Schartz-Metterklume method to make children understand history by acting it themselves; fixes it in their memory, you know. Of course, if, thanks to your interference, your boys go through life thinking that the Sabine women ultimately escaped, I really cannot be held responsible.'

'You may be very clever and modern, Miss Hope,' said Mrs Quabarl firmly, 'but I should like you to leave here by the next train. Your luggage will be sent after you as soon as it arrives.'

'I'm not certain exactly where I shall be for the next few days,' said the dismissed instructress of youth; 'you might keep my luggage till I wire my address. There are only a couple of trunks and some golf-clubs and a leopard cub.'

'A leopard cub!' gasped Mrs Quabarl. Even in her departure this extraordinary person seemed destined to leave a trail of embarrassment behind her.

'Well, it's rather left off being a cub; it's more than half-grown, you know. A fowl every day and a rabbit on Sundays is what it usually gets. Raw beef makes it too excitable. Don't trouble about getting the car for me, I'm rather inclined for a walk.'

And Lady Carlotta strode out of the Quabarl horizon.

The advent of the genuine Miss Hope, who had made a mistake as to the day on which she was due to arrive, caused a turmoil which that good lady was quite unused to inspiring. Obviously the Quabarl family had been woefully befooled, but a certain amount of relief came with the knowledge.

'How tiresome for you, dear Carlotta,' said her hostess, when the overdue guest ultimately arrived; 'how very tiresome losing your train and having to stop overnight in a strange place.'

'Oh, dear, no,' said Lady Carlotta; 'not at all tiresome—for me.'

THE SEVENTH PULLET

'IT's NOT the daily grind that I complain of,' said Blenkinthrope resentfully; 'it's the dull grey sameness of my life outside of office hours. Nothing of interest comes my way, nothing remarkable or out of the common. Even the little things that I do try to find some interest in don't seem to interest other people. Things in my garden, for instance.'

'The potato that weighed just over two pounds,' said his friend Gorworth.

'Did I tell you about that?' said Blenkinthrope; 'I was telling the others in the train this morning. I forgot if I'd told you.'

'To be exact you told me that it weighed just under two pounds, but I took into account the fact that abnormal vegetables and freshwater fish have an after-life, in which growth is not arrested.'

'You're just like the others,' said Blenkinthrope sadly, 'you only make fun of it.'

'The fault is with the potato, not with us,' said Gorworth; 'we are not in the least interested in it because it is not in the least interesting. The men you go up in the train with every day are just in the same case as yourself; their lives are commonplace and not very interesting to themselves, and they certainly are not going to wax enthusiastic over the commonplace events in other men's lives. Tell them something startling, dramatic, piquant, that has happened to yourself or to some one in your family, and you will capture their interest at once. They will talk about you with a certain personal pride to all their acquaintances. "Man I know intimately, fellow called Blenkinthrope, lives down my way, had two of his fingers clawed clean off by a lobster he was carrying home to supper. Doctor says entire hand may have to come off." Now that is conversation of a very high order. But imagine walking into a tennis club with the remark: 'I know a man who has grown a potato weighing two and a quarter pounds." '

'But hang it all, my dear fellow,' said Blenkinthrope impatiently, 'haven't I just told you that nothing of a remarkable nature ever happens to me?'

'Invent something,' said Gorworth. Since winning a prize for excellence in Scriptural knowledge at a preparatory school he had felt licensed to be a little more unscrupulous than the circle he moved in. Much might surely be excused to one who in early life could give a list of seventeen trees mentioned in the Old Testament.

'What sort of thing?' asked Blenkinthrope, somewhat snappishly.

'A snake got into your hen-run yesterday morning and killed six out of seven pullets, first mesmerizing them with its eyes and then biting them as they stood helpless. The seventh pullet was one of that French sort, with feathers all over its eyes, so it escaped the mesmeric snare, and just flew at what it could see of the snake and pecked it to pieces.'

'Thank you,' said Blenkinthrope stiffly; 'it's a very clever invention. If such a thing had really happened in my poultry-run I admit I should have been proud and interested to tell people about it. But I'd rather stick to fact, even if it is plain fact.' All the same his mind dwelt wistfully on the story of the Seventh Pullet. He could picture himself telling it in the train amid the absorbed interest of his fellow-passengers. Unconsciously all sorts of little details and improvements began to suggest themselves.

Wistfulness was still his dominant mood when he took his seat in the railway carriage the next morning. Opposite him sat Stevenham, who had attained to a recognized brevet of importance through the fact of an uncle having dropped dead in the act of voting at a Parliamentary election. That had happened three years ago, but Stevenham was still deferred to on all questions of home and foreign politics.

'Hullo, how's the giant mushroom, or whatever it was?'

was all the notice Blenkinthrope got from his fellow-travellers.

Young Duckby, whom he mildly disliked, speedily monopolized the general attention by an account of a domestic bereavement.

'Had four pigeons carried off last night by a whacking big rat. Oh, a monster he must have been; you could tell by the size of the hole he made breaking into the loft.'

No moderate-sized rat ever seemed to carry out any predatory operations in these regions; they were all enormous in their enormity.

'Pretty hard lines that,' continued Duckby, seeing that he had secured the attention and respect of the company; 'four squeakers carried off at one swoop. You'd find it rather hard to match that in the way of unlooked-for bad luck.'

'I had six pullets out of a pen of seven killed by a snake yesterday afternoon,' said Blenkinthrope, in a voice which he hardly recognized as his own.

'By a snake?' came in excited chorus.

'It fascinated them with its deadly, glittering eyes, one after the other, and struck them down while they stood helpless. A bedridden neighbour, who wasn't able to call for assistance, witnessed it all from her bedroom window.'

'Well, I never!' broke in the chorus, with variations.

'The interesting part of it is about the seventh pullet, the one that didn't get killed,' resumed Blenkinthrope, slowly lighting a cigarette. His diffidence had left him, and he was beginning to realize how safe and easy depravity can seem once one has the courage to begin. 'The six dead birds were Minorcas; the seventh was a Houdan with a mop of feathers all over its eyes. It could hardly see the snake at all, so of course, it wasn't mesmerized like the others. It just could see something wriggling on the ground, and went for it and pecked it to death.'

'Well, I'm blessed!' exclaimed the chorus.

In the course of the next few days Blenkinthrope discovered how little the loss of one's self-respect affects one when one has gained the esteem of the world. His story found its way into one of the poultry papers, and was copied thence into a daily news-sheet as a matter of general interest. A lady wrote from the North of Scotland recounting a similar episode which she had witnessed as occurring between a stoat and a blind grouse. Somehow a lie seems so much less reprehensible when one can call it a lee.

For a while the adapter of the Seventh Pullet story enjoyed to the full his altered standing as a person of consequence, one who had had some share in the strange events of his times. Then he was thrust once again into the cold grey background by the sudden blossoming into importance of Smith-Paddon, a daily fellow traveller, whose little girl had been knocked down and nearly hurt by a car belonging to a musical-comedy actress. The actress was not in the car at the time, but she was in numerous photographs which appeared in the illustrated papers of Zoto Dobreen inquiring after the well-being of Maisie, daughter of Edmund Smith-Paddon, Esq. With this new human interest to absorb them the travelling companions were almost rude when Blenkinthrope tried to explain his contrivance for keeping vipers and peregrine falcons out of his chicken-run.

Gorworth, to whom he unburdened himself in private, gave him the same counsel as theretofore.

'Invent something.'

'Yes, but what?'

The ready affirmative coupled with the question betrayed a significant shifting of the ethical standpoint.

It was a few days later that Blenkinthrope revealed a chapter of family history to the customary gathering in the railway carriage.

'Curious thing happened to my aunt, the one who lives in Paris,' he began. He had several aunts, but they were all geographically distributed over Greater London.

'She was sitting on a seat in the Bois the other afternoon, after lunching at the Roumanian Legation.'

Whatever the story gained in picturesqueness for the dragging-in of diplomatic 'atmosphere,' it ceased from that moment to command any acceptance as a record of current events. Gorworth had warned his neophyte that this would be the case, but the traditional enthusiasm of the neophyte had triumphed over discretion.

'She was feeling rather drowsy, the effect probably of the champagne, which she's not in the habit of taking in the middle of the day.'

A subdued murmur of admiration went round the company. Blenkinthrope's aunts were not used to taking champagne in the middle of the year, regarding it exclusively as a Christmas and New Year accessory.

'Presently a rather portly gentleman passed by her seat and paused an instant to light a cigar. At that moment a youngish man came up behind him, drew the blade from a swordstick, and stabbed him half a dozen times through and through. "Scoundrel," he cried to his victim, "you do not know me. My name is Henri Leturc.' The elder man wiped away some of the blood that was spattering his clothes, turned to his assailant, and said: "And since when has an attempted assassination been considered an introduction?" Then he finished lighting his cigar and walked away. My aunt had intended screaming for the police, but seeing the indifference with which the principal in the affair treated the matter she felt that it would be an impertinence on her part to interfere. Of course I need hardly say she put the whole thing down to the effects of a warm, drowsy afternoon and the Legation champagne. Now comes the astonishing part of my story. A fortnight later a bank manager was stabbed to death with a swordstick in that very part of the Bois. His assassin was the son of a charwoman formerly working at the bank, who had been dismissed from her job by the manager on account of chronic intemperance. His name was Henri Leturc.'

From that moment Blenkinthrope was tacitly accepted as the Munchausen of the party. No effort was spared to draw him out from day to day in the exercise of testing their powers of credulity, and Blenkinthrope, in the false security of an assured and receptive audience, waxed industrious and ingenious in supplying the demand for marvels. Duckby's satirical story of a tame otter that had a tank in the garden to swim in, and whined restlessly whenever the water-rate was overdue, was scarcely an unfair parody of some of Blenkinthrope's wilder efforts. And then one day came Nemesis.

Returning to his villa one evening Blenkinthrope found his wife sitting in front of a pack of cards, which she was scrutinizing with unusual concentration.

'The same old patience-game?' he asked carelessly.

'No, dear; this is the Death's Head patience, the most difficult of them all. I've never got it to work out, and somehow I should be rather frightened if I did. Mother only got it out once in her life; she was afraid of it, too. Her great-aunt had done it once and fallen dead from excitement the next moment, and mother always had a feeling that she would die if she ever got it out. She died the same night that she did it. She was in bad health at the time, certainly, but it was a strange coincidence.'

'Don't do it if it frightens you,' was Blenkinthrope's practical comment as he left the room. A few minutes later his wife called to him.

'John, it gave me such a turn, I nearly got it out. Only the five of diamonds held me up at the end. I really thought I'd done it.'

'Why, you can do it,' said Blenkinthrope, who had come back to the room; 'if you shift the eight of clubs on to that open nine the five can be moved on to the six.'

His wife made the suggested move with hasty, trembling fingers, and piled the outstanding cards on to their respective packs. Then she followed the example of her mother and great-grand-aunt.

Blenkinthrope had been genuinely fond of his wife, but in the midst of his bereavement one dominant thought obtruded itself. Something sensational and real had at last come into his life; no longer was it a grey, colourless record. The headlines which might appropriately describe his domestic tragedy kept shaping themselves in his brain. 'Inherited presentiment comes true.' 'The Death's Head patience: Card-game that justified its sinister name in three generations.' He wrote out a full story of the fatal occurrence for the *Essex Vedette*, the editor of which was a friend of his, and to another friend he gave a condensed account, to be taken up to the office of one of the half-penny dailies. But in both cases his reputation as a romancer stood fatally in the way of the fulfilment of his ambitions. 'Not the right thing to be Munchausening in a time of sorrow,' agreed his friends among themselves, and a brief note of regret at the 'sudden death of the wife of our respected neighbour, Mr John Blenkinthrope, from heart failure,' appearing in the news column of the local paper was the forlorn outcome of his visions of widespread publicity.

Blenkinthrope shrank from the society of his erstwhile travelling companions and took to travelling townwards by an earlier train. He sometimes tries to enlist the sympathy and attention of a chance acquaintance in details of the whistling prowess of his best canary or the dimensions of his largest beetroot; he scarcely recognizes himself as the man who was once spoken about and pointed out as the owner of the Seventh Pullet.

COUSIN TERESA

BASSET HARROWCLUFF returned to the home of his fathers, after an absence of four years, distinctly well pleased with himself. He was only thirty-one, but he had put in some useful service in an out-of-the-way, though not unimportant, corner of the world. He had quieted a province, kept open a trade route, enforced the tradition of respect which is worth the ransom of many kings in out-of-the-way regions, and done the whole business on rather less expenditure than would be requisite for organizing a charity in the home country. In Whitehall and places where they think, they doubtless thought well of him. It was not inconceivable, his father allowed himself to imagine, that Basset's name might figure in the next list of Honours.

Basset was inclined to be rather contemptuous of his half-brother, Lucas, whom he found feverishly engrossed in the same medley of elaborate futilities that had claimed his whole time and energies, such as they were, four years ago, and almost as far back before that as he could remember. It was the contempt of the man of action for the man of activities, and it was probably reciprocated. Lucas was an over-well nourished individual, some nine years Basset's senior, with a colouring that would have been accepted as a sign of intensive culture in an asparagus, but probably meant in this case mere abstention from exercise. His hair and forehead furnished a recessional note in a personality that was in all other respects obtrusive and assertive. There was certainly no Semitic blood in Lucas's parentage, but his appearance contrived to convey at least a suggestion of Jewish extraction. Clovis Sangrail, who knew most of his associates by sight, said it was undoubtedly a case of protective mimicry.

Two days after Basset's return, Lucas frisked in to lunch in a state of twittering excitement that could not be restrained even for the immediate consideration of soup, but had to be verbally discharged in spluttering competition with mouthfuls of vermicelli.

'I've got hold of an idea for something immense,' he babbled, 'something that is simply It.'

Basset gave a short laugh that would have done equally well as a snort, if one had wanted to make the exchange. His half-brother was in the habit of discovering futilities that were 'simply It' at frequently recurring intervals. The discovery generally meant that he flew up to town, preceded by glowingly worded telegrams, to see some one connected with the stage or the publishing world, got together one or two momentous luncheon parties, flitted in and out of 'Gambrinus' for one or two evenings, and returned home with an air of subdued importance and the asparagus tint slightly intensified. The great idea was generally forgotten a few weeks later in the excitement of some new discovery.

'The inspiration came to me whilst I was dressing,' announced Lucas; 'it will be *the* thing in the next music-hall *revue*. All London will go mad over it. It's just a couplet; of course there will be other words, but they won't matter. Listen:

> Cousin Teresa takes out Caesar,
> Fido, Jock, and the big borzoi.

A lilting, catchy sort of refrain, you see, and big-drum business on the two syllables of bor-zoi. It's immense. And I've thought out all the business of it; the singer will sing the first verse alone, then during the second verse Cousin Teresa will walk through, followed by four wooden dogs on wheels; Caesar will be an Irish terrier, Fido a black poodle, Jock a fox-terrier, and the borzoi, of course, will be a borzoi. During the third verse Cousin Teresa will come on alone, and the dogs will be drawn across by themselves from the opposite wing; then Cousin Teresa will catch on to the singer and go off-stage in one direction, while dogs' procession goes off in the other, crossing *en route*, which is always very effective. There'll be a lot of applause there, and for the fourth verse Cousin Teresa will come on in sables and the dogs will all have coats on. Then I've got a great idea for the fifth verse; each of the dogs will be led on by a Nut, and Cousin Teresa will come on from the opposite side, crossing *en route*, always effective, and then she turns round and leads the whole lot

of them off on a string, and all the time every one singing
like mad:

> Cousin Teresa takes out Caesar,
> Fido, Jock, and the big borzoi.

Tum-Tum! Drum business on the two last syllables. I'm
so excited, I shan't sleep a wink tonight. I'm off tomorrow
by the ten-fifteen. I've wired to Hermanova to lunch with
me.'

If any of the rest of the family felt any excitement over
the creation of Cousin Teresa, they were signally successful in concealing the fact.

'Poor Lucas does take his silly little ideas seriously,'
said Colonel Harrowcluff afterwards in the smoking-room.

'Yes,' said his younger son, in a slightly less tolerant
tone, 'in a day or two he'll come back and tell us that his
sensational masterpiece is above the heads of the public,
and in about three weeks' time he'll be wild with enthusiasm over a scheme to dramatize the poems of Herrick
or something equally promising.'

And then an extraordinary thing befell. In defiance of
all precedent Lucas's glowing anticipations were justified
and endorsed by the course of events. If Cousin Teresa
was above the heads of the public, the public heroically
adapted itself to her altitude. Introduced as an experiment
at a dull moment in a new *revue*, the success of the item
was unmistakable; the calls were so insistent and uproarious
that even Lucas's ample devisings of additional 'business'
scarcely sufficed to keep pace with the demand. Packed
houses on successive evenings confirmed the verdict of the
first night audience, stalls and boxes filled significantly
just before the turn came on, and emptied significantly after
the last *encore* had been given. The manager tearfully
acknowledged that Cousin Teresa was It. Stage hands and
supers and programme sellers acknowledged it to one
another, without the least reservation. The name of the
revue dwindled to secondary importance, and vast letters
of electric blue blazoned the words 'Cousin Teresa' from

the front of the great palace of pleasure. And, of course, the magic of the famous refrain laid its spell all over the Metropolis. Restaurant proprietors were obliged to provide the members of their orchestras with painted wooden dogs on wheels, in order that the much-demanded and always conceded melody should be rendered with the necessary spectacular effects, and the crash of bottles and forks on the tables at the mention of the big borzoi usually drowned the sincerest efforts of drum or cymbals. Nowhere and at no time could one get away from the double thump that brought up the rear of the refrain; revellers reeling home at night banged it on doors and hoardings, milkmen clashed their cans to its cadence, messenger boys hit smaller messenger boys resounding double smacks on the same principle. And the more thoughtful circles of the great city were not deaf to the claims and significance of the popular melody. An enterprising and emancipated preacher discoursed from his pulpit on the inner meaning of 'Cousin Teresa,' and Lucas Harrowcluff was invited to lecture on the subject of his great achievement to members of the Young Men's Endeavour League, the Nine Arts Club, and other learned and willing-to-learn bodies. In Society it seemed to be the one thing people really cared to talk about; men and women of middle age and average education might be seen together in corners earnestly discussing, not the question whether Servia should have an outlet on the Adriatic, or the possibilities of a British success in international polo contests, but the more absorbing topic of the problematic Aztec or Nilotic origin of the Teresa *motif*.

'Politics and patriotism are so boring and so out of date,' said a revered lady who had some pretensions to oracular utterance 'we are too cosmopolitan nowadays to be really moved by them. That is why one welcomes an intelligible production like "Cousin Teresa," that has a genuine message for one. One can't understand the message all at once, of course, but one felt from the very first that it was there. I've been to see it eighteen times and I'm going again tomorrow and on Thursday. One can't see it often enough.'

'It would be rather a popular move if we gave this Harrowcluff person a knighthood or something of the sort,' said the Minister reflectively.

'Which Harrowcluff?' asked his secretary.

'Which? There is only one, isn't there?' said the Minister; 'the "Cousin Teresa" man, of course, I think every one would be pleased if we knighted him. Yes, you can put him down on the list of certainties—under the letter L.'

'The letter L,' said the secretary, who was new to his job: 'does that stand for Liberalism or liberality?'

Most of the recipients of Ministerial favour were expected to qualify in both of those subjects.

'Literature,' explained the Minister.

And thus, after a fashion, Colonel Harrowcluff's expectation of seeing his son's name in the list of Honours was gratified.

THE BYZANTINE OMELETTE

SOPHIE CHATTEL-MONKHEIM was a Socialist by conviction and a Chattel-Monkheim by marriage. The particular member of that wealthy family whom she had married was rich, even as his relatives counted riches. Sophie had very advanced and decided views as to the distribution of money: it was a pleasing and fortunate circumstance that she also had the money. When she inveighed eloquently against the evils of capitalism at drawing-room meetings and Fabian conferences she was conscious of a comfortable feeling that the system, with all its inequalities and iniquities, would probably last her time.

It is one of the consolations of middle-aged reformers that the good they inculcate must live after them if it is to live at all.

On a certain spring evening, somewhere towards the dinner-hour, Sophie sat tranquilly between her mirror and her maid, undergoing the process of having her hair built into an elaborate reflection of the prevailing fashion. She was hedged round with a great peace, the peace of one who has attained a desired end with much effort and perseverance, and who has found it still eminently desirable in its attainment. The Duke of Syria had consented to come beneath her roof as a guest, was even now installed beneath her roof, and would shortly be sitting at her dining-table. As a good Socialist, Sophie disapproved of social distinctions, and derided the idea of a princely caste, but if there were to be these artificial gradations of rank and dignity she was pleased and anxious to have an exalted specimen of an exalted order included in her house-party. She was broad-minded enough to love the sinner while hating the sin—not that she entertained any warm feeling of personal affection for the Duke of Syria, who was a comparative stranger, but still, as Duke of Syria, he was very, very welcome beneath her roof. She could not have explained why, but no one was likely to ask her for an explanation, and most hostesses envied her.

'You must surpass yourself tonight, Richardson,' she said complacently to her maid; 'I must be looking my very best. We must all surpass ourselves.'

The maid said nothing, but from the concentrated look in her eyes and the deft play of her fingers it was evident that she was beset with the ambition to surpass herself.

A knock came at the door, a quiet but peremptory knock, as of some one who would not be denied.

'Go and see who it is,' said Sophie; 'it may be something about the wine.'

Richardson held a hurried conference with an invisible messenger at the door; when she returned there was noticeable a curious listlessness in place of her hitherto alert manner.

'What is it?' asked Sophie.

'The household servants have "downed tools," madame,' said Richardson.

'Downed tools!' exclaimed Sophie; 'do you mean to say they've gone on strike?'

'Yes, madame,' said Richardson, adding the information: 'It's Gaspare that the trouble is about.'

'Gaspare?' said Sophie wonderingly; 'the emergency chef! The omelette specialist!'

'Yes, madame. Before he became an omelette specialist he was a valet, and he was one of the strike-breakers in the great strike at Lord Grimford's two years ago. As soon as the household staff here learned that you had engaged him they resolved to "down tools" as a protest. They haven't got any grievance against you personally, but they demand that Gaspare should be immediately dismissed.'

'But,' protested Sophie, 'he is the only man in England who understands how to make a Byzantine omelette. I engaged him specially for the Duke of Syria's visit, and it would be impossible to replace him at short notice. I should have to send to Paris, and the Duke loves Byzantine omelettes. It was the one thing we talked about coming from the station.'

'He was one of the strike-breakers at Lord Grimford's,' reiterated Richardson.

'This is too awful,' said Sophie; 'a strike of servants at a moment like this, with the Duke of Syria staying in the house. Something must be done immediately. Quick, finish my hair and I'll go and see what I can do to bring them round.'

'I can't finish your hair, madame,' said Richardson quietly, but with immense decision. 'I belong to the union and I can't do another half-minute's work till the strike is settled. I'm sorry to be disobliging.'

'But this is inhuman!' exclaimed Sophie tragically; 'I've always been a model mistress and I've refused to employ any but union servants, and this is the result. I can't finish my hair myself; I don't know how to. What am I to do? It's wicked!'

'Wicked is the word,' said Richardson; 'I'm a good Conservative, and I've no patience with this Socialist foolery, asking your pardon. It's tyranny, that's what it is, all along the line, but I've my living to make, same as other people, and I've got to belong to the union. I couldn't touch another hair-pin without a strike permit, not if you was to double my wages.'

The door burst open and Catherine Malsom raged into the room.

'Here's a nice affair,' she screamed, 'a strike of household servants without a moment's warning, and I'm left like this! I can't appear in public in this condition.'

After a very hasty scrutiny Sophie assured her that she could not.

'Have they *all* struck?' she asked her maid.

'Not the kitchen staff,' said Richardson, 'they belong to a different union.'

'Dinner at least will be assured,' said Sophie, 'that is something to be thankful for.'

'Dinner!' snorted Catherine, 'what on earth is the good of dinner when none of us will be able to appear at it? Look at your hair—and look at me! or rather, don't.'

'I know it's difficult to manage without a maid; can't your husband be any help to you?' asked Sophie despairingly.

'Henry? He's in worse case than any of us. His man is the only person who really understands that ridiculous newfangled Turkish bath that he insists on taking with him everywhere.'

'Surely he could do without a Turkish bath for one evening,' said Sophie; 'I can't appear without hair, but a Turkish bath is a luxury.'

'My good woman,' said Catherine, speaking with a fearful intensity, 'Henry was *in* the bath when the strike started. *In* it, do you understand? He's there now.'

'Can't he get out?'

'He doesn't know how to. Every time he pulls the lever marked "release" he only releases hot steam. There are two kinds of steam in the bath, "bearable" and "scarcely bearable"; he has released them both. By this time I'm probably a widow.'

'I simply can't send away Gaspare,' wailed Sophie; 'I should never be able to secure another omelette specialist.'

'Any difficulty that I may experience in securing another husband is of course a trifle beneath any one's consideration,' said Catherine bitterly.

Sophie capitulated. 'Go,' she said to Richardson, 'and tell the Strike Committee, or whoever are directing this affair, that Gaspare is herewith dismissed. And ask Gaspare to see me presently in the library, when I will pay him what is due to him and make what excuses I can; and then fly back and finish my hair.'

Some half an hour later Sophie marshalled her guests in the Grand Salon preparatory to the formal march to the dining-room. Except that Henry Malsom was of the ripe raspberry tint that one sometimes sees at private theatricals representing the human complexion, there was little outward sign among those assembled of the crisis that had just been encountered and surmounted. But the tension had been too stupefying while it lasted not to leave some mental effects behind it. Sophie talked at random to her illustrious guest, and found her eyes straying with increasing frequency towards the great doors through which would presently come the blessed announcement that dinner was served. Now and again she glanced mirror-ward at the reflection of her wonderfully coiffed hair, as an insurance underwriter might gaze thankfully at an overdue vessel that had ridden safely into harbour in the wake of a devastating hurricane. Then the doors opened and the welcome figure of the butler entered the room. But he made no general announcement of a banquet in readiness, and the doors closed behind him; his message was for Sophie alone.

'There is no dinner, madame,' he said gravely; 'the kitchen staff have "downed tools." Gaspare belongs to the Union of Cooks and Kitchen Employés, and as soon as they heard of his summary dismissal at a moment's notice they struck work. They demand his instant reinstatement and an apology to the union. I may add, madame, that they are very firm; I've been obliged even to hand back the dinner rolls that were already on the table.'

After the lapse of eighteen months Sophie Chattel-Monkheim is beginning to go about again among her old haunts and associates, but she still has to be very careful. The doctors will not let her attend anything at all exciting, such as a drawing-room meeting or a Fabian conference; it is doubtful, indeed, whether she wants to.

THE FORBIDDEN BUZZARDS

'IS MATCHMAKING at all in your line?'

Hugo Peterby asked the question with a certain amount of personal interest.

'I don't specialize in it,' said Clovis; 'it's all right while you're doing it, but the after-effects are sometimes so disconcerting—the mute reproachful looks of the people you've aided and abetted in matrimonial experiments. It's as bad as selling a man a horse with half a dozen latent vices and watching him discover them piecemeal in the course of the hunting season. I suppose you're thinking of the Coulterneb girl. She's certainly jolly, and quite all right as far as looks go, and I believe a certain amount of money adheres to her. What I don't see is how you will ever manage to propose to her. In all the time I've known her I don't remember her to have stopped talking for three consecutive minutes. You'll have to race her six times round the grass paddock for a bet, and then blurt your proposal out before she's got her wind back. The paddock is laid up for hay, but if you're really in love with her you won't let a consideration of that sort stop you, especially as it's not your hay.'

'I think I could manage the proposing part right enough,' said Hugo, 'if I could count on being left alone with her for four or five hours. The trouble is that I'm not likely to get anything like that amount of grace. That fellow Lanner is showing signs of interesting himself in the same quarter. He's quite heartbreakingly rich and is rather a swell in his way; in fact, our hostess is obviously a bit flattered at having him here. If she gets wind of the fact that he's inclined to be attracted by Betty Coulterneb she'll think it a splendid match and throw them into each other's arms all day long, and then where will my opportunities come in? My one anxiety is to keep him out of the girl's way as much as possible, and if you could help me——'

'If you want me to trot Lanner round the countryside, inspecting alleged Roman remains and studying local methods of bee culture and crop raising, I'm afraid I can't oblige you,' said Clovis. 'You see, he's taken something like an aversion to me since the other night in the smoking-room.'

'What happened in the smoking-room?'

'He trotted out some well-worn chestnut as the latest thing in good stories, and I remarked, quite innocently, that I never could remember whether it was George II or James II who was so fond of that particular story, and now he regards me with politely draped dislike. I'll do my best for you, if the opportunity arises, but it will have to be in a roundabout, impersonal manner.'

'It's so nice having Mr Lanner here,' confided Mrs Olston to Clovis the next afternoon; 'he's always been engaged when I've asked him before. Such a nice man; he really ought to be married to some nice girl. Between you and me, I have an idea that he came down here for a certain reason.'

'I've had much the same idea,' said Clovis, lowering his voice; 'in fact, I'm almost certain of it.'

'You mean he's attracted by——' began Mrs Olston eagerly.

'I mean he's here for what he can get,' said Clovis.

'For what he can *get*?' said the hostess with a touch of indignation in her voice; 'what do you mean? He's a very rich man. What should he want to get here?'

'He has one ruling passion,' said Clovis, 'and there's something he can get here that is not to be had for love nor for money anywhere else in the country, as far as I know.'

'But what? Whatever do you mean? What is his ruling passion?'

'Egg-collecting,' said Clovis. 'He has agents all over the world getting rare eggs for him, and his collection is one of the finest in Europe; but his great ambition is to collect his treasures personally. He stops at no expense nor trouble to achieve that end.'

'Good heavens! The buzzards, the rough-legged buzzards!' exclaimed Mrs Olston; 'you don't think he's going to raid their nest?'

'What do you think yourself?' asked Clovis; 'the only pair of rough-legged buzzards known to breed in this country are nesting in your woods. Very few people know about them, but as a member of the league for protecting rare birds that information would be at his disposal. I came down in the train with him, and I noticed that a bulky volume of Dresser's *Birds of Europe* was one of the requisites that he had packed in his travelling-kit. It was the volume dealing with short-winged hawks and buzzards.'

Clovis believed that if a lie was worth telling it was worth telling well.

'This is appalling,' said Mrs Olston; 'my husband would never forgive me if anything happened to those birds. They've been seen about the woods for the last year or two, but this is the first time they've nested. As you say, they are almost the only pair known to be breeding in the whole of Great Britain; and now their nest is going to be harried by a guest staying under my roof. I must do something to stop it. Do you think if I appealed to him——?'

Clovis laughed.

'There is a story going about, which I fancy is true in most of its details, of something that happened not long ago somewhere on the coast of the Sea of Marmora, in which our friend had a hand. A Syrian nightjar, or some such bird, was known to be breeding in the olive gardens of a rich Armenian, who for some reason or other wouldn't allow Lanner to go in and take the eggs though he offered cash down for the permission. The Armenian was found beaten nearly to death a day or two later, and his fences levelled. It was assumed to be a case of Mussulman aggression, and noted as such in all the Consular reports, but the eggs are in the Lanner collection. No, I don't think I should appeal to his better feelings if I were you.'

'I must do something,' said Mrs Olston tearfully; 'my husband's parting words when he went off to Norway were an injunction to see that those birds were not disturbed, and he's asked about them every time he's written. Do suggest something.'

'I was going to suggest picketing,' said Clovis.

'Picketing! You mean setting guards round the birds?'

'No; round Lanner. He can't find his way through those woods by night, and you could arrange that you or Evelyn or Jack or the German governess should be by his side in relays all day long. A fellow guest he could get rid of, but he couldn't very well shake off members of the household, and even the most determined collector would hardly go climbing after forbidden buzzards' eggs with a German governess hanging round his neck, so to speak.'

Lanner, who had been lazily watching for an opportunity for prosecuting his courtship of the Coulterneb girl, found presently that his chances of getting her to himself for ten minutes even were non-existent. If the girl was ever alone he never was. His hostess had changed suddenly, as far as he was concerned, from the desirable type that lets her guests do nothing in the way that best pleases them, to the sort that drags them over the ground like so many harrows. She showed him the herb garden and the greenhouses, the village church, some water-colour sketches that her sister had done in Corsica, and the place where it was hoped that celery would grow later in the year. He was shown all the Aylesbury ducklings and the row of wooden hives where there would have been bees if there had not been bee disease. He was also taken to the end of a long lane and shown a distant mound whereon local tradition reported that the Danes had once pitched a camp. And when his hostess had to desert him temporarily for other duties he would find Evelyn walking solemnly by his side. Evelyn was fourteen and talked chiefly about good and evil, and of how much one might accomplish in the way of regenerating the world if one was thoroughly determined to do one's utmost. It was generally rather a relief when she was displaced by Jack, who was nine years old, and talked exclusively about the Balkan War without throwing any fresh light on its political or military history. The German governess told Lanner more about Schiller than he had ever heard in his life about any one person; it was perhaps his own fault for having told her that he was not interested in Goethe. When the governess went off picket duty the hostess was again on hand with a not-to-be-gainsaid invitation to visit the cottage of an old woman who remembered Charles James Fox; the woman had been dead for two or three years, but the cottage was still there. Lanner was called back to town earlier than he had originally intended.

Hugo did not bring off his affair with Betty Coulterneb. Whether she refused him or whether, as was more generally supposed, he did not get a chance of saying three consecutive words, has never been exactly ascertained. Anyhow, she is still the jolly Coulterneb girl.

The buzzards successfully reared two young ones, which were shot by a local hairdresser.

THE STAKE

'RONNIE IS a great trial to me,' said Mrs Attray plaintively. 'Only eighteen years old last February and already a confirmed gambler. I am sure I don't know where he inherits it from; his father never touched cards, and you know how little I play—a game of bridge on Wednesday afternoons in the winter, for threepence a hundred, and even that I shouldn't do if it wasn't that Edith always wants a fourth and would be certain to ask that detestable Jenkinham woman if she couldn't get me. I would much rather sit and talk any day than play bridge; cards are such a waste of time, I think. But as to Ronnie, bridge and baccarat and poker-patience are positively all that he thinks about. Of course I've done my best to stop it; I've asked the Norridrums not to let him play cards when he's over there, but you might as well ask the Atlantic Ocean to keep quiet for a crossing as expect them to bother about a mother's natural anxieties.'

'Why do you let him go there?' asked Eleanor Saxelby.

'My dear,' said Mrs Attray, 'I don't want to offend them. After all, they are my landlords and I have to look to them for anything I want done about the place; they were very accommodating about the new roof for the orchid house. And they lend me one of their cars when mine is out of order; you know how often it gets out of order.'

'I don't know how often,' said Eleanor, 'but it must happen very frequently. Whenever I want you to take me anywhere in your car I am always told that there is something wrong with it, or else that the chauffeur has got neuralgia and you don't like to ask him to go out.'

'He suffers quite a lot from neuralgia,' said Mrs Attray hastily. 'Anyhow,' she continued, 'you can understand that I don't want to offend the Norridrums. Their household is the most rackety one in the county, and I believe no one ever knows to an hour or two when any particular meal will appear on the table or what it will consist of when it does appear.'

Eleanor Saxelby shuddered. She liked her meals to be of regular occurrence and assured proportions.

'Still,' pursued Mrs Attray, 'whatever their own home life may be, as landlords and neighbours they are considerate and obliging, so I don't want to quarrel with them. Besides, if Ronnie didn't play cards there he'd be playing somewhere else.'

'Not if you were firm with him,' said Eleanor; 'I believe in being firm.'

'Firm? I am firm,' exclaimed Mrs Attray; 'I am more than firm—I am farseeing. I've done everything I can think of to prevent Ronnie from playing for money. I've stopped his allowance for the rest of the year, so he can't even gamble on credit, and I've subscribed a lump sum to the church offertory in his name instead of giving him instalments of small silver to put in the bag on Sundays. I wouldn't even let him have the money to tip the hunt servants with, but sent it by postal order. He was furiously sulky about it, but I reminded him of what happened to the ten shillings that I gave him for the Young Men's Endeavour League "Self-Denial Week." '

'What did happen to it?' asked Eleanor.

'Well, Ronnie did some preliminary endeavouring with it, on his own account, in connection with the Grand National. If it had come off, as he expressed it, he would have given the League twenty-five shillings and netted a comfortable commission for himself; as it was, that ten shillings was one of the things the League had to deny itself. Since then I've been careful not to let him have a penny piece in his hands.'

'He'll get round that in some way,' said Eleanor with quiet conviction; 'he'll sell things.'

'My dear, he's done all that is to be done in that direction already. He's got rid of his wrist-watch and his hunting flask and both his cigarette cases, and I shouldn't be surprised if he's wearing imitation-gold sleeve links instead of those his Aunt Rhoda gave him on his seventeenth birthday. He can't sell his clothes, of course, except his winter overcoat, and I've locked that up in the camphor cupboard on the pretext of preserving it from moth. I really don't see what else he can raise money on. I consider that I've been both firm and farseeing.'

'Has he been at the Norridrums lately?' asked Eleanor.

'He was there yesterday afternoon and stayed to dinner,' said Mrs Attray. 'I don't quite know when he came home, but I fancy it was late.'

'Then depend on it he was gambling,' said Eleanor, with the assured air of one who has few ideas and makes the most of them. 'Late hours in the country always mean gambling.'

'He can't gamble if he has no money and no chance of getting any,' argued Mrs Attray; 'even if one plays for small stakes one must have a decent prospect of paying one's losses.'

'He may have sold some of the Amherst pheasant chicks,' suggested Eleanor; 'they would fetch about ten or twelve shillings each, I dare say.'

'Ronnie wouldn't do such a thing,' said Mrs Attray; 'and anyhow I went and counted them this morning and they're all there. No,' she continued, with the quiet satisfaction that comes from a sense of painstaking and merited achievement, 'I fancy that Ronnie had to content himself with the rôle of onlooker last night, as far as the card-table was concerned.'

'Is that clock right?' asked Eleanor, whose eyes had been straying restlessly towards the mantelpiece for some little time; 'lunch is usually so punctual in your establishment.'

'Three minutes past the half-hour,' exclaimed Mrs Attray; 'cook must be preparing something unusually sumptuous in your honour. I am not in the secret; I've been out all the morning, you know.'

Eleanor smiled forgivingly. A special effort by Mrs Attray's cook was worth waiting a few minutes for.

As a matter of fact, the luncheon fare, when it made its tardy appearance, was distinctly unworthy of the reputation which the justly treasured cook had built up for herself. The soup alone would have sufficed to cast a gloom over any meal that it had inaugurated, and it was not redeemed by anything that followed. Eleanor said little, but when she spoke there was a hint of tears in her voice that was far more eloquent than outspoken denunciation would have been, and even the insouciant Ronald showed traces of depression when he tasted the rognons Saltikoff.

'Not quite the best luncheon I've enjoyed in your house,' said Eleanor at last, when her final hope had flickered out with the savoury.

'My dear, it's the worst meal I've sat down to for years,' said her hostess; 'that last dish tasted principally of red pepper and wet toast. I'm awfully sorry. Is anything the matter in the kitchen, Pellin?' she asked of the attendant maid.

'Well, ma'am, the new cook hadn't hardly time to see to things properly, coming in so sudden——' commenced Pellin by way of explanation.

'The *new* cook!' screamed Mrs Attray.

'Colonel Norridrum's cook, ma'am,' said Pellin.

'What on earth do you mean? What is Colonel Norridrum's cook doing in my kitchen—and where is *my* cook?'

'Perhaps I can explain better than Pellin can,' said Ronald hurriedly: 'the fact is, I was dining at the Norridrums' yesterday, and they were wishing they had a swell cook like yours, just for today and tomorrow, while they've got some gourmet staying with them; their own cook is no earthly good—well, you've seen what she turns out when she's at all flurried. So I thought it would be rather sporting to play them at baccarat for the loan of our cook against a money stake, and I lost, that's all. I have had rotten luck at baccarat all this year.'

The remainder of his explanation, of how he had assured the cooks that the temporary transfer had his mother's sanction, and had smuggled the one out and the other in during the maternal absence, was drowned in the outcry of scandalized upbraiding.

'If I had sold the woman into slavery there couldn't have been a bigger fuss about it,' he confided afterwards to Bertie Norridrum, 'and Eleanor Saxelby raged and ramped the louder of the two. I tell you what, I'll bet you two of the Amherst pheasants to five shillings that she refuses to have me as a partner at the croquet tournament. We're drawn together, you know.'

This time he won his bet.

THE STALLED OX

THEOPHIL ESHLEY was an artist by profession, a cattle painter by force of environment. It is not to be supposed that he lived on a ranch or a dairy farm, in an atmosphere pervaded with horn and hoof, milking-stool, and branding-iron. His home was in a park-like, villa-dotted district that only just escaped the reproach of being suburban. On one side of his garden there abutted a small, picturesque meadow, in which an enterprising neighbour pastured some small picturesque cows of the Channel Island persuasion. At noonday in summertime the cows stood knee-deep in tall meadow-grass under the shade of a group of walnut trees, with the sunlight falling in dappled patches on their mouse-sleek coats. Eshley had conceived and executed a dainty picture of two reposeful milch-cows in a setting of walnut tree and meadow-grass and filtered sunbeam, and the Royal Academy had duly exposed the same on the walls of its Summer Exhibition. The Royal Academy encourages orderly, methodical habits in its children. Eshley had painted a successful and acceptable picture of cattle drowsing picturesquely under walnut trees, and as he had begun, so, of necessity, he went on. His 'Noontide Peace,' a study of two dun cows under a walnut tree, was followed by 'A Mid-day Sanctuary,' a study of a walnut tree, with two dun cows under it. In due succession there came 'Where the Gad-Flies Cease from Troubling,' 'The Haven of the Herd,' and 'A Dream in Dairyland,' studies of walnut trees and dun cows. His two attempts to break away from his own tradition were signal failures: 'Turtle Doves Alarmed by Sparrow-hawk' and 'Wolves on the Roman Campagna' came back to his studio in the guise of abominable heresies, and Eshley climbed back into grace and the public gaze with 'A Shaded Nook Where Drowsy Milkers Dream.'

On a fine afternoon in late autumn he was putting some finishing touches to a study of meadow weeds when his neighbour, Adela Pingsford, assailed the outer door of his studio with loud peremptory knockings.'

'There is an ox in my garden,' she announced, in explanation of the tempestuous intrusion.

'An ox,' said Eshley blankly, and rather fatuously; 'what kind of ox?'

'Oh, I don't know what kind,' snapped the lady. 'A common or garden ox, to use the slang expression. It is the garden part of it that I object to. My garden has just been put straight for the winter, and an ox roaming about in it won't improve matters. Besides, there are the chrysanthemums just coming into flower.'

'How did it get into the garden?' asked Eshley.

'I imagine it came in by the gate,' said the lady impatiently; 'it couldn't have climbed the walls, and I don't suppose any one dropped it from an aeroplane as a Bovril advertisement. The immediately important question is not how it got in, but how to get it out.'

'Won't it go?' said Eshley.

'If it was anxious to go,' said Adela Pingsford rather angrily, 'I should not have come here to chat with you about it. I'm practically all alone; the housemaid is having her afternoon out and the cook is lying down with an attack of neuralgia. Anything that I may have learned at school or in after life about how to remove a large ox from a small garden seems to have escaped from my memory now. All I could think of was that you were a near neighbour and a cattle painter, presumably more or less familiar with the subjects that you painted, and that you might be of some slight assistance. Possibly I was mistaken.'

'I paint dairy cows, certainly,' admitted Eshley, 'but I cannot claim to have had any experience in rounding up stray oxen. I've seen it done on a cinema film, of course, but there were always horses and lots of other accessories; besides, one never knows how much of those pictures are faked.'

Adela Pingsford said nothing, but led the way to her garden. It was normally a fair-sized garden, but it looked small in comparison with the ox, a huge mottled brute, dull red about the head and shoulders, passing to dirty white on the flanks and hind-quarters, with shaggy ears and large blood-shot eyes. It bore about as much resemblance to the dainty paddock heifers that Eshley was accustomed to paint as the chief of a Kurdish nomad clan would to a Japanese tea-shop girl. Eshley stood very near the gate while he studied the animal's appearance and demeanour. Adela Pingsford continued to say nothing.

'It's eating a chrysanthemum,' said Eshley at last, when the silence had become unbearable.

'How observant you are,' said Adela bitterly. 'You seem to notice everything. As a matter of fact, it has got six chrysanthemums in its mouth at the present moment.'

The necessity for doing something was becoming imperative. Eshley took a step or two in the direction of the animal, clapped his hands, and made noises of the 'Hish' and 'Shoo' variety. If the ox heard them it gave no outward indication of the fact.

'If any hens should ever stray into my garden,' said Adela, 'I should certainly send for you to frighten them out. You 'shoo' beautifully. Meanwhile, do you mind trying to drive that ox away? That is a *Mademoiselle Louise Bichot* that he's begun on now,' she added in icy calm, as a glowing orange head was crushed into the huge munching mouth.

'Since you have been so frank about the variety of the chrysanthemum,' said Eshley, 'I don't mind telling you that this is an Ayrshire ox.'

The icy calm broke down; Adela Pingsford used language that sent the artist instinctively a few feet nearer to the ox. He picked up a pea-stick and flung it with some determination against the animal's mottled flanks. The operation of mashing *Mademoiselle Louise Bichot* into a petal salad was suspended for a long moment, while the ox gazed with concentrated inquiry at the stick-thrower. Adela gazed with equal concentration and more obvious hostility at the same focus. As the beast neither lowered its head nor stamped its feet Eshley ventured on another javelin exercise with another pea-stick. The ox seemed to realize at once that it was to go; it gave a hurried final pluck at the bed where the chrysanthemums had been, and strode swiftly up the garden. Eshley ran to head it towards the gate, but only succeeded in quickening its pace from a walk to a lumbering trot. With an air of inquiry, but with no real hesitation, it crossed the tiny strip of turf that the charitable called the croquet lawn, and pushed its way through the open French window into the morning-room. Some chrysanthemums and other autumn herbage stood about the room in vases, and the animal resumed its browsing operations; all the same, Eshley fancied that the beginnings of a hunted look had come into its eyes, a look that counselled respect. He discontinued his attempt to interfere with its choice of surroundings.

'Mr Eshley,' said Adela in a shaking voice, 'I asked you to drive that beast out of my garden, but I did not ask you to drive it into my house. If I must have it anywhere on the premises, I prefer the garden to the morning-room.'

'Cattle drives are not in my line,' said Eshley; 'if I remember, I told you so at the outset.'

'I quite agree,' retorted the lady, 'painting pretty pictures of pretty little cows is what you're suited for. Perhaps you'd like to do a nice sketch of that ox making itself at home in my morning-room?'

This time it seemed as if the worm had turned; Eshley began striding away.

'Where are you going?' screamed Adela.

'To fetch implements,' was the answer.

'Implements? I won't have you use a lasso. The room will be wrecked if there's a struggle.'

But the artist marched out of the garden. In a couple of minutes he returned, laden with easel, sketching-stool, and painting materials.

'Do you mean to say that you're going to sit quietly down and paint that brute while it's destroying my morning-room?' gasped Adela.

'It was your suggestion,' said Eshley, setting his canvas in position.

'I forbid it; I absolutely forbid it!' stormed Adela.

'I don't see what standing you have in the matter,' said the artist; 'you can hardly pretend that it's your ox, even by adoption.'

'You seem to forget that it's in my morning-room, eating my flowers,' came the raging retort.

'You seem to forget that the cook has neuralgia,' said Eshley; 'she may be just dozing off into a merciful sleep and your outcry will waken her. Consideration for others should be the guiding principle of people in our station of life.'

'The man is mad!' exclaimed Adela tragically. A moment later it was Adela herself who appeared to go mad. The ox had finished the vase-flowers and the cover of *Israel Kalisch*, and appeared to be thinking of leaving its rather restricted quarters. Eshley noticed its restlessness and promptly flung it some bunches of Virginia creeper leaves as an inducement to continue the sitting.

'I forget how the proverb runs,' he observed; 'something about "better a dinner of herbs than a stalled ox where hate is." We seem to have all the ingredients for the proverb ready to hand.'

'I shall go to the Public Library and get them to telephone for the police,' announced Adela, and, raging audibly, she departed.

Some minutes later the ox, awakening probably to the suspicion that oil cake and chopped mangold was waiting for it in some appointed byre, stepped with much precaution out of the morning-room, stared with grave inquiry at the no longer obtrusive and pea-stick-throwing human, and then lumbered heavily but swiftly out of the garden. Eshley packed up his tools and followed the animal's example and 'Larkdene' was left to neuralgia and the cook.

The episode was the turning-point in Eshley's artistic career. His remarkable picture, 'Ox in a Morning-room, Late Autumn,' was one of the sensations and successes of the next Paris Salon, and when it was subsequently exhibited at Munich it was bought by the Bavarian Government, in the teeth of the spirited bidding of three meat-extract firms. From that moment his success was continuous and assured, and the Royal Academy was thankful, two years later, to give a conspicuous position on its walls to his large canvas 'Barbary Apes Wrecking a Boudoir.'

Eshley presented Adela Pingsford with a new copy of *Israel Kalisch*, and a couple of finely flowering plants of *Madame André Blusset*, but nothing in the nature of a real reconciliation has taken place between them.

THE STORY-TELLER

IT WAS a hot afternoon, and the railway carriage was correspondingly sultry, and the next stop was at Templecombe, nearly an hour ahead. The occupants of the carriage were a small girl, and a smaller girl, and a small boy. An aunt belonging to the children occupied one corner seat, and the further corner seat on the opposite side was occupied by a bachelor who was a stranger to their party, but the small girls and the boy emphatically occupied the compartment. Both the aunt and the children were conversational in a limited, persistent way, reminding one of the attentions of a housefly that refused to be discouraged. Most of the aunt's remarks seemed to begin with 'Don't,' and nearly all of the children's remarks began with 'Why?' The bachelor said nothing out loud.

'Don't, Cyril, don't,' exclaimed the aunt, as the small boy began smacking the cushions of the seat, producing a cloud of dust at each blow.

'Come and look out of the window,' she added.

The child moved reluctantly to the window. 'Why are those sheep being driven out of that field?' he asked.

'I expect they are being driven to another field where there is more grass,' said the aunt weakly.

'But there is lots of grass in that field,' protested the boy; 'there's nothing else but grass there. Aunt, there's lots of grass in that field.'

'Perhaps the grass in the other field is better,' suggested the aunt fatuously.

'Why is it better?' came the swift, inevitable question.

'Oh, look at those cows!' exclaimed the aunt. Nearly every field along the line had contained cows or bullocks, but she spoke as though she were drawing attention to a rarity.

'Why is the grass in the other field better?' persisted Cyril.

The frown on the bachelor's face was deepening to a scowl. He was a hard, unsympathetic man, the aunt decided in her mind. She was utterly unable to come to any satisfactory decision about the grass in the other field.

The smaller girl created a diversion by beginning to recite 'On the Road to Mandalay.' She only knew the first line, but she put her limited knowledge to the fullest possible use. She repeated the line over and over again in a dreamy but resolute and very audible voice; it seemed to the bachelor as though some one had had a bet with her that she could not repeat the line aloud two thousand times without stopping. Whoever it was who had made the wager was likely to lose his bet.

'Come over here and listen to a story,' said the aunt, when the bachelor had looked twice at her and once at the communication cord.

The children moved listlessly towards the aunt's end of the carriage. Evidently her reputation as a story-teller did not rank high in their estimation.

In a low, confidential voice, interrupted at frequent intervals by loud, petulant questions from her listeners, she began an unenterprising and deplorably uninteresting story about a little girl who was good, and made friends with every one on account of her goodness, and was finally saved from a mad bull by a number of rescuers who admired her moral character.

'Wouldn't they have saved her if she hadn't been good?' demanded the bigger of the small girls. It was exactly the question that the bachelor had wanted to ask.

'Well, yes,' admitted the aunt lamely, 'but I don't think they would have run quite so fast to her help if they had not liked her so much.'

'It's the stupidest story I've ever heard,' said the bigger of the small girls, with immense conviction.

'I didn't listen after the first bit, it was so stupid,' said Cyril.

The smaller girl made no actual comment on the story,

but she had long ago recommenced a murmured repetition of her favourite line.

'You don't seem to be a success as a story-teller,' said the bachelor suddenly from his corner.

The aunt bristled in instant defence at this unexpected attack.

'It's a very difficult thing to tell stories that children can both understand and appreciate,' she said stiffly.

'I don't agree with you,' said the bachelor.

'Perhaps *you* would like to tell them a story,' was the aunt's retort.

'Tell us a story,' demanded the bigger of the small girls.

'Once upon a time,' began the bachelor, 'there was a little girl called Bertha, who was extraordinarily good.'

The children's momentarily-aroused interest began at once to flicker; all stories seemed dreadfully alike, no matter who told them.

'She did all that she was told, she was always truthful, she kept her clothes clean, ate milk puddings as though they were jam tarts, learned her lessons perfectly, and was polite in her manners.'

'Was she pretty?' asked the bigger of the small girls.

'Not as pretty as any of you,' said the bachelor, 'but she was horribly good.'

There was a wave of reaction in favour of the story; the word horrible in connection with goodness was a novelty that commended itself. It seemed to introduce a ring of truth that was absent from the aunt's tales of infant life.

'She was so good,' continued the bachelor, 'that she won several medals for goodness, which she always wore, pinned on to her dress. There was a medal for obedience, another medal for punctuality, and a third for good behaviour. They were large metal medals and they clinked against one another as she walked. No other child in the town where she lived had as many as three medals, so everybody knew that she must be an extra good child.'

'Horribly good,' quoted Cyril.

'Everybody talked about her goodness, and the Prince of the country got to hear about it, and he said that as she was so very good she might be allowed once a week to walk in his park, which was just outside the town. It was a beautiful park, and no children were ever allowed in it, so it was a great honour for Bertha to be allowed to go there.'

'Were there any sheep in the park?' demanded Cyril.

'No,' said the bachelor, 'there were no sheep.'

'Why weren't there any sheep?' came the inevitable question arising out of that answer.

The aunt permitted herself a smile, which might almost have been described as a grin.

'There were no sheep in the park,' said the bachelor, 'because the Prince's mother had once had a dream that her son would either be killed by a sheep or else by a clock falling on him. For that reason the Prince never kept a sheep in his park or a clock in his palace.'

The aunt suppressed a gasp of admiration.

'Was the Prince killed by a sheep or by a clock?' asked Cyril.

'He's still alive, so we can't tell whether the dream will come true,' said the bachelor unconcernedly; anyway, there were no sheep in the park, but there were lots of little pigs running all over the place.'

'What colour were they?'

'Black with white faces, white with black spots, black all over, grey with white patches, and some were white all over.'

The story-teller paused to let a full idea of the park's treasures sink into the children's imaginations; then he resumed:

'Bertha was rather sorry to find that there were no flowers in the park. She had promised her aunts, with tears in her eyes, that she would not pick any of the kind Prince's flowers, and she had meant to keep her promise, so of course it made her feel silly to find that there were no flowers to pick.'

'Why weren't there any flowers?'

'Because the pigs had eaten them all,' said the bachelor promptly. 'The gardeners had told the Prince that you couldn't have pigs and flowers, so he decided to have pigs and no flowers.'

There was a murmur of approval at the excellence of the Prince's decision; so many people would have decided the other way.

'There were lots of other delightful things in the park. There were ponds with gold and blue and green fish in them, and trees with beautiful parrots that said clever things at a moment's notice, and humming birds that hummed all the popular tunes of the day. Bertha walked up and down and enjoyed herself immensely, and thought to herself: "If I were not so extraordinarily good I should not have been allowed to come into this beautiful park and enjoy all that there is to be seen in it," and her three medals clinked against one another as she walked and helped to remind her how very good she really was. Just then an enormous wolf came prowling into the park to see if it could catch a fat little pig for its supper.'

'What colour was it?' asked the children, amid an immediate quickening of interest.

'Mud-colour all over, with a black tongue and pale grey eyes that gleamed with unspeakable ferocity. The first thing that it saw in the park was Bertha; her pinafore was so spotlessly white and clean that it could be seen from a great distance. Bertha saw the wolf and saw that it was stealing towards her, and she began to wish that she had never been allowed to come into the park. She ran as hard as she could, and the wolf came after her with huge leaps and bounds. She managed to reach a shrubbery of myrtle bushes and she hid herself in one of the thickest of the bushes. The wolf came sniffing among the branches, its black tongue lolling out of its mouth and its pale grey eyes glaring with rage. Bertha was terribly frightened, and thought to herself: "If I had not been so extraordinarily good I should have been safe in the town at this moment." However, the scent of the myrtle was so strong that the wolf could not sniff out where Bertha was hiding, and the bushes were so thick that he might have hunted about in them for a long time without catching sight of her, so he thought he might as well go off and catch a little pig instead. Bertha was trembling very much at having the wolf prowling and sniffing so near her, and as she trembled the medal for obedience clinked against the medals for good conduct and punctuality. The wolf was just moving away when he heard the sound of the medals clinking and stopped to listen; they clinked again in a bush quite near him. He dashed into the bush, his pale grey eyes gleaming with ferocity and triumph and dragged Bertha out and devoured her to the last morsel. All that was left of her were her shoes, bits of clothing, and the three medals for goodness.'

'Were any of the little pigs killed?'

'No, they all escaped.'

'The story began badly,' said the smaller of the small girls, 'but it had a beautiful ending.'

'It is the most beautiful story that I ever heard,' said the bigger of the small girls, with immense decision.

'It is the *only* beautiful story I have ever heard,' said Cyril.

A dissentient opinion came from the aunt.

'A most improper story to tell to young children! You have undermined the effect of years of careful teaching.'

'At any rate,' said the bachelor, collecting his belongings preparatory to leaving the carriage, 'I kept them quiet for ten minutes, which was more than you were able to do.'

'Unhappy woman!' he observed to himself as he walked down the platform of Templecombe station; 'for the next six months or so those children will assail her in public with demands for an improper story!'

A DEFENSIVE DIAMOND

TREDDLEFORD SAT in an easeful arm-chair in front of a slumberous fire, with a volume of verse in his hand and the comfortable consciousness that outside the club windows the rain was dripping and pattering with persistent purpose. A chill, wet October afternoon was emerging into a black, wet October evening, and the club smoking-room seemed warmer and cosier by contrast. It was an afternoon on which to be wafted away from one's climatic surroundings, and *The Golden Journey to Samarkand* promised to bear Treddleford well and bravely into other lands and under other skies. He had already migrated from London the rain-swept to Bagdad the Beautiful, and stood by the Sun Gate 'in the olden time' when an icy breath of imminent annoyance seemed to creep between the book and himself. Amblecope, the man with the restless, prominent eyes and the mouth ready mobilized for conversational openings, had planted himself in a neighbouring arm-chair. For a twelve-month and some odd weeks Treddleford had skilfully avoided making the acquaintance of his voluble fellow-clubman; he had marvellously escaped from the infliction of his relentless record of tedious personal achievements, or alleged achievements, on golf links, turf, and gaming table, by flood and field and covert-side. Now his season of immunity was coming to an end. There was no escape; in another moment he would be numbered among those who knew Amblecope to speak to—or rather, to suffer being spoken to.

The intruder was armed with a copy of *Country Life*, not for purposes of reading, but as an aid to conversational ice-breaking.

'Rather a good portrait of Throstlewing,' he remarked explosively, turning his large challenging eyes on Treddleford; 'somehow it reminds me very much of Yellowstep, who was supposed to be such a good thing for the Grand

Prix in 1903. Curious race that was; I suppose I've seen every race for the Grand Prix for the last——'

'Be kind enough never to mention the Grand Prix in my hearing,' said Treddleford desperately; 'it awakens acutely distressing memories. I can't explain why without going into a long and complicated story.'

'Oh, certainly, certainly,' said Amblecope hastily; long and complicated stories that were not told by himself were abominable in his eyes. He turned the pages of *Country Life* and became spuriously interested in the picture of a Mongolian pheasant.

'Not a bad representation of the Mongolian variety,' he exclaimed, holding it up for his neighbour's inspection. 'They do very well in some covers. Take some stopping too once they're fairly on the wing. I suppose the biggest bag I ever made in two successive days——'

'My aunt, who owns the greater part of Lincolnshire,' broke in Treddleford, with dramatic abruptness, 'possesses perhaps the most remarkable record in the way of a pheasant bag that has ever been achieved. She is seventy-five and can't hit a thing, but she always goes out with the guns. When I say she can't hit a thing, I don't mean to say that she doesn't occasionally endanger the lives of her fellow-guns, because that wouldn't be true. In fact, the chief Government Whip won't allow Ministerial M.P.s to go out with her; "We don't want to incur by-elections needlessly," he quite reasonably observed. Well, the other day she winged a pheasant, and brought it to earth with a feather or two knocked out of it; it was a runner, and my aunt saw herself in danger of being done out of about the only bird she'd hit during the present reign. Of course she wasn't going to stand that; she followed it through bracken and brushwood, and when it took to the open country and started across a ploughed field she jumped on to the shooting pony and went after it. The chase was a long one, and when my aunt at last ran the bird to a standstill she was nearer home than she was to the shooting party; she had left that some five miles behind her.'

'Rather a long run for a wounded pheasant,' snapped Amblecope.

'The story rests on my aunt's authority,' said Treddleford coldly, 'and she is local vice-president of the Young Women's Christian Association. She trotted three miles or so to her home, and it was not till the middle of the afternoon that it was discovered that the lunch for the entire shooting party was in a pannier attached to the pony's saddle. Anyway, she got her bird.'

'Some birds, of course, take a lot of killing,' said Amblecope; 'so do fish. I remember once I was fishing in the Exe, lovely trout stream, lots of fish, though they don't run to any great size——'

'One of them did,' announced Treddleford, with emphasis. 'My uncle, the Bishop of Southmolton, came across a giant trout in a pool just off the main stream of the Exe near Ugworthy; he tried it with every kind of fly and worm every day for three weeks without an atom of success, and then Fate intervened on his behalf. There was a low stone bridge just over this pool, and on the last day of his fishing holiday a motor van ran violently into the parapet and turned completely over; no one was hurt, but part of the parapet was knocked away, and the entire load that the van was carrying was pitched over and fell a little way into the pool. In a couple of minutes the giant trout was flapping and twisting on bare mud at the bottom of a waterless pool, and my uncle was able to walk down to him and fold him to his breast. The van-load consisted of blotting-paper, and every drop of water in that pool had been sucked up into the mass of spilt cargo.'

There was silence for nearly half a minute in the smoking-room, and Treddleford began to let his mind steal back towards the golden road that led to Samarkand. Amblecope, however, rallied, and remarked in a rather tired and dispirited voice:

'Talking of motor accidents, the narrowest squeak I ever had was the other day, motoring with old Tommy

Yarby in North Wales. Awfully good sort, old Yarby, thorough good sportsman, and the best——'

'It was in North Wales,' said Treddleford, 'that my sister met with her sensational carriage accident last year. She was on her way to a garden-party at Lady Nineveh's, about the only garden-party that ever comes to pass in those parts in the course of the year, and therefore a thing that she would have been very sorry to miss. She was driving a young horse that she'd only bought a week or two previously, warranted to be perfectly steady with motor traffic, bicycles, and other common objects of the roadside. The animal lived up to its reputation, and passed the most explosive of motor-bikes with an indifference that almost amounted to apathy. However, I suppose we all draw the line somewhere, and this particular cob drew it at travelling wild beast shows. Of course my sister didn't know that, but she knew it very distinctly when she turned a sharp corner and found herself in a mixed company of camels, piebald horses, and canary-coloured vans. The dog-cart was overturned in a ditch and kicked to splinters, and the cob went home across country. Neither my sister nor the groom was hurt, but the problem of how to get to the Nineveh garden-party, some three miles distant, seemed rather difficult to solve; once there, of course, my sister would easily find some one to drive her home. "I suppose you wouldn't care for the loan of a couple of my camels?" the showman suggested, in humorous sympathy. "I would," said my sister, who had ridden camel-back in Egypt, and she overruled the objections of the groom, who hadn't. She picked out two of the most presentable-looking of the beasts and had them dusted and made as tidy as was possible at short notice, and set out for the Nineveh mansion. You may imagine the sensation that her small but imposing caravan created when she arrived at the hall door. The entire garden-party flocked up to gape. My sister was rather glad to slip down from her camel, and the groom was thankful to scramble down from his. Then young Billy Doulton, of the Dragoon Guards, who has been a lot at Aden and thinks he knows camel-language backwards, thought he would show off by making the beasts kneel down in orthodox fashion. Unfortunately camel words-of-command are not the same all the world over; these were magnificent Turkestan camels, accustomed to stride up the stony terraces of mountain passes, and when Doulton shouted at them they went side by side up the front steps, into the entrance hall, and up the grand staircase. The German governess met them just at the turn of the corridor. The Ninevehs nursed her with devoted attention for weeks, and when I last heard from them she was well enough to go about her duties again, but the doctor says she will always suffer from Hagenbeck heart.'

Amblecope got up from his chair and moved to another part of the room. Treddleford reopened his book and betook himself once more across

The dragon-green, the luminous, the dark, the serpent-
    haunted sea.

For a blessed half-hour he disported himself in imagination by the 'gay Aleppo-Gate,' and listened to the bird-voiced singing-man. Then the world of today called him back; a page summoned him to speak with a friend on the telephone.

As Treddleford was about to pass out of the room he encountered Amblecope, also passing out, on his way to the billiard-room, where, perchance, some luckless wight might be secured and held fast to listen to the number of his attendances at the Grand Prix, with subsequent remarks on Newmarket and the Cambridgeshire. Amblecope made as if to pass out first, but a new-born pride was surging in Treddleford's breast and he waved him back.

'I believe I take precedence,' he said coldly; 'you are merely the club Bore; I am the club Liar.'

THE LUMBER-ROOM

THE CHILDREN were to be driven, as a special treat, to
the sands at Jagborough. Nicholas was not to be of the
party; he was in disgrace. Only that morning he had
refused to eat his wholesome bread-and-milk on the seemingly frivolous ground that there was a frog in it. Older
and wiser and better people had told him that there could
not possibly be a frog in his bread-and-milk and that he
was not to talk nonsense; he continued, nevertheless, to
talk what seemed the veriest nonsense, and described with
much detail the coloration and markings of the alleged
frog. The dramatic part of the incident was that there
really was a frog in Nicholas' basin of bread-and-milk; he
had put it there himself, so he felt entitled to know something about it. The sin of taking a frog from the garden
and putting it into a bowl of wholesome bread-and-milk
was enlarged on at great length, but the fact that stood
out clearest in the whole affair, as it presented itself to the
mind of Nicholas, was that the older, wiser, and better
people had been proved to be profoundly in error in
matters about which they had expressed the utmost
assurance.

'You said there couldn't possibly be a frog in my bread-
and-milk; there *was* a frog in my bread-and-milk,' he
repeated, with the insistence of a skilled tactician who does
not intend to shift from favourable ground.

So his boy-cousin and girl-cousin and his quite uninteresting younger brother were to be taken to Jagborough
sands that afternoon and he was to stay at home. His
cousins' aunt, who insisted, by an unwarranted stretch of
imagination, in styling herself his aunt also, had hastily
invented the Jagborough expedition in order to impress on
Nicholas the delights that he had justly forfeited by his
disgraceful conduct at the breakfast-table. It was her habit,
whenever one of the children fell from grace, to improvise
something of a festival nature from which the offender

would be rigorously debarred; if all the children sinned collectively they were suddenly informed of a circus in a neighbouring town, a circus of unrivalled merit and un-counted elephants, to which, but for their depravity, they would have been taken that very day.

A few decent tears were looked for on the part of Nicholas when the moment for the departure of the expedition arrived. As a matter of fact, however, all the crying was done by his girl-cousin, who scraped her knee rather painfully against the step of the carriage as she was scrambling in.

'How she did howl,' said Nicholas cheerfully, as the party drove off without any of the elation of high spirits that should have characterized it.

'She'll soon get over that,' said the *soi-disant* aunt; 'it will be a glorious afternoon for racing about over those beautiful sands. How they will enjoy themselves!'

'Bobby won't enjoy himself much, and he won't race much either,' said Nicholas with a grim chuckle; 'his boots are hurting him. They're too tight.'

'Why didn't he tell me they were hurting?' asked the aunt with some asperity.

'He told you twice, but you weren't listening. You often don't listen when we tell you important things.'

'You are not to go into the gooseberry garden,' said the aunt, changing the subject.

'Why not?' demanded Nicholas.

'Because you are in disgrace,' said the aunt loftily.

Nicholas did not admit the flawlessness of the reasoning; he felt perfectly capable of being in disgrace and in a gooseberry garden at the same moment. His face took on an expression of considerable obstinacy. It was clear to his aunt that he was determined to get into the gooseberry garden, 'only,' as she remarked to herself, 'because I have told him he is not to.'

Now the gooseberry garden had two doors by which it might be entered, and once a small person like Nicholas could slip in there he could effectually disappear from view amid the masking growth of artichokes, raspberry canes, and fruit bushes. The aunt had many other things to do that afternoon, but she spent an hour or two in trivial gardening operations among flower beds and shrubberies, whence she could keep a watchful eye on the two doors that led to the forbidden paradise. She was a woman of few ideas, with immense powers of concentration.

Nicholas made one or two sorties into the front garden, wriggling his way with obvious stealth of purpose towards one or other of the doors, but never able for a moment to evade the aunt's watchful eye. As a matter of fact, he had no intention of trying to get into the gooseberry garden, but it was extremely convenient for him that his aunt should believe that he had; it was a belief that would keep her on self-imposed sentry-duty for the greater part of the afternoon. Having thoroughly confirmed and fortified her suspicions, Nicholas slipped back into the house and rapidly put into execution a plan of action that had long germinated in his brain. By standing on a chair in the library one could reach a shelf on which reposed a fat, important-looking key. The key was as important as it looked; it was the instrument which kept the mysteries of the lumber-room secure from unauthorized intrusion, which opened a way only for aunts and such-like privileged persons. Nicholas had not had much experience of the art of fitting keys into keyholes and turning locks, but for some days past he had practised with the key of the schoolroom door; he did not believe in trusting too much to luck and accident. The key turned stiffly in the lock, but it turned. The door opened, and Nicholas was in an unknown land, compared with which the gooseberry garden was a stale delight, a mere material pleasure.

Often and often Nicholas had pictured to himself what the lumber-room might be like, that region that was so carefully sealed from youthful eyes and concerning which no questions were ever answered. It came up to his expectations. In the first place it was large and dimly lit, one high window opening on to the forbidden garden being

its only source of illumination. In the second place it was
a storehouse of unimagined treasures. The aunt-by-asser-
tion was one of those people who think that things spoil
by use and consign them to dust and damp by way of
preserving them. Such parts of the house as Nicholas
knew best were rather bare and cheerless, but here there
were wonderful things for the eye to feast on. First and
foremost there was a piece of framed tapestry that was
evidently meant to be a fire-screen. To Nicholas it was a
living, breathing story; he sat down on a roll of Indian
hangings, glowing in wonderful colours beneath a layer of
dust, and took in all the details of the tapestry picture.
A man, dressed in the hunting costume of some remote
period, had just transfixed a stag with an arrow; it could
not have been a difficult shot because the stag was only
one or two paces away from him; in the thickly growing
vegetation that the picture suggested it would not have
been difficult to creep up to a feeding stag, and the two
spotted dogs that were springing forward to join in the
chase had evidently been trained to keep to heel till the
arrow was discharged. That part of the picture was simple,
if interesting, but did the huntsman see, what Nicholas
saw, that four galloping wolves were coming in his direction through the wood? There might be more than four
of them hidden behind the trees, and in any case would
the man and his dogs be able to cope with the four wolves
if they made an attack? The man had only two arrows
left in his quiver, and he might miss with one or both of
them; all one knew about his skill in shooting was that
he could hit a large stag at a ridiculously short range.
Nicholas sat for many golden minutes revolving the possibilities of the scene; he was inclined to think that there
were more than four wolves and that the man and his
dogs were in a tight corner.

But there were other objects of delight and interest
claiming his instant attention; there were quaint twisted
candlesticks in the shape of snakes, and a teapot fashioned
like a china duck, out of whose open beak the tea was sup-

posed to come. How dull and shapeless the nursery teapot seemed in comparison! And there was a carved sandal-wood box packed tight with aromatic cotton-wool, and between the layers of cotton-wool were little brass figures, hump-necked bulls, and peacocks and goblins, delightful to see and to handle. Less promising in appearance was a large square book with plain black covers; Nicholas peeped into it, and, behold, it was full of coloured pictures of birds. And such birds! In the garden, and in the lanes when he went for a walk, Nicholas came across a few birds, of which the largest were an occasional magpie or wood-pigeon; here were herons and bustards, kites, toucans, tiger-bitterns, brush turkeys, ibises, golden pheasants, a whole portrait gallery of undreamed-of creatures. And as he was admiring the colouring of the mandarin duck and assigning a life-history to it, the voice of his aunt in shrill vociferation of his name came from the gooseberry garden without. She had grown suspicious of his long disappearance, and had leapt to the conclusion that he had climbed over the wall behind the sheltering screen of the lilac bushes; she was now engaged in energetic and rather hopeless search for him among the artichokes and rasp-berry canes.

'Nicholas, Nicholas!' she screamed, 'you are to come out of this at once. It's no use trying to hide there; I can see you all the time.'

It was probably the first time for twenty years that any one had smiled in that lumber-room.

Presently the angry repetitions of Nicholas' name gave way to a shriek, and a cry for somebody to come quickly. Nicholas shut the book, restored it carefully to its place in a corner, and shook some dust from a neighbouring pile of newspapers over it. Then he crept from the room, locked the door, and replaced the key exactly where he had found it. His aunt was still calling his name when he sauntered into the front garden.

'Who's calling?' he asked.

'Me,' came the answer from the other side of the wall;

'didn't you hear me? I've been looking for you in the gooseberry garden, and I've slipped into the rain-water tank. Luckily there's no water in it, but the sides are slippery and I can't get out. Fetch the little ladder from under the cherry tree——'

'I was told I wasn't to go into the gooseberry garden,' said Nicholas promptly.

'I told you not to, and now I tell you that you may,' came the voice from the rain-water tank, rather impatiently.

'Your voice doesn't sound like aunt's,' objected Nicholas; 'you may be the Evil One tempting me to be disobedient. Aunt often tells me that the Evil One tempts me and that I always yield. This time I'm not going to yield.'

'Don't talk nonsense,' said the prisoner in the tank; 'go and fetch the ladder.'

'Will there be strawberry jam for tea?' asked Nicholas innocently.

'Certainly there will be,' said the aunt, privately resolving that Nicholas should have none of it.

'Now I know that you are the Evil One and not aunt,' shouted Nicholas gleefully; 'when we asked aunt for strawberry jam yesterday she said there wasn't any. I know there are four jars of it in the store cupboard, because I looked, and of course you know it's there, but *she* doesn't, because she said there wasn't any. Oh, Devil, you *have* sold yourself!'

There was an unusual sense of luxury in being able to talk to an aunt as though one was talking to the Evil One, but Nicholas knew, with childish discernment, that such luxuries were not to be over-indulged in. He walked noisily away, and it was a kitchenmaid, in search of parsley, who eventually rescued the aunt from the rain-water tank.

Tea that evening was partaken of in a fearsome silence. The tide had been at its highest when the children had arrived at Jagborough Cove, so there had been no sands to play on—a circumstance that the aunt had overlooked in the haste of organizing her punitive expedition. The tightness of Bobby's boots had had disastrous effect on his temper the whole of the afternoon, and altogether the children could not have been said to have enjoyed themselves. The aunt maintained the frozen muteness of one who has suffered undignified and unmerited detention in a rain-water tank for thirty-five minutes. As for Nicholas, he, too, was silent, in the absorption of one who has much to think about; it was just possible, he considered, that the huntsman would escape with his hounds while the wolves feasted on the stricken stag.

FUR

'YOU LOOK worried, dear,' said Eleanor.

'I am worried,' admitted Suzanne; 'not worried exactly, but anxious. You see, my birthday happens next week——'

'You lucky person,' interrupted Eleanor; 'my birthday doesn't come till the end of March.'

'Well, old Bertram Kneyght is over in England just now from the Argentine. He's a kind of distant cousin of my mother's and so enormously rich that we've never let the relationship drop out of sight. Even if we don't see him or hear from him for years he is always Cousin Bertram when he does turn up. I can't say he's ever been of much solid use to us, but yesterday the subject of my birthday cropped up, and he asked me to let him know what I wanted for a present.'

'Now, I understand the anxiety,' observed Eleanor.

'As a rule when one is confronted with a problem like that,' said Suzanne, 'all one's ideas vanish; one doesn't seem to have a desire in the world. Now it so happens that I have been very keen on a little Dresden figure that I saw somewhere in Kensington; about thirty-six shillings, quite beyond my means. I was very nearly describing the figure, and giving Bertram the address of the shop. And then it suddenly struck me that thirty-six shillings was such a ridiculously inadequate sum for a man of his immense wealth to spend on a birthday present. He could give thirty-six pounds as easily as you or I could buy a bunch of violets. I don't want to be greedy, of course, but I don't like being wasteful.'

'The question is,' said Eleanor, 'what are his ideas as to present-giving? Some of the wealthiest people have curiously cramped views on that subject. When people grow gradually rich their requirements and standard of living expand in proportion, while their present-giving instincts often remain in the undeveloped condition of their earlier days. Something showy and not-too-expensive in a shop is their only conception of the ideal gift. That is why even quite good shops have their counters and windows crowded with things worth about four shillings that look as if they might be worth seven-and-six, and are priced at ten shillings and labelled "seasonable gifts." '

'I know,' said Suzanne; 'that is why it is so risky to be vague when one is giving indications of one's wants. Now if I say to him: "I am going out to Davos this winter, so anything in the travelling line would be acceptable," he *might* give me a dressing-bag with gold-mounted fittings, but, on the other hand, he might give me Baedeker's *Switzerland*, or *Ski-ing without Tears*, or something of that sort.'

'He would be more likely to say: "She'll be going to lots of dances, a fan will be sure to be useful." '

'Yes, and I've got tons of fans, so you see where the danger and anxiety lies. Now if there is one thing more than another that I really urgently want it is furs. I simply haven't any. I'm told that Davos is full of Russians, and they are sure to wear the most lovely sables and things. To be among people who are smothered in furs when one hasn't any oneself makes one want to break most of the Commandments.'

'If it's furs that you're out for,' said Eleanor, 'you will have to superintend the choice of them in person. You can't be sure that your cousin knows the difference between silver-fox and ordinary squirrel.'

'There are some heavenly silver-fox stoles at Goliath and Mastodon's,' said Suzanne, with a sigh; 'if I could only inveigle Bertram into their building and take him for a stroll through the fur department!'

'He lives somewhere near there, doesn't he?' said Eleanor. 'Do you know what his habits are? Does he take a walk at any particular time of day?'

'He usually walks down to his club about three o'clock, if it's a fine day. That takes him right past Goliath and Mastodon's.'

'Let us two meet him accidentally at the street corner tomorrow,' said Eleanor; 'we can walk a little way with him, and with luck we ought to be able to side-track him into the shop. You can say you want to get a hair-net or something. When we're safely there I can say: "I wish you'd tell me what you want for your birthday." Then you'll have everything ready to hand—the rich cousin, the fur department, and the topic of birthday presents.'

'It's a great idea,' said Suzanne; 'you really are a brick. Come round tomorrow at twenty to three; don't be late, we must carry out our ambush to the minute.'

At a few minutes to three the next afternoon the fur-trappers walked warily towards the selected corner. In the near distance rose the colossal pile of Messrs Goliath and Mastodon's famed establishment. The afternoon was brilliantly fine, exactly the sort of weather to tempt a gentleman of advancing years into the discreet exercise of a leisurely walk.

'I say, dear, I wish you'd do something for me this evening,' said Eleanor to her companion; 'just drop in after dinner on some pretext or other, and stay on to make a fourth at bridge with Adela and the aunts. Otherwise I shall have to play, and Harry Scarisbrooke is going to come in unexpectedly about nine-fifteen, and I particularly wanted to be free to talk to him while the others are playing.'

'Sorry, my dear, no can do,' said Suzanne; 'ordinary bridge at threepence a hundred, with such dreadfully slow players as your aunts, bores me to tears. I nearly go to sleep over it.'

'But I most particularly want an opportunity to talk with Harry,' urged Eleanor, an angry glint coming into her eyes.

'Sorry, anything to oblige, but not that,' said Suzanne cheerfully; the sacrifices of friendship were beautiful in her eyes as long as she was not asked to make them.

Eleanor said nothing further on the subject, but the corners of her mouth rearranged themselves.

'There's our man!' exclaimed Suzanne suddenly; 'hurry!'

Mr Bertram Kneyght greeted his cousin and her friend with genuine heartiness, and readily accepted their invitation to explore the crowded mart that stood temptingly at their elbow. The plate-glass doors swung open and the trio plunged bravely into the jostling throng of buyers and loiterers.

'Is it always as full as this?' asked Bertram of Eleanor.

'More or less, and autumn sales are on just now,' she replied.

Suzanne, in her anxiety to pilot her cousin to the desired haven of the fur department, was usually a few paces ahead of the others, coming back to them now and then if they lingered for a moment at some attractive counter, with the nervous solicitude of a parent rook encouraging its young ones on their first flying expedition.

'It's Suzanne's birthday on Wednesday next,' confided Eleanor to Bertram Kneyght at a moment when Suzanne had left them unusually far behind; 'my birthday comes the day before, so we are both on the look-out for something to give each other.'

'Ah,' said Bertram. 'Now, perhaps you can advise me on that very point. I want to give Suzanne something, and I haven't the least idea what she wants.'

'She's rather a problem,' said Eleanor. 'She seems to have everything one can think of, lucky girl. A fan is always useful; she'll be going to a lot of dances at Davos this winter. Yes, I should think a fan would please her more than anything. After our birthdays are over we inspect each other's muster of presents, and I always feel dreadfully humble. She gets such nice things, and I never have anything worth showing. You see, none of my relations or any of the people who give me presents are at all well off, so I can't expect them to do anything more than just remember the day with some little trifle. Two years ago an uncle on my mother's side of the family, who had come into a small legacy, promised me a silver-fox stole for my birthday. I can't tell you how excited I was about it, and I pictured myself showing it off to all my friends and enemies. Then just at that moment his wife died, and, of course, poor man, he could not be expected to think of birthday presents at such a time. He has lived abroad ever since, and I never got my fur. Do you know, to this day I can scarcely look at a silver-fox pelt in a shop window or round any one's neck without feeling ready to burst into tears. I suppose if I hadn't had the prospect of getting one I shouldn't feel that way. Look, there is the fan counter, on your left; you can easily slip away in the crowd. Get her as nice a one as you can see—she is such a dear, dear girl.'

'Hullo, I thought I had lost you,' said Suzanne, making her way through an obstructive knot of shoppers. Where is Bertram?'

'I got separated from him long ago. I thought he was on ahead with you,' said Eleanor. 'We shall never find him in this crush.'

Which turned out to be a true prediction.

'All our trouble and forethought thrown away,' said Suzanne sulkily, when they had pushed their way fruitlessly through half a dozen departments.

'I can't think why you didn't grab him by the arm,' said Eleanor; 'I would have if I'd known him longer, but I'd only just been introduced. It's nearly four now, we'd better have tea.'

Some days later Suzanne rang Eleanor up on the telephone.

'Thank you very much for the photograph frame. It was just what I wanted. Very good of you. I say, do you know what that Kneyght person has given me? Just what you said he would—a wretched fan. What? Oh, yes, quite a good enough fan in its way, but still . . .'

'You must come and see what he's given me,' came in Eleanor's voice over the 'phone.

'You! Why should he give you anything?'

'Your cousin appears to be one of those rare people of wealth who take a pleasure in giving good presents,' came the reply.

'I wondered why he was so anxious to know where she lived,' snapped Suzanne to herself as she rang off.

A cloud has arisen between the friendships of the two young women; as far as Eleanor is concerned the cloud has a silver-fox lining.

THE PHILANTHROPIST
AND THE HAPPY CAT

JOCANTHA BESSBURY was in the mood to be serenely and graciously happy. Her world was a pleasant place, and it was wearing one of its pleasantest aspects. Gregory had managed to get home for a hurried lunch and a smoke afterwards in the little snuggery; the lunch had been a good one, and there was just time to do justice to the coffee and cigarettes. Both were excellent in their way, and Gregory was, in his way, an excellent husband. Jocantha rather suspected herself of making him a very charming wife, and more than suspected herself of having a first-rate dressmaker.

'I don't suppose a more thoroughly contented personality is to be found in all Chelsea,' observed Jocantha in allusion to herself; 'except perhaps Attab,' she continued, glancing towards the large tabby-marked cat that lay in considerable ease in a corner of the divan. 'He lies there, purring and dreaming, shifting his limbs now and then in an ecstasy of cushioned comfort. He seems the incarnation of everything soft and silky and velvety, without a sharp edge in his composition, a dreamer whose philosophy is sleep and let sleep; and then, as evening draws on, he goes out into the garden with a red glint in his eyes and slays a drowsy sparrow.'

'As every pair of sparrows hatches out ten or more young ones in the year, while their food supply remains stationary, it is just as well that the Attabs of the community should have that idea of how to pass an amusing afternoon,' said Gregory. Having delivered himself of this sage comment he lit another cigarette, bade Jocantha a playfully affectionate good-bye, and departed into the outer world.

'Remember, dinner's a wee bit earlier tonight, as we're going to the Haymarket,' she called after him.

Left to herself, Jocantha continued the process of looking at her life with placid, introspective eyes. If she had not everything she wanted in this world, at least she was very well pleased with what she had got. She was very well pleased, for instance, with the snuggery, which contrived somehow to be cosy and dainty and expensive all at once. The porcelain was rare and beautiful, the Chinese enamels took on wonderful tints in the firelight, the rugs and hangings led the eye through sumptuous harmonies of colouring. It was a room in which one might have suitably entertained an ambassador or an archbishop, but it was also a room in which one could cut out pictures for a scrap-book without feeling that one was scandalizing the deities of the place with one's litter. And as with the snuggery, so with the rest of the house, and as with the house, so with the other departments of Jocantha's life;

she really had good reason for being one of the most contented women in Chelsea.

From being in a mood of simmering satisfaction with her lot she passed to the phase of being generously commiserating for those thousands around her whose lives and circumstances were dull, cheap, pleasureless, and empty. Work girls, shop assistants and so forth, the class that have neither the happy-go-lucky freedom of the poor nor the leisured freedom of the rich, came specially within the range of her sympathy. It was sad to think that there were young people who, after a long day's work, had to sit alone in chill, dreary bedrooms because they could not afford the price of a cup of coffee and a sandwich in a restaurant, still less a shilling for a theatre gallery.

Jocantha's mind was still dwelling on this theme when she started forth on an afternoon campaign of desultory shopping; it would be rather a comforting thing, she told herself, if she could do something, on the spur of the moment, to bring a gleam of pleasure and interest into the life of even one or two wistful-hearted, empty-pocketed workers; it would add a good deal to her sense of enjoyment at the theatre that night. She would get two upper circle tickets for a popular play, make her way into some cheap tea-shop, and present the tickets to the first couple of interesting work girls with whom she could casually drop into conversation. She could explain matters by saying that she was unable to use the tickets herself and did not want them to be wasted, and, on the other hand, did not want the trouble of sending them back. On further reflection she decided that it might be better to get only one ticket and give it to some lonely-looking girl sitting eating her frugal meal by herself; the girl might scrape acquaintance with her next-seat neighbour at the theatre and lay the foundations of a lasting friendship.

With the Fairy Godmother impulse strong upon her, Jocantha marched into a ticket agency and selected with immense care an upper circle seat for the 'Yellow Peacock,' a play that was attracting a considerable amount of discus-

sion and criticism. Then she went forth in search of a
tea-shop and philanthropic adventure, at about the same
time that Attab sauntered into the garden with a mind
attuned to sparrow stalking. In a corner of an A.B.C.
shop she found an unoccupied table, whereat she promptly
installed herself, impelled by the fact that at the next table
was sitting a young girl, rather plain of feature, with tired,
listless eyes and a general air of uncomplaining forlornness.
Her dress was of poor material, but aimed at being in the
fashion, her hair was pretty, and her complexion bad; she
was finishing a modest meal of tea and scone, and she was
not very different in her way from thousands of other girls
who were finishing, or beginning, or continuing their teas
in London tea-shops at that exact moment. The odds
were enormously in favour of the supposition that she had
never seen the 'Yellow Peacock'; obviously she supplied
excellent material for Jocantha's first experiment in haphazard benefaction.

Jocantha ordered some tea and a muffin, and then turned
a friendly scrutiny on her neighbour with a view to catching her eye. At that precise moment the girl's face lit up
with sudden pleasure, her eyes sparkled, a flush came into
her cheeks, and she looked almost pretty. A young man,
whom she greeted with an affectionate 'Hullo, Bertie' came
up to her table and took his seat in a chair facing her.
Jocantha looked hard at the new-comer; he was in appearance a few years younger than herself, very much better-
looking than Gregory, rather better-looking, in fact, than
any of the young men of her set. She guessed him to be
a well-mannered young clerk in some wholesale warehouse,
existing and amusing himself as best he might on a tiny
salary, and commanding a holiday of about two weeks
in the year. He was aware, of course, of his good looks, but
with the shy self-consciousness of the Anglo-Saxon, not the
blatant complacency of the Latin or Semite. He was
obviously on terms of friendly intimacy with the girl he
was talking to, probably they were drifting towards a
formal engagement. Jocantha pictured the boy's home, in a

rather narrow circle, with a tiresome mother who always wanted to know how and where he spent his evenings. He would exchange that humdrum thraldom in due course for a home of his own, dominated by a chronic scarcity of pounds, shillings, and pence, and a dearth of most of the things that made life attractive or comfortable. Jocantha felt extremely sorry for him. She wondered if he had seen the 'Yellow Peacock'; the odds were enormously in favour of the supposition that he had not. The girl had finished her tea, and would shortly be going back to her work; when the boy was alone it would be quite easy for Jocantha to say: 'My husband has made other arrangements for me this evening; would you care to make use of this ticket, which would otherwise be wasted?' Then she could come there again one afternoon for tea, and, if she saw him, ask him how he liked the play. If he was a nice boy and improved on acquaintance he could be given more theatre tickets and perhaps asked to come one Sunday to tea at Chelsea. Jocantha made up her mind that he would improve on acquaintance, and that Gregory would like him, and that the Fairy Godmother business would prove far more entertaining than she had originally anticipated. The boy was distinctly presentable; he knew how to brush his hair, which was possibly an imitative faculty; he knew what colour of tie suited him, which might be intuition; he was exactly the type that Jocantha admired, which of course was accident. Altogether she was rather pleased when the girl looked at the clock and bade a friendly but unhurried farewell to her companion. Bertie nodded 'good-bye,' gulped down a mouthful of tea, and then produced from his overcoat pocket a paper-covered book, bearing the title *Sepoy and Sahib, a Tale of the Great Mutiny*.

The laws of tea-shop etiquette forbid that you should offer theatre tickets to a stranger without having first caught the stranger's eye. It is even better if you can ask to have a sugar basin passed to you, having previously concealed the fact that you have a large and well-filled sugar basin on your own table; this is not difficult to manage, as the printed menu is generally nearly as large as the table, and can be made to stand on end. Jocantha set to work hopefully; she had a long and rather high-pitched discussion with the waitress concerning alleged defects in an altogether blameless muffin, she made loud and plaintive inquiries about the tube service to some impossibly remote suburb, she talked with brilliant insincerity to the tea-shop kitten, and as a last resort she upset a milk-jug and swore at it daintily. Altogether she attracted a good deal of attention, but never for a moment did she attract the attention of the boy with the beautifully brushed hair, who was some thousands of miles away in the baking plains of Hindostan, amid deserted bungalows, seething bazaars, and riotous barrack squares, listening to the throbbing of tom-toms and the distant rattle of musketry.

Jocantha went back to her house in Chelsea, which struck her for the first time as looking dull and over-furnished. She had a resentful conviction that Gregory would be uninteresting at dinner, and that the play would be stupid after dinner. On the whole her frame of mind showed a marked divergence from the purring complacency of Attab, who was again curled up in his corner of the divan with a great peace radiating from every curve of his body.

But then he had killed his sparrow.

From

THE TOYS
OF PEACE
[1919]

QUAIL SEED

'THE OUTLOOK is not encouraging for us smaller businesses,' said Mr Scarrick to the artist and his sister, who had taken rooms over his suburban grocery store. 'These big concerns are offering all sorts of attractions to the shopping public which we couldn't afford to imitate, even on a small scale—reading-rooms and play-rooms and gramophones and Heaven knows what. People don't care to buy half a pound of sugar nowadays unless they can listen to Harry Lauder and have the latest Australian cricket scores ticked off before their eyes. With the big Christmas stock we've got in we ought to keep half a dozen assistants hard at work, but as it is my nephew Jimmy and myself can pretty well attend to it ourselves. It's a nice stock of goods, too, if I could only run it off in a few weeks' time, but there's no chance of that—not unless the London line was to get snowed up for a fortnight before Christmas. I did have a sort of idea of engaging Miss Luffcombe to give recitations during afternoons; she made a great hit at the Post Office entertainments with her rendering of "Little Beatrice's Resolve." '

'Anything less likely to make your shop a fashionable shopping centre I can't imagine,' said the artist, with a very genuine shudder; 'if I were trying to decide between the merits of Carlsbad plums and confected figs as a winter dessert it would infuriate me to have my train of thought entangled with little Beatrice's resolve to be an Angel of Light or a girl scout. No,' he continued, 'the desire to get something thrown in for nothing is a ruling passion with the feminine shopper, but you can't afford to pander effectively to it. Why not appeal to another instinct, which dominates not only the woman shopper but the male shopper—in fact, the entire human race?'

'What is that instinct, sir?' said the grocer.

. . .

Mrs Greyes and Miss Fritten had missed the 2.18 to Town, and as there was not another train till 3.12 they thought that they might as well make their grocery purchases at Scarrick's. It would not be sensational, they agreed, but it would still be shopping.

For some minutes they had the shop almost to themselves, as far as customers were concerned, but while they were debating the respective virtues and blemishes of two competing brands of anchovy paste they were startled by an order, given across the counter, for six pomegranates and a packet of quail seed. Neither commodity was in general demand in that neighbourhood. Equally unusual was the style and appearance of the customer; about sixteen years old, with dark olive skin, large dusky eyes, and thick, low-growing, blue-black hair, he might have made his living as an artist's model. As a matter of fact he did. The bowl of beaten brass that he produced for the reception of his purchases was distinctly the most astonishing variation on the string bag or marketing basket of suburban civilization that his fellow-shoppers had ever seen. He threw a gold piece, apparently of some exotic currency, across the counter, and did not seem disposed to wait for any change that might be forthcoming.

'The wine and figs were not paid for yesterday,' he said; 'keep what is over of the money for our future purchases.'

'A very strange-looking boy?' said Mrs Greyes interrogatively to the grocer as soon as his customer had left.

'A foreigner, I believe,' said Mr Scarrick, with a shortness that was entirely out of keeping with his usually communicative manner.

'I wish for a pound and a half of the best coffee you have,' said an authoritative voice a moment or two later. The speaker was a tall, authoritative-looking man of rather outlandish aspect, remarkable among other things for a full black beard, worn in a style more in vogue in early Assyria than in a London suburb of the present day.

'Has a dark-faced boy been here buying pomegranates?'

he asked suddenly, as the coffee was being weighed out to him.

The two ladies almost jumped on hearing the grocer reply with an unblushing negative.

'We have a few pomegranates in stock,' he continued, 'but there has been no demand for them.'

'My servant will fetch the coffee as usual,' said the purchaser, producing a coin from a wonderful metal-work purse. As an apparent afterthought he fired out the question: 'Have you, perhaps, any quail seed?'

'No,' said the grocer, without hesitation, 'we don't stock it.'

'What will he deny next?' asked Mrs Greyes under her breath. What made it seem so much worse was the fact that Mr Scarrick had quite recently presided at a lecture on Savonarola.

Turning up the deep astrakhan collar of his long coat, the stranger swept out of the shop, with the air, as Miss Fritten afterwards described it, of a Satrap proroguing a Sanhedrin. Whether such a pleasant function ever fell to a Satrap's lot she was not quite certain, but the simile faithfully conveyed her meaning to a large circle of acquaintances.

'Don't let's bother about the 3.12,' said Mrs Greyes; 'let's go and talk this over at Laura Lipping's. It's her day.'

When the dark-faced boy arrived at the shop next day with his brass marketing bowl there was quite a fair gathering of customers, most of whom seemed to be spinning out their purchasing operations with the air of people who had very little to do with their time. In a voice that was heard all over the shop, perhaps because everybody was intently listening, he asked for a pound of honey and a packet of quail seed.

'More quail seed!' said Miss Fritten. 'Those quails must be voracious, or else it isn't quail seed at all.'

'I believe it's opium, and the bearded man is a detective,' said Mrs Greyes brilliantly.

'I don't,' said Laura Lipping; 'I'm sure it's something to do with the Portuguese Throne.'

'More likely to be a Persian intrigue on behalf of the ex-Shah,' said Miss Fritten; 'the bearded man belongs to the Government Party. The quail seed is a countersign, of course; Persia is almost next door to Palestine, and quails come into the Old Testament, you know.'

'Only as a miracle,' said her well-informed younger sister; 'I've thought all along it was part of a love intrigue.'

The boy who had so much interest and speculation centred on him was on the point of departing with his purchases when he .was waylaid by Jimmy, the nephew-apprentice, who, from his post at the cheese and bacon counter, commanded a good view of the street.

'We have some very fine Jaffa oranges,' he said hurriedly, pointing to a corner where they were stored, behind a high rampart of biscuit tins. There was evidently more in the remark than met the ear. The boy flew at the oranges with the enthusiasm of a ferret finding a rabbit family at home after a long day of fruitless subterranean research. Almost at the same moment the bearded stranger stalked into the shop, and flung an order for a pound of dates and a tin of the best Smyrna halva across the counter. The most adventurous housewife in the locality had never heard of halva, but Mr Scarrick was apparently able to produce the best Smyrna variety of it without a moment's hesitation.

'We might be living in the Arabian Nights,' said Miss Fritten excitedly.

'Hush! Listen,' beseeched Mrs Greyes.

'Has the dark-faced boy, of whom I spoke yesterday, been here today?' asked the stranger.

'We've had rather more people than usual in the shop today,' said Mr Scarrick, 'but I can't recall a boy such as you describe.'

Mrs Greyes and Miss Fritten looked round triumphantly at their friends. It was, of course, deplorable that any one should treat the truth as an article temporarily and excusably out of stock, but they felt gratified that the vivid accounts they had given of Mr Scarrick's traffic in falsehoods should receive confirmation at first hand.

'I shall never again be able to believe what he tells me about the absence of colouring matter in the jam,' whispered an aunt of Mrs Greyes tragically.

The mysterious stranger took his departure; Laura Lipping distinctly saw a snarl of baffled rage reveal itself behind his heavy moustache and upturned astrakhan collar. After a cautious interval the seeker after oranges emerged from behind the biscuit tins, having apparently failed to find any individual orange that satisfied his requirements. He, too, took his departure, and the shop was slowly emptied of its parcel- and gossip-laden customers. It was Emily Yorling's 'day,' and most of the shoppers made their way to her drawing-room. To go direct from a shopping expedition to a tea-party was what was known locally as 'living in a whirl.'

Two extra assistants had been engaged for the following afternoon, and their services were in brisk demand; the shop was crowded. People bought and bought, and never seemed to get to the end of their lists. Mr Scarrick had never had so little difficulty in persuading customers to embark on new experiences in grocery wares. Even those women whose purchases were of modest proportions dawdled over them as though they had brutal drunken husbands to go home to. The afternoon had dragged uneventfully on, and there was a distinct buzz of unpent excitement when a dark-eyed boy carrying a brass bowl entered the shop. The excitement seemed to have communicated itself to Mr Scarrick; abruptly deserting a lady who was making insincere inquiries about the home life of the Bombay duck, he intercepted the new-comer on his way to the accustomed counter and informed him, amid a deathlike hush, that he had run out of quail seed.

The boy looked nervously round the shop, and turned hesitatingly to go. He was again intercepted, this time by the nephew, who darted out from behind his counter and said something about a better line of oranges. The boy's hesitation vanished; he almost scuttled into the obscurity of the orange corner. There was an expectant turn of public attention towards the door, and the tall bearded stranger made a really effective entrance. The aunt of Mrs Greyes declared afterwards that she found herself subconsciously repeating 'The Assyrian came down like a wolf on the fold' under her breath, and she was generally believed.

The new-comer, too, was stopped before he reached the counter, but not by Mr Scarrick or his assistant. A heavily veiled lady, whom no one had hitherto noticed, rose languidly from a seat and greeted him in a clear, penetrating voice.

'Your Excellency does his shopping himself?' she said.

'I order the things myself,' he explained; 'I find it difficult to make my servants understand.'

In a lower, but still perfectly audible, voice the veiled lady gave him a piece of casual information.

'They have some excellent Jaffa oranges here.' Then with a tingling laugh she passed out of the shop.

The man glared all round the shop, and then, fixing his eyes instinctively on the barrier of biscuit tins, demanded loudly of the grocer: 'You have, perhaps, some good Jaffa oranges?'

Every one expected an instant denial on the part of Mr Scarrick of any such possession. Before he could answer, however, the boy had broken forth from his sanctuary. Holding his empty brass bowl before him he passed out into the street. His face was variously described afterwards as masked with studied indifference, overspread with ghastly pallor, and blazing with defiance. Some said that his teeth chattered, others that he went out whistling the Persian National Hymn. There was no mistaking, however, the effect produced by the encounter on the man who had seemed to force it. If a rabid dog or a rattlesnake had suddenly thrust its companionship on him he could scarcely have displayed a greater access of terror. His air of

authority and assertiveness had gone, his masterful stride
had given way to a furtive pacing to and fro, as of an
animal seeking an outlet for escape. In a dazed perfunctory
manner, always with his eyes turning to watch the shop
entrance, he gave a few random orders, which the grocer
made a show of entering in his book. Now and then he
walked out into the street, looked anxiously in all directions, and hurried back to keep up his pretence of shopping. From one of these sorties he did not return; he had
dashed away into the dusk, and neither he nor the dark-
faced boy nor the veiled lady were seen again by the
expectant crowds that continued to throng the Scarrick
establishment for days to come.

'I can never thank you and your sister sufficiently,' said
the grocer.
'We enjoyed the fun of it,' said the artist modestly, 'and
as for the model, it was a welcome variation on posing for
hours for 'The Lost Hylas.'
'At any rate,' said the grocer, 'I insist on paying for the
hire of the black beard.'

EXCEPTING MRS PENTHERBY

IT WAS Reggie Bruttle's own idea for converting what had
threatened to be an albino elephant into a beast of burden
that should help him along the stony road of his finances.
'The Limes,' which had come to him by inheritance without any accompanying provision for its upkeep, was one
of those pretentious, unaccommodating mansions which
none but a man of wealth could afford to live in, and which
not one wealthy man in a hundred would choose on its
merits. It might easily languish in the estate market for

years, set round with notice-boards proclaiming it, in the eyes of a sceptical world, to be an eminently desirable residence.

Reggie's scheme was to turn it into the headquarters of a prolonged country-house party, in session during the months from October till the end of March—a party consisting of young or youngish people of both sexes, too poor to be able to do much hunting or shooting on a serious scale, but keen on getting their fill of golf, bridge, dancing, and occasional theatre-going. No one was to be on the footing of a paying guest, but every one was to rank as a paying host; a committee would look after the catering and expenditure, and an informal sub-committee would make itself useful in helping forward the amusement side of the scheme.

As it was only an experiment, there was to be a general agreement on the part of those involved in it to be as lenient and mutually helpful to one another as possible. Already a promising nucleus, including one or two young married couples, had been got together, and the thing seemed to be fairly launched.

'With good management and a little unobtrusive hard work, I think the thing ought to be a success,' said Reggie, and Reggie was one of those people who are painstaking first and optimistic afterwards.

'There is one rock on which you will unfailingly come to grief, manage you never so wisely,' said Major Dagberry cheerfully: 'the women will quarrel. Mind you,' continued this prophet of disaster, 'I don't say that some of the men won't quarrel too, probably they will; but the women are bound to. You can't prevent it; it's in the nature of the sex. The hand that rocks the cradle rocks the world, in a volcanic sense. A woman will endure discomforts, and make sacrifices, and go without things to an heroic extent, but the one luxury she will not go without is her quarrels. No matter where she may be, or how transient her appearance on a scene, she will install her feminine feuds as assuredly as a Frenchman would concoct

soup in the waste of the Arctic regions. At the commencement of a sea voyage, before the male traveller knows half
a dozen of his fellow-passengers by sight, the average
woman will have started a couple of enmities, and laid in
material for one or two more—provided, of course, that
there are sufficient women aboard to permit quarrelling in
the plural. If there's no one else she will quarrel with the
stewardess. This experiment of yours is to run for six
months; in less than five weeks there will be war to the
knife declaring itself in half a dozen different directions.'

'Oh, come, there are only eight women in the party; they
won't all pick quarrels quite as soon as that,' protested
Reggie.

'They won't all originate quarrels, perhaps,' conceded
the Major, 'but they will all take sides, and just as
Christmas is upon you, with its conventions of peace and
good will, you will find yourself in for a glacial epoch
of cold, unforgiving hostility, with an occasional Etna
flare of open warfare. You can't help it, old boy; but, at
any rate, you can't say you were not warned.'

The first five weeks of the venture falsified Major Dagberry's prediction and justified Reggie's optimism. There
were, of course, occasional small bickerings, and the existence of certain jealousies might be detected below the
surface of everyday intercourse; but, on the whole, the
womenfolk got on remarkably well together. There was,
however, a notable exception. It had not taken five weeks
for Mrs Pentherby to get herself cordially disliked by the
members of her own sex; five days had been amply sufficient. Most of the women declared that they had detested
her the moment they set eyes on her; but that was probably
an afterthought.

With the menfolk she got on well enough, without being
of the type of woman who can only bask in male society;
neither was she lacking in the general qualities which make
an individual useful and desirable as a member of a co-
operative community. She did not try to 'get the better of'
her fellow-hosts by snatching little advantages or cleverly

evading her just contributions; she was not inclined to be boring or snobbish in the way of personal reminiscence. She played a fair game of bridge, and her card-room manners were irreproachable. But wherever she came in contact with her own sex the light of battle kindled at once; her talent for arousing animosity seemed to border on positive genius.

Whether the object of her attentions was thick-skinned or sensitive, quick-tempered or good-natured, Mrs. Pentherby managed to achieve the same effect. She exposed little weaknesses, she prodded sore places, she snubbed enthusiasms, she was generally right in a matter of argument, or, if wrong, she somehow contrived to make her adversary appear foolish and opinionated. She did, and said, horrible things in a matter-of-fact innocent way, and she did, and said, matter-of-fact innocent things in a horrible way. In short, the unanimous feminine verdict on her was that she was objectionable.

There was no question of taking sides, as the Major had anticipated; in fact, dislike of Mrs Pentherby was almost a bond of union between the other women, and more than one threatening disagreement had been rapidly dissipated by her obvious and malicious attempts to inflame and extend it; and the most irritating thing about her was her successful assumption of unruffled composure at moments when the tempers of her adversaries were with difficulty kept under control. She made her most scathing remarks in the tone of a tube conductor announcing that the next station is Brompton Road—the measured, listless tone of one who knows he is right, but is utterly indifferent to the fact that he proclaims.

On one occasion Mrs Val Gwepton, who was not blessed with the most reposeful of temperaments, fairly let herself go, and gave Mrs Pentherby a vivid and truthful *résumé* of her opinion of her. The object of this unpent storm of accumulated animosity waited patiently for a lull, and then remarked quietly to the angry little woman—

'And now, my dear Mrs Gwepton, let me tell you

something that I've been wanting to say for the last two or three minutes, only you wouldn't give me a chance; you've got a hairpin dropping out on the left side. You thin-haired women always find it difficult to keep your hairpins in.'

'What can one do with a woman like that?' Mrs Val demanded afterwards of a sympathizing audience.

Of course, Reggie received numerous hints as to the unpopularity of this jarring personality. His sister-in-law openly tackled him on the subject of her many enormities. Reggie listened with the attenuated regret that one bestows on an earthquake disaster in Bolivia or a crop failure in Eastern Turkestan, events which seem so distant that one can almost persuade oneself they haven't happened.

'That woman has got some hold over him,' opined his sister-in-law darkly; 'either she is helping him to finance the show, and presumes on the fact, or else, which Heaven forbid, he's got some queer infatuation for her. Men do take the most extraordinary fancies.'

Matters never came exactly to a crisis. Mrs Pentherby, as a source of personal offence, spread herself over so wide an area that no one woman of the party felt impelled to rise up and declare that she absolutely refused to stay another week in the same house with her. What is everybody's tragedy is nobody's tragedy. There was even a certain consolation in comparing notes as to specific acts of offence. Reggie's sister-in-law had the added interest of trying to discover the secret bond which blunted his condemnation of Mrs Pentherby's long catalogue of misdeeds. There was little to go on from his manner towards her in public, but he remained obstinately unimpressed by anything that was said against her in private.

With the one exception of Mrs Pentherby's unpopularity, the house-party scheme was a success on its first trial, and there was no difficulty about reconstructing it on the same lines for another winter session. It so happened that most of the women of the party, and two or three of the men, would not be available on this occasion, but Reggie had laid his plans well ahead and booked plenty of 'fresh blood' for the new departure. It would be, if anything, rather a larger party than before.

'I'm so sorry I can't join this winter,' said Reggie's sister-in-law, 'but we must go to our cousins in Ireland; we've put them off so often. What a shame! You'll have none of the same women this time.'

'Excepting Mrs Pentherby,' said Reggie demurely.

'Mrs Pentherby! *Surely*, Reggie, you're not going to be so idiotic as to have that woman again! She'll set all the women's backs up just as she did this time. What *is* this mysterious hold she's got over you?'

'She's invaluable,' said Reggie; 'she's my official quarreller.'

'Your—what did you say?' gasped his sister-in-law.

'I introduced her into the house-party for the express purpose of concentrating the feuds and quarrelling that would otherwise have broken out in all directions among the womenkind. I didn't need the advice and warning of sundry friends to foresee that we shouldn't get through six months of close companionship without a certain amount of pecking and sparring, so I thought the best thing was to localize and sterilize it in one process. Of course, I made it well worth the lady's while, and as she didn't know any of you from Adam, and you don't even know her real name, she didn't mind getting herself disliked in a useful cause.'

'You mean to say she was in the know all the time?'

'Of course she was, and so were one or two of the men, so she was able to have a good laugh with us behind the scenes when she'd done anything particularly outrageous. And she really enjoyed herself. You see, she's in the position of poor relation in a rather pugnacious family, and her life has been largely spent in smoothing over other people's quarrels. You can imagine the welcome relief of being able to go about saying and doing perfectly exasperating things to a whole houseful of women—and all in the cause of peace.'

'I think you are the most odious person in the whole world,' said Reggie's sister-in-law. Which was not strictly true; more than anybody, more than ever she disliked Mrs Pentherby. It was impossible to calculate how many quarrels that woman had done her out of.

THE MAPPINED LIFE

'THESE Mappin Terraces at the Zoological Gardens are a great improvement on the old style of wild-beast cage,' said Mrs James Gurtleberry, putting down an illustrated paper; 'they give one the illusion of seeing the animals in their natural surroundings. I wonder how much of the illusion is passed on to the animals?'

'That would depend on the animal,' said her niece; 'a jungle-fowl, for instance, would no doubt think its lawful jungle surroundings were faithfully reproduced if you gave it a sufficiency of wives, a goodly variety of seed food and ants' eggs, a commodious bank of loose earth to dust itself in, a convenient roosting tree, and a rival or two to make matters interesting. Of course there ought to be jungle-cats and birds of prey and other agencies of sudden death to add to the illusion of liberty, but the bird's own imagination is capable of inventing those—look how a domestic fowl will squawk an alarm note if a rook or a wood-pigeon passes over its run when it has chickens.'

'You think, then, they really do have a sort of illusion, if you give them space enough——'

'In a few cases only. Nothing will make me believe that an acre or so of concrete enclosure will make up to a wolf or a tiger-cat for the range of night-prowling that would belong to it in a wild state. Think of the dictionary of sound and scent and recollection that unfolds before a real wild beast as it comes out from its lair every evening, with the knowledge that in a few minutes it will be hieing

along to some distant hunting ground where all the joy
and fury of the chase awaits it; think of the crowded
sensations of the brain when every rustle, every cry, every
bent twig, and every whiff across the nostrils means
something, something to do with life and death and dinner.
Imagine the satisfaction of stealing down to your own
particular drinking spot, choosing your own particular tree
to scrape your claws on, finding your own particular bed
of dried grass to roll on. Then, in the place of all that, put
a concrete promenade, which will be of exactly the same
dimensions whether you race or crawl across it, coated
with stale, unvarying scents and surrounded with cries and
noises that have ceased to have the least meaning or
interest. As a substitute for a narrow cage the new en-
closures are excellent, but I should think they are a poor
imitation of a life of liberty.'

'It's rather depressing to think that,' said Mrs Gurtleberry; 'they look so spacious and so natural, but I suppose
a good deal of what seems natural to us would be meaningless to a wild animal.'

'That is where our superior powers of self-deception
come in,' said the niece; 'we are able to live our unreal,
stupid little lives on our particular Mappin terrace, and
persuade ourselves that we really are untrammelled men
and women leading a reasonable existence in a reasonable
sphere.'

'But good gracious,' exclaimed the aunt, bouncing into
an attitude of scandalized defence, 'we are leading reasonable existences! What on earth do you mean by trammels?
We are merely trammelled by the ordinary decent conventions of civilized society.'

'We are trammelled,' said the niece, calmly and pitilessly,
'by restrictions of income and opportunity, and above all
by lack of initiative. To some people a restricted income
doesn't matter a bit, in fact it often seems to help as a
means for getting a lot of reality out of life; I am sure
there are men and women who do their shopping in little
back streets of Paris, buying four carrots and a shred of

beef for their daily sustenance, who lead a perfectly real and eventful existence. Lack of initiative is the thing that really cripples one, and that is where you and I and Uncle James are so hopelessly shut in. We are just so many animals stuck down on a Mappin terrace, with this difference in our disfavour, that the animals are there to be looked at, while nobody wants to look at us. As a matter of fact there would be nothing to look at. We get colds in winter and hay-fever in summer, and if a wasp happens to sting one of us, well, that is the wasp's initiative, not ours; all we do is to wait for the swelling to go down. Whenever we do climb into local fame and notice, it is by indirect methods; if it happens to be a good flowering year for magnolias the neighbourhood observes, "Have you seen the Gurtleberrys' magnolia? It is a perfect mass of flowers"; and we go about telling people that there are fifty-seven blossoms as against thirty-nine the previous year.'

'In Coronation year there were as many as sixty,' put in the aunt; 'your uncle has kept a record for the last eight years.'

'Doesn't it ever strike you,' continued the niece relentlessly, 'that if we moved away from here or were blotted out of existence our local claim to fame would pass on automatically to whoever happened to take the house and garden? People would say to one another, "Have you seen the Smith-Jenkinses' magnolia? It is a perfect mass of flowers," or else, "Smith-Jenkins tells me there won't be a single blossom on their magnolia this year; the east winds have turned all the buds black." Now if, when we had gone, people still associated our names with the magnolia tree, no matter who temporarily possessed it, if they said, "Ah, that's the tree on which the Gurtleberrys hung their cook because she sent up the wrong kind of sauce with the asparagus," that would be something really due to our own initiative, apart from anything east winds or magnolia vitality might have to say in the matter.'

'We should never do such a thing,' said the aunt. The niece gave a reluctant sigh.

'I can't imagine it,' she admitted. 'Of course,' she continued, 'there are heaps of ways of leading a real existence without committing sensational deeds of violence. It's the dreadful little everyday acts of pretended importance that give the Mappin stamp to our life. It would be entertaining, if it wasn't so pathetically tragic, to hear Uncle James fuss in here in the morning and announce, "I must just go down into the town and find out what the men there are saying about Mexico. Matters are beginning to look serious there." Then he patters away into the town, and talks in a highly serious voice to the tobacconist, incidentally buying an ounce of tobacco; perhaps he meets one or two others of the world's thinkers and talks to them in a highly serious voice, then he patters back here and announces with increased importance, "I've just been talking to some men in the town about the condition of affairs in Mexico. They agree with the view that I have formed, that things there will have to get worse before they get better." Of course nobody in the town cared in the least little bit what his views about Mexico were or whether he had any. The tobacconist wasn't even fluttered at his buying the ounce of tobacco; he knows that he purchases the same quantity of the same sort of tobacco every week. Uncle James might just as well have lain on his back in the garden and chattered to the lilac tree about the habits of caterpillars.'

'I really will not listen to such things about your uncle,' protested Mrs James Gurtleberry angrily.

'My own case is just as bad and just as tragic,' said the niece dispassionately; 'nearly everything about me is conventional make-believe. I'm not a good dancer, and no one could honestly call me good-looking, but when I go to one of our dull little local dances I'm conventionally supposed to "have a heavenly time," to attract the ardent homage of the local cavaliers, and to go home with my head awhirl with pleasurable recollections. As a matter of fact, I've merely put in some hours of indifferent dancing, drunk some badly made claret cup, and listened to an enormous amount of laborious light conversation. A moon-light hen-stealing raid with the merry-eyed curate would be infinitely more exciting; imagine the pleasure of carrying off all those white Minorcas that the Chibfords are always bragging about. When we had disposed of them we could give the proceeds to a charity, so there would be nothing really wrong about it. But nothing of that sort lies within the Mappined limits of my life. One of these days some-body dull and decorous and undistinguished will "make himself agreeable" to me at a tennis party, as the saying is, and all the dull old gossips of the neighbourhood will begin to ask when we are to be engaged, and at last we shall be engaged, and people will give us butter-dishes and blotting-cases and framed pictures of young women feeding swans. Hullo, Uncle, are you going out?'

'I'm just going down to the town,' announced Mr James Gurtleberry, with an air of some importance: 'I want to hear what people are saying about Albania. Affairs there are beginning to take on a serious look. It's my opinion that we haven't seen the worst of things yet.'

In this he was probably right, but there was nothing in the immediate or prospective condition of Albania to warrant Mrs Gurtleberry in bursting into tears.

THE BULL

TOM YORKFIELD had always regarded his half-brother, Laurence, with a lazy instinct of dislike, toned down, as years went on, to a tolerant feeling of indifference. There was nothing very tangible to dislike him for; he was just a blood-relation, with whom Tom had no single taste or interest in common, and with whom, at the same time, he had had no occasion for quarrel. Laurence had left the farm early in life, and had lived for a few years on a small sum of money left him by his mother; he had taken up painting as a profession, and was reported to be doing fairly well at it, well enough, at any rate, to keep body and soul together. He specialized in painting animals, and he was successful in finding a certain number of people to buy his pictures. Tom felt a comforting sense of assured superiority in contrasting his position with that of his half-brother; Laurence was an artist-chap, just that and nothing more, though you might make it sound more important by calling him an animal painter; Tom was a farmer, not in a very big way, it was true, but the Helsery farm had been in the family for some generations, and it had a good reputation for the stock raised on it. Tom had done his best, with the little capital at his command, to maintain and improve the standard of his small herd of cattle, and in Clover Fairy he had bred a bull which was something rather better than any that his immediate neighbours could show. It would not have made a sensation in the judging-ring at an important cattle show, but it was as vigorous, shapely and healthy a young animal as any small practical farmer could wish to possess. At the King's Head on market days Clover Fairy was very highly spoken of, and Yorkfield used to declare that he would not part with him for a hundred pounds; a hundred pounds is a lot of money in the small farming line, and probably anything over eighty would have tempted him.

It was with some especial pleasure that Tom took advantage of one of Laurence's rare visits to the farm to lead him down to the enclosure where Clover Fairy kept solitary state—the grass widower of a grazing harem. Tom felt some of his old dislike for his half-brother reviving; the artist was becoming more languid in his manner, more unsuitably turned-out in attire, and he seemed inclined to impart a slightly patronizing tone to his conversation. He took no heed of a flourishing potato crop, but waxed enthusiastic over a clump of yellow-flowering weed that stood in a corner by a gateway, which was rather galling to the owner of a really very well weeded farm; again, when he might have been duly complimentary about a

group of fat, black-faced lambs, that simply cried aloud
for admiration, he became eloquent over the foliage tints
of an oak copse on the hill opposite. But now he was being
taken to inspect the crowning pride and glory of Helsery;
however grudging he might be in his praises, however backward and niggardly with his congratulations, he would
have to see and acknowledge the many excellencies of that
redoubtable animal. Some weeks ago, while on a business
journey to Taunton, Tom had been invited by his half-
brother to visit a studio in that town, where Laurence
was exhibiting one of his pictures, a large canvas representing a bull standing knee-deep in some marshy ground; it
had been good of its kind, no doubt, and Laurence had
seemed inordinately pleased with it; 'the best thing I've
done yet,' he had said over and over again, and Tom had
generously agreed that it was fairly life-like. Now, the
man of pigments was going to be shown a real picture, a
living model of strength and comeliness, a thing to feast
the eyes on, a picture that exhibited new pose and action
with every shifting minute, instead of standing glued into
one unvarying attitude between the four walls of a frame.
Tom unfastened a stout wooden door and led the way
into a straw-bedded yard.

'Is he quiet?' asked the artist, as a young bull with a
curly red coat came inquiringly towards them.

'He's playful at times,' said Tom, leaving his half-brother
to wonder whether the bull's ideas of play were of the
catch-as-catch-can order. Laurence made one or two perfunctory comments on the animal's appearance and asked
a question or so as to his age and such-like details; then
he coolly turned the talk into another channel.

'Do you remember the picture I showed you at Taunton?' he asked.

'Yes,' grunted Tom; 'a white-faced bull standing in
some slush. Don't admire those Herefords much myself;
bulky-looking brutes, don't seem to have much life in
them. Daresay they're easier to paint that way; now, this

young beggar is on the move all the time, aren't you, Fairy?'

'I've sold that picture,' said Laurence, with considerable complacency in his voice.

'Have you?' said Tom; 'glad to hear it, I'm sure. Hope you're pleased with what you've got for it.'

'I got three hundred pounds for it,' said Laurence.

Tom turned towards him with a slowly rising flush of anger in his face. Three hundred pounds! Under the most favourable market conditions that he could imagine his prized Clover Fairy would hardly fetch a hundred, yet here was a piece of varnished canvas, painted by his half-brother, selling for three times that sum. It was a cruel insult that went home with all the more force because it emphasized the triumph of the patronizing, self-satisfied Laurence. The young farmer had meant to put his relative just a little out of conceit with himself by displaying the jewel of his possessions, and now the tables were turned, and his valued beast was made to look cheap and insignificant beside the price paid for a mere picture. It was so monstrously unjust; the painting would never be anything more than a dexterous piece of counterfeit life, while Clover Fairy was the real thing, a monarch in his little world, a personality in the countryside. After he was dead, even, he would still be something of a personality; his descendants would graze in those valley meadows and hillside pastures, they would fill stall and byre and milking-shed, their good red coats would speckle the landscape and crowd the market-place; men would note a promising heifer or a well-proportioned steer, and say: 'Ah, that one comes of good old Clover Fairy's stock.' All that time the picture would be hanging, lifeless and unchanging, beneath its dust and varnish, a chattel that ceased to mean anything if you chose to turn it with its face to the wall. These thoughts chased themselves angrily through Tom York-field's mind, but he could not put them into words. When he gave tongue to his feelings he put matters bluntly and harshly.

'Some soft-witted fools may like to throw away three hundred pounds on a bit of paintwork; can't say as I envy them their taste. I'd rather have the real thing than a picture of it.'

He nodded towards the young bull, that was alternately staring at them with nose held high and lowering his horns with a half-playful, half-impatient shake of the head.

Laurence laughed a laugh of irritating, indulgent amusement.

'I don't think the purchaser of my bit of paintwork, as you call it, need worry about having thrown his money away. As I get to be better known and recognized my pictures will go up in value. That particular one will probably fetch four hundred in a sale-room five or six years hence; pictures aren't a bad investment if you know enough to pick out the work of the right men. Now you can't say your precious bull is going to get more valuable the longer you keep him; he'll have his little day, and then, if you go on keeping him, he'll come down at last to a few shillingsworth of hoofs and hide, just at a time, perhaps, when *my* bull is being bought for a big sum for some important picture gallery.'

It was too much. The united force of truth and slander and insult put over heavy a strain on Tom Yorkfield's powers of restraint. In his right hand he held a useful oak cudgel, with his left he made a grab at the loose collar of Laurence's canary-coloured silk shirt. Laurence was not a fighting man; the fear of physical violence threw him off his balance as completely as overmastering indignation had thrown Tom off his, and thus it came to pass that Clover Fairy was regaled with the unprecedented sight of a human being scudding and squawking across the enclosure, like the hen that would persist in trying to establish a nesting-place in the manger. In another crowded happy moment the bull was trying to jerk Laurence over his left shoulder, to prod him in the ribs while still in the air, and to kneel on him when he reached the ground. It was only the

vigorous intervention of Tom that induced him to relin-
quish the last item of his programme.

Tom devotedly and ungrudgingly nursed his half-brother
to a complete recovery from his injuries, which consisted of
nothing more serious than a dislocated shoulder, a broken
rib or two, and a little nervous prostration. After all, there
was no further occasion for rancour in the young farmer's
mind; Laurence's bull might sell for three hundred, or for
six hundred, and be admired by thousands in some big picture gallery, but it would never toss a man over one shoulder
and catch him a jab in the ribs before he had fallen on the
other side. That was Clover Fairy's noteworthy achievement, which could never be taken away from him.

Laurence continues to be popular as an animal artist,
but his subjects are always kittens or fawns or lambkins—
never bulls.

MORLVERA

THE Olympic Toy Emporium occupied a conspicuous
frontage in an important West End street. It was happily
named Toy Emporium, because one would never have
dreamed of according it the familiar and yet pulse-quicken-
ing name of toyshop. There was an air of cold splendour
and elaborate failure about the wares that were set out in
its ample windows; they were the sort of toys that a tired
shop-assistant displays and explains at Christmas-time to
exclamatory parents and bored, silent children. The animal
toys looked more like natural history models than the comfortable, sympathetic companions that one would wish, at
a certain age, to take to bed with one, and to smuggle
into the bathroom. The mechanical toys incessantly did
things that no one could want a toy to do more than half
a dozen times in its lifetime; it was a merciful reflection

that in any right-minded nursery the lifetime would certainly be short.

Prominent among the elegantly dressed dolls that filled an entire section of the window frontage was a large hobble-skirted lady in a confection of peach-coloured velvet, elaborately set off with leopard-skin accessories, if one may use such a conveniently comprehensive word in describing an intricate feminine toilette. She lacked nothing that is to be found in a carefully detailed fashion-plate—in fact, she might be said to have something more than the average fashion-plate female possesses; in place of a vacant, expressionless stare she had character in her face. It must be admitted that it was bad character, cold, hostile, inquisitorial, with a sinister lowering of one eyebrow and a merciless hardness about the corners of the mouth. One might have imagined histories about her by the hour, histories in which unworthy ambition, the desire for money, and an entire absence of all decent feeling would play a conspicuous part.

As a matter of fact, she was not without her judges and biographers, even in this shop-window stage of her career. Emmeline, aged ten, and Bert, aged seven, had halted on the way from their obscure back street to the minnow-stocked water of St James's Park, and were critically examining the hobble-skirted doll, and dissecting her character in no very tolerant spirit. There is probably a latent enmity between the necessarily under-clad and the unnecessarily over-dressed, but a little kindness and good-fellowship on the part of the latter will often change the sentiment to admiring devotion; if the lady in peach-coloured velvet and leopard-skin had worn a pleasant expression in addition to her other elaborate furnishings, Emmeline at least might have respected and even loved her. As it was, she gave her a horrible reputation, based chiefly on a second-hand knowledge of gilded depravity derived from the conversation of those who were skilled in the art of novelette reading; Bert filled in a few damaging details from his own limited imagination.

'She's a bad lot, that one is,' declared Emmeline, after a long unfriendly stare; ' 'er 'usbind 'ates 'er.'

' 'E knocks 'er abart,' said Bert with enthusiasm.

'No, 'e don't, cos 'e's dead; she poisoned 'im slow and gradual, so that nobody didn't know. Now she wants to marry a lord, with 'eaps and 'eaps of money. 'E's got a wife already, but she's going to poison 'er, too.'

'She's a bad lot,' said Bert with growing hostility.

' 'Er mother 'ates her, and she's afraid of 'er, too, cos she's got a serkestic tongue; always talking serkesms, she is. She's greedy, too; if there's fish going, she eats 'er own share and 'er little girl's as well, though the little girl is dellikit.'

'She 'ad a little boy once,' said Bert, 'but she pushed 'im into the water when nobody wasn't looking.'

'No, she didn't,' said Emmeline, 'she sent 'im away to be kep' by poor people, so 'er husbind wouldn't know where 'e was. They ill-treat 'im somethink cruel.'

'Wot's 'er nime?' asked Bert, thinking that it was time that so interesting a personality should be labelled.

' 'Er nime?' said Emmeline, thinking hard, ' 'er nime's Morlvera.' It was as near as she could get to the name of an adventuress who figured prominently in a cinema drama. There was silence for a moment while the possibilities of the name were turned over in the children's minds.

'Those clothes she's got on ain't paid for, and never won't be,' said Emmeline; 'she thinks she'll get the rich lord to pay for 'em, but 'e won't. 'E's given 'er jools, 'underds of pounds' worth.'

' 'E won't pay for the clothes,' said Bert with conviction. Evidently there was some limit to the weak good nature of wealthy lords.

At that moment a motor carriage with liveried servants drew up at the emporium entrance; a large lady, with a penetrating and rather hurried manner of talking, stepped out, followed slowly and sulkily by a small boy, who had a very black scowl on his face and a very white sailor suit over the rest of him. The lady was continuing an argument which had probably commenced in Portman Square.

'Now, Victor, you are to come in and buy a nice doll for your cousin Bertha. She gave you a beautiful box of soldiers on your birthday, and you must give her a present on hers.'

'Bertha is a fat little fool,' said Victor, in a voice that was as loud as his mother's and had more assurance in it.

'Victor, you are not to say such things. Bertha is not a fool, and she is not in the least fat. You are to come in and choose a doll for her.'

The couple passed into the shop, out of view and hearing of the two back-street children.

'My, he is in a wicked temper,' exclaimed Emmeline, but both she and Bert were inclined to side with him against the absent Bertha, who was doubtless as fat and foolish as he had described her to be.

'I want to see some dolls,' said the mother of Victor to the nearest assistant; 'it's for a little girl of eleven.'

'A fat little girl of eleven,' added Victor by way of supplementary information.

'Victor, if you say such rude things about your cousin, you shall go to bed the moment we get home, without having any tea.'

'This is one of the newest things we have in dolls,' said the assistant, removing a hobble-skirted figure in peach-coloured velvet from the window; 'leopard-skin toque and stole, the latest fashion. You won't get anything newer than that anywhere. It's an exclusive design.'

'Look!' whispered Emmeline outside; 'they've bin and took Morlvera.'

There was a mingling of excitement and a certain sense of bereavement in her mind; she would have liked to gaze at that embodiment of overdressed depravity for just a little longer.

'I 'spect she's going away in a kerridge to marry the rich lord,' hazarded Bert.

'She's up to no good,' said Emmeline vaguely.

Inside the shop the purchase of the doll had been decided on.

'It's a beautiful doll, and Bertha will be delighted with it,' asserted the mother of Victor loudly.

'Oh, very well,' said Victor sulkily; 'you needn't have it stuck in a box and wait an hour while it's being done up into a parcel. I'll take it as it is, and we can go round to Manchester Square and give it to Bertha, and get the thing done with. That will save me the trouble of writing, "For dear Bertha, with Victor's love," on a bit of paper.'

'Very well,' said his mother, 'we can go to Manchester Square on our way home. You must wish her many happy returns of tomorrow, and give her the doll.'

'I won't let the little beast kiss me,' stipulated Victor.

His mother said nothing; Victor had not been half as troublesome as she had anticipated. When he chose he could really be dreadfully naughty.

Emmeline and Bert were just moving away from the window when Morlvera made her exit from the shop, very carefully held in Victor's arms. A look of sinister triumph seemed to glow in her hard, inquisitorial face. As for Victor, a certain scornful serenity had replaced the earlier scowls; he had evidently accepted defeat with a contemptuous good grace.

The tall lady gave a direction to the footman and settled herself in the carriage. The little figure in the white sailor suit clambered in beside her, still carefully holding the elegantly garbed doll.

The car had to be backed a few yards in the process of turning. Very stealthily, very gently, very mercilessly Victor sent Morlvera flying over his shoulder, so that she fell into the road just behind the retrogressing wheel. With a soft, pleasant-sounding scrunch the car went over the prostrate form, then it moved forward again with another scrunch. The carriage moved off and left Bert and Emmeline gazing in scared delight at a sorry mess of petrol-smeared velvet, sawdust, and leopard-skin, which was all that remained of the hateful Morlvera. They gave a shrill cheer, and then raced away shuddering from the scene of so much rapidly enacted tragedy.

Later that afternoon, when they were engaged in the pursuit of minnows by the waterside in St James's Park, Emmeline said in a solemn undertone to Bert——

'I've bin finking. Do you know oo 'e was? 'E was 'er little boy wot she'd sent away to live wiv poor folks. 'E come back and done that.'

THE CUPBOARD
OF THE YESTERDAYS

'WAR IS a cruelly destructive thing' said the Wanderer, dropping his newspaper to the floor and staring reflectively into space.

'Ah, yes, indeed,' said the Merchant, responding readily to what seemed like a safe platitude; 'when one thinks of the loss of life and limb, the desolated homesteads, the ruined——'

'I wasn't thinking of anything of the sort,' said the Wanderer; 'I was thinking of the tendency that modern war has to destroy and banish the very elements of picturesqueness and excitement that are its chief excuse and charm. It is like a fire that flares up brilliantly for a while and then leaves everything blacker and bleaker than before. After every important war in South-East Europe in recent times there has been a shrinking of the area of chronically disturbed territory, a stiffening of frontier lines, an intrusion of civilized monotony. And imagine what may happen at the conclusion of this war if the Turk should really be driven out of Europe.'

'Well, it would be a gain to the cause of good government, I suppose,' said the Merchant.

'But have you counted the loss?' said the other. 'The

Balkans have long been the last surviving shred of happy hunting-ground for the adventurous, a playground for passions that are fast becoming atrophied for want of exercise. In old bygone days we had the wars in the Low Countries always at our doors, as it were; there was no need to go far afield into malaria-stricken wilds if one wanted a life of boot and saddle and licence to kill and be killed. Those who wished to see life had a decent opportunity for seeing death at the same time.'

'It is scarcely right to talk of killing and bloodshed in that way,' said the Merchant reprovingly; 'one must remember that all men are brothers.'

'One must also remember that a large percentage of them are younger brothers; instead of going into bankruptcy, which is the usual tendency of the younger brother nowadays, they gave their families a fair chance of going into mourning. Every bullet finds a billet, according to a rather optimistic proverb, and you must admit that nowadays it is becoming increasingly difficult to find billets for a lot of young gentlemen who would have adorned, and probably thoroughly enjoyed, one of the old-time happy-go-lucky wars. But that is not exactly the burden of my complaint. The Balkan lands are especially interesting to us in these rapidly moving days because they afford us the last remaining glimpse of a vanishing period of European history. When I was a child one of the earliest events of the outside world that forced itself coherently under my notice was a war in the Balkans; I remember a sunburnt, soldierly man putting little pin-flags in a war-map, red flags for the Turkish forces and yellow flags for the Russians. It seemed a magical region, with its mountain passes and frozen rivers and grim battlefields, its drifting snows, and prowling wolves; there was a great stretch of water that bore the sinister but engaging name of the Black Sea—nothing that I ever learned before or after in a geography lesson made the same impression on me as that strange-named inland sea, and I don't think its magic has ever faded out of my imagination. And there was a battle called

Plevna that went on and on with varying fortunes for what seemed like a great part of a lifetime; I remember the day of wrath and mourning when the little red flag had to be taken away from Plevna—like other maturer judges, I was backing the wrong horse, at any rate the losing horse. And now today we are putting little pin-flags again into maps of the Balkan region, and the passions are being turned loose once more in their playground.'

'The war will be localized,' said the Merchant vaguely; 'at least every one hopes so.'

'It couldn't wish for a better locality,' said the Wanderer; 'there is a charm about those countries that you find nowhere else in Europe, the charm of uncertainty and landslide, and the little dramatic happenings that make all the difference between the ordinary and the desirable.'

'Life is held very cheap in those parts,' said the Merchant.

'To a certain extent, yes,' said the Wanderer. 'I remember a man at Sofia who used to teach me Bulgarian in a rather inefficient manner, interspersed with a lot of quite wearisome gossip. I never knew what his personal history was, but that was only because I didn't listen; he told it to me many times. After I left Bulgaria he used to send me Sofia newspapers from time to time. I felt that he would be rather tiresome if I ever went there again. And then I heard afterwards that some men came in one day from Heaven knows where, just as things do happen in the Balkans, and murdered him in the open street, and went away as quietly as they had come. You will not understand it, but to me there was something rather piquant in the idea of such a thing happening to such a man; after his dullness and his long-winded small-talk it seemed a sort of brilliant *esprit d'escalier* on his part to meet with an end of such ruthlessly planned and executed violence.'

The Merchant shook his head; the piquancy of the incident was not within striking distance of his comprehension.

'I should have been shocked at hearing such a thing about any one I had known,' he said.

'The present war,' continued his companion, without stopping to discuss two hopelessly divergent points of view, 'may be the beginning of the end of much that has hitherto survived the resistless creeping-in of civilization. If the Balkan lands are to be finally parcelled out between the competing Christian Kingdoms and the haphazard rule of the Turk banished to beyond the Sea of Marmora, the old order, or disorder if you like, will have received its death-blow. Something of its spirit will linger perhaps for a while in the old charmed regions where it bore sway; the Greek villagers will doubtless be restless and turbulent and unhappy where the Bulgars rule, and the Bulgars will certainly be restless and turbulent and unhappy under Greek administration, and the rival flocks of the Exarchate and Patriarchate will make themselves intensely disagreeable to one another wherever the opportunity offers; the habits of a lifetime, of several lifetimes, are not laid aside all at once. And the Albanians, of course, we shall have with us still, a troubled Moslem pool left by the receding wave of Islam in Europe. But the old atmosphere will have changed, the glamour will have gone; the dust of formality and bureaucratic neatness will slowly settle down over the time-honoured landmarks; the Sanjak of Novi Bazar, the Muersteg Agreement, the Komitadje bands, the Vilayet of Adrianople, all those familiar outlandish names and things and places, that we have known so long as part and parcel of the Balkan Question, will have passed away into the cupboard of yesterdays, as completely as the Hansa League and the wars of the Guises.

'They were the heritage that history handed down to us, spoiled and diminished no doubt, in comparison with yet earlier days that we never knew, but still something to thrill and enliven one little corner of our Continent, something to help us to conjure up in our imagination the days when the Turk was thundering at the gates of Vienna. And what shall we have to hand down to our children? Think of what their news from the Balkans will be in the course of another ten or fifteen years. Socialist Congress at

Uskub, election riot at Monastir, great dock strike at Salonika, visit of the Y.M.C.A. to Varna. Varna—on the coast of that enchanted sea! They will drive out to some suburb for tea, and write home about it as the Bexhill of the East.

'War is a wickedly destructive thing.'

'Still, you must admit——' began the Merchant. But the Wanderer was not in the mood to admit anything. He rose impatiently and walked to where the tape-machine was busy with the news from Adrianople.

THE
UNBEARABLE
BASSINGTON
[1912]

THE UNBEARABLE
BASSINGTON

CHAPTER I

FRANCESCA BASSINGTON sat in the drawing-room of her house in Blue Street, W., regaling herself and her estimable brother Henry with China tea and small cress sandwiches. The meal was of that elegant proportion which, while ministering sympathetically to the desires of the moment, is happily reminiscent of a satisfactory luncheon and blessedly expectant of an elaborate dinner to come.

In her younger days Francesca had been known as the beautiful Miss Greech; at forty, although much of the original beauty remained, she was just dear Francesca Bassington. No one would have dreamed of calling her sweet, but a good many people who scarcely knew her were punctilious about putting in the 'dear.'

Her enemies, in their honester moments, would have admitted that she was svelte and knew how to dress, but they would have agreed with her friends in asserting that she had no soul. When one's friends and enemies agree on any particular point they are usually wrong. Francesca herself, if pressed in an unguarded moment to describe her soul, would probably have described her drawing-room. Not that she would have considered that the one had stamped the impress of its character on the other, so that close scrutiny might reveal its outstanding features, and even suggest its hidden places, but because she might have dimly recognized that her drawing-room was her soul.

Francesca was one of those women towards whom Fate appears to have the best intentions and never to carry them into practice. With the advantages put at her disposal she might have been expected to command a more than average share of feminine happiness. So many of the things that make for fretfulness, disappointment and discouragement in a woman's life were removed from her path that she might well have been considered the fortunate Miss Greech, or later, lucky Francesca Bassington. And she was not of the perverse band of those who make a rock-garden of their souls by dragging into them all the stony griefs and unclaimed troubles they can find lying around them. Francesca loved the smooth ways and pleasant places of life; she liked not merely to look on the bright side of things, but to live there and stay there. And the fact that things had, at one time and another, gone badly with her and cheated her of some of her early illusions made her cling the closer to such good fortune as remained to her now that she seemed to have reached a calmer period of her life. To undiscriminating friends she appeared in the guise of a rather selfish woman, but it was merely the selfishness of one who had seen the happy and unhappy sides of life and wished to enjoy to the utmost what was left to her of the former. The vicissitudes of fortune had not soured her, but they had perhaps narrowed her in the sense of making her concentrate much of her sympathies on things that immediately pleased and amused her, or that recalled and perpetuated the pleasing and successful incidents of other days. And it was her drawing-room in particular that enshrined the memorials or tokens of past and present happiness.

Into that comfortable quaint-shaped room of angles and bays and alcoves had sailed, as into a harbour, those precious personal possessions and trophies that had survived the buffetings and storms of a not very tranquil married life. Wherever her eyes might turn she saw the embodied results of her successes, economies, good luck, good management, or good taste. The battle had more than once gone against her, but she had somehow always contrived to save her baggage train, and her complacent gaze could roam over object after object that represented the spoils of victory or the salvage of honourable defeat. The delicious bronze Fremiet on the mantelpiece had been the outcome of a Grand Prix sweepstake of many years ago; a group of Dresden figures of some considerable value had been bequeathed to her by a discreet admirer, who had added death to his other kindnesses; another group had been a self-bestowed present, purchased in blessed and unfading memory of a wonderful nine-days' bridge winnings at a country-house party. There were old Persian and Bokharan rugs and Worcester tea-services of glowing colour, and little treasures of antique silver that each enshrined a history or a memory in addition to its own intrinsic value. It amused her at times to think of the bygone craftsmen and artificers who had hammered and wrought and woven in far distant countries and ages, to produce the wonderful and beautiful things that had come, one way and another, into her possession. Workers in the studios of medieval Italian towns and of later Paris, in the bazaars of Bagdad and of Central Asia, in old-time English workshops and German factories, in all manner of queer hidden corners where craft secrets were jealously guarded, nameless unremembered men and men whose names were world-renowned and deathless.

And above all her other treasures, dominating in her estimation every other object that the room contained, was the great Van der Meulen that had come from her father's home as part of her wedding dowry. It fitted exactly into the central wall panel above the narrow buhl cabinet, and filled exactly its right space in the composition and balance of the room. From wherever you sat it seemed to confront you as the dominating feature of its surroundings. There was a pleasing serenity about the great pompous battle scene with its solemn courtly warriors bestriding their heavily prancing steeds, grey or skewbald or dun, all gravely in earnest, and yet somehow conveying the impression that their campaigns were but vast serious picnics arranged in the grand manner. Francesca could not imagine the drawing-room without the crowning complement of the stately well-hung picture, just as she could not imagine

herself in any other setting than this house in Blue Street
with its crowded Pantheon of cherished household gods.

And herein sprouted one of the thorns that obtruded
through the rose-leaf damask of what might otherwise
have been Francesca's peace of mind. One's happiness
always lies in the future rather than in the past. With due
deference to an esteemed lyrical authority one may safely
say that a sorrow's crown of sorrow is anticipating un-
happier things. The house in Blue Street had been left
to her by her old friend Sophie Chetrof, but only until
such time as her niece Emmeline Chetrof should marry,
when it was to pass to her as a wedding present. Emmeline
was now seventeen and passably good-looking, and four
or five years were all that could be safely allotted to the
span of her continued spinsterhood. Beyond that period
lay chaos, the wrenching asunder of Francesca from the
sheltering habitation that had grown to be her soul. It is
true that in imagination she had built herself a bridge
across the chasm, a bridge of a single span. The bridge in
question was her schoolboy son Comus, now being educated somewhere in the southern counties, or rather one
should say the bridge consisted of the possibility of his
eventual marriage with Emmeline, in which case Francesca
saw herself still reigning, a trifle squeezed and incommoded
perhaps, but still reigning in the house in Blue Street.
The Van der Meulen would still catch its requisite afternoon light in its place of honour, the Fremiet and the
Dresden and Old Worcester would continue undisturbed
in their accustomed niches. Emmeline could have the
Japanese snuggery, where Francesca sometimes drank her
after-dinner coffee, as a separate drawing-room, where she
could put her own things. The details of the bridge structure had all been carefully thought out. Only—it was
an unfortunate circumstance that Comus should have been
the span on which everything balanced.

Francesca's husband had insisted on giving the boy that
strange Pagan name, and had not lived long enough to
judge as to the appropriateness, or otherwise, of its signifi-

cance. In seventeen years and some odd months Francesca had had ample opportunity for forming an opinion concerning her son's characteristics. The spirit of mirthfulness which one associates with the name certainly ran riot in the boy, but it was a twisted wayward sort of mirth of which Francesca herself could seldom see the humorous side. In her brother Henry, who sat eating small cress sandwiches as solemnly as though they had been ordained in some immemorial Book of Observances, fate had been undisguisedly kind to her. He might so easily have married some pretty, helpless little woman, and lived at Notting Hill Gate, and been the father of a long string of pale, clever, useless children, who would have had birthdays and the sort of illnesses that one is expected to send grapes to, and who would have painted fatuous objects in a South Kensington manner as Christmas offerings to an aunt whose cubic space for lumber was limited. Instead of committing these unbrotherly actions, which are so frequent in family life that they might almost be called brotherly, Henry had married a woman who had both money and a sense of repose, and their one child had the brilliant virtue of never saying anything which even its parents could consider worth repeating. Then he had gone into Parliament, possibly with the idea of making his home life seem less dull; at any rate it redeemed his career from insignificance, for no man whose death can produce the item 'another by-election' on the news posters can be wholly a nonentity. Henry, in short, who might have been an embarrassment and a handicap, had chosen rather to be a friend and counsellor, at times even an emergency bank balance; Francesca on her part, with partiality which a clever and lazily-inclined woman often feels for a reliable fool, not only sought his counsel but frequently followed it. When convenient, moreover, she repaid his loans.

Against this good service on the part of Fate in providing her with Henry for a brother, Francesca could well set the plaguy malice of the destiny that had given her Comus for a son. The boy was one of those untamable young lords of misrule that frolic and chafe themselves through nursery and preparatory and public-school days with the utmost allowance of storm and dust and dislocation and the least possible amount of collar-work, and come somehow with a laugh through a series of catastrophes that has reduced every one else concerned to tears or Cassandra-like forebodings. Sometimes they sober down in after-life and become uninteresting, forgetting that they were ever lords of anything; sometimes Fate plays royally into their hands, and they do great things in a spacious manner, and are thanked by Parliaments and the Press and acclaimed by gala-day crowds. But in most cases their tragedy begins when they leave school and turn themselves loose in a world that has grown too civilized and too crowded and too empty to have any place for them. And they are very many.

Henry Greech had made an end of biting small sandwiches, and settled down like a dust-storm refreshed, to discuss one of the fashionably prevalent topics of the moment, the prevention of destitution.

'It is a question that is only being nibbled at, smelt at, one might say, at the present moment,' he observed, 'but it is one that will have to engage our serious attention and consideration before long. The first thing that we shall have to do is to get out of the dilettante and academic way of approaching it. We must collect and assimilate hard facts. It is a subject that ought to appeal to all thinking minds, and yet, you know, I find it surprisingly difficult to interest people in it.'

Francesca made some monosyllabic response, a sort of sympathetic grunt which was meant to indicate that she was, to a certain extent, listening and appreciating. In reality she was reflecting that Henry possibly found it difficult to interest people in any topic that he enlarged on. His talents lay so thoroughly in the direction of being uninteresting, that even as an eye witness of the massacre of St Bartholomew he would probably have infused a flavour of boredom into his descriptions of the event.

'I was speaking down in Leicestershire the other day on this subject,' continued Henry, 'and I pointed out at some length a thing that few people ever stop to consider——'

Francesca went over immediately but decorously to the majority that will not stop to consider.

'Did you come across any of the Barnets when you were down there?' she interrupted; 'Eliza Barnet is rather taken up with all those subjects.'

In the propagandist movements of Sociology, as in other arenas of life and struggle, the fiercest competition and rivalry is frequently to be found between closely allied types and species. Eliza Barnet shared many of Henry Greech's political and social views, but she also shared his fondness for pointing things out at some length; there had been occasions when she had extensively occupied the strictly limited span allotted to the platform oratory of a group of speakers of whom Henry Greech had been an impatient unit. He might see eye to eye with her on the leading questions of the day, but he persistently wore mental blinkers as far as her estimable qualities were concerned, and the mention of her name was a skilful lure drawn across the trail of his discourse; if Francesca had to listen to his eloquence on any subject she much preferred that it should be a disparagement of Eliza Barnet rather than the prevention of destitution.

'I've no doubt she means well,' said Henry, 'but it would be a good thing if she could be induced to keep her own personality a little more in the background, and not to imagine that she is the necessary mouthpiece of all the progressive thought in the countryside. I fancy Canon Besomley must have had her in his mind when he said that some people came into the world to shake empires and others to move amendments.'

Francesca laughed with genuine amusement.

'I suppose she is really wonderfully well up in all the subjects she talks about,' was her provocative comment.

Henry grew possibly conscious of the fact that he was being drawn out on the subject of Eliza Barnet, and he presently turned on to a more personal topic.

'From the general air of tranquillity about the house I presume Comus has gone back to Thaleby,' he observed.

'Yes,' said Francesca, 'he went back yesterday. Of course, I'm very fond of him, but I bear the separation well. When he's here it's rather like having a live volcano in the house, a volcano that in its quietest moments asks incessant questions and uses strong scent.'

'It is only a temporary respite,' said Henry; 'in a year or two he will be leaving school, and then what?'

Francesca closed her eyes with the air of one who seeks to shut out a distressing vision. She was not fond of looking intimately at the future in the presence of another person, especially when the future was draped in doubtfully auspicious colours.

'And then what?' persisted Henry.

'Then I suppose he will be upon my hands.'

'Exactly.'

'Don't sit there looking judicial. I'm quite ready to listen to suggestions if you've any to make.'

'In the case of any ordinary boy,' said Henry, 'I might make lots of suggestions as to the finding of suitable employment. From what we know of Comus it would be rather a waste of time for either of us to look for jobs which he wouldn't look at when we'd got them for him.'

'He must do something,' said Francesca.

'I know he must; but he never will. At least, he'll never stick to anything. The most hopeful thing to do with him will be to marry him to an heiress. That would solve the financial side of his problem. If he had unlimited money at his disposal, he might go to the wilds somewhere and shoot big game. I never know what the big game have done to deserve it, but they do help to deflect the destructive energies of some of our social misfits.'

Henry, who never killed anything larger or fiercer than a

trout, was scornfully superior on the subject of big game shooting.

Francesca brightened at the matrimonial suggestion. 'I don't know about an heiress,' she said reflectively. 'There's Emmeline Chetrof, of course. One could hardly call her an heiress, but she's got a comfortable little income of her own, and I suppose something more will come to her from her grandmother. Then, of course, you know this house goes to her when she marries.'

'That would be very convenient,' said Henry, probably following a line of thought that his sister had trodden many hundreds of times before him. 'Do she and Comus hit it off at all well together?'

'Oh, well enough in boy and girl fashion,' said Francesca. 'I must arrange for them to see more of each other in future. By the way, that little brother of hers that she dotes on, Lancelot, goes to Thaleby this term. I'll write and tell Comus to be especially kind to him; that will be a sure way to Emmeline's heart. Comus has been made a prefect, you know. Heaven knows why.'

'It can only be for prominence in games,' sniffed Henry; 'I think we may safely leave work and conduct out of the question.'

Comus was not a favourite with his uncle.

Francesca had turned to her writing cabinet and was scribbling a letter to her son in which the delicate health, timid disposition and other inevitable attributes of the new boy were brought to his notice, and commended to his care. When she had sealed and stamped the envelope Henry uttered a belated caution.

'Perhaps on the whole it would be wiser to say nothing about the boy to Comus. He doesn't always respond to directions, you know.'

Francesca did know, and already was more than half of her brother's opinion; but the woman who can sacrifice a clean unspoiled penny stamp is probably yet unborn.

CHAPTER II

Lancelot Chetrof stood at the end of a long bare passage, restlessly consulting his watch and fervently wishing himself half an hour older with a certain painful experience already registered in the past; unfortunately it still belonged to the future, and what was still more horrible, to the immediate future. Like many boys new to a school he had cultivated an unhealthy passion for obeying rules and requirements, and his zeal in this direction had proved his undoing. In his hurry to be doing two or three estimable things at once he had omitted to study the notice-board in more than a perfunctory fashion and had thereby missed a football practice specially ordained for newly-joined boys. His fellow-juniors of a term's longer standing had graphically enlightened him as to the inevitable consequences of his lapse; the dread which attaches to the unknown was, at any rate, deleted from his approaching doom, though at the moment he felt scarcely grateful for the knowledge placed at his disposal with such lavish solicitude.

'You'll get six of the very best, over the back of a chair,' said one.

'They'll draw a chalk line across you, of course, you know,' said another.

'A chalk line?'

'Rather. So that every cut can be aimed exactly at the same spot. It hurts more that way.'

Lancelot tried to nourish a wan hope that there might be an element of exaggeration in this uncomfortably realistic description.

Meanwhile in the prefects' room at the other end of the passage, Comus Bassington and a fellow-prefect sat also waiting on time, but in a mood of far more pleasurable expectancy. Comus was one of the most junior of the prefect caste, but by no means the least well known, and outside the masters' common-room he enjoyed a certain fitful popularity, or at any rate admiration. At football he was too erratic to be a really brilliant player, but he tackled as if the act of bringing his man headlong to the ground was in itself a sensuous pleasure, and his weird swear-words whenever he got hurt were eagerly treasured by those who were fortunate enough to hear them. At athletics in general he was a showy performer, and although new to the functions of a prefect he had already established a reputation as an effective and artistic caner. In appearance he exactly fitted his fanciful Pagan name. His large green-grey eyes seemed for ever asparkle with goblin mischief and the joy of revelry, and the curved lips might have been those of some wickedly-laughing faun; one almost expected to see embryo horns fretting the smoothness of his sleek dark hair. The chin was firm, but one looked in vain for a redeeming touch of ill-temper in the handsome, half-mocking, half-petulant face. With a strain of sourness in him Comus might have been leavened into something creative and masterful; fate had fashioned him with a certain whimsical charm, and left him all unequipped for the greater purposes of life. Perhaps no one would have called him a lovable character, but in many respects he was adorable; in all respects he was certainly damned.

Rutley, his companion of the moment, sat watching him and wondering, from the depths of a very ordinary brain, whether he liked or hated him; it was easy to do either.

'It's not really your turn to cane,' he said.

'I know it's not,' said Comus, fingering a very service-able-looking cane as lovingly as a pious violinist might handle his Strad. 'I gave Greyson some mint-chocolate to let me toss whether I caned or him, and I won. He was rather decent over it and let me have half the chocolate back.'

The droll lightheartedness which won Comus Bassington such measure of popularity as he enjoyed among his fellows did not materially help to endear him to the succession of masters with whom he came in contact during the course of his schooldays. He amused and interested such of them as had the saving grace of humour at their disposal, but if they sighed when he passed from their immediate responsibility it was a sigh of relief rather than of regret. The more enlightened and experienced of them realized that he was something outside the scope of the things that they were called upon to deal with. A man who has been trained to cope with storms, to foresee their coming, and to minimize their consequences, may be pardoned if he feels a certain reluctance to measure himself against a tornado.

Men of more limited outlook and with a correspondingly larger belief in their own powers were ready to tackle the tornado had time permitted.

'I think I could tame young Bassington if I had your opportunities,' a form-master once remarked to a colleague whose House had the embarrassing distinction of numbering Comus among its inmates.

'Heaven forbid that I should try,' replied the housemaster.

'But why?' asked the reformer.

'Because Nature hates any interference with her own arrangements, and if you start in to tame the obviously untamable you are taking a fearful responsibility on yourself.'

'Nonsense; boys are Nature's raw material.'

'Millions of boys are. There are just a few, and Bassington is one of them, who are Nature's highly finished product when they are in the schoolboy stage, and we, who are supposed to be moulding raw material, are quite helpless when we come in contact with them.'

'But what happens to them when they grow up?'

'They never do grow up,' said the housemaster; 'that is their tragedy. Bassington will certainly never grow out of his present stage.'

'Now you are talking in the language of Peter Pan,' said the form-master.

'I am not thinking in the manner of Peter Pan,' said the other. 'With all reverence for the author of that masterpiece I should say he had a wonderful and tender insight into the child mind and knew nothing whatever about boys. To make only one criticism on that particular work, can you imagine a lot of British boys, or boys of any country that one knows of, who would stay contentedly playing children's games in an underground cave when there were wolves and pirates and Red Indians to be had for the asking on the other side of the trap-door?'

The form-master laughed. 'You evidently think that the "Boy who would not grow up" must have been written by a "grown-up who could never have been a boy." Perhaps that is the meaning of the "Never-never Land." I daresay you're right in your criticism, but I don't agree with you about Bassington. He's a handful to deal with, as any one knows who has come in contact with him, but if one's hands weren't full with a thousand and one other things I hold to my opinion that he could be tamed.'

And he went his way, having maintained a form-master's inalienable privilege of being in the right.

In the prefects' room, Comus busied himself with the exact position of a chair planted out in the middle of the floor.

'I think everything's ready,' he said.

Rutley glanced at the clock with the air of a Roman elegant in the Circus, languidly awaiting the introduction of an expected Christian to an expectant tiger.

'The kid is due in two minutes,' he said.

'He'd jolly well better not be late,' said Comus.

Comus had gone through the mill of many scorching castigations in his earlier schooldays, and was able to appreciate to the last ounce the panic that must be now possessing his foredoomed victim, probably at this moment hovering miserably outside the door. After all, that was part of the fun of the thing, and most things have their amusing side if one knows where to look for it.

There was a knock at the door, and Lancelot entered in response to a hearty friendly summons to 'come in.'

'I've come to be caned,' he said breathlessly; adding by way of identification, 'my name's Chetrof.'

'That's quite bad enough in itself,' said Comus, 'but there is probably worse to follow. You are evidently keeping something back from us.'

'I missed a footer practice,' said Lancelot.

'Six,' said Comus briefly, picking up his cane.

'I didn't see the notice on the board,' hazarded Lancelot as a forlorn hope.

'We are always pleased to listen to excuses, and our charge is two extra cuts. That will be eight. Get over.'

And Comus indicated the chair that stood in sinister isolation in the middle of the room. Never had an article of furniture seemed more hateful in Lancelot's eyes. Comus could well remember the time when a chair stuck in the middle of a room had seemed to him the most horrible of manufactured things.

'Lend me a piece of chalk,' he said to his brother prefect.

Lancelot ruefully recognized the truth of the chalk-line story.

Comus drew the desired line with an anxious exactitude which he would have scorned to apply to a diagram of Euclid or a map of the Russo-Persian frontier.

'Bend a little more forward,' he said to the victim, 'and much tighter. Don't trouble to look pleasant, because I can't see your face anyway. It may sound unorthodox to say so, but this is going to hurt you much more than it will hurt me.'

There was a carefully measured pause, and then Lancelot was made vividly aware of what a good cane can be made to do in really efficient hands. At the second cut he projected himself hurriedly off the chair.

'Now I've lost count,' said Comus; 'we shall have to begin all over again. Kindly get back into the same position. If you get down again before I've finished Rutley will hold you over and you'll get a dozen.'

Lancelot got back on to the chair, and was re-arranged to the taste of his executioner. He stayed there somehow or other while Comus made eight accurate and agonizingly effective shots at the chalk line.

'By the way,' he said to his gasping and gulping victim when the infliction was over, 'you said Chetrof, didn't you? I believe I've been asked to be kind to you. As a beginning you can clean out my study this afternoon. Be awfully careful how you dust the old china. If you break any don't come and tell me, but just go and drown yourself somewhere; it will save you from a worse fate.'

'I don't know where your study is,' said Lancelot between his chokes.

'You'd better find it or I shall have to beat you, really hard this time. Here, you'd better keep this chalk in your pocket, it's sure to come in handy later on. Don't stop to thank me for all I've done, it only embarrasses me.'

As Comus hadn't got a study Lancelot spent a feverish half-hour in looking for it, incidentally missing another footer practice.

'Everything is very jolly here,' wrote Lancelot to his sister Emmeline. 'The prefects can give you an awful hot time if they like, but most of them are rather decent. Some are Beasts. Bassington is a prefect, though only a junior one. He is the Limit as Beasts go. At least, I think so.'

Schoolboy reticence went no further, but Emmeline filled in the gaps for herself with the lavish splendour of feminine imagination. Francesca's bridge went crashing into the abyss.

CHAPTER III

On the evening of a certain November day, two years after the events heretofore chronicled, Francesca Bassington steered her way through the crowd that filled the rooms of her friend Serena Golackly, bestowing nods of vague recognition as she went, but with eyes that were obviously intent on focusing one particular figure. Parliament had pulled its energies together for an Autumn Session, and both political Parties were fairly well represented in the throng. Serena had a harmless way of inviting a number of more or less public men and women to her house, and hoping that if you left them together long enough they would constitute a *salon*. In pursuance of the same instinct she planted the flower borders at her week-end cottage retreat in Surrey with a large mixture of bulbs, and called the result a Dutch garden. Unfortunately, though you may bring brilliant talkers into your home, you cannot always make them talk brilliantly, or even talk at all; what is worse, you cannot restrict the output of those starling-voiced dullards who seem to have, on all subjects, so much to say that was well worth leaving unsaid. One group that Francesca passed was discussing a Spanish painter, who was forty-three, and had painted thousands of square yards of canvas in his time, but of whom no one in London had heard till a few months ago; now the starling-voices seemed determined that one should hear of very little else. Three women knew how his name was pronounced, another always felt that she must go into a forest and pray whenever she saw his pictures, another had noticed that there were always pomegranates in his later compositions, and a man with an indefensible collar knew what the pomegranates 'meant.' 'What I think so splendid about him,' said a stout lady in a loud challenging voice, 'is the way he defies all the conventions of art while retaining all that the conventions stand for.' 'Ah, but have you noticed——' put in the man with the atrocious collar, and Francesca pushed desperately on, wondering dimly as she went what people found so unsupportable in the affliction of deafness. Her progress was impeded for a moment by a couple engaged in earnest and voluble discussion of some smouldering question of the day; a thin spectacled young man, with the receding forehead that so often denotes advanced opinions, was talking to a spectacled young woman with a similar type of forehead and exceedingly untidy hair. It was her ambition in life to be taken for a

Russian girl-student, and she had spent weeks of patient research in trying to find out exactly where you put the tea-leaves in a samovar. She had once been introduced to a young Jewess from Odessa, who had died of pneumonia the following week; the experience, slight as it was, constituted the spectacled young lady an authority on all things Russian in the eyes of her immediate set.

'Talk is helpful, talk is needful,' the young man was saying, 'but what we have got to do is to lift the subject out of the furrow of undisciplined talk and place it on the threshing-floor of practical discussion.'

The young woman took advantage of the rhetorical full-stop to dash in with the remark which was already marshalled on the tip of her tongue.

'In emancipating the serfs of poverty we must be careful to avoid the mistakes which Russian bureaucracy stumbled into when liberating the serfs of the soil.'

She paused in her turn for the sake of declamatory effect, but recovered her breath quickly enough to start afresh on level terms with the young man, who had jumped into the stride of his next sentence.

'They got off to a good start that time,' said Francesca to herself; 'I suppose it's the Prevention of Destitution they're hammering at. What on earth would become of these dear good people if any one started a crusade for the prevention of mediocrity?'

Midway through one of the smaller rooms, still questing for an elusive presence, she caught sight of some one that she knew, and the shadow of a frown passed across her face. The object of her faintly signalled displeasure was Courtenay Youghal, a political spur-winner who seemed absurdly youthful to a generation that had never heard of Pitt. It was Youghal's ambition—or perhaps his hobby— to infuse into the greyness of modern political life some of the colour of Disraelian dandyism, tempered with the correctness of Anglo-Saxon taste, and supplemented by the flashes of wit that were inherent from the Celtic strain in him. His success was only a half-measure. The public missed in him that touch of blatancy which it looks for in its rising public men; the decorative smoothness of his chestnut-golden hair, and the lively sparkle of his epigrams were counted to him for good, but the restrained sumptuousness of his waistcoats and cravats was as wasted efforts. If he had habitually smoked cigarettes in a pink coral mouthpiece, or worn spats of Mackenzie tartan, the great heart of the voting-man and the gush of the paragraph-makers might have been unreservedly his. The art of public life consists to a great extent of knowing exactly where to stop and going a bit farther.

It was not Youghal's lack of political sagacity that had brought the momentary look of disapproval into Francesca's face. The fact was that Comus, who had left off being a schoolboy and was now a social problem, had lately enrolled himself among the young politician's associates and admirers, and as the boy knew and cared nothing about politics, and merely copied Youghal's waistcoats, and, less successfully, his conversation, Francesca felt herself justified in deploring the intimacy. To a woman who dressed well on comparatively nothing a year it was an anxious experience to have a son who dressed sumptuously on absolutely nothing.

The cloud that had passed over her face when she caught sight of the offending Youghal was presently succeeded by a smile of gratified achievement, as she encountered a bow of recognition and welcome from a portly middle-aged gentleman, who seemed genuinely anxious to include her in the rather meagre group that he had gathered about him.

'We were just talking about my new charge,' he observed genially, including in the 'we' his somewhat depressed-looking listeners, who in all human probability had done none of the talking. 'I was just telling them, and you may be interested to hear this——'

Francesca, with Spartan stoicism, continued to wear an ingratiating smile, though the character of the deaf adder that stoppeth her ear and will not hearken seemed to her at that moment a beautiful one.

Sir Julian Jull had been a member of a House of Commons distinguished for its high standard of well-informed mediocrity, and had harmonized so thoroughly with his surroundings that the most attentive observer of Parliamentary proceedings could scarcely have told even on which side of the House he sat. A baronetcy bestowed on him by the Party in power had at least removed that doubt; some weeks later he had been made Governor of some West Indian dependency, whether as a reward for having accepted the baronetcy, or as an application of a theory that West Indian islands get the Governors they deserve, it would have been hard to say. To Sir Julian the appointment was, doubtless, one of some importance; during the span of his Governorship the island might possibly be visited by a member of the Royal Family, or at the least by an earthquake, and in either case his name would get into the papers. To the public the matter was one of absolute indifference; 'Who is he and where is it?' would have correctly epitomized the sum total of general information on the personal and geographical aspects of the case.

Francesca, however, from the moment she had heard of the likelihood of the appointment, had taken a deep and lively interest in Sir Julian. As a Member of Parliament he had not filled any very pressing social want in her life, and on the rare occasions when she took tea on the Terrace of the House she was wont to lapse into rapt contemplation of St Thomas's Hospital whenever she saw him within bowing distance. But as Governor of an island he would, of course, want a private secretary, and as a friend and colleague of Henry Greech, to whom he was indebted for many little acts of political support (they had once jointly drafted an amendment which had been ruled out of order), what was more natural and proper than that he should let his choice fall on Henry's nephew Comus? While privately doubting whether the boy would make the sort of secretary that any public man would esteem a treasure, Henry was thoroughly in agreement with Francesca as to the excellence and desirability of an arrangement which would transplant that troublesome young animal from the too restricted and conspicuous area that centres in the parish of St James's to some misty corner of the British dominion overseas. Brother and sister had conspired to give an elaborate and at the same time cosy little luncheon to Sir Julian on the very day that his appointment was officially announced, and the question of the secretaryship had been mooted and sedulously fostered as occasion permitted, until all that was now needed to clinch the matter was a formal interview between His Excellency and Comus. The boy had from the first shown very little gratification at the prospect of his deportation. To live on a remote shark-girt island, as he expressed it, with the Jull family as his chief social mainstay, and Sir Julian's conversation as a daily item of his existence, did not inspire him with the same degree of enthusiasm as was displayed by his mother and uncle, who, after all, were not making the experiment. Even the necessity for an entirely new outfit did not appeal to his imagination with the force that might have been expected. But, however lukewarm his adhesion to the project might be, Francesca and her brother were clearly determined that no lack of deft persistence on their part should endanger its success. It was for the purpose of reminding Sir Julian of his promise to meet Comus at lunch on the following day, and definitely settle the matter of the secretaryship, that Francesca was now enduring the ordeal of a long harangue on the value of the West Indian group as an Imperial asset. Other listeners dexterously detached themselves one by one, but Francesca's patience outlasted even Sir Julian's flow of commonplaces, and her devotion was duly rewarded by a renewed acknowledgment of the lunch engagement and its purpose. She pushed her way back through the throng of starling-voiced chatterers fortified by a sense of well-earned victory. Dear Serena's absurd *salons* served some good purpose after all.

Francesca was not an early riser, and her breakfast was only just beginning to mobilize on the breakfast-table next morning when a copy of *The Times*, sent by special mes-

senger from her brother's house, was brought up to her
room. A heavy margin of blue pencilling drew her attention to a prominently-printed letter which bore the ironical
heading: 'Julian Jull, Proconsul.' The matter of the letter
was a cruel disinterment of some fatuous and forgotten
speeches made by Sir Julian to his constituents not many
years ago, in which the value of some of our Colonial
possessions, particularly certain West Indian islands, was
decried in a medley of pomposity, ignorance and amazingly
cheap humour. The extracts given sounded weak and
foolish enough, taken by themselves, but the writer of the
letter had interlarded them with comments of his own,
which sparkled with an ironical brilliance that was Cer-
vantes-like in its polished cruelty. Remembering her ordeal
of the previous evening Francesca permitted herself a
certain feeling of amusement as she read the merciless
stabs inflicted on the newly-appointed Governor; then she
came to the signature at the foot of the letter, and the
laughter died out of her eyes. 'Comus Bassington' stared
at her from above a thick layer of blue pencil lines marked
by Henry Greech's shaking hand.

Comus could no more have devised such a letter than he
could have written an Episcopal charge to the clergy of
any given diocese. It was obviously the work of Courtenay
Youghal, and Comus, for a palpable purpose of his own,
had wheedled him into forgoing for once the pride of
authorship in a clever piece of political raillery, and letting
his young friend stand sponsor instead. It was a daring
stroke, and there could be no question as to its success;
the secretaryship and the distant shark-girt island faded
away into the horizon of impossible things. Francesca,
forgetting the golden rule of strategy which enjoins a careful choosing of ground and opportunity before entering
on hostilities, made straight for the bathroom door, behind
which a lively din of splashing betokened that Comus had
at least begun his toilet.

'You wicked boy, what have you done?' she cried
reproachfully.

'Me washee,' came a cheerful shout; 'me washee from the neck all the way down to the merrythought, and now washee down from the merrythought to——'

'You have ruined your future. *The Times* has printed that miserable letter with your signature.'

A loud squeal of joy came from the bath. 'Oh, Mummy! Let me see!'

There were sounds as of a sprawling dripping body clambering hastily out of the bath. Francesca fled. One cannot effectively scold a moist nineteen-year-old boy clad only in a bath-towel and a cloud of steam.

Another messenger arrived before Francesca's breakfast was over. This one brought a letter from Sir Julian Jull, excusing himself from fulfilment of the luncheon engagement.

CHAPTER IV

Francesca prided herself on being able to see things from other people's points of view, which meant, as it usually does, that she could see her own point of view from various aspects. As regards Comus, whose doings and non-doings bulked largely in her thoughts at the present moment, she had mapped out in her mind so clearly what his outlook in life ought to be, that she was peculiarly unfitted to understand the drift of his feelings or the impulses that governed them. Fate had endowed her with a son; in limiting the endowment to a solitary offspring Fate had certainly shown a moderation which Francesca was perfectly willing to acknowledge and be thankful for; but then, as she pointed out to a certain complacent friend of hers who cheerfully sustained an endowment of half a dozen male offsprings and a girl or two, her one child was Comus. Moderation in numbers was more than counterbalanced in his case by extravagance in characteristics.

Francesca mentally compared her son with hundreds of other young men whom she saw around her, steadily, and no doubt happily, engaged in the process of transforming themselves from nice boys into useful citizens. Most of them had occupations, or were industriously engaged in qualifying for such; in their leisure moments they smoked reasonably-priced cigarettes, went to the cheaper seats at music-halls, watched an occasional cricket match at Lord's with apparent interest, saw most of the world's spectacular events through the medium of the cinematograph, and were wont to exchange at parting seemingly superfluous injunctions to 'be good.' The whole of Bond Street and many of the tributary thoroughfares of Piccadilly might have been swept off the face of modern London without in any way interfering with the supply of their daily wants. They were doubtless dull as acquaintances, but as sons they would have been eminently restful. With a growing sense of irritation Francesca compared these deserving young men with her own intractable offspring, and wondered why Fate should have singled her out to be the parent of such a vexatious variant from a comfortable and desirable type. As far as remunerative achievement was concerned, Comus copied the insouciance of the field lily with a dangerous fidelity. Like his mother he looked round with wistful irritation at the example afforded by contemporary youth, but he concentrated his attention exclusively on the richer circles of his acquaintance, young men who bought cars and polo ponies as unconcernedly as he might purchase a carnation for his buttonhole, and went for trips to Cairo or the Tigris valley with less difficulty and finance-stretching than he encountered in contriving a week-end at Brighton.

Gaiety and good looks had carried Comus successfully and, on the whole, pleasantly, through schooldays and a recurring succession of holidays; the same desirable assets were still at his service to advance him along his road, but it was a disconcerting experience to find that they could not be relied on to go all distances at all times. In an animal world, and a fiercely competitive animal world at that, something more was needed than the decorative *abandon* of the field lily, and it was just that something more which Comus seemed unable or unwilling to provide on his own account; it was just the lack of that something more which left him sulking with Fate over the numerous breakdowns and stumbling-blocks that held him up on what he expected to be a triumphal or, at any rate, unimpeded progress.

Francesca was, in her own way, fonder of Comus than of any one else in the world, and if he had been browning his skin somewhere east of Suez she would probably have kissed his photograph with genuine fervour every night before going to bed; the appearance of a cholera scare or rumour of native rising in the columns of her daily newssheet would have caused her a flutter of anxiety, and she would have mentally likened herself to a Spartan mother sacrificing her best-beloved on the altar of State necessities. But with the best-beloved installed under her roof, occupying an unreasonable amount of cubic space, and demanding daily sacrifices instead of providing the raw material for one, her feelings were tinged with irritation rather than affection. She might have forgiven Comus generously for misdeeds of some gravity committed in another continent, but she could never overlook the fact that out of a dish of five plovers' eggs he was certain to take three. The absent may be always wrong, but they are seldom in a position to be inconsiderate.

Thus a wall of ice had grown up gradually between mother and son, a barrier across which they could hold converse, but which gave a wintry chill even to the sparkle of their lightest words. The boy had the gift of being irresistibly amusing when he chose to exert himself in that direction, and after a long series of moody or jangling meal-sittings he would break forth into a torrential flow of small-talk, scandal and malicious anecdote, true or more generally invented, to which Francesca listened with a relish and appreciation that was all the more flattering from being so unwillingly bestowed.

'If you chose your friends from a rather more reputable

set you would be doubtless less amusing, but there would be compensating advantages.'

Francesca snapped the remark out at lunch one day when she had been betrayed into a broader smile than she considered the circumstances of her attitude towards Comus warranted.

'I'm going to move in quite decent society tonight,' replied Comus with a pleased chuckle; 'I'm going to meet you and Uncle Henry and heaps of nice dull God-fearing people at dinner.'

Francesca gave a little gasp of surprise and annoyance.

'You don't mean to say Caroline has asked you to dinner tonight?' she said; 'and of course without telling me. How exceedingly like her!'

Lady Caroline Benaresq had reached that age when you can say and do what you like in defiance of people's most sensitive feelings and most cherished antipathies. Not that she had waited to attain her present age before pursuing that line of conduct; she came of a family whose individual members went through life, from the nursery to the grave, with as much tact and consideration as a cactus-hedge might show in going through a crowded bathing tent. It was a compensating mercy that they disagreed rather more among themselves than they did with the outside world; every known variety and shade of religion and politics had been pressed into the family service to avoid the possibility of any agreement on the larger essentials of life, and such unlooked-for happenings as the Home Rule schism, the Tariff-Reform upheaval and the Suffragette crusade were thankfully seized on as furnishing occasion for further differences and subdivisions. Lady Caroline's favourite scheme of entertaining was to bring jarring and antagonistic elements into close contact and play them remorselessly one against the other. 'One gets much better results under those circumstances,' she used to observe, 'than by asking people who wish to meet each other. Few people talk as brilliantly to impress a friend as they do to depress an enemy.'

She admitted that her theory broke down rather badly if you applied it to Parliamentary debates. At her own dinner table its success was usually triumphantly vindicated.

'Who else is to be there?' Francesca asked, with some pardonable misgiving.

'Courtenay Youghal. He'll probably sit next to you, so you'd better think out a lot of annihilating remarks in readiness. And Elaine de Frey.'

'I don't think I've heard of her. Who is she?'

'Nobody in particular, but rather nice-looking in a solemn sort of way, and almost indecently rich.'

'Marry her' was the advice which sprang to Francesca's lips, but she choked it back with a salted almond, having a rare perception of the fact that words are sometimes given to us to defeat our purposes.

'Caroline has probably marked her down for Toby or one of the grand-nephews,' she said carelessly; 'a little money would be rather useful in that quarter, I imagine.'

Comus tucked in his underlip with just the shade of pugnacity that she wanted to see.

An advantageous marriage was so obviously the most sensible course for him to embark on that she scarcely dared to hope that he would seriously entertain it; yet there was just a chance that if he got as far as the flirtation stage with an attractive (and attracted) girl who was also an heiress, the sheer perversity of his nature might carry him on to more definite courtship, if only from the desire to thrust other more genuinely enamoured suitors into the background. It was a forlorn hope; so forlorn that the idea even crossed her mind of throwing herself on the mercy of her *bête noire*, Courtenay Youghal, and trying to enlist the influence which he seemed to possess over Comus for the purpose of furthering her hurriedly conceived project. Anyhow, the dinner promised to be more interesting than she had originally anticipated.

Lady Caroline was a professed Socialist in politics, chiefly, it was believed, because she was thus enabled to disagree with most of the Liberals and Conservatives, and all the Socialists of the day. She did not permit her Socialism, however to penetrate below stairs; her cook and butler had every encouragement to be Individualists. Francesca, who was a keen and intelligent food critic, harboured no misgivings as to her hostess's kitchen and cellar departments; some of the human side-dishes at the feast gave her more ground for uneasiness. Courtenay Youghal, for instance, would probably be brilliantly silent; her brother Henry would almost certainly be the reverse.

The dinner-party was a large one, and Francesca arrived late with little time to take preliminary stock of the guests; a card with the name 'Miss de Frey,' immediately opposite her own place at the other side of the table, indicated, however, the whereabouts of the heiress. It was characteristic of Francesca that she first carefully read the menu from end to end, and then indulged in an equally careful, though less open, scrutiny of the girl who sat opposite her, the girl who was nobody in particular, but whose income was everything that could be desired. She was pretty in a restrained nut-brown fashion, and had a look of grave reflective calm that probably masked a speculative unsettled temperament. Her pose, if one wished to be critical, was just a little too elaborately careless. She wore some excellently set rubies with that indefinable air of having more at home that is so difficult to improvise. Francesca was distinctly pleased with her survey.

'You seem interested in your *vis-à-vis*,' said Courtenay Youghal.

'I almost think I've seen her before,' said Francesca; 'her face seems familiar to me.'

'The narrow gallery at the Louvre: attributed to Leonardo da Vinci,' said Youghal.

'Of course,' said Francesca, her feelings divided between satisfaction at capturing an elusive impression and annoyance that Youghal should have been her helper. A stronger tinge of annoyance possessed her when she heard the voice of Henry Greech raised in painful prominence at Lady Caroline's end of the table.

'I called on the Trudhams yesterday,' he announced; 'it was their Silver Wedding, you know, at least the day before was. Such lots of silver presents, quite a show. Of course there were a great many duplicates, but still, very nice to have. I think they were very pleased to get so many.'

'We must not grudge them their show of presents after their twenty-five years of married life,' said Lady Caroline gently; 'it is the silver lining to their cloud.'

A third of the guests present were related to the Trudhams.

'Lady Caroline is beginning well,' murmured Courtenay Youghal.

'I should hardly call twenty-five years of married life a cloud,' said Henry Greech lamely.

'Don't let's talk about married life,' said a tall handsome woman, who looked like some modern painter's conception of the goddess Bellona; 'it's my misfortune to write eternally about husbands and wives and their variants. My public expects it of me. I do so envy journalists who can write about plagues and strikes and Anarchist plots, and other pleasing things, instead of being tied down to one stale old topic.'

'Who is that woman and what has she written?' Francesca asked Youghal; she dimly remembered having seen her at one of Serena Golackly's gatherings, surrounded by a little court of admirers.

'I forget her name; she has a villa at San Remo or Mentone, or somewhere where one does have villas, and plays an extraordinary good game of bridge. Also she has the reputation, rather rare in your sex, of being a wonderfully sound judge of wine.'

'But what has she written?'

'Oh, several novels of the thinnish ice order. Her last one, *The Woman who Wished it was Wednesday*, has been banned at all the libraries. I expect you've read it.'

'I don't see why you should think so,' said Francesca coldly.

'Only because Comus lent me your copy yesterday,' said Youghal. He threw back his handsome head and gave her a sidelong glance of quizzical amusement. He knew that she hated his intimacy with Comus, and he was secretly rather proud of his influence over the boy, shallow and negative though he knew it to be. It had been, on his part, an unsought intimacy, and it would probably fall to pieces the moment he tried seriously to take up the rôle of mentor. The fact that Comus's mother openly disapproved of the friendship gave it perhaps its chief interest in the young politician's eyes.

Francesca turned her attention to her brother's end of the table. Henry Greech had willingly availed himself of the invitation to leave the subject of married life, and had launched forthwith into the equally well-worn theme of current politics. He was not a person who was in much demand for public meetings, and the House showed no great impatience to hear his views on the topics of the moment; its impatience, indeed, was manifested rather in the opposite direction. Hence he was prone to unburden himself of accumulated political wisdom as occasion presented itself—sometimes, indeed, to assume an occasion that was hardly visible to the naked intelligence.

'Our opponents are engaged in a hopelessly uphill struggle, and they know it,' he chirruped defiantly; 'they've become possessed, like the Gadarene swine, with a whole legion of——'

'Surely the Gadarene swine went down-hill?' put in Lady Caroline in a gently inquiring voice.

Henry Greech hastily abandoned simile and fell back on platitude and the safer kinds of fact.

Francesca did not regard her brother's views on statecraft either in the light of gospel or revelation; as Comus once remarked, they more usually suggested exodus. In the present instance she found distraction in a renewed scrutiny of the girl opposite her, who seemed to be only

moderately interested in the conversational efforts of the
diners on either side of her. Comus, who was looking and
talking his best, was sitting at the farther end of the table,
and Francesca was quick to notice in which direction the
girl's glances were continually straying. Once or twice the
eyes of the young people met and a swift flush of pleasure
and a half-smile that spoke of good understanding came
to the heiress's face. It did not need the gift of the traditional intuition of her sex to enable Francesca to guess
that the girl with the desirable banking account was already
considerably attracted by the lively young Pagan who
had, when he cared to practise it, such an art of winning
admiration. For the first time for many, many months
Francesca saw her son's prospects in a rose-coloured
setting, and she began, unconsciously, to wonder exactly
how much wealth was summed up in the expressive label
'almost indecently rich.' A wife with a really large fortune
and a correspondingly big dower of character and ambition,
might, perhaps, succeed in turning Comus's latent energies
into a groove which would provide him, if not with a
career, at least with an occupation, and the young serious
face opposite looked as if its owner lacked neither character nor ambition. Francesca's speculations took a more
personal turn. Out of the well-filled coffers with which
her imagination was toying, an inconsiderable sum might
eventually be devoted to the leasing, or even perhaps the
purchase, of the house in Blue Street when the present
convenient arrangement should have come to an end, and
Francesca and the Van der Meulen would not be obliged
to seek fresh quarters.

A woman's voice, talking in a discreet undertone on the
other side of Courtenay Youghal, broke in on her bridge-
building.

'Tons of money and really very presentable. Just the
wife for a rising young politician. Go in and win her before
she's snapped up by some fortune hunter.'

Youghal and his instructress in worldly wisdom were
looking straight across the table at the Leonardo da Vinci

girl with the grave reflective eyes and the over-emphasized air of repose. Francesca felt a quick throb of anger against her matchmaking neighbour; why, she asked herself, must some women, with no end or purpose of their own to serve, except the sheer love of meddling in the affairs of others, plunge their hands into plots and schemings of this sort, in which the happiness of more than one person was concerned? And more clearly than ever she realized how thoroughly she detested Courtenay Youghal. She had disliked him as an evil influence, setting before her son an example of showy ambition that he was not in the least likely to follow, and providing him with a model of extravagant dandyism that he was only too certain to copy. In her heart she knew that Comus would have embarked just as surely on his present course of idle self-indulgence if he had never known of the existence of Youghal, but she chose to regard that young man as her son's evil genius, and now he seemed likely to justify more than ever the character she had fastened on to him. For once in his life Comus appeared to have an idea of behaving sensibly and making some use of his opportunities, and almost at the same moment Courtenay Youghal arrived on the scene as a possible and very dangerous rival. Against the good looks and fitful powers of fascination that Comus could bring into the field, the young politician could match half a dozen dazzling qualities which would go far to recommend him in the eyes of a woman of the world, still more in those of a young girl in search of an ideal. Good-looking in his own way, if not on such showy lines as Comus, always well turned-out, witty, self-confident without being bumptious, with a conspicuous Parliamentary career alongside him, and Heaven knew what else in front of him, Courtenay Youghal certainly was not a rival whose chances could be held very lightly. Francesca laughed bitterly to herself as she remembered that a few hours ago she had entertained the idea of begging for his good offices in helping on Comus's wooing. One consolation, at least, she found for herself: if Youghal really meant to step in and try and cut out his young friend, the latter at any rate had snatched a useful start. Comus had mentioned Miss de Frey at luncheon that day, casually and dispassionately; if the subject of the dinner guests had not come up he would probably not have mentioned her at all. But they were obviously already very good friends. It was part and parcel of the state of domestic tension at Blue Street that Francesca should only have come to know of this highly interesting heiress by an accidental sorting of guests at a dinner party.

Lady Caroline's voice broke in on her reflections; it was a gentle purring voice, that possessed an uncanny quality of being able to make itself heard down the longest dinner table.

'The dear Archdeacon is getting *so* absent-minded. He read a list of box-holders for the opera as the First Lesson the other Sunday, instead of the families and lots of the tribes of Israel that entered Canaan. Fortunately no one noticed the mistake.'

CHAPTER V

On a conveniently secluded bench facing the Northern Pheasantry in the Zoological Society's Gardens, Regent's Park, Courtenay Youghal sat immersed in mature flirtation with a lady, who, though certainly young in fact and appearance, was some four or five years his senior. When he was a schoolboy of sixteen, Molly McQuade had personally conducted him to the Zoo and stood him dinner afterwards at Kettner's, and whenever the two of them happened to be in town on the anniversary of that bygone festivity they religiously repeated the programme in its entirety. Even the menu of the dinner was adhered to as nearly as possible; the original selection of food and wine that schoolboy exuberance, tempered by schoolboy shyness, had pitched on those many years ago, confronted Youghal on those occasions, as a drowning man's past life

is said to rise up and parade itself in his last moments of consciousness.

The flirtation which was thus perennially restored to its old-time footing owed its longevity more to the enterprising solicitude of Miss McQuade than to any conscious sentimental effort on the part of Youghal himself. Molly McQuade was known to her neighbours in a minor hunting shire as a hard-riding conventionally unconventional type of young woman, who came naturally into the classification, 'a good sort.' She was just sufficiently good-looking, sufficiently reticent about her own illnesses, when she had any, and sufficiently appreciative of her neighbour's gardens, children and hunters to be generally popular. Most men liked her, and the percentage of women who disliked her was not inconveniently high. One of these days, it was assumed, she would marry a brewer or a Master of Otter Hounds, and, after a brief interval, be known to the world as the mother of a boy or two at Malvern or some similar seat of learning. The romantic side of her nature was altogether unguessed by the countryside.

Her romances were mostly in serial form, and suffered perhaps in fervour from their disconnected course what they gained in length of days. Her affectionate interest in the several young men who figured in her affairs of the heart was perfectly honest, and she certainly made no attempt either to conceal their separate existences, or to play them off one against the other. Neither could it be said that she was a husband hunter; she had made up her mind what sort of man she was likely to marry, and her forecast did not differ very widely from that formed by her local acquaintances. If her married life were eventually to turn out a failure, at least she looked forward to it with very moderate expectations. Her love affairs she put on a very different footing, and apparently they were the all-absorbing element in her life. She possessed the happily constituted temperament which enables a man or woman to be a 'pluralist,' and to observe the sage precaution of not putting all one's eggs into one basket. Her demands were not exacting: she required of her affinity that he should be young, good-looking, and at least moderately amusing; she would have preferred him to be invariably faithful, but, with her own example before her, she was prepared for the probability, bordering on certainty, that he would be nothing of the sort. The philosophy of the 'Garden of Kama' was the compass by which she steered her barque, and thus far, if she had encountered some storms and buffeting, she had at least escaped being either shipwrecked or becalmed.

Courtenay Youghal had not been designed by Nature to fulfil the rôle of an ardent or devoted lover, and he scrupulously respected the limits which Nature had laid down. For Molly, however, he had a certain responsive affection. She had always obviously admired him, and at the same time she never beset him with crude flattery; the principal reason why the flirtation had stood the test of so many years was the fact that it only flared into active existence at convenient intervals. In an age when the telephone has undermined almost every fastness of human privacy, and the sanctity of one's seclusion depends often on the ability for tactful falsehood shown by a club page-boy, Youghal was duly appreciative of the circumstance that his lady fair spent a large part of the year pursuing foxes, in lieu of pursuing him. Also the honestly admitted fact that, in her human hunting, she rode after more than one quarry, made the inevitable break-up of the affair a matter to which both could look forward without a sense of coming embarrassment and recrimination. When the time for gathering ye rosebuds should be over, neither of them could accuse the other of having wrecked his or her entire life. At the most they would only have disorganized a week-end.

On this particular afternoon, when old reminiscences had been gone through, and the intervening gossip of past months duly recounted, a lull in the conversation made itself rather obstinately felt. Molly had already guessed that matters were about to slip into a new phase; the affair had reached maturity long ago, and a new phase must be in the nature of a wane.

'You're a clever brute,' she said suddenly, with an air of affectionate regret; 'I always knew you'd get on in the House, but I hardly expected you to come to the front so soon.'

'I'm coming to the front,' admitted Youghal judicially; 'the problem is, shall I be able to stay there? Unless something happens in the financial line before long, I don't see how I'm to stay in Parliament at all. Economy is out of the question. It would open people's eyes, I fancy, if they knew how little I exist on as it is. And I'm living so far beyond my income that we may almost be said to be living apart.'

'It will have to be a rich wife, I suppose,' said Molly slowly; 'that's the worst of success, it imposes so many conditions. I rather knew, from something in your manner, that you were drifting that way.'

Youghal said nothing in the way of contradiction; he gazed steadfastly at the aviary in front of him as though exotic pheasants were for the moment the most absorbing study in the world. As a matter of fact, his mind was centred on the image of Elaine de Frey, with her clear untroubled eyes and her Leonardo da Vinci air. He was wondering whether he was likely to fall into a frame of mind concerning her which would be in the least like falling in love.

'I shall mind horribly,' continued Molly, after a pause, 'but, of course, I have always known that something of the sort would have to happen one of these days. When a man goes into politics he can't call his soul his own, and I suppose his heart becomes an impersonal possession in the same way.'

'Most people who know me would tell you that I haven't got a heart,' said Youghal.

'I've often felt inclined to agree with them,' said Molly;

'and then, now and again, I think you have a heart tucked away somewhere.'

'I hope I have,' said Youghal, 'because I'm trying to break to you the fact that I think I'm falling in love with somebody.'

Molly McQuade turned sharply to look at her companion, who still fixed his gaze on the pheasant run in front of him.

'Don't tell me you're losing your head over somebody useless, some one without money,' she said; 'I don't think I could stand that.'

For the moment she feared that Courtenay's selfishness might have taken an unexpected turn, in which ambition had given way to the fancy of the hour; he might be going to sacrifice his Parliamentary career for a life of stupid lounging in momentarily attractive company. He quickly undeceived her.

'She's got heaps of money.'

Molly gave a grunt of relief. Her affection for Courtenay had produced the anxiety which underlay her first question; a natural jealousy prompted the next one.

'Is she young and pretty and all that sort of thing, or is she just a good sort with a sympathetic manner and nice eyes? As a rule that's the kind that goes with a lot of money.'

'Young and quite good-looking in her way, and a distinct style of her own. Some people would call her beautiful. As a political hostess I should think she'd be splendid. I imagine I'm rather in love with her.'

'And is she in love with you?'

Youghal threw back his head with the slight assertive movement that Molly knew and liked.

'She's a girl who I fancy would let judgment influence her a lot. And without being stupidly conceited I think I may say she might do worse than throw herself away on me. I'm young and quite good-looking, and I'm making a name for myself in the House; she'll be able to read all sorts of nice and horrid things about me in the papers at breakfast-time. I can be brilliantly amusing at times, and I understand the value of silence; there is no fear that I shall ever degenerate into that fearsome thing—a cheerful talkative husband. For a girl with money and social ambitions I should think I was rather a good thing.'

'You are certainly in love, Courtenay,' said Molly, 'but it's the old love and not a new one. I'm rather glad. I should have hated to have you head-over-heels in love with a pretty woman, even for a short time. You'll be much happier as it is. And I'm going to put all my feelings in the background, and tell you to go in and win. You've got to marry a rich woman, and if she's nice and will make a good hostess, so much the better for everybody. You'll be happier in your married life than I shall be in mine, when it comes; you'll have other interests to absorb you. I shall just have the garden and dairy and nursery and lending library, as like as two peas to all the gardens and dairies and nurseries for hundreds of miles round. You won't care for your wife enough to be worried every time she has a finger-ache, and you'll like her well enough to be pleased to meet her sometimes at your own house. I shouldn't wonder if you were quite happy. She will probably be miserable, but any woman who married you would be.'

There was a short pause; they were both staring at the pheasant cages. Then Molly spoke again, with the swift nervous tone of a general who is hurriedly altering the disposition of his forces for a strategic retreat.

'When you are safely married and honeymooned and all that sort of thing, and have put your wife through her paces as a political hostess, some time, when the House isn't sitting, you must come down by yourself, and do a little hunting with us. Will you? It won't be quite the same as old times, but it will be something to look forward to when I'm reading the endless paragraphs about your fashionable political wedding.'

'You're looking forward pretty far,' laughed Youghal; 'the lady may take your view as to the probable unhappiness of a future shared with me, and I may have to content myself with penurious political bachelorhood. Anyhow, the present is still with us. We dine at Kettner's tonight, don't we?'

'Rather,' said Molly, 'though it will be more or less a throat-lumpy feast as far as I am concerned. We shall have to drink to the health of the future Mrs Youghal. By the way, it's rather characteristic of you that you haven't told me who she is, and of me that I haven't asked. And now, like a dear boy, trot away and leave me. I haven't got to say good-bye to you yet, but I'm going to take a quiet farewell of the Pheasantry. We've had some jolly good talks, you and I, sitting on this seat, haven't we? And I know, as well as I know anything, that this is the last of them. Eight o'clock tonight, as punctually as possible.'

She watched his retreating figure with eyes that grew slowly misty; he had been such a jolly, comely boy-friend, and they had had such good times together. The mist deepened on her lashes as she looked round at the familiar rendezvous where they had so often kept tryst since the day when they had first come there together, he a school-boy and she but lately out of her teens. For the moment she felt herself in the thrall of a very real sorrow.

Then, with the admirable energy of one who is only in town for a fleeting fortnight, she raced away to have tea with a world-faring naval admirer at his club. Pluralism is a merciful narcotic.

CHAPTER VI

Elaine de Frey sat at ease—at bodily ease, at any rate—in a low wicker chair placed under the shade of a group of cedars in the heart of a stately spacious garden that had almost made up its mind to be a park. The shallow stone basin of an old fountain, on whose wide ledge a leaden-moulded otter for ever preyed on a leaden salmon, filled a conspicuous place in the immediate foreground.

Around its rim ran an inscription in Latin, warning mortal man that time flows as swiftly as water and exhorting him to make the most of his hours; after which piece of Jacobean moralizing it set itself shamelessly to beguile all who might pass that way into an abandonment of contemplative repose. On all sides of it a stretch of smooth turf spread away, broken up here and there by groups of dwarfish chestnut and mulberry trees, whose leaves and branches cast a laced pattern of shade beneath them. On one side the lawn sloped gently down to a small lake, whereon floated a quartet of swans, their movements suggestive of a certain mournful listlessness, as though a weary dignity of caste held them back from the joyous bustling life of the lesser waterfowl. Elaine liked to imagine that they re-embodied the souls of happy boys who had been forced by family interests to become high ecclesiastical dignitaries and had grown prematurely Right Reverend. A low stone balustrade fenced part of the shore of the lake, making a miniature terrace above its level, and here roses grew in a rich multitude. Other rose bushes, carefully pruned and tended, formed little oases of colour and perfume amid the restful green of the sward, and in the distance the eye caught the variegated blaze of a many-hued hedge of rhododendron. With these favoured exceptions flowers were hard to find in this well-ordered garden; the misguided tyranny of staring geranium beds and beflowered archways leading to nowhere, so dear to the suburban gardener, found no expression here. Magnificent Amherst pheasants, whose plumage challenged and almost shamed the peacock on his own ground, stepped to and fro over the emerald turf with the assured self-conscious pride of reigning sultans. It was a garden where summer seemed a part-proprietor rather than a hurried visitor.

By the side of Elaine's chair under the shadow of the cedars a wicker table was set out with the paraphernalia of afternoon tea. On some cushions at her feet reclined Courtenay Youghal, smoothly preened and youthfully elegant, the personification of decorative repose; equally decorative, but with the showy restlessness of a dragonfly, Comus disported his flannelled person over a considerable span of the available foreground.

The intimacy existing between the two young men had suffered no immediate dislocation from the circumstance that they were tacitly paying court to the same lady. It was an intimacy founded not in the least on friendship or community of tastes and ideas, but owed its existence to the fact that each was amused and interested by the other. Youghal found Comus, for the time being at any rate, just as amusing and interesting as a rival for Elaine's favour as he had been in the rôle of scapegrace boy-about-town; Comus for his part did not wish to lose touch with Youghal, who among other attractions possessed the recommendation of being under the ban of Comus's mother. She disapproved, it is true, of a great many of her son's friends and associates, but this particular one was a special and persistent source of irritation to her from the fact that he figured prominently and more or less successfully in the public life of the day. There was something peculiarly exasperating in reading a brilliant and incisive attack on the Government's rash handling of public expenditure delivered by a young man who encouraged her son in every imaginable extravagance. The actual extent of Youghal's influence over the boy was of the slightest; Comus was quite capable of deriving encouragement to rash outlay and frivolous conversation from an anchorite or an East End parson if he had been thrown into close companionship with such an individual. Francesca, however, exercised a mother's privilege in assuming her son's bachelor associates to be industrious in labouring to achieve his undoing. Therefore the young politician was a source of unconcealed annoyance to her, and in the same degree as she expressed her disapproval of him Comus was careful to maintain and parade the intimacy. Its existence, or rather its continued existence, was one of the things that faintly puzzled the young lady whose sought-for favour might have been expected to furnish an occasion for its rapid dissolution.

With two suitors, one of whom at least she found markedly attractive, courting her at the same moment, Elaine should have had reasonable cause for being on good terms with the world, and with herself in particular. Happiness was not, however, at this auspicious moment, her dominant mood. The grave calm of her face masked as usual a certain degree of grave perturbation. A succession of well-meaning governesses, and a plentiful supply of moralizing aunts on both sides of her family, had impressed on her young mind the theoretical fact that wealth is a great responsibility. The consciousness of her responsibility set her continually wondering, not as to her own fitness to discharge her 'stewardship,' but as to the motives and merits of people with whom she came in contact. The knowledge that there was so much in the world that she could buy invited speculation as to how much there was that was worth buying. Gradually she had come to regard her mind as a sort of appeal court before whose secret sittings were examined and judged the motives and actions, the motives especially, of the world in general. In her schoolroom days she had sat in conscientious judgment on the motives that guided or misguided Charles and Cromwell and Monck, Wallenstein and Savonarola. In her present stage she was equally occupied in examining the political sincerity of the Secretary for Foreign Affairs, the good-faith of a honey-tongued but possibly loyal-hearted waiting-maid, and the disinterestedness of a whole circle of indulgent and flattering acquaintances. Even more absorbing, and, in her eyes, more urgently necessary, was the task of dissecting and appraising the characters of the two young men who were favouring her with their attentions. And herein lay cause for much thinking and some perturbation. Youghal, for example, might have baffled a more experienced observer of human nature. Elaine was too clever to confound his dandyism with foppishness or self-advertisement. He admired his own toilet effect in a mirror from a genuine sense of pleasure in a thing good to look upon, just as he would feel a sensuous appreciation of the sight of a well-bred, well-matched, well-turned-out pair of horses. Behind his careful political flippancy and cynicism one might also detect a certain careless sincerity, which would probably in the long run save him from moderate success, and turn him into one of the brilliant failures of his day. Beyond this it was difficult to form an exact appreciation of Courtenay Youghal, and Elaine, who liked to have her impressions distinctly labelled and pigeonholed, was perpetually scrutinizing the outer surface of his characteristics and utterances, like a baffled art critic vainly searching beneath the varnish and scratches of a doubtfully assigned picture for an enlightening signature. The young man added to her perplexities by his deliberate policy of never trying to show himself in a favourable light even when most anxious to impart a favourable impression. He preferred that people should hunt for his good qualities, and merely took very good care that as far as possible they should never draw blank; even in the matter of selfishness, which was the anchor-sheet of his existence, he contrived to be noted, and justly noted, for doing remarkably unselfish things. As a ruler he would have been reasonably popular; as a husband he would probably be unendurable.

Comus was to a certain extent as great a mystification as Youghal, but here Elaine was herself responsible for some of the perplexity which enshrouded his character in her eyes. She had taken more than a passing fancy for the boy—for the boy as he might be, that was to say—and she was desperately unwilling to see him and appraise him as he really was. Thus the mental court of appeal was constantly engaged in examining witnesses as to character, most of whom signally failed to give any testimony which would support the favourable judgment which the tribunal was so anxious to arrive at. A woman with wider experience of the world's ways and shortcomings would probably have contented herself with an endeavour to find out whether her liking for the boy outweighed her dislike of his characteristics; Elaine took her judgments too seriously to approach the matter from such a simple and convenient standpoint. The fact that she was much more than half in love with Comus made it dreadfully important that she should discover him to have a lovable soul, and Comus, it must be confessed, did little to help forward the discovery.

'At any rate he is honest,' she would observe to herself, after some outspoken admission of unprincipled conduct on his part, and then she would ruefully recall certain episodes in which he had figured, from which honesty had been conspicuously absent. What she tried to label honesty in his candour was probably only a cynical defiance of the laws of right and wrong.

'You look more than usually thoughtful this afternoon,' said Comus to her, 'as if you had invented this summer day and were trying to think out improvements.'

'If I had the power to create improvements anywhere I think I should begin with you,' retorted Elaine.

'I'm sure it's much better to leave me as I am,' protested Comus; 'you're like a relative of mine up in Argyllshire, who spends his time producing improved breeds of sheep and pigs and chickens. So patronizing and irritating to the Almighty, I should think, to go about putting superior finishing touches to Creation.'

Elaine frowned, and then laughed, and finally gave a little sigh.

'It's not easy to talk sense to you,' she said.

'Whatever else you take in hand,' said Youghal, 'you must never improve this garden. It's what our idea of heaven might be like if the Jews hadn't invented one for us on totally different lines. It's dreadful that we should accept them as the impresarios of our religious dreamland instead of the Greeks.'

'You are not very fond of the Jews,' said Elaine.

'I've travelled and lived a good deal in Eastern Europe, said Youghal.

'It seems largely a question of geography,' said Elaine; 'in England no one really is anti-Semitic.'

Youghal shook his head. 'I know a great many Jews who are.'

Servants had quietly, almost reverently, placed tea and its accessories on the wicker table, and quietly receded from the landscape. Elaine sat like a grave young goddess about to dispense some mysterious potion to her devotees. Her mind was still sitting in judgment on the Jewish question.

Comus scrambled to his feet.

'It's too hot for tea,' he said; 'I shall go and feed the swans.'

And he walked off with a little silver basket-dish containing brown bread-and-butter.

Elaine laughed quietly.

'It's so like Comus,' she said, 'to go off with our one dish of bread-and-butter.'

Youghal chuckled responsively. It was an undoubted opportunity for him to put in some disparaging criticism of Comus, and Elaine sat alert in readiness to judge the critic and reserve judgment on the criticized.

'His selfishness is splendid but absolutely futile,' said Youghal; 'now my selfishness is commonplace, but always thoroughly practical and calculated. He will have great difficulty in getting the swans to accept his offering, and he incurs the odium of reducing us to a bread-and-butterless condition. Incidentally, he will get very hot.'

Elaine again had the sense of being thoroughly baffled. If Youghal had said anything unkind it was about himself.

'If my cousin Suzette had been here,' she observed, with the shadow of a malicious smile on her lips, 'I believe she would have gone into a flood of tears at the loss of her bread-and-butter, and Comus would have figured ever after in her mind as something black and destroying and hateful. In fact, I don't really know why we took our loss so unprotestingly.'

'For two reasons,' said Youghal: 'you are rather fond of Comus. And I—am not very fond of bread-and-butter.'

The jesting remark brought a throb of pleasure to

Elaine's heart. She had known full well that she cared for Comus, but now that Courtenay Youghal had openly proclaimed the fact as something unchallenged and understood, matters seemed placed at once on a more advanced footing. The warm sunlit garden grew suddenly into a heaven that held the secret of eternal happiness. Youth and comeliness would always walk here, under the low-boughed mulberry trees, as unchanging as the leaden otter that for ever preyed on the leaden salmon on the edge of the old fountain, and somehow the lovers would always wear the aspect of herself and the boy who was talking to the four white swans by the water steps. Youghal was right; this was the real heaven of one's dreams and longings, immeasurably removed from that Rue de la Paix Paradise about which one professed utterly insincere hankerings in places of public worship. Elaine drank her tea in a happy silence; besides being a brilliant talker Youghal understood the rarer art of being a non-talker on occasion.

Comus came back across the grass swinging the empty basket-dish in his hand.

'Swans were very pleased,' he cried gaily, 'and said they hoped I would keep the bread-and-butter dish as a souvenir of a happy tea-party. I may really have it, mayn't I?' he continued in an anxious voice; 'it will do to keep studs and things in. You don't want it.'

'It's got the family crest on it,' said Elaine. Some of the happiness had died out of her eyes.

'I'll have that scratched off and my own put on,' said Comus.

'It's been in the family for generations,' protested Elaine, who did not share Comus's view that because you were rich your lesser possessions could have no value in your eyes.

'I want it dreadfully,' said Comus sulkily, 'and you've heaps of other things to put bread-and-butter in.'

For the moment he was possessed by an overmastering desire to keep the dish at all costs; a look of greedy determination dominated his face, and he had not for an instant relaxed his grip of the coveted object.

Elaine was genuinely angry by this time, and was busily telling herself that it was absurd to be put out over such a trifle; at the same moment a sense of justice was telling her that Comus was displaying a good deal of rather shabby selfishness. And somehow her chief anxiety at the moment was to keep Courtenay Youghal from seeing that she was angry.

'I know you don't really want it, so I'm going to keep it,' persisted Comus.

'It's too hot to argue,' said Elaine.

'Happy mistress of your destinies,' laughed Youghal; 'you can suit your disputations to the desired time and temperature. I have to go and argue, or what is worse, listen to other people's arguments, in a hot and doctored atmosphere suitable to an invalid lizard.'

'You haven't got to argue about a bread-and-butter dish,' said Elaine.

'Chiefly about bread-and-butter,' said Youghal; 'our great preoccupation is other people's bread-and-butter. They earn or produce the material, but we busy ourselves with making rules how it shall be cut up, and the size of the slices, and how much butter shall go on how much bread. That is what is called legislation. If we could only make rules as to how the bread-and-butter should be digested we should be quite happy.'

Elaine had been brought up to regard Parliaments as something to be treated with cheerful solemnity, like illness or family reunions. Youghal's flippant disparagement of the career in which he was involved did not, however, jar on her susceptibilities. She knew him to be not only a lively and effective debater but an industrious worker on committees. If he made light of his labours, at least he afforded no one else a loophole for doing so. And certainly the Parliamentary atmosphere was not uninviting on this hot afternoon.

'When must you go?' she asked sympathetically.

Youghal looked ruefully at his watch. Before he could answer, a cheerful hoot came through the air, as of an owl joyfully challenging the sunlight with a foreboding of the coming night. He sprang laughing to his feet.

'Listen! My summons back to my galley,' he cried. 'The Gods have given me an hour in this enchanted garden, so I must not complain.'

Then in a lower voice he almost whispered, 'It's the Persian debate tonight.'

It was the one hint he had given in the midst of his talking and laughing that he was really keenly enthralled in the work that lay before him. It was the one little intimate touch that gave Elaine the knowledge that he cared for her opinion of his work.

Comus, who had emptied his cigarette-case, became suddenly clamorous at the prospect of being temporarily stranded without a smoke. Youghal took the last remaining cigarette from his own case and gravely bisected it.

'Friendship could go no farther,' he observed, as he gave one-half to the doubtfully appeased Comus, and lit the other himself.

'There are heaps more in the hall,' said Elaine.

'It was only done for the Saint Martin of Tours effect,' said Youghal; 'I hate smoking when I'm rushing through the air. Good-bye.'

The departing galley-slave stepped forth into the sunlight, radiant and confident. A few minutes later Elaine could see glimpses of his white car as it rushed past the rhododendron bushes. He woos best who leaves first, particularly if he goes forth to battle or the semblance of battle.

Somehow Elaine's garden of Eternal Youth had already become clouded in its imagery. The girl-figure who walked in it was still distinctly and unchangingly herself, but her companion was more blurred and undefined, as a picture that has been superimposed on another.

Youghal sped townward well satisfied with himself. To-morrow, he reflected, Elaine would read his speech in her morning paper, and he knew in advance that it was not going to be one of his worst efforts. He knew almost exactly where the punctuations of laughter and applause would burst in, he knew that nimble fingers in the Press Gallery would be taking down each gibe and argument as he flung it at the impassive Minister confronting him, and that the fair lady of his desire would be able to judge what manner of young man this was who spent his afternoon in her garden, lazily chaffing himself and his world.

And he further reflected, with an amused chuckle, that she would be vividly reminded of Comus for days to come, when she took her afternoon tea, and saw the bread-and-butter reposing in an unaccustomed dish.

CHAPTER VII

Towards four o'clock on a hot afternoon Francesca stepped out from a shop entrance near the Piccadilly end of Bond Street and ran almost into the arms of Merla Blathlington. The afternoon seemed to get instantly hotter. Merla was one of those human flies that buzz; in crowded streets, at bazaars and in warm weather, she attained to the proportions of a human bluebottle. Lady Caroline Benaresq had openly predicted that a special fly-paper was being reserved for her accommodation in another world; others, however, held the opinion that she would be miraculously multiplied in a future state, and that four or more Merla Blathlingtons, according to deserts, would be in perpetual and unremitting attendance on each lost soul.

'Here we are,' she cried, with a glad eager buzz, 'popping in and out of shops like rabbits; not that rabbits do pop in and out of shops very extensively.'

It was evidently one of her bluebottle days.

'Don't you love Bond Street?' she gabbled on. 'There's something so unusual and distinctive about it; no other street anywhere else is quite like it. Don't you know those ikons and images and things scattered up and down Europe, that are supposed to have been painted or carved, as the case may be, by St Luke or Zaccheus, or somebody of that sort; I always like to think that some notable person of those times designed Bond Street. St Paul, perhaps. He travelled about a lot.'

'Not in Middlesex, though,' said Francesca.

'One can't be sure,' persisted Merla; 'when one wanders about as much as he did one gets mixed up and forgets where one *has* been. I can never remember whether I've been to the Tyrol twice and St Moritz once, or the other way about; I always have to ask my maid. And there's something about the name Bond that suggests St Paul; didn't he write a lot about the bond and the free?'

'I fancy he wrote in Hebrew or Greek,' objected Francesca; 'the word wouldn't have the least resemblance.'

'So dreadfully non-committal to go about pamphleteering in those bizarre languages,' complained Merla; 'that's what makes all those people so elusive. As soon as you try to pin them down to a definite statement about anything you're told that some vitally important word has fifteen other meanings in the original. I wonder our Cabinet Ministers and politicians don't adopt a sort of dog-Latin or Esperanto jargon to deliver their speeches in; what a lot of subsequent explaining away would be saved! But to go back to Bond Street—not that we've left it——'

'I'm afraid I must leave it now,' said Francesca, preparing to turn up Grafton Street. 'Good-bye.'

'Must you be going? Come and have tea somewhere. I know of a cosy little place where one can talk undisturbed.'

Francesca repressed a shudder and pleaded an urgent engagement.

'I know where you're going,' said Merla, with the resentful buzz of a bluebottle that finds itself thwarted by the cold unreasoning resistance of a windowpane. 'You're going to play bridge at Serena Golackly's. She never asks me to her bridge parties.'

Francesca shuddered openly this time; the prospect of having to play bridge anywhere in the near neighbourhood of Merla's voice was not one that could be contemplated with ordinary calmness.

'Good-bye,' she said again firmly, and passed out of ear-shot; it was rather like leaving the machinery section of an exhibition. Merla's diagnosis of her destination had been a correct one; Francesca made her way slowly through the hot streets in the direction of Serena's Golackly's house on the far side of Berkeley Square. To the blessed certainty of finding a game of bridge she hopefully added the possibility of hearing some fragments of news which might prove interesting and enlightening. And of enlightenment on a particular subject, in which she was acutely and personally interested, she stood in some need. Comus of late had been provokingly reticent as to his movements and doings; partly, perhaps, because it was his nature to be provoking, partly because the daily bickerings over money matters were gradually choking other forms of conversation. Francesca had seen him once or twice in the Park in the desirable company of Elaine de Frey, and from time to time she heard of the young people as having danced together at various houses; on the other hand, she had seen and heard quite as much evidence to connect the heiress's name with that of Courtenay Youghal. Beyond this meagre and conflicting and altogether tantalizing information, her knowledge of the present position of affairs did not go. If either of the young men was seriously 'making the running,' it was probable that she would hear some sly hint or open comment about it from one of Serena's gossip-laden friends, without having to go out of her way to introduce the subject and unduly disclose her own state of ignorance. And a game of bridge, played for moderately high points, gave ample excuse for convenient lapses into reticence; if questions took an embarrassingly inquisitive turn, one could always find refuge in a defensive spade.

The afternoon was too warm to make bridge a generally popular diversion, and Serena's party was a comparatively small one. Only one table was incomplete when Francesca made her appearance on the scene; at it was seated Serena herself, confronted by Ada Spelvexit, whom every one was wont to explain as 'one of the Cheshire Spelvexits,' as though any other variety would have been intolerable. Ada Spelvexit was one of those naturally stagnant souls who take infinite pleasure in what are called 'movements.' 'Most of the really great lessons I have learned have been taught me by the Poor,' was one of her favourite statements. The one great lesson that the Poor in general would have liked to have taught her, that their kitchens and sickrooms were not unreservedly at her disposal as private lecture halls, she had never been able to assimilate. She was ready to give them unlimited advice as to how they should keep the wolf from their doors, but in return she claimed and enforced for herself the penetrating powers of an east wind or a dust-storm. Her visits among her wealthier acquaintances were equally extensive and enterprising, and hardly more welcome; in country-house parties, while partaking to the fullest extent of the hospitality offered her, she made a practice of unburdening herself of homilies on the evils of leisure and luxury, which did not particularly endear her to her fellow-guests. Hostesses regarded her philosophically as a form of social measles which every one had to have once.

The third prospective player, Francesca noted without any special enthusiasm, was Lady Caroline Benaresq. Lady Caroline was far from being a remarkably good bridge player, but she always managed to domineer mercilessly over any table that was favoured with her presence, and generally managed to win. A domineering player usually inflicts the chief damage and demoralization on his partner; Lady Caroline's special achievement was to harass and demoralize partner and opponents alike.

'Weak and weak,' she announced in her gentle voice, as she cut her hostess for a partner; 'I suppose we had better play only five shillings a hundred.'

Francesca wondered at the old woman's moderate assessment of the stake, knowing her fondness for highish play and her usual good luck in card holding.

'I don't mind what we play,' said Ada Spelvexit, with an

incautious parade of elegant indifference; as a matter of fact she was inwardly relieved and rejoicing at the reasonable figure proposed by Lady Caroline, and she would certainly have demurred if a higher stake had been suggested. She was not as a rule a successful player, and money lost at cards was always a poignant bereavement to her.

'Then as you don't mind we'll make it ten shillings a hundred,' said Lady Caroline, with the pleased chuckle of one who has spread a net in the sight of a bird and disproved the vanity of the proceeding.

It proved a tiresome ding-dong rubber, with the strength of the cards slightly on Francesca's side, and the luck of the table going mostly the other way. She was too keen a player not to feel a certain absorption in the game once it had started, but she was conscious today of a distracting interest that competed with the momentary importance of leads and discards and declarations. The little accumulations of talk that were unpent during the dealing of the hands became as noteworthy to her alert attention as the play of the hands themselves.

'Yes, quite a small party this afternoon,' said Serena, in reply to a seemingly casual remark on Francesca's part; 'and two or three non-players, which is unusual on a Wednesday. Canon Besomley was here just before you came; you know, the big preaching man.'

'I've been to hear him scold the human race once or twice,' said Francesca.

'A strong man with a wonderfully strong message,' said Ada Spelvexit, in an impressive and assertive tone.

'The sort of popular pulpiteer who spanks the vices of his age and lunches with them afterwards,' said Lady Caroline.

'Hardly a fair summary of the man and his work,' protested Ada. 'I've been to hear him many times when I've been depressed or discouraged, and I simply can't tell you the impression his words leave—   '

'At least you can tell us what you intend to make trumps,' broke in Lady Caroline gently.

'Diamonds,' pronounced Ada, after a rather flurried survey of her hand.

'Doubled,' said Lady Caroline, with increased politeness, and a few minutes later she was pencilling an addition of twenty-four to her score.

'I stayed with his people down here in Herefordshire last May,' said Ada, returning to the unfinished theme of the Canon; 'such an exquisite rural retreat, and so restful and healing to the nerves. Real country scenery; apple blossom everywhere.'

'Surely only on the apple trees!' said Lady Caroline.

Ada Spelvexit gave up the attempt to reproduce the decorative setting of the Canon's home-life, and fell back on the small but practical consolation of scoring the odd trick in her opponent's declaration of hearts.

'If you had led your highest club to start with, instead of the nine, we should have saved the trick,' remarked Lady Caroline to her partner in a tone of coldly gentle reproof; 'it's no use, my dear,' she continued, as Serena flustered out a halting apology, 'no earthly use to attempt to play bridge at one table and try to see and hear what's going on at two or three other tables.'

'I can generally manage to attend to more than one thing at a time,' said Serena rashly; 'I think I must have a sort of double brain.'

'Much better to economize and have one really good one,' observed Lady Caroline.

'*La belle dame sans merci* scoring a verbal trick or two as usual,' said a player at another table in a discreet undertone.

'Did I tell you Sir Edward Roan is coming to my next big evening?' said Serena hurriedly, by way, perhaps, of restoring herself a little in her own esteem.

'Poor, dear, good Sir Edward! What have you made trumps?' asked Lady Caroline, in one breath.

'Clubs,' said Francesca; 'and pray, why these adjectives of commiseration?'

Francesca was a Ministerialist by family interest and allegiance, and was inclined to take up the cudgels at the suggested disparagement aimed at the Foreign Secretary.

'He amuses me so much,' purred Lady Caroline. Her amusement was usually of the sort that a sporting cat derives from watching the Swedish exercises of a well-spent and carefully thought-out mouse.

'Really? He has been rather a brilliant success at the Foreign Office, you know,' said Francesca.

'He reminds one so of a circus elephant—infinitely more intelligent than the people who direct him, but quite content to go on putting his foot down or taking it up as may be required, quite unconcerned whether he steps on a meringue or a hornet's nest in the process of going where he's expected to go.'

'How can you say such things!' protested Francesca.

'I can't,' said Lady Caroline; 'Courtenay Youghal said it in the House last night. Didn't you read the debate? He was really rather in form. I disagree entirely with his point of view, of course, but some of the things he says have just enough truth behind them to redeem them from being merely smart; for instance, his summing up of the Government's attitude towards our embarrassing Colonial Empire in the wistful phrase "Happy is the country that has no geography." '

'What an absurdly unjust thing to say!' put in Francesca; 'I daresay some of our Party at some time have taken up that attitude, but every one knows that Sir Edward is a sound Imperialist at heart.'

'Most politicians are something or other at heart, but no one would be rash enough to insure a politician against heart failure. Particularly when he happens to be in office.'

'Anyhow, I don't see that the Opposition leaders would have acted any differently in the present case,' said Francesca.

'One should always speak guardedly of the Opposition leaders,' said Lady Caroline, in her gentlest voice; 'one never knows what a turn in the situation may do for them.'

'You mean they may one day be at the head of affairs?' asked Serena briskly.

'I mean they may one day lead the Opposition. One never knows.'

Lady Caroline had just remembered that her hostess was on the Opposition side in politics.

Francesca and her partner scored four tricks in clubs; the game stood irresolutely at twenty-four all.

'If you had followed the excellent lyrical advice given to the Maid of Athens and returned my heart we should have made two more tricks and gone game,' said Lady Caroline to her partner.

'Mr Youghal seems to be pushing himself to the fore of late,' remarked Francesca, as Serena took up the cards to deal. Since the young politician's name had been introduced into the conversation the opportunity for turning the talk more directly on him and his affairs was too good to be missed.

'I think he's got a career before him,' said Serena; 'the House always fills when he's speaking, and that's a good sign. And then he's young and got rather an attractive personality, which is always something in the political world.'

'His lack of money will handicap him, unless he can find himself a rich wife or persuade some one to die and leave him a fat legacy,' said Francesca; 'since M.P.s have become the recipients of a salary rather more is expected and demanded of them in the expenditure line than before.'

'Yes, the House of Commons still remains rather at the opposite pole to the Kingdom of Heaven as regards entrance qualifications,' observed Lady Caroline.

'There ought to be no difficulty about Youghal picking up a girl with money,' said Serena; 'with his prospects he would make an excellent husband for any woman with social ambitions.'

And she half sighed, as though she almost regretted that a previous matrimonial arrangement precluded her from entering into the competition on her own account.

Francesca, under an assumption of languid interest, was watching Lady Caroline narrowly for some hint of suppressed knowledge of Youghal's courtship of Miss de Frey.

'Whom are you marrying and giving in marriage?'

The question came from George St Michael, who had strayed over from a neighbouring table, attracted by the fragments of small-talk that had reached his ears.

St Michael was one of those dapper, bird-like, illusorily-active men, who seem to have been in a certain stage of middle-age for as long as human memory can recall them. A close-cut peaked beard lent a certain dignity to his appearance—a loan which the rest of his features and mannerisms were continually and successfully repudiating. His profession, if he had one, was submerged in his hobby, which consisted of being an advance-agent for small happenings or possible happenings that were or seemed imminent in the social world around him; he found a perpetual and unflagging satisfaction in acquiring and retailing any stray items of gossip or information, particularly of a matrimonial nature, that chanced to come his way. Given the bare outline of an officially announced engagement, he would immediately fill it in with all manner of details, true or, at any rate, probable, drawn from his own imagination or from some equally exclusive source. The *Morning Post* might content itself with the mere statement of the arrangement which would shortly take place, but it was St Michael's breathless little voice that proclaimed how the contracting parties had originally met over a salmon-fishing incident, why the Guards' Chapel would not be used, why her Aunt Mary had at first opposed the match, how the question of the children's religious upbringing had been compromised, etc., etc., to all whom it might interest and to many whom it might not. Beyond his industrially-earned pre-eminence in this special branch of intelligence, he was chiefly noteworthy for having a wife reputed to be the tallest and thinnest woman in the Home Counties. The two were sometimes seen together in Society, where they passed under the collective name of St Michael and All Angles.

'We are trying to find a rich wife for Courtenay Youghal,' said Serena, in answer to St Michael's question.

'Ah, there I'm afraid you're a little late,' he observed, glowing with the importance of pending revelation; 'I'm afraid you're a little late,' he repeated, watching the effect of his words as a gardener might watch the development of a bed of carefully tended asparagus. 'I think the young gentleman has been before you and already found himself a rich mate in prospect.'

He lowered his voice as he spoke, not with a view to imparting impressive mystery to his statement, but because there were other table groups within hearing to whom he hoped presently to have the privilege of re-disclosing his revelation.

'Do you mean——?' began Serena.

'Miss de Frey,' broke in St Michael hurriedly, fearful lest his revelation should be forestalled, even in guesswork; 'quite an ideal choice, the very wife for a man who means to make his mark in politics. Twenty-four thousand a year, with prospects of more to come, and a charming place of her own not too far from town. Quite the type of girl, too, who will make a good political hostess, brains without being brainy, you know. Just the right thing. Of course, it would be premature to make any definite announcement at present——'

'It would hardly be premature for my partner to announce what she means to make trumps,' interrupted Lady Caroline, in a voice of such sinister gentleness that St Michael fled headlong back to his own table.

'Oh, is it me? I beg your pardon. I leave it,' said Serena.

'Thank you. No trumps,' declared Lady Caroline. The hand was successful, and the rubber ultimately fell to her with a comfortable margin of honours. The same partners cut together again, and this time the cards went distinctly against Francesca and Ada Spelvexit, and a heavily piled-up score confronted them at the close of the rubber.

Francesca was conscious that a certain amount of rather erratic play on her part had at least contributed to the result. St Michael's incursion into the conversation had proved rather a powerful distraction to her ordinarily sound bridge-craft.

Ada Spelvexit emptied her purse of several gold pieces, and infused a corresponding degree of superiority into her manner.

'I must be going now,' she announced; 'I'm dining early. I have to give an address to some charwomen afterwards.'

'Why?' asked Lady Caroline, with a disconcerting directness that was one of her most formidable characteristics.

'Oh, well, I have some things to say to them that I daresay they will like to hear,' said Ada, with a thin laugh.

Her statement was received with a silence that betokened profound unbelief in any such probability.

'I go about a good deal among working-class women,' she added.

'No one has ever said it,' observed Lady Caroline, 'but how painfully true it is that the poor have us always with them!'

Ada Spelvexit hastened her departure; the marred impressiveness of her retreat came as a culminating discomfiture on the top of her ill-fortune at the card-table. Possibly, however, the multiplication of her own annoyances enabled her to survey charwomen's troubles with increased cheerfulness. None of them, at any rate, had spent an afternoon with Lady Caroline.

Francesca cut in at another table and, with better fortune attending on her, succeeded in winning back most of her losses. A sense of satisfaction was distinctly dominant as she took leave of her hostess. St Michael's gossip, or rather the manner in which it had been received, had given her a clue to the real state of affairs, which, however slender and conjectural, at least pointed in the desired direction. At first she had been horribly afraid lest she should be listening to a definite announcement which would have been the death-blow to her hopes, but as the recitation went on

without any of those assured little minor details which
St Michael so loved to supply, she had come to the conclusion that it was merely a piece of intelligent guesswork.
And if Lady Caroline had really believed in the story of
Elaine de Frey's virtual engagement to Courtenay Youghal
she would have taken a malicious pleasure in encouraging
St Michael in his confidences, and in watching Francesca's
discomfiture under the recital. The irritated manner in
which she had cut short the discussion betrayed the fact
that, as far as the old woman's information went, it was
Comus, and not Courtenay Youghal, who held the field.
And in this particular case Lady Caroline's information
was likely to be nearer the truth than St Michael's confident gossip.

Francesca always gave a penny to the first crossing-
sweeper or match-seller she chanced across after a
successful sitting at bridge. This afternoon she had come
out of the fray some fifteen shillings to the bad, but she
gave two pennies to a crossing-sweeper at the north-west
corner of Berkeley Square as a sort of thank-offering to the
gods.

CHAPTER VIII

It was a fresh rain-repentant afternoon, following a morning that had been sultry and torrentially wet by turns:
the sort of afternoon that impels people to talk graciously
of the rain as having done a lot of good, its chief merit in
their eyes probably having been its recognition of the
art of moderation. Also it was an afternoon that invited
bodily activity after the convalescent languor of the earlier
part of the day. Elaine had instinctively found her way into
her riding-habit and sent an order down to the stables—
a blessed oasis that still smelt sweetly of horse and hay and
cleanliness in a world that reeked of petrol, and now she
set her mare at a smart pace through a succession of long-
stretching country lanes. She was due some time that

afternoon at a garden party, but she rode with determination in an opposite direction. In the first place, neither Comus nor Courtenay would be at the party, which fact seemed to remove any valid reason that could be thought of for inviting her attendance thereat; in the second place about a hundred human beings would be gathered there, and human gatherings were not her most crying need at the present moment. Since her last encounter with her wooers, under the cedars in her own garden, Elaine realized that she was either very happy or cruelly unhappy, she could not quite determine which. She seemed to have what she most wanted in the world lying at her feet, and she was dreadfully uncertain in her more reflective moments whether she really wanted to stretch out her hand and take it. It was all very like some situation in an *Arabian Nights* tale or a story of Pagan Hellas, and consequently the more puzzling and disconcerting to a girl brought up on the methodical lines of Victorian Christianity. Her appeal court was in permanent session these last few days, but it gave no decisions, at least none that she would listen to. And the ride on her fast light-stepping little mare, alone and unattended, through the fresh-smelling leafy lanes into unexplored country, seemed just what she wanted at the moment. The mare made some small delicate pretence of being road-shy, not the staring dolt-like kind of nervousness that shows itself in an irritating hanging-back as each conspicuous wayside object presents itself, but the nerve-flutter of an imaginative animal that merely results in a quick whisk of the head and a swifter bound forward. She might have paraphrased the mental attitude of the immortalized Peter Bell into

> A basket underneath a tree
> A yellow tiger is to me,
> If it is nothing more.

The more really alarming episodes of the road, the hoot and whir of a passing motor-car or the loud vibrating hum of a wayside threshing-machine, were treated with indifference.

On turning a corner out of a narrow coppice-bordered lane into a wider road that sloped steadily upward in a long stretch of hill, Elaine saw, coming toward her at no great distance, a string of yellow-painted vans, drawn for the most part by skewbald or speckled horses. A certain rakish air about these oncoming road-craft proclaimed them as belonging to a travelling wild-beast show, decked out in the rich primitive colouring that one's taste in childhood would have insisted on before it had been schooled in the artistic value of dullness. It was an unlooked-for and distinctly unwelcome encounter. The mare had already commenced a sixfold scrutiny with nostrils, eyes, and daintily-pricked ears; one ear made hurried little backward movements to hear what Elaine was saying about the eminent niceness and respectability of the approaching caravan, but even Elaine felt that she would be unable satisfactorily to explain the elephants and camels that could certainly form part of the procession. To turn back would seem rather craven, and the mare might take fright at the manœuvre and try to bolt; a gate standing ajar at the entrance to a farmyard lane provided a convenient way out of the difficulty.

As Elaine pushed her way through she became aware of a man standing just inside the lane, who made a movement forward to open the gate for her.

'Thank you. I'm just getting out of the way of a wild-beast show,' she explained; 'my mare is tolerant of motors and traction-engines, but I expect camels—hallo!' she broke off, recognizing the man as an old acquaintance, 'I heard you had taken rooms in a farmhouse somewhere. Fancy meeting you in this way!'

In the not very distant days of her little-girlhood Tom Keriway had been a man to be looked upon with a certain awe and envy; indeed the glamour of his roving career would have fired the imagination, and wistful desire to do likewise, of many young Englishmen. It seemed to be the grown-up realization of the games played in dark rooms in winter firelit evenings, and the dreams dreamed over favourite books of adventure. Making Vienna his headquarters, almost his home, he had rambled where he listed through the lands of the Near and Middle East as leisurely and thoroughly as tamer souls might explore Paris. He had wandered through Hungarian horse-fairs, hunted shy crafty beasts on lonely Balkan hillsides, dropped himself pebble-wise into the stagnant human pool of some Bulgarian monastery, threaded his way through the strange racial mosaic of Salonika, listened with amused politeness to the shallow ultra-modern opinions of a voluble editor or lawyer in some wayside Russian town, or learned wisdom from a chance tavern companion, one of the atoms of the busy ant-stream of men and merchandise that moves untiringly round the shores of the Black Sea. And far and wide as he might roam, he always managed to turn up at frequent intervals, at ball and supper and theatre, in the gay Hauptstadt of the Habsburgs, haunting his favourite cafés and wine-vaults, skimming through his favourite news-sheets, greeting old acquaintances and friends, from ambassadors down to cobblers in the social scale. He seldom talked of his travels, but it might be said that his travels talked of him; there was an air about him that a German diplomat once summed up in a phrase: 'a man that wolves have sniffed at.'

And then two things happened, which he had not mapped out in his route; a severe illness shook half the life and all the energy out of him, and a heavy money loss brought him almost to the door of destitution. With something, perhaps, of the impulse which drives a stricken animal away from its kind, Tom Keriway left the haunts where he had known so much happiness, and withdrew into the shelter of a secluded farmhouse lodging; more than ever he became to Elaine a hearsay personality. And now the chance meeting with the caravan had flung her across the threshold of his retreat.

'What a charming little nook you've got hold of!' she exclaimed with instinctive politeness, and then looked searchingly round, and discovered that she had spoken the truth; it really was charming. The farmhouse had that intensely English look that one seldom sees out of Normandy. Over the whole scene of rickyard, garden, outbuildings, horsepond, and orchard, brooded that air which seems rightfully to belong to out-of-the-way farmyards, an air of wakeful dreaminess which suggests that here man and beast and bird have got up so early that the rest of the world has never caught them up and never will.

Elaine dismounted, and Keriway led the mare round to a little paddock by the side of a great grey barn. At the end of the lane they could see the show go past, a string of lumbering vans and great striding beasts that seemed to link the vast silences of the desert with the noises and sights and smells, the naphtha-flares and advertisement hoardings and trampled orange-peel, of an endless succession of towns.

'You had better let the caravan pass well on its way before you get on the road again,' said Keriway; 'the smell of the beasts may make your mare nervous and restive going home.'

Then he called to a boy, who was busy with a hoe among some defiantly prosperous weeds, to fetch the lady a glass of milk and a piece of currant loaf.

'I don't know when I've seen anything so utterly charming and peaceful,' said Elaine, propping herself on a seat that a pear-tree had obligingly designed in the fantastic curve of its trunk.

'Charming, certainly,' said Keriway, 'but too full of the stress of its own little life struggle to be peaceful. Since I have lived here I've learnt, what I've always suspected, that a country farmhouse, set away in a world of its own, is one of the most wonderful studies of interwoven happenings and tragedies that can be imagined. It is like the old chronicles of medieval Europe in the days when there was a sort of ordered anarchy between feudal lords and overlords, and burg-grafs, and mitred abbots, and prince-bishops, robber barons and merchant guilds, and Electors and so forth, all striving and contending and counter-plotting and interfering with each other under some vague code of loosely-applied rules. Here one sees it reproduced under one's eyes, like a musty page of black-letter come to life. Look at one little section of it, the poultry-life on the farm. Villa poultry, dull egg-machines, with records kept of how many ounces of food they eat, and how many pennyworths of eggs they lay, give you no idea of the wonder-life of these farm-birds; their feuds and jealousies, and carefully maintained prerogatives, their unsparing tyrannies and persecutions, their calculated courage and bravado or sedulously hidden cowardice, it might all be some human chapter from the annals of the old Rhineland or medieval Italy. And then, outside their own bickering wars and hates, the grim enemies that come up against them from the woodlands: the hawk that dashes among the coops like a moss-trooper raiding the border, knowing well that a charge of shot may tear him to bits at any moment. And the stoat, a creeping slip of brown fur a few inches long, intently and unstayably out for blood. And the hunger-taught master of craft, the red fox, who has waited perhaps half the afternoon for his chance while the fowls were dusting themselves under the hedge, and just as they were turning supper-ward to the yard one has stopped a moment to give her feathers a final shake and found death springing upon her. Do you know,' he continued, as Elaine fed herself and the mare with morsels of currant-loaf, 'I don't think any tragedy in litera-ture that I have ever come across impressed me so much as the first one that I spelled out slowly for myself in words of three letters: the bad fox has got the red hen. There was something so dramatically complete about it; the badness of the fox, added to all the traditional guile of his race, seemed to heighten the horror of the hen's fate, and there was such a suggestion of masterful malice about the word 'got.' One felt that a countryside in arms would not get that hen away from the bad fox. They used to think me a slow dull reader for not getting on with my lesson, but I used to sit and picture to myself the red hen, with its wings beating helplessly, screeching in terrified protest, or perhaps, if he had got it by the neck, with beak wide agape and silent, and eyes staring, as it left the farmyard for ever. I have seen blood-spilling and down-crushings and abject defeat here and there in my time, but the red hen has remained in my mind as the type of helpless tragedy.' He was silent for a moment as if he were again musing over the three-letter drama that had so dwelt in his childhood's imagination.

'Tell me some of the things you have seen in your time,' was the request that was nearly on Elaine's lips, but she hastily checked herself and substituted another.

'Tell me more about the farm, please.'

And he told her of a whole world, or rather of several intermingled worlds, set apart in this sleepy hollow in the hills, of beast lore and wood lore and farm craft, at times touching almost the border of witchcraft—passing lightly here, not with the probing eagerness of those who know nothing, but with the averted glance of those who fear to see too much. He told her of those things that slept and those that prowled when the dusk fell, of strange hunting cats, of the yard swine and the stalled cattle, of the farm folk themselves, as curious and remote in their way, in their ideas and fears and wants and tragedies, as the brutes and feathered stock that they tended. It seemed to Elaine as if a musty store of old-world children's books had been fetched down from some cobwebbed lumber-room and brought to life. Sitting there in the little pad-dock, grown thickly with tall weeds and rank grasses, and shadowed by the weather-beaten old grey barn, listening to this chronicle of wonderful things, half fanciful, half very real, she could scarcely believe that a few miles away there was a garden party in full swing, with smart frocks and smart conversation, fashionable refreshments and fashionable music, and a fevered undercurrent of social strivings and snubbings. Did Vienna and the Balkan Mountains and the Black Sea seem as remote and hard to believe in, she wondered, to the man sitting by her side, who had discovered or invented this wonderful fairyland? Was it a true and merciful arrangement of fate and life that the things of the moment thrust out the after-taste of the things that had been? Here was one who had held much that was priceless in the hollow of his hand and lost it all, and he was happy and absorbed and well content with the little wayside corner of the world into which he had crept. And Elaine, who held so many desirable things in the hollow of her hand, could not make up her mind to be even moderately happy. She did not even know whether to take this hero of her childhood down from his pedestal, or to place him on a higher one; on the whole she was inclined to resent rather than approve the idea that ill-health and misfortune could so completely subdue and tame an erstwhile bold and roving spirit.

The mare was showing signs of delicately-hinted impatience; the paddock, with its teasing insects and very indifferent grazing, had not thrust out the image of her own comfortable well-foddered loose-box. Elaine divested her habit of some remaining crumbs of bun-loaf and jumped lightly on to her saddle. As she rode slowly down the lane, with Keriway escorting her as far as its gate, she looked round at what had seemed to her, a short while ago, just a picturesque old farmstead, a place of bee-hives and hollyhocks and gabled cart-sheds; now it was in her eyes a magic city, with an undercurrent of reality beneath its magic.

'You are a person to be envied,' she said to Keriway; 'you have created a fairyland, and you are living in it yourself.'

'Envied?'

He shot the question out with sudden bitterness. She looked down and saw the wistful misery that had come into his face.

'Once,' he said to her, 'in a German paper I read a short story about a tame crippled crane that lived in the park of some small town. I forget what happened in the story, but there was one line that I shall always remember: "it was lame, that is why it was tame." '

He had created a fairyland, but assuredly he was not living in it.

CHAPTER IX

IN the warmth of a late June morning the long shaded stretch of raked earth, gravel-walk, and rhododendron bush that is known affectionately as the Row was alive with the monotonous movement and alert stagnation appropriate to the time and place. The seekers after health, the seekers after notoriety and recognition, and the lovers of good exercise were all well represented on the galloping ground; the gravel-walk and chairs and long seats held a population whose varied instincts and motives would have baffled a social catalogue-maker. The children, handled or in perambulators, might be excused from instinct or motive; they were brought.

Pleasingly conspicuous among a bunch of indifferent riders pacing along by the rails where the onlookers were thickest was Courtenay Youghal, on his handsome plum-roan gelding Anne de Joyeuse. That delicately stepping animal had taken a prize at Islington and nearly taken the life of a stable-boy of whom he disapproved, but his strongest claims to distinction were his good looks and his high opinion of himself. Youghal evidently believed in thorough accord between horse and rider.

'Please stop and talk to me,' said a quiet beckoning voice from the other side of the rails, and Youghal drew rein and greeted Lady Veula Croot. Lady Veula had married into a family of commercial solidity and enterprising political nonentity. She had a devoted husband, some blond teachable children, and a look of unutterable weariness in her eyes. To see her standing at the top of an expensively horticultured staircase receiving her husband's guests was rather like watching an animal performing on a music-hall stage. One always tells oneself that the animal likes it, and one always knows that it doesn't.

'Lady Veula is an ardent Free Trader, isn't she?' some one once remarked to Lady Caroline.

'I wonder,' said Lady Caroline, in her gently questioning voice; 'a woman whose dresses are made in Paris and whose marriage has been made in heaven might be equally biased for and against free imports.'

Lady Veula looked at Youghal and his mount with slow critical appraisement, and there was a note of blended raillery and wistfulness in her voice.

'You two dear things, I should love to stroke you both, but I'm not sure how Joyeuse would take it. So I'll stroke you down verbally instead. I admired your attack on Sir Edward immensely, though of course I don't agree with a word of it. Your description of him building a hedge round the German cuckoo and hoping he was isolating it was rather sweet. Seriously though, I regard him as one of the pillars of the Administration.'

'So do I,' said Youghal; 'the misfortune is that he is merely propping up a canvas roof. It's just his regrettable solidity and integrity that make him so expensively dangerous. The average Briton arrives at the same judgment about Roan's handling of foreign affairs as Omar does of the Supreme Being in his dealings with the world: "He's a good fellow and 'twill all be well." '

Lady Veula laughed lightly. 'My Party is in power, so I may exercise the privilege of being optimistic. Who is that who bowed to you?' she continued, as a dark young man with an inclination to stoutness passed by them on foot; 'I've seen him about a good deal lately. He's been to one or two of my dances.'

'Andrei Drakoloff,' said Youghal; 'he's just produced a play that has had a big success in Moscow and is certain to be extremely popular all over Russia. In the first three acts the heroine is supposed to be dying of consumption; in the last act they find she is really dying of cancer.'

'Are the Russians really such a gloomy people?'

'Gloom-loving, but not in the least gloomy. They merely take their sadness pleasurably, just as we are accused of taking our pleasures sadly. Have you noticed that dreadful Klopstock youth has been pounding past us at shortening intervals? He'll come up and talk if he half catches your eye.'

'I only just know him. Isn't he at an agricultural college or something of the sort?'

'Yes, studying to be a gentleman farmer, he told me. I didn't ask if both subjects were compulsory.'

'You're really rather dreadful,' said Lady Veula, trying to look as if she thought so; 'remember, we are all equal in the sight of Heaven.'

For a preacher of wholesome truths her voice rather lacked conviction.

'If I and Ernest Klopstock are really equal in the sight of Heaven,' said Youghal, with intense complacency, 'I should recommend Heaven to consult an eye specialist.'

There was a heavy spattering of loose earth, and a squelching of saddle-leather, as the Klopstock youth lumbered up to the rails and delivered himself of loud, cheerful greetings. Joyeuse laid his ears well back as the ungainly bay cob and his appropriately matched rider drew up beside him; his verdict was reflected and endorsed by the cold stare of Youghal's eyes.

'I've been having a nailing fine time,' recounted the newcomer with clamorous enthusiasm; 'I was over in Paris last month and had lots of strawberries there, then I had a lot more in London, and now I've been having a late crop of them in Herefordshire, so I've had quite a lot this year.' And he laughed as one who had deserved well and received well of Fate.

'The charm of that story,' said Youghal, 'is that it can be told in any drawing-room.' And with a sweep of his wide-brimmed hat to Lady Veula he turned the impatient Joyeuse into the moving stream of horses and horsemen.

'That woman reminds me of some verse I've read and liked,' thought Youghal, as Joyeuse sprang into a light showy canter that gave full recognition to the existence of observant human beings along the side-walk. 'Ah, I have it.'

And he quoted almost aloud, as one does in the exhilaration of a canter:

> 'How much I loved that way you had
> Of smiling most, when very sad,
> A smile which carried tender hints
> Of sun and spring,
> And yet, more than all other thing,
> Of weariness beyond all words.'

And having satisfactorily fitted Lady Veula on to a quotation he dismissed her from his mind. With the constancy of her sex she thought about him, his good looks and his youth and his railing tongue, till late in the afternoon.

While Youghal was putting Joyeuse through his paces under the elm trees of the Row a little drama in which he was directly interested was being played out not many hundred yards away. Elaine and Comus were indulging themselves in two pennyworths of Park chair, drawn aside just a little from the serried rows of sitters who were set out like bedded plants over an acre or so of turf. Comus was, for the moment, in a mood of pugnacious gaiety, disbursing a fund of pointed criticism and unsparing anecdote concerning those of the promenaders or loungers whom he knew personally or by sight. Elaine was rather quieter than usual, and the grave serenity of the Leonardo da Vinci portrait seemed intensified in her face this morning. In his leisurely courtship Comus had relied almost exclusively on his physical attraction and the fitful drollery of his wit and high spirits, and these graces had gone far to make him seem a very desirable and rather lovable thing in Elaine's eyes. But he had left out of account the disfavour which he constantly risked and sometimes incurred from his frank and undisguised indifference to other people's interests and wishes, including, at times, Elaine's. And the more that she felt that she liked him the more she was irritated by his lack of consideration for her. Without expecting that her every wish should become a law to him, she would at least have liked it to reach the formality of a Second Reading. Another important factor he had also left out of his reckoning, namely the presence on the scene of another suitor, who also had youth and wit to recommend him, and who certainly did not lack physical attractions. Comus, marching carelessly through unknown country to effect what seemed already an assured victory, made the mistake of disregarding the existence of an unbeaten army on his flank.

Today Elaine felt that, without having actually quarrelled, she and Comus had drifted a little bit out of sympathy with one another. The fault she knew was scarcely hers, in fact from the most good-natured point of view it could hardly be denied that it was almost entirely his. The incident of the silver dish had lacked even the attraction of novelty; it had been one of a series, all bearing a strong connecting likeness. There had been small unrepaid loans which Elaine would not have grudged in themselves, though the application for them brought a certain qualm of distaste; with the perversity which seemed inseparable from his doings, Comus had always flung away a portion of his borrowings in some ostentatious piece of glaring and utterly profitless extravagance, which outraged all the canons of her upbringing without bringing him an atom of understandable satisfaction. Under these repeated discouragements it was not surprising that some small part of her affection should have slipped away, but she had come to the Park that morning with an unconfessed expectation of being gently wooed back to the mood of gracious forgetfulness that she was only too eager to assume. It was almost worth while being angry with Comus for the sake of experiencing the pleasure of being coaxed into friendliness again with the charm which he knew so well how to exert. It was delicious here under the trees on this perfect June morning, and Elaine had the blessed assurance that most of the women within range were envying her the companionship of the handsome merry-hearted youth who sat by her side. With special complacence she contemplated her cousin Suzette, who was self-consciously but not very elatedly basking in the attentions of her fiancé, an earnest-looking young man who was superintendent of a People's something-or-other on the south side of the river, and whose clothes Comus had described as having been made in Southwark rather than in anger.

Most of the pleasures in life must be paid for, and the chair-ticket vendor in due time made his appearance in quest of pennies. Comus paid him from out of a varied assortment of coins and then balanced the remainder in the palm of his hand. Elaine felt a sudden foreknowledge of something disagreeable about to happen, and a red spot deepened in her cheeks.

'Four shillings and fivepence and a halfpenny,' said Comus reflectively. 'It's a ridiculous sum to last me for the next three days, and I owe a card debt of over two pounds.'

'Yes?' commented Elaine dryly and with an apparent lack of interest in his exchequer statement. Surely, she was thinking hurriedly to herself, he could not be foolish enough to broach the matter of another loan.

'The card debt is rather a nuisance,' pursued Comus, with fatalistic persistency.

'You won seven pounds last week, didn't you?' asked Elaine. 'Don't you put any of your winnings to balance losses?'

'The four shillings and the fivepence and the halfpenny represent the rearguard of the seven pounds,' said Comus; 'the rest have fallen by the way. If I can pay the two pounds today I daresay I shall win something more to go on with; I'm holding rather good cards just now. But if I can't pay it, of course I shan't show up at the club. So you see the fix I am in.'

Elaine took no notice of this indirect application. The Appeal Court was assembling in haste to consider new evidence, and this time there was the rapidity of sudden determination about its movement.

The conversation strayed away from the fateful topic for a few moments, and then Comus brought it deliberately back to the danger zone.

'It would be awfully nice if you would let me have a fiver for a few days, Elaine,' he said quickly; 'if you don't I really don't know what I shall do.'

'If you are really bothered about your card debt I will send you the two pounds by messenger boy this afternoon.' She spoke quietly and with great decision. 'And I shall not be at the Connors' dance tonight,' she continued; 'it's too hot for dancing. I'm going home now; please don't bother to accompany me, I particularly wish to go alone.'

Comus saw that he had overstepped the mark of her good nature. Wisely he made no immediate attempt to force himself back into her good graces. He would wait till her indignation had cooled.

His tactics would have been excellent if he had not forgotten that unbeaten army on his flank.

Elaine de Frey had known very clearly what qualities she had wanted in Comus, and she had known, against all efforts at self-deception, that he fell far short of those qualities. She had been willing to lower her standard of moral requirements in proportion as she was fond of the boy, but there was a point beyond which she would not go. He had hurt her pride, besides alarming her sense of caution. Suzette, on whom she felt a thoroughly justified tendency to look down, had at any rate an attentive and considerate lover. Elaine walked towards the Park gates feeling that in one essential Suzette possessed something that had been denied to her, and at the gates she met

Joyeuse and his spruce young rider preparing to turn homeward.

'Get rid of Joyeuse and come and take me out to lunch somewhere,' demanded Elaine.

'How jolly!' said Youghal. 'Let's go to the Corridor Restaurant. The head-waiter there is an old Viennese friend of mine and looks after me beautifully. I've never been there with a lady before, and he's sure to ask me afterwards, in his fatherly way, if we're engaged.'

The lunch was a success in every way. There was just enough orchestral effort to immerse the conversation without drowning it, and Youghal was an attentive and inspired host. Through an open doorway Elaine could see the café reading-room, with its imposing array of *Neue Freie Presse, Berliner Tageblatt*, and other exotic newspapers hanging on the wall. She looked across at the young man seated opposite her, who gave one the impression of having centred the most serious efforts of his brain on his toilet and his food, and recalled some of the flattering remarks that the Press had bestowed on his recent speeches.

'Doesn't it make you conceited, Courtenay,' she asked, 'to look at all those foreign newspapers hanging there and know that most of them have got paragraphs and articles about your Persian speech?'

Youghal laughed.

'There's always a chastening corrective in the thought that some of them may have printed your portrait. When once you've seen your features hurriedly reproduced in the *Matin*, for instance, you feel you would like to be a veiled Turkish woman for the rest of your life.'

And Youghal gazed long and lovingly at his reflection in the nearest mirror, as an antidote against possible incitements to humility in the portrait gallery of fame.

Elaine felt a certain soothed satisfaction in the fact that this young man, whose knowledge of the Middle East was an embarrassment to Ministers at question time and in debate, was showing himself equally well informed on the subject of her culinary likes and dislikes. If Suzette could have been forced to attend as a witness at a neighbouring table she would have felt even happier.

'Did the head-waiter ask if we were engaged?' asked Elaine, when Courtenay had settled the bill, and she had finished collecting her sunshade and gloves and other impedimenta from the hands of obsequious attendants.

'Yes,' said Youghal, 'and he seemed quite crestfallen when I had to say "No."'

'It would be horrid to disappoint him when he's looked after us so charmingly,' said Elaine; 'tell him that we are.'

CHAPTER X

The Rutland Galleries were crowded, especially in the neighbourhood of the tea-buffet, by a fashionable throng of art-patrons which had gathered to inspect Mervyn Quentock's collection of Society portraits. Quentock was a young artist whose abilities were just receiving due recognition from the critics; that the recognition was not overdue he owed largely to his perception of the fact that if one hides one's talent under a bushel one must be careful to point out to every one the exact bushel under which it is hidden. There are two manners of receiving recognition: one is to be discovered so long after one's death that one's grandchildren have to write to the papers to establish their relationship; the other is to be discovered, like the infant Moses, at the very outset of one's career. Mervyn Quentock had chosen the latter and happier manner. In an age when many aspiring young men strive to advertise their wares by imparting to them a freakish imbecility, Quentock turned out work that was characterized by a pleasing delicate restraint, but he contrived to herald his output with a certain fanfare of personal eccentricity, thereby compelling an attention which might otherwise have strayed past his studio. In appearance he was the ordinary cleanly young Englishman, except, perhaps, that his eyes rather suggested a library edition of the

Arabian Nights; his clothes matched his appearance and showed no taint of the sartorial disorder by which the bourgeois of the garden-city and the Latin Quarter anxiously seeks to proclaim his kinship with art and thought. His eccentricity took the form of flying in the face of some of the prevailing social currents of the day, but as a reactionary, never as a reformer. He produced a gasp of admiring astonishment in fashionable circles by efusing to paint actresses—except, of course, those who had left the legitimate drama to appear between the boards of Debrett. He absolutely declined to execute portraits of Americans unless they hailed from certain favoured States. His 'water-colour line,' as a New York paper phrased it, earned for him a crop of angry criticism and a shoal of Transatlantic commissions, and criticism and commissions were the things that Quentock most wanted.

'Of course he is perfectly right,' said Lady Caroline Benaresq, calmly rescuing a piled-up plate of caviare sandwiches from the neighbourhood of a trio of young ladies who had established themselves hopefully within easy reach of it. 'Art,' she continued, addressing herself to the Rev. Poltimore Vardon, 'has always been geographically exclusive. London may be more important from most points of view than Venice, but the art of portrait painting, which would never concern itself with a Lord Mayor, simply grovels at the feet of the Doges. As a Socialist I'm bound to recognize the right of Ealing to compare itself with Avignon, but one cannot expect the Muses to put the two on a level.'

'Exclusiveness,' said the Reverend Poltimore, 'has been the salvation of Art, just as the lack of it is proving the downfall of religion. My colleagues of the cloth go about zealously proclaiming the fact that Christianity, in some form or other, is attracting shoals of converts among all sorts of races and tribes that one had scarcely ever heard of, except in reviews of books of travel that one never read. That sort of thing was all very well when the world was more sparsely populated, but nowadays, when it simply teems with human beings, no one is particularly impressed by the fact that a few million, more or less, of converts, of a low stage of mental development, have accepted the teachings of some particular religion. It not only chills one's enthusiasm, it positively shakes one's convictions when one hears that the things one has been brought up to believe as true are being very favourably spoken of by Buriats and Samoyeds and Kanakas.'

The Rev. Poltimore Vardon had once seen a resemblance in himself to Voltaire, and had lived alongside the comparison ever since.

'No modern cult or fashion,' he continued, 'would be favourably influenced by considerations based on statistics; fancy adopting a certain style of hat or cut of coat, because it was being largely worn in Lancashire and the Midlands; fancy favouring a certain brand of champagne because it was being extensively patronized in German summer resorts! No wonder that religion is falling into disuse in this country under such ill-directed methods.'

'You can't prevent the heathen being converted if they choose to be,' said Lady Caroline; 'this is an age of toleration.'

'You could always deny it,' said the Reverend Poltimore, 'like the Belgians do with regrettable occurrences in the Congo. But I would go further than that. I would stimulate the waning enthusiasm for Christianity in this country by labelling it as the exclusive possession of a privileged few. If one could induce the Duchess of Pelm, for instance, to assert that the Kingdom of Heaven, as far as the British Isles are concerned, is strictly limited to herself, two of the under-gardeners at Pelmby, and, possibly, but not certainly, the Dean of Dunster, there would be an instant reshaping of the popular attitude towards religious convictions and observances. Once let the idea get about that the Christian Church is rather more exclusive than the Lawn at Ascot, and you would have a quickening of religious life such as this generation has never witnessed. But as long as the clergy and the religious organizations advertise their creed on the lines of "Everybody ought to believe in us: millions do," one can expect nothing but indifference and waning faith.'

'Time is just as exclusive in its way as Art,' said Lady Caroline.

'In what way?' said the Reverend Poltimore.

'Your pleasantries about religion would have sounded quite clever and advanced in the early 'nineties. Today they have a dreadfully warmed-up flavour. That is the great delusion of you would-be advanced satirists; you imagine you can sit down comfortably for a couple of decades saying daring and startling things about the age you live in, which, whatever other defects it may have, is certainly not standing still. The whole of the Sherard Blaw school of discursive drama suggests, to my mind, Early Victorian furniture in a travelling circus. However, you will always have relays of people from the suburbs to listen to the Mocking Bird of yesterday, and sincerely imagine it is the harbinger of something new and revolutionizing.'

'*Would* you mind passing that plate of sandwiches?' asked one of the trio of young ladies, emboldened by famine.

'With pleasure,' said Lady Caroline, deftly passing her a nearly empty plate of bread-and-butter.

'I meant the plate of caviare sandwiches. So sorry to trouble you,' persisted the young lady.

Her sorrow was misapplied; Lady Caroline had turned her attention to a new-comer.

'A very interesting exhibition,' Ada Spelvexit was saying; 'faultless technique, as far as I am a judge of technique, and quite a master-touch in the way of poses. But have you noticed how very animal his art is? He seems to shut out the soul from his portraits. I nearly cried when I saw dear Winifred depicted simply as a good-looking healthy blonde.'

'I wish you had,' said Lady Caroline; 'the spectacle of a strong, brave woman weeping at a private view in the

Rutland Galleries would have been so sensational. It would certainly have been reproduced in the next Drury Lane drama. And I'm so unlucky; I never see these sensational events. I was ill with appendicitis, you know, when Lulu Braminguard dramatically forgave her husband, after seventeen years of estrangement, during a State luncheon party at Windsor. The old Queen was furious about it. She said it was so disrespectful to the cook to be thinking of such a thing at such a time.'

Lady Caroline's recollections of things that hadn't happened at the Court of Queen Victoria were notoriously vivid; it was the very widespread fear that she might one day write a book of reminiscences that made her so universally respected.

'As for his full-length picture of Lady Brickfield,' continued Ada, ignoring Lady Caroline's commentary as far as possible, 'all the expression seems to have been deliberately concentrated in the feet; beautiful feet, no doubt, but still, hardly the most distinctive part of a human being.'

'To paint the right people at the wrong end may be an eccentricity, but it is scarcely an indiscretion,' pronounced Lady Caroline.

One of the portraits which attracted more than a passing flutter of attention was a costume study of Francesca Bassington. Francesca had secured some highly desirable patronage for the young artist, and in return he had enriched her pantheon of personal possessions with a clever piece of work into which he had thrown an unusual amount of imaginative detail. He had painted her in a costume of the Great Louis's brightest period, seated in front of a tapestry that was so prominent in the composition that it could scarcely be said to form part of the background. Flowers and fruit, in exotic profusion, were its dominant note; quinces, pomegranates, passion-flowers, giant convolvulus, great mauve-pink roses, and grapes that were already being pressed by gleeful cupids in a riotous Arcadian vintage, stood out on its woven texture. The same note was struck in the beflowered satin of the lady's kirtle, and in the pomegranate pattern of the brocade that draped the couch on which she was seated. The artist had called his picture 'Recolte.' And after one had taken in all the details of fruit and flower and foliage that earned the composition its name, one noted the landscape that showed through a broad casement in the left-hand corner. It was a landscape clutched in the grip of winter, naked, bleak, black-frozen; a winter in which things died and knew no reawakening. If the picture typified harvest, it was a harvest of artificial growth.

'It leaves a great deal to the imagination, doesn't it?' said Ada Spelvexit, who had edged away from the range of Lady Caroline's tongue.

'At any rate one can tell who it's meant for,' said Serena Golackly.

'Oh, yes, it's a good likeness of dear Francesca,' admitted Ada; 'of course, it flatters her.'

'That, too, is a fault on the right side in portrait painting,' said Serena; 'after all, if posterity is going to stare at one for centuries it's only kind and reasonable to be looking just a little better than one's best.'

'What a curiously unequal style the artist has!' continued Ada, almost as if she felt a personal grievance against him. 'I was just noticing what a lack of soul there was in most of his portraits. Dear Winifred, you know, who speaks so beautifully and feelingly at my gatherings for old women, he's made her look just an ordinary dairy-maidish blonde; and Francesca, who is quite the most soulless woman I've ever met, well, he's given her quite——'

'Hush!' said Serena, 'the Bassington boy is just behind you.'

Comus stood looking at the portrait of his mother with the feeling of one who comes suddenly across a once-familiar, half-forgotten acquaintance in unfamiliar surroundings. The likeness was undoubtedly a good one, but the artist had caught an expression in Francesca's eyes which few people had ever seen there. It was the expression of a woman who had forgotten for one short moment to be absorbed in the small cares and excitements of her life, the money worries and little social plannings, and had found time to send a look of half-wistful friendliness to some sympathetic companion. Comus could recall that look, fitful and fleeting, in his mother's eyes when she had been a few years younger, before her world had grown to be such a committee-room of ways and means. Almost as a re-discovery, he remembered that she had once figured in his boyish mind as a 'rather good sort,' more ready to see the laughable side of a piece of mischief than to labour forth a reproof. That the bygone feeling of good-fellowship had been stamped out was, he knew, probably in great part his own doing, and it was possible that the old friendliness was still there under the surface of things, ready to show itself again if he willed it, and friends were becoming scarcer with him than enemies in these days. Looking at the picture with its wistful hint of a long-ago comradeship, Comus made up his mind that he very much wanted things to be back on their earlier footing, and to see again on his mother's face the look that the artist had caught and perpetuated in its momentary flitting. If the projected Elaine marriage came off, and in spite of recent maladroit behaviour on his part he still counted it an assured thing, much of the immediate cause for estrangement between himself and his mother would be removed, or at any rate easily removable. With the influence of Elaine's money behind him, he promised himself that he would find some occupation that would remove from himself the reproach of being a waster and idler. There were lots of careers, he told himself, that were open to a man with solid financial backing and good connexions. There might yet be jolly times ahead, in which his mother would have her share of the good things that were going, and carking thin-lipped Henry Greech and other of Comus's detractors could take their sour looks and words out of sight and hearing. Thus, staring at the picture as though he were studying its every detail, and seeing really only that wistful friendly smile,

Comus made his plans and dispositions for a battle that was already fought and lost.

The crowd grew thicker in the galleries, cheerfully enduring an amount of overcrowding that would have been fiercely resented in a railway carriage. Near the entrance Mervyn Quentock was talking to a Serene Highness, a lady who led a life of obtrusive usefulness, largely imposed on her by a good-natured inability to say 'No.' 'That woman creates a positive draught with the number of bazaars she opens,' a frivolously-spoken ex-Cabinet Minister had once remarked. At the present moment she was being whimsically apologetic.

'When I think of the legions of well-meaning young men and women to whom I've given away prizes for proficiency in art-school curriculum. I feel that I ought not to show my face inside a picture gallery. I always imagine that my punishment in another world will be perpetually sharpening pencils and cleaning palettes for unending relays of misguided young people whom I deliberately encouraged in their artistic delusions.'

'Do you suppose we shall all get appropriate punishments in another world for our sins in this?' asked Quentock.

'Not so much for our sins as for our indiscretions; they are the things which do the most harm and cause the greatest trouble. I feel certain that Christopher Columbus will undergo the endless torment of being discovered by parties of American tourists. You see I am quite old-fashioned in my ideas about the terrors and inconveniences of the next world. And now I must be running away; I've got to open a Free Library somewhere. You know the sort of thing that happens—one unveils a bust of Carlyle and makes a speech about Ruskin, and then people come in their thousands and read *Rabid Ralph, or Should He Have Bitten Her?* Don't forget, please, I'm going to have the medallion with the fat cupid sitting on a sundial. And just one thing more—perhaps I ought not to ask you, but you have such nice kind eyes, you embolden one to make daring requests, *would* you send me the recipe for those lovely chestnut-and-chicken-liver sandwiches? I know the ingredients, of course, but it's the proportions that make such a difference—just how much liver to how much chestnut, and what amount of red pepper and other things. Thank you so much. I really am going now.'

Staring round with a vague half-smile at everybody within nodding distance, Her Serene Highness made one of her characteristic exits, which Lady Caroline declared always reminded her of a scrambled egg slipping off a piece of toast. At the entrance she stopped for a moment to exchange a word or two with a young man who had just arrived. From a corner where he was momentarily hemmed in by a group of tea-consuming dowagers, Comus recognized the new-comer as Courtenay Youghal, and began slowly to labour his way towards him. Youghal was not at the moment the person whose society he most craved for in the world, but there was at least the possibility that he might provide an opportunity for a game of bridge, which was the dominant desire of the moment. The young politician was already surrounded by a group of friends and acquaintances, and was evidently being made the recipient of a salvo of congratulation—presumably on his recent performances in the Foreign Office debate, Comus concluded. But Youghal himself seemed to be announcing the event with which the congratulations were connected. Had some dramatic catastrophe overtaken the Government? Comus wondered. And then, as he pressed nearer, a chance word, the coupling of two names, told him the news.

CHAPTER XI

After the momentous lunch at the Corridor Restaurant, Elaine had returned to Manchester Square (where she was staying with one of her numerous aunts) in a frame of mind that embraced a tangle of competing emotions. In the first place she was conscious of a dominant feeling of relief;

in a moment of impetuosity, not wholly uninfluenced by pique, she had settled the problem which hours of hard thinking and serious heart-searching had brought no nearer to solution, and, although she felt just a little inclined to be scared at the headlong manner of her final decision, she had now very little doubt in her own mind that the decision had been the right one. In fact, the wonder seemed rather that she should have been so long in doubt as to which of her wooers really enjoyed her honest approval. She had been in love these many weeks past with an imaginary Comus, but now that she had definitely walked out of her dreamland she saw that nearly all the qualities that had appealed to her on his behalf had been absent from, or only fitfully present in, the character of the real Comus. And now that she had installed Youghal in the first place of her affections he had rapidly acquired in her eyes some of the qualities which ranked highest in her estimation. Like the proverbial buyer she had the happy feminine tendency of magnifying the worth of her possession as soon as she had acquired it. And Courtenay Youghal gave Elaine some justification for her sense of having chosen wisely. Above all other things, selfish and cynical though he might appear at times, he was unfailingly courteous and considerate towards her. That was a circumstance which would always have carried weight with her in judging any man; in this case its value was enormously heightened by contrast with the behaviour of her other wooer. And Youghal had in her eyes the advantage which the glamour of combat, even the combat of words and wire-pulling, throws over the fighter. He stood well in the forefront of a battle which however carefully stage-managed, however honeycombed with personal insincerities and overlaid with calculated mock-heroics, really meant something, really counted for good or wrong in the nation's development and the world's history. Shrewd parliamentary observers might have warned her that Youghal would never stand much higher in the political world than he did at present, as a brilliant Opposition freelance, leading lively and rather meaningless forays against the dull and rather purposeless foreign policy of a Government that was scarcely either to be blamed for or congratulated on its handling of foreign affairs. The young politician had not the strength of character or convictions that keeps a man naturally in the forefront of affairs and gives his counsels a sterling value, and on the other hand his insincerity was not deep enough to allow him to pose artificially and successfully as a leader of men and shaper of movements. For the moment, however, his place in public life was sufficiently marked out to give him a secure footing in that world where people are counted individually and not in herds. The woman whom he would make his wife would have the chance, too, if she had the will and the skill, to become an individual who counted.

There was balm to Elaine in this reflection, yet it did not wholly suffice to drive out the feeling of pique which Comus had called into being by his slighting view of her as a convenient cash supply in moments of emergency. She found a certain satisfaction in scrupulously observing her promise, made earlier on that eventful day, and sent off a messenger with the stipulated loan. Then a reaction of compunction set in, and she reminded herself that in fairness she ought to write and tell her news in as friendly a fashion as possible to her dismissed suitor before it burst upon him from some other quarter. They parted on more or less quarrelling terms, it was true, but neither of them had foreseen the finality of the parting nor the permanence of the breach between them; Comus might even now be thinking himself half-forgiven, and the awakening would be rather cruel. The letter, however, did not prove an easy one to write; not only did it present difficulties of its own, but it suffered from the competing urgency of a desire to be doing something far pleasanter than writing explanatory and valedictory phrases. Elaine was possessed with an unusual but quite overmastering hankering to visit her cousin Suzette Brankley. They met but rarely at each other's houses and very seldom anywhere

else, and Elaine for her part was never conscious of feeling
that their opportunities for intercourse lacked anything in
the way of adequacy. Suzette accorded her just that touch
of patronage which a moderately well-off and immoderately
dull girl will usually try to mete out to an acquaintance
who is known to be wealthy and suspected of possessing
brains. In return Elaine armed herself with that particular
brand of mock humility which can be so terribly disconcerting if properly wielded. No quarrel of any description
stood between them and one could not legitimately have
described them as enemies, but they never disarmed in one
another's presence. A misfortune of any magnitude falling
on one of them would have been sincerely regretted by
the other, but any minor discomfiture would have produced
a feeling very much akin to satisfaction. Human nature
knows millions of these inconsequent little feuds, springing
up and flourishing apart from any basis of racial, political,
religious or economic causes, as a hint perhaps to crass
unseeing altruists that enmity has its place and purpose
in the world as well as benevolence.

Elaine had not personally congratulated Suzette since
the formal announcement of her engagement to the young
man with the dissentient tailoring effects. The impulse to
go and do so now overmastered her sense of what was due
to Comus in the way of explanation. The letter was still
in its blank unwritten stage, an unmarshalled sequence of
sentences forming in her brain, when she ordered her car
and made a hurried but well-thought-out change into
her most sumptuously sober afternoon toilette. Suzette, she
felt tolerably sure, would still be in the costume that she
had worn in the Park that morning, a costume that aimed
at elaboration of detail, and was damned with overmuch
success.

Suzette's mother welcomed her unexpected visitor with
obvious satisfaction. Her daughter's engagement, she explained, was not so brilliant from the social point of view
as a girl of Suzette's attractions and advantages might have
legitimately aspired to, but Egbert was a thoroughly com-

mendable and dependable young man, who would very probably win his way before long to membership of the County Council.

'From there, of course, the road would be open to him to higher things.'

'Yes,' said Elaine, 'he might become an alderman.'

'Have you seen their photographs, taken together?' asked Mrs Brankley, abandoning the subject of Egbert's prospective career.

'No; do show me,' said Elaine, with a flattering show of interest; 'I've never seen that sort of thing before. It used to be the fashion once for engaged couples to be photographed together, didn't it?'

'It's *very* much the fashion now,' said Mrs Brankley assertively, but some of the complacency had filtered out of her voice.

Suzette came into the room, wearing the dress that she had worn in the Park that morning.

'Of course, you've been hearing all about *the* engagement from mother,' she cried, and then set to work conscientiously to cover the same ground.

'We met at Grindelwald, you know. He always calls me his Ice Maiden because we first got to know each other on the skating-rink. Quite romantic, wasn't it? Then we asked him to tea one day, and we got to be quite friendly. Then he proposed.'

'He wasn't the only one who was smitten with Suzette,' Mrs Brankley hastened to put in, fearful lest Elaine might suppose that Egbert had had things all his own way. 'There was an American millionaire who was quite taken with her, and a Polish count of a very old family. I assure you I felt quite nervous at some of our tea-parties.'

Mrs Brankley had given Grindelwald a sinister but rather alluring reputation among a large circle of untravelled friends as a place where the insolence of birth and wealth was held in precarious check from breaking forth into scenes of savage violence.

'My marriage with Egbert will, of course, enlarge the sphere of my life enormously,' pursued Suzette.

'Yes,' said Elaine; her eyes were rather remorselessly taking in the details of her cousin's toilette. It is said that nothing is sadder than victory except defeat. Suzette began to feel that the tragedy of both was concentrated in the creation which had given her such unalloyed gratification till Elaine had come on the scene.

'A woman can be so immensely helpful in the social way to a man who is making a career for himself. And I'm so glad to find that we've a great many ideas in common. We each made out a list of our idea of the hundred best books, and quite a number of them were the same.'

'He looks bookish,' said Elaine, with a critical glance at the photograph.

'Oh, he's not at all a bookworm,' said Suzette quickly, 'though he's tremendously well-read. He's quite the man of action.'

'Does he hunt?' asked Elaine.

'No, he doesn't get much time or opportunity for riding.'

'What a pity!' commented Elaine. 'I don't think I could marry a man who wasn't fond of riding.'

'Of course that's a matter of taste,' said Suzanne stiffly; 'horsey men are not usually gifted with overmuch brains, are they?'

'There is as much difference between a horseman and a horsey man as there is between a well-dressed man and a dressy one,' said Elaine judicially; 'and you may have noticed how seldom a dressy woman really knows how to dress. As an old lady of my acquaintance observed the other day, some people are born with a sense of how to clothe themselves, others acquire it, others look as if their clothes had been thrust upon them.'

She gave Lady Caroline her due quotation marks, but the sudden tactfulness with which she looked away from her cousin's frock was entirely her own idea.

A young man entering the room at this moment caused a diversion that was rather welcome to Suzette.

'Here comes Egbert,' she announced, with an air of subdued triumph; it was at least a satisfaction to be able to produce the captive of her charms, alive and in good condition, on the scene. Elaine might be as critical as she pleased, but a live lover outweighed any number of well-dressed straight-riding cavaliers who existed only as a distant vision of the delectable husband.

Egbert was one of those men who have no small-talk, but possess an inexhaustible supply of the larger variety. In whatever society he happened to be, and particularly in the immediate neighbourhood of an afternoon-tea table, with a limited audience of womenfolk, he gave the impression of some one who was addressing a public meeting, and would be happy to answer questions afterwards. A suggestion of gaslit mission-halls, wet umbrellas, and discreet applause seemed to accompany him everywhere. He was an exponent, among other things, of what he called New Thought, which seemed to lend itself conveniently to the employment of a good deal of rather stale phraseology. Probably in the course of some thirty odd years of existence he had never been of any notable use to man, woman, child, or animal, but it was his firmly-announced intention to leave the world a better, happier, purer place than he had found it; against the danger of any relapse to earlier conditions after his disappearance from the scene, he was, of course, powerless to guard. 'Tis not in mortals to ensure succession, and Egbert was admittedly mortal.

Elaine found him immensely entertaining, and would certainly have exerted herself to draw him out if such a proceeding had been at all necessary. She listened to his conversation with the complacent appreciation that one bestows on a stage tragedy, from whose calamities one can escape at any moment by the simple process of leaving one's seat. When at last he checked the flow of his opinions by a hurried reference to his watch, and declared that he must be moving on elsewhere, Elaine almost expected a vote of thanks to be accorded him, or to be asked to signify herself in favour of some resolution by holding up her hand.

When the young man had bidden the company a rapid business-like farewell, tempered in Suzette's case by the exact degree of tender intimacy that it would have been considered improper to omit or overstep, Elaine turned to her expectant cousin with an air of cordial congratulation.

'He is exactly the husband I should have chosen for you, Suzette.'

For the second time that afternoon Suzette felt a sense of waning enthusiasm for one of her possessions.

Mrs Brankley detected the note of ironical congratulation in her visitor's verdict.

'I suppose she means he's not her idea of a husband, but he's good enough for Suzette,' she observed to herself, with a snort that expressed itself somewhere in the nostrils of the brain. Then with a smiling air of heavy patronage she delivered herself of her one idea of a damaging counterstroke.

'And when are we to hear of your engagement, my dear?'

'Now,' said Elaine quietly, but with electrical effect; 'I came to announce it to you but I wanted to hear all about Suzette first. It will be formally announced in the papers in a day or two.'

'But who is it? Is it the young man who was with you in the Park this morning?' asked Suzette.

'Let me see, who was I with in the Park this morning? A very good-looking dark boy? Oh, no, not Comus Bassington. Some one you know by name, anyway, and I expect you've seen his portrait in the papers.'

'A flying-man?' asked Mrs Brankley.

'Courtenay Youghal,' said Elaine.

Mrs Brankley and Suzette had often rehearsed in the privacy of their minds the occasion when Elaine should come to pay her personal congratulations to her engaged cousin. It had never been in the least like this.

On her return from her enjoyable afternoon visit Elaine

found an express messenger letter waiting for her. It was
from Comus, thanking her for her loan—and returning it.

'I suppose I ought never to have asked you for it,' he
wrote, 'but you are always so deliciously solemn about
money matters that I couldn't resist. Just heard the news
of your engagement to Courtenay. Congrats. to you both.
I'm far too stony broke to buy you a wedding-present so
I'm going to give you back the bread-and-butter dish.
Luckily it still has your crest on it. I shall love to think
of you and Courtenay eating bread-and-butter out of it for
the rest of your lives.'

That was all he had to say on the matter about which
Elaine had been preparing to write a long and kindly-
expressed letter, closing a rather momentous chapter in her
life and his. There was not a trace of regret or upbraiding
in his note; he had walked out of their mutual fairyland
as abruptly as she had, and to all appearances far more
unconcernedly. Reading the letter again and again, Elaine
could come to no decision as to whether this was merely
a courageous gibe at defeat, or whether it represented the
real value that Comus set on the thing that he had lost.

And she would never know. If Comus possessed one
useless gift to perfection it was the gift of laughing at Fate
even when it had struck him hardest. One day, perhaps, the
laughter and mockery would be silent on his lips, and Fate
would have the advantage of laughing last.

CHAPTER XII

A door closed and Francesca Bassington sat alone in her
well-beloved drawing-room. The visitor who had been enjoying the hospitality of her afternoon-tea table had just
taken his departure. The *tête-à-tête* had not been a pleasant
one, at any rate as far as Francesca was concerned, but at
least it had brought her the information for which she had
been seeking. Her rôle of looker-on from a tactful distance
had necessarily left her much in the dark concerning the

progress of the all-important wooing, but during the last few hours she had, on slender though significant evidence, exchanged her complacent expectancy for a conviction that something had gone wrong. She had spent the previous evening at her brother's house, and had naturally seen nothing of Comus in that uncongenial quarter; neither had he put in an appearance at the breakfast table the following morning. She had met him in the hall at eleven o'clock, and he had hurried past her, merely imparting the information that he would not be in till dinner that evening. He spoke in his sulkiest tone, and his face wore a look of defeat, thinly masked by an air of defiance; it was not the defiance of a man who is losing, but of one who has already lost.

Francesca's conviction that things had gone wrong between Comus and Elaine de Frey grew in strength as the day wore on. She lunched at a friend's house, but it was not a quarter where special social information of any importance was likely to come early to hand. Instead of the news she was hankering for, she had to listen to trivial gossip and speculation on the flirtations and 'cases' and 'affairs' of a string of acquaintances whose matrimonial projects interested her about as much as the nesting arrangements of the wildfowl in St James's Park.

'Of course,' said her hostess, with the duly impressive emphasis of a privileged chronicler, 'we've always regarded Claire as the marrying one of the family, so when Emily came to us and said, "I've got some news for you," we all said, "Claire's engaged!" "Oh, no," said Emily, "it's not Claire this time, it's me." So then we had to guess who the lucky man was. "It can't be Captain Parminter," we all said, "because he's always been sweet on Joan." And then Emily said——'

The recording voice reeled off the catalogue of inane remarks with a comfortable purring complacency that held out no hope of an early abandoning of the topic. Francesca sat and wondered why the innocent acceptance of a cutlet and a glass of indifferent claret should lay one open to such unsparing punishment.

A stroll homeward through the Park after lunch brought no further enlightenment on the subject that was uppermost in her mind; what was worse, it brought her, without possibility of escape, within hailing distance of Merla Blathlington, who fastened on to her with the enthusiasm of a lonely tsetse fly encountering an outpost of civilization.

'Just think,' she buzzed inconsequently, 'my sister in Cambridgeshire has hatched out thirty-three White Orpington chickens in her incubator!'

'What eggs did she put in it?' asked Francesca.

'Oh, some very special strain of White Orpington.'

'Then I don't see anything remarkable in the result. If she had put in crocodiles' eggs and hatched out White Orpingtons, there might have been something to write to *Country Life* about.'

'What funny fascinating things these little green parkchairs are,' said Merla, starting off on a fresh topic; 'they always look so quaint and knowing when they're stuck away in pairs by themselves under the trees, as if they were having a heart-to-heart talk or discussing a piece of very private scandal. If they could only speak, what tragedies and comedies they could tell us of, what flirtations and proposals!'

'Let us be devoutly thankful that they can't,' said Francesca, with a shuddering recollection of the luncheon-table conversation.

'Of course, it would make one very careful what one said before them—or above them rather,' Merla rattled on, and then, to Francesca's infinite relief, she espied another acquaintance sitting in unprotected solitude, who promised to supply a more durable audience than her present rapidly moving companion. Francesca was free to return to her drawing-room in Blue Street to await with such patience as she could command the coming of some visitor who might be able to throw light on the subject that was puzzling and disquieting her. The arrival of George St Michael boded bad news, but at any rate news, and she gave him an almost cordial welcome.

'Well, you see I wasn't far wrong about Miss de Frey and Courtenay Youghal, was I?' he chirruped, almost before he had seated himself. Francesca was to be spared any further spinning-out of her period of uncertainty. 'Yes, it's officially given out,' he went on, 'and it's to appear in the *Morning Post* tomorrow. I heard it from Colonel Deel this morning, and he had it direct from Youghal himself. Yes, please, one lump; I'm not fashionable, you see.' He had made the same remark about the sugar in his tea with unfailing regularity for at least thirty years. Fashions in sugar are apparently stationary. 'They say,' he continued hurriedly, 'that he proposed to her on the Terrace of the House, and a division bell rang and he had to hurry off before she had time to give her answer, and when he got back she simply said, "The Ayes have it." ' St Michael paused in his narrative to give an appreciative giggle.

'Just the sort of inanity that would go the rounds,' remarked Francesca, with the satisfaction of knowing that she was making the criticism direct to the author and begetter of the inanity in question. Now that the blow had fallen and she knew the full extent of its weight, her feeling towards the bringer of bad news, who sat complacently nibbling at her tea-cakes and scattering crumbs of tiresome small-talk at her feet, was one of whole-hearted dislike. She could sympathize with, or at any rate understand, the tendency of Oriental despots to inflict death or ignominious chastisement on messengers bearing tidings of misfortune and defeat, and St Michael, she perfectly well knew, was thoroughly aware of the fact that her hopes and wishes had been centred on the possibility of having Elaine for a daughter-in-law; every purring remark that his mean little soul prompted him to contribute to the conversation had an easily recognizable undercurrent of malice. Fortunately for her powers of polite endurance, which had been put to such searching and repeated tests that day, St Michael

had planned out for himself a busy little time-table of afternoon visits, at each of which his self-appointed task of
forestalling and embellishing the newspaper announce-
ments of the Youghal-de Frey engagement would be hurriedly but thoroughly performed.

'They'll be quite one of the best-looking and most interesting couples of the season, won't they?' he cried, by way
of farewell. The door closed, and Francesca Bassington sat
alone in her drawing-room.

Before she could give way to the bitter luxury of reflection on the downfall of her hopes, it was prudent to take
precautionary measures against unwelcome intrusion. Sum-
moning the maid who had just speeded the departing St
Michael, she gave the order: 'I am not at home this afternoon to Lady Caroline Benaresq.' On second thoughts she
extended the taboo to all possible callers, and sent a
telephone message to catch Comus at his club, asking him
to come and see her as soon as he could manage before
it was time to dress for dinner. Then she sat down to
think, and her thinking was beyond the relief of tears.

She had built herself a castle of hopes, and it had not
been a castle in Spain, but a structure well on the probable
side of the Pyrenees. There had been a solid foundation on
which to build. Miss de Frey's fortune was an assured and
unhampered one, her liking for Comus had been an obvious
fact; his courtship of her a serious reality. The young
people had been much together in public, and their names
had naturally been coupled in the match-making gossip
of the day. The only serious shadow cast over the scene
had been the persistent presence, in foreground or background, of Courtenay Youghal. And now the shadow suddenly stood forth as the reality, and the castle of hopes
was a ruin, a hideous mortification of dust and debris,
with the skeleton outlines of its chambers still standing
to make mockery of its discomfited architect. The daily
anxiety about Comus and his extravagant ways and intractable disposition had been gradually lulled by the prospect
of his making an advantageous marriage, which would have

transformed him from a ne'er-do-well and adventurer into a wealthy idler. He might even have been moulded, by the resourceful influence of an ambitious wife, into a man with some definite purpose in life. The prospect had vanished with cruel suddenness, and the anxieties were crowding back again, more insistent than ever. The boy had had his one good chance in the matrimonial market and missed it; if he were to transfer his attentions to some other well-dowered girl he would be marked down at once as a fortune-hunter, and that would constitute a heavy handicap to the most plausible of wooers. His liking for Elaine had evidently been genuine in its way, though perhaps it would have been rash to read any deeper sentiment into it, but even with the spur of his own inclination to assist him he had failed to win the prize that had seemed so temptingly within his reach. And in the dashing of his prospects, Francesca saw the threatening of her own. The old anxiety as to her precarious tenure of her present quarters put on again all its familiar terrors. One day, she foresaw, in the horribly near future, George St Michael would come pattering up her stairs with the breathless intelligence that Emmeline Chetrof was going to marry somebody or other in the Guards or the Record Office, as the case might be, and then there would be an uprooting of her life from its home and haven in Blue Street and a wandering forth to some cheap unhappy far-off dwelling, where the stately Van der Meulen and its companion host of beautiful and desirable things would be stuffed and stowed away in soulless surroundings, like courtly *émigrés* fallen on evil days. It was unthinkable, but the trouble was that it had to be thought about. And if Comus had played his cards well and transformed himself from an encumbrance into a son with wealth at his command, the tragedy which she saw looming in front of her might have been avoided, or at the worst whittled down to easily bearable proportions. With money behind one, the problem of where to live approaches more nearly to the simple question of where do you wish to live, and a rich daughter-in-law would have surely seen to it that she did not have to leave her square mile of Mecca and go out into the wilderness of bricks and mortar. If the house in Blue Street could not have been compounded for, there were other desirable residences which would have been capable of consoling Francesca for her lost Eden. And now the detested Courtenay Youghal, with his mocking eyes and air of youthful cynicism, had stepped in and overthrown those golden hopes and plans whose non-fulfilment would make such a world of change in her future. Assuredly she had reason to feel bitter against that young man, and she was not disposed to take a very lenient view of Comus's own mismanagement of the affair; her greeting when he at last arrived was not couched in a sympathetic strain.

'So you have lost your chance with the heiress,' she remarked abruptly.

'Yes,' said Comus coolly; 'Courtenay Youghal has added her to his other successes.'

'And you have added her to your other failures,' pursued Francesca relentlessly; her temper had been tried that day beyond ordinary limits.

'I thought you seemed getting along so well with her,' she continued, as Comus remained uncommunicative.

'We hit it off rather well together,' said Comus, and added with deliberate bluntness, 'I suppose she got rather sick at my borrowing money from her. She thought it was all I was after.'

'You borrowed money from her!' said Francesca; 'you were fool enough to borrow money from a girl who was favourably disposed towards you, and with Courtenay Youghal in the background waiting to step in and oust you!'

Francesca's voice trembled with misery and rage. This great stroke of good luck that had seemed about to fall into their laps had been thrust aside by an act or series of acts of wanton paltry folly. The good ship had been lost for the sake of the traditional ha'p'orth of tar. Comus had paid some pressing tailor's or tobacconist's bill with a loan unwillingly put at his disposal by the girl he was courting, and had flung away his chances of securing a wealthy and in every way desirable bride. Elaine de Frey and her fortune might have been the making of Comus, but he had hurried in as usual to effect his own undoing. Calmness did not in this case come with reflection; the more Francesca thought about the matter, the more exasperated she grew. Comus threw himself down in a low chair and watched her without a trace of embarrassment or concern at her mortification. He had come to her feeling rather sorry for himself, and bitterly conscious of his defeat, and she had met him with a taunt and without the least hint of sympathy; he determined that she should be tantalized with the knowledge of how small and stupid a thing had stood between the realization and ruin of her hopes for him.

'And to think she should be captured by Courtenay Youghal,' said Francesca bitterly; 'I've always deplored your intimacy with that young man.'

'It's hardly my intimacy with him that's made Elaine accept him,' said Comus.

Francesca realized the futility of further upbraiding. Through the tears of vexation that stood in her eyes she looked across at the handsome boy who sat opposite her, mocking at his own misfortune, perversely indifferent to his folly, seemingly almost indifferent to its consequences.

'Comus,' she said quietly and wearily, 'you are an exact reversal of the legend of Pandora's Box. You have all the charm and advantages that a boy could want to help him on in the world, and behind it all there is the fatal damning gift of utter hopelessness.'

'I think,' said Comus, 'that is the best description that any one has ever given of me.'

For the moment there was a flush of sympathy and something like outspoken affection between mother and son. They seemed very much alone in the world just now, and in the general overturn of hopes and plans there flickered a chance that each might stretch out a hand to the other, and summon back to their lives an old dead love that was the best and strongest feeling either of them had known. But the sting of disappointment was too keen, and the flood of resentment mounted too high on either side to allow the chance more than a moment in which to flicker away into nothingness. The old fatal topic of estrangement came to the fore, the question of immediate ways and means, and mother and son faced themselves again as antagonists on a well-disputed field.

'What is done is done,' said Francesca, with a movement of tragic impatience that belied the philosophy of her words; 'there is nothing to be gained by crying over spilt milk. There is the present and the future to be thought about, though. One can't go on indefinitely as a tenant-for-life in a fools' paradise.' Then she pulled herself together and proceeded to deliver an ultimatum which the force of circumstances no longer permitted her to hold in reserve.

'It's not much use talking to you about money, as I know from long experience, but I can only tell you this, that in the middle of the season I'm already obliged to be thinking of leaving town. And you, I'm afraid, will have to be thinking of leaving England at equally short notice. Henry told me the other day that he can get you something out in West Africa. You've had your chance of doing something better for yourself from the financial point of view, and you've thrown it away for the sake of borrowing a little ready money for your luxuries, so now you must take what you can get. The pay won't be very good at first, but living is not dear out there.'

'West Africa,' said Comus reflectively; 'it's a sort of modern substitute for the old-fashioned *oubliette*, a convenient depository for tiresome people. Dear Uncle Henry may talk lugubriously about the burden of Empire, but he evidently recognizes its use as a refuse consumer.'

'My dear Comus, you are talking of the West Africa of yesterday. While you have been wasting your time at school, and worse than wasting your time in the West End, other people have been grappling with the study of tropical diseases, and the West African coast country is being rapidly transformed from a lethal chamber into a sanatorium.'

Comus laughed mockingly.

'What a beautiful bit of persuasive prose! It reminds one of the Psalms, and even more of a company prospectus. If you were honest you'd confess that you lifted it straight out of a rubber or railway promotion scheme. Seriously, mother, if I must grub about for a living, why can't I do it in England? I could go into a brewery, for instance.'

Francesca shook her head decisively; she could foresee the sort of steady work Comus was likely to accomplish, with the lodestone of town and the minor attractions of race-meetings and similar festivities always beckoning to him from a conveniently attainable distance, but apart from that aspect of the case there was a financial obstacle in the way of his obtaining any employment at home.

'Breweries and all those sort of things necessitate money to start with; one has to pay premiums or invest capital in the undertaking and so forth. And as we have no money available, and can scarcely pay our debts as it is, it's no use thinking about it.'

'Can't we sell something?' asked Comus.

He made no actual suggestion as to what should be sacrificed, but he was looking straight at the Van der Meulen.

For a moment Francesca felt a stifling sensation of weakness, as though her heart was going to stop beating. Then she sat forward in her chair and spoke with energy, almost fierceness.

'When I am dead my things can be sold and dispersed. As long as I am alive I prefer to keep them by me.'

In her holy place, with all her treasured possessions around her, this dreadful suggestion had been made. Some of her cherished household gods, souvenirs and keepsakes from past days, would, perhaps, not have fetched a very considerable sum in the auction-room, others had a distinct value of their own, but to her they were all precious. And the Van der Meulen, at which Comus had looked with impious appraising eyes, was the most sacred of them all. When Francesca had been away from her town residence or had been confined to her bedroom through illness, the great picture with its stately solemn representation of a long-ago battle-scene, painted to flatter the flattery-loving soul of a warrior-king who was dignified even in his campaigns—this was the first thing she visited on her return to town or convalescence. If an alarm of fire had been raised it would have been the first thing for whose safety she would have troubled. And Comus had almost suggested that it should be parted with, as one sold railway shares and other soulless things.

Scolding, she had long ago realized, was a useless waste of time and energy where Comus was concerned, but this evening she unloosed her tongue for the mere relief that it gave to her surcharged feelings. He sat listening without comment, though she purposely let fall remarks that she hoped might sting him into self-defence or protest. It was an unsparing indictment, the more damaging in that it was so irrefutably true, the more tragic in that it came from perhaps the one person in the world whose opinion he had ever cared for. And he sat through it as silent and seemingly unmoved as though she had been rehearsing a speech for some drawing-room comedy. When she had had her say his method of retort was not the soft answer that turneth away wrath, but the inconsequent one that shelves it.

'Let's go and dress for dinner.'

The meal, like so many that Francesca and Comus had eaten in each other's company of late, was a silent one. Now that the full bearings of the disaster had been discussed in all its aspects, there was nothing more to be said. Any attempt at ignoring the situation and passing on to less controversial topics would have been a mockery and pretence which neither of them would have troubled to sustain. So the meal went forward with its dragged-out dreary intimacy of two people who were separated by a

gulf of bitterness, and whose hearts were hard with resentment against one another.

Francesca felt a sense of relief when she was able to give
the maid the order to serve her coffee upstairs. Comus
had a sullen scowl on his face, but he looked up as she
rose to leave the room, and gave his half-mocking little
laugh.

'You needn't look so tragic,' he said. 'You're going to
have your own way. I'll go out to that West African hole.'

CHAPTER XIII

Comus found his way to his seat in the stalls of the Straw
Exchange Theatre, and turned to watch the stream of
distinguished and distinguishable people who made their
appearance as a matter of course at a First Night in the
height of the season. Pit and gallery were already packed
with a throng, tense, expectant and alert, that waited for
the rise of the curtain with the eager patience of a terrier
watching a dilatory human prepare for outdoor exercises.
Stalls and boxes filled slowly and hesitatingly with a crowd
whose component units seemed for the most part to
recognize the probability that they were quite as interesting
as any play they were likely to see. Those who bore no
particular face-value themselves derived a certain amount
of social dignity from the near neighbourhood of obvious
notabilities; if one could not obtain recognition oneself
there was some vague pleasure in being able to recognize
notoriety at intimately close quarters.

'Who is that woman with the auburn hair and a rather
effective belligerent gleam in her eyes?' asked a man sitting
just behind Comus. 'She looks as if she might have created
the world in six days and destroyed it on the seventh.'

'I forget her name,' said his neighbour; 'she writes. She's
the author of that book, *The Woman Who Wished it was
Wednesday*, you know. It used to be the convention that
women writers should be plain and dowdy; now we have

gone to the other extreme and build them on extravagantly decorative lines.'

A buzz of recognition came from the front rows of the pit, together with a craning of necks on the part of those in less favoured seats. It heralded the arrival of Sherard Blaw, the dramatist who had discovered himself, and who had given so ungrudgingly of his discovery to the world. Lady Caroline, who was already directing little conversational onslaughts from her box, gazed gently for a moment at the new arrival, and then turned to the silver-haired Archdeacon sitting beside her.

'They say the poor man is haunted by the fear that he will die during a general election, and that his obituary notices will be seriously curtailed by the space taken up by the election results. The curse of our party system, from his point of view, is that it takes up so much room in the Press.'

The Archdeacon smiled indulgently. As a man he was so exquisitely worldly that he fully merited the name of the Heavenly Worldling bestowed on him by an admiring duchess, and withal his texture was shot with a pattern of such genuine saintliness that one felt that whoever else might hold the keys of Paradise he, at least, possessed a private latchkey to that abode.

'Is it not significant of the altered grouping of things,' he observed, 'that the Church, as represented by me, sympathizes with the message of Sherard Blaw, while neither the man nor his message find acceptance with unbelievers like you, Lady Caroline?'

Lady Caroline blinked her eyes. 'My dear Archdeacon,' she said, 'no one can be an unbeliever nowadays. The Christian Apologists have left one nothing to disbelieve.'

The Archdeacon rose with a delighted chuckle. 'I must go and tell that to De la Poulett,' he said, indicating a clerical figure sitting in the third row of the stalls; 'he spends his life explaining from his pulpit that the glory of Christianity consists in the fact that though it is not true it has been found necessary to invent it.'

The door of the box opened and Courtenay Youghal entered, bringing with him a subtle suggestion of chaminade and an atmosphere of political tension. The Government had fallen out of the good graces of a section of its supporters, and those who were not in the know were busy predicting a serious crisis over a forthcoming division in the Committee stage of an important Bill. This was Saturday night, and unless some successful cajolery were effected between now and Monday afternoon, Ministers would be, seemingly, in danger of defeat.

'Ah, here is Youghal,' said the Archdeacon; 'he will be able to tell us what going to happen in the next forty-eight hours. I hear the Prime Minister says it is a matter of conscience, and they will stand or fall by it.'

His hopes and sympathies were notoriously on the Ministerial side.

Youghal greeted Lady Caroline and subsided gracefully into a chair well in the front of the box. A buzz of recognition rippled slowly across the house.

'For the Government to fall on a matter of conscience,' he said, 'would be like a man cutting himself with a safety razor.'

Lady Caroline purred a gentle approval.

'I'm afraid it's true, Archdeacon,' she said.

No one can effectively defend a Government when it's been in office several years. The Archdeacon took refuge in light skirmishing.

'I believe Lady Caroline sees the makings of a great Socialist statesman in you, Youghal,' he observed.

'Great Socialist statesmen aren't made, they're stillborn,' replied Youghal.

'What is the play about tonight?' asked a pale young woman who had taken no part in the talk.

'I don't know,' said Lady Caroline, 'but I hope it's dull. If there is any brilliant conversation in it I shall burst into tears.'

In the front row of the upper circle a woman with a restless starling-voice was discussing the work of a temporarily fashionable composer, chiefly in relation to her own emotions, which she seemed to think might prove generally interesting to those around her.

'Whenever I hear his music I feel that I want to go up into a mountain and pray. Can you understand that feeling?'

The girl to whom she was unburdening herself shook her head.

'You see, I've heard his music chiefly in Switzerland, and we were up among the mountains all the time, so it wouldn't have made any difference.'

'In that case,' said the woman, who seemed to have emergency emotions to suit all geographical conditions, 'I should have wanted to be in a great silent plain by the side of a rushing river.'

'What I think is so splendid about his music——' commenced another starling-voice on the farther side of the girl. Like sheep that feed greedily before the coming of a storm, the starling-voices seemed impelled to extra effort by the knowledge of four imminent intervals of acting during which they would be hushed into constrained silence.

In the back row of the dress circle a late-comer, after a cursory glance at the programme, had settled down into a comfortable narrative, which was evidently the resumed thread of an unfinished taxi-drive monologue.

'We all said, "It can't be Captain Parminter, because he's always been sweet on Joan," and then Emily said——'

The curtain went up, and Emily's contribution to the discussion had to be held over till the entr'acte.

The play promised to be a success. The author, avoiding the pitfall of brilliancy, had aimed at being interesting; and as far as possible, bearing in mind that his play was a comedy, he had striven to be amusing. Above all he had remembered that in the laws of stage proportions it is permissible and generally desirable that the part should be greater than the whole; hence he had been careful to give the leading lady such a clear and commanding lead over the other characters of the play that it was impossible for any of them ever to get on level terms with her. The action of the piece was now and then delayed thereby, but the duration of its run would be materially prolonged.

The curtain came down on the first act amid an encouraging instalment of applause, and the audience turned its back on the stage and began to take a renewed interest in itself. The authoress of *The Woman Who Wished it was Wednesday* had swept like a convalescent whirlwind, subdued but potentially tempestuous, into Lady Caroline's box.

'I've just trodden with all my weight on the foot of an eminent publisher as I was leaving my seat,' she cried, with a peal of delighted laughter. 'He was such a dear about it; I said I hoped I hadn't hurt him, and he said, "I suppose you think, who drives hard bargains should himself be hard." Wasn't it pet lamb of him?'

'I've never trodden on a pet lamb,' said Lady Caroline, 'so I've no idea what its behaviour would be under the circumstances.'

'Tell me,' said the authoress, coming to the front of the box, the better to survey the house, and perhaps also with a charitable desire to make things easy for those who might pardonably wish to survey her, 'tell me, please, where is the girl sitting whom Courtenay Youghal is engaged to?'

Elaine was pointed out to her, sitting in the fourth row of the stalls, on the opposite side of the house to where Comus had his seat. Once during the interval she had turned to give him a friendly nod of recognition as he stood in one of the side gangways, but he was absorbed at the moment in looking at himself in the glass panel. The grave brown eyes and the mocking green-grey ones had looked their last into each other's depths.

For Comus this first-night performance, with its brilliant gathering of spectators, its groups and coteries of lively talkers, even its counterfoil of dull chatterers, its pervading atmosphere of stage and social movement, and its intruding undercurrent of political flutter, all this composed a tragedy

in which he was the chief character. It was the life he knew
and loved and basked in, and it was the life he was leaving.
It would go on reproducing itself again and again, with its
stage interest and social interest and intruding outside
interests, with the same lively chattering crowd, the people
who had done things being pointed out by people who
recognized them to people who didn't—it would all go on
with unflagging animation and sparkle and enjoyment, and
for him it would have stopped utterly. He would be in
some unheard-of sun-blistered wilderness, where natives
and pariah dogs and raucous-throated crows fringed round
mockingly on one's loneliness, where one rode for sweltering miles for the chance of meeting a collector or police
officer, with whom most likely on closer acquaintance one
had hardly two ideas in common, where female society was
represented at long intervals by some climate-withered
woman missionary or official's wife, where food and sickness and veterinary lore became at last the three outstanding subjects on which the mind settled, or rather sank.
That was the life he foresaw and dreaded, and that was
the life he was going to. For a boy who went out to it from
the dullness of some country rectory, from a neighbourhood where a flower show and a cricket match formed the
social landmarks of the year, the feeling of exile might
not be very crushing, might indeed be lost in the sense of
change and adventure. But Comus had lived too thoroughly
in the centre of things to regard life in a backwater as anything else than stagnation, and stagnation while one is
young he justly regarded as an offence against nature and
reason, in keeping with the perverted mockery that sends
decrepit invalids touring painfully about the world and
shuts panthers up in narrow cages. He was being put aside,
as wine is put aside, but to deteriorate instead of gaining
in the process, to lose the best time of his youth and health
and good looks in a world where youth and health and
good looks count for much and where time never returns
lost possessions. And thus, as the curtain swept down on
the close of each act, Comus felt a sense of depression and

deprivation sweep down on himself; bitterly he watched his last evening of social gaiety slipping away to its end. In less than an hour it would be over; in a few months' time it would be an unreal memory.

In the third interval, as he gazed round at the chattering house, some one touched him on the arm. It was Lady Veula Croot.

'I suppose in a week's time you'll be on the high seas?' she said. 'I'm coming to your farewell dinner, you know; your mother has just asked me. I'm not going to talk the usual rot to you about how much you will like it and so on. I sometimes think that one of the advantages of hell will be that no one will have the impertinence to point out to you that you're really better off than you would be anywhere else. What do you think of the play? Of course one can foresee the end; she will come to her husband with the announcement that their longed-for child is going to be born, and that will smooth over everything. So conveniently effective to wind up a comedy with the commencement of some one else's tragedy. And every one will go away saying, "I'm glad it had a happy ending." '

Lady Veula moved back to her seat, with her pleasant smile on her lips and the look of infinite weariness in her eyes.

The interval, the last interval, was drawing to a close, and the house began to turn with fidgety attention towards the stage for the unfolding of the final phase of the play. Francesca sat in Serena Golackly's box listening to Colonel Springfield's story of what happened to a pigeon-cote in his compound at Poona. Every one who knew the Colonel had to listen to that story a good many times, but Lady Caroline had mitigated the boredom of the infliction, and in fact invested it with a certain sporting interest, by offering a prize to the person who heard it oftenest in the course of the season, the competitors being under an honourable understanding not to lead up to the subject. Ada Spelvexit and a boy in the Foreign Service were at present at the top of the list with five recitals each to their score, but the former was suspected of doubtful adherence to the rules and spirit of the competition.

'And there, dear lady,' concluded the Colonel, 'were the eleven dead pigeons. What had become of the bandicoot no one ever knew.'

Francesca thanked him for his story, and complacently inscribed the figure 4 on the margin of her theatre programme. Almost at the same moment she heard George St Michael's voice pattering out a breathless piece of intelligence for the edification of Serena Golackly and any one else who might care to listen. Francesca galvanized into sudden attention.

'... Emmeline Chetrof to a fellow in the Indian Forest Department. He's got nothing but his pay, and they can't be married for four or five years: an absurdly long engagement, don't you think so? All very well to wait seven years for a wife in patriarchal times when you probably had others to go on with, and you lived long enough to celebrate your own tercentenary, but under modern conditions it seems a foolish arrangement.'

St Michael spoke almost with a sense of grievance. A marriage project that tied up all the small pleasant nuptial gossip-items about bridesmaids and honeymoon and recalcitrant aunts and so forth for an indefinite number of years seemed scarcely decent in his eyes, and there was little satisfaction or importance to be derived from early and special knowledge of an event which loomed as far distant as a Presidential Election or a change of Viceroy. But to Francesca, who had listened with startled apprehension at the mention of Emmeline Chetrof's name, the news came in a flood of relief and thankfulness. Short of entering a nunnery and taking celibate vows, Emmeline could hardly have behaved more conveniently than in tying herself up to a lover whose circumstances made it necessary to relegate marriage to the distant future. For four or five years Francesca was assured of undisturbed possession of the house in Blue Street, and after that period who knew what might happen? The engagement might stretch on indefinitely, it might even come to nothing under the weight of its accumulated years, as sometimes happened with these protracted affairs. Emmeline might lose her fancy for her absentee lover, and might never replace him with another. A golden possibility of perpetual tenancy of her present home began to float once more through Francesca's mind. As long as Emmeline had been unbespoken in the marriage market there had always been the haunting likelihood of seeing the dreaded announcement, 'A marriage has been arranged and will shortly take place,' in connexion with her name. And now a marriage had been arranged and would *not* shortly take place, might indeed never take place. St Michael's information was likely to be correct in this instance; he would never have invented a piece of matrimonial intelligence which gave such little scope for supplementary detail of the kind he loved to supply. As Francesca turned to watch the fourth act of the play, her mind was singing a paean of thankfulness and exultation. It was as though some artificer sent by the gods had reinforced with a substantial cord the horsehair thread that held up the sword of Damocles over her head. Her love for her home, for her treasured household possessions and her pleasant social life, was able to expand once more in present security, and feed on future hope. She was still young enough to count four or five years as a long time, and tonight she was optimistic enough to prophesy smooth things of the future that lay beyond that span. Of the fourth act, with its carefully held back but obviously imminent reconciliation between the leading characters, she took in but little, except that she vaguely understood it to have a happy ending. As the lights went up she looked round on the dispersing audience with a feeling of friendliness uppermost in her mind; even the sight of Elaine de Frey and Courtenay Youghal leaving the theatre together did not inspire her with a tenth part of the annoyance that their entrance had caused her. Serena's invitation to go on to the Savoy for supper fitted in exactly with her mood of exhilaration. It would be a fit and appropriate wind-up to an auspicious evening. The cold chicken and modest brand of Chablis waiting for her at home should give way to a banquet of more festive nature.

In the crush of the vestibule, friends and enemies, personal and political, were jostled and locked together in the general effort to rejoin temporarily estranged garments and secure the attendance of elusive vehicles. Lady Caroline found herself at close quarters with the estimable Henry Greech, and experienced some of the joy which comes to the homeward wending sportsman when a chance shot presents itself on which he may expend his remaining cartridges.

'So the Government's going to climb down, after all,' she said, with a provocative assumption of private information on the subject.

'I assure you the Government will do nothing of the kind,' replied the Member of Parliament with befitting dignity; 'the Prime Minister told me last night that under no circumstances——'

'My dear Mr Greech,' said Lady Caroline, 'we all know that Prime Ministers are wedded to the truth, but like other wedded couples they sometimes live apart.'

For her, at any rate, the comedy had had a happy ending.

Comus made his way slowly and lingeringly from the stalls, so slowly that the lights were already being turned down and great shroud-like dustcloths were being swathed over the ornamental gilt-work. The laughing, chattering, yawning throng had filtered out of the vestibule, and was melting away in final groups from the steps of the theatre. An impatient attendant gave him his coat and locked up the cloak-room. Comus stepped out under the portico; he looked at the posters announcing the play, and in anticipation he could see other posters announcing its 200th performance. Two hundred performances; by that time the Straw Exchange Theatre would be to him something so remote and unreal that it would hardly seem to exist or to have ever existed except in his fancy. And to the laughing, chattering throng that would pass in under that portico to the 200th performance, he would be, to those that had known him, something equally remote and non-existent. 'The good-looking Bassington boy? Oh, dead, or rubber-growing or sheep-farming, or something of that sort.'

CHAPTER XIV

The farewell dinner which Francesca had hurriedly organized in honour of her son's departure threatened from the outset to be a doubtfully successful function. In the first place, as he observed privately, there was very little of Comus and a good deal of farewell in it. His own particular friends were unrepresented. Courtenay Youghal was out of the question; and though Francesca would have stretched a point and welcomed some of his other male associates of whom she scarcely approved, he himself had been opposed to including any of them in the invitations. On the other hand, as Henry Greech had provided Comus with this job that he was going out to, and was, moreover, finding part of the money for the necessary outfit, Francesca had felt it her duty to ask him and his wife to the dinner; the obtuseness that seems to cling to some people like a garment throughout their life had caused Mr Greech to accept the invitation. When Comus heard of the circumstance he laughed long and boisterously; his spirits, Francesca noted, seemed to be rising fast as the hour for departure drew near.

The other guests included Serena Golackly and Lady Veula, the latter having been asked on the inspiration of the moment at the theatrical first night. In the height of the season it was not easy to get together a goodly selection of guests at short notice, and Francesca had gladly fallen in with Serena's suggestion of bringing with her Stephen Thorle, who was alleged, in loose feminine phrasing, to 'know all about' tropical Africa. His travels and experiences in those regions probably did not cover much ground or stretch over any great length of time, but he was one of those individuals who can describe a continent on the strength of a few days' stay in a coast town as intimately and dogmatically as a palaeontologist will reconstruct an extinct mammal from the evidence of a stray shinbone. He had the loud penetrating voice and the prominent penetrating eyes of a man who can do no listening in the ordinary way and whose eyes have to perform the function of listening for him. His vanity did not necessarily make him unbearable, unless one had to spend much time in his society, and his need for a wide field of audience and admiration was mercifully calculated to spread his operations over a considerable human area. Moreover, his craving for attentive listeners forced him to interest himself in a wonderful variety of subjects on which he was able to discourse fluently and with a certain semblance of special knowledge. Politics he avoided; the ground was too well known, and there was a definite No to every definite Yes that could be put forward. Moreover, argument was not congenial to his disposition, which preferred an unchallenged flow of dissertation modified by occasional helpful questions which formed the starting-point for new off-shoots of word-spinning. The promotion of cottage industries, the prevention of juvenile street trading, the extension of the Borstal prison system, the furtherance of vague talkative religious movements, the fostering of inter-racial *ententes*, all found in him a tireless exponent, a fluent and entertaining, though perhaps not very convincing, advocate. With the real motive power behind these various causes he was not very closely identified; to the spade-workers who carried on the actual labours of each particular movement he bore the relation of a trowel-worker, delving superficially at the surface, but able to devote a proportionately far greater amount of time to the advertisement of his progress and achievements. Such was Stephen Thorle, a governess in the nursery of Chelsea-bred religions, a skilled window-dresser in the emporium of his own personality, and, needless to say, evanescently popular amid a wide but shifting circle of acquaintances. He improved on the record of a socially much-travelled individual whose experience has become classical, and went to most of the best houses—twice.

His inclusion as a guest at this particular dinner-party was not a very happy inspiration. He was inclined to patronize Comus, as well as the African continent, and on even slighter acquaintance. With the exception of Henry Greech, whose feelings towards his nephew had been soured by many years of overt antagonism, there was an uncomfortable feeling among those present that the topic of the black-sheep export trade, as Comus would have himself expressed it, was being given undue prominence in what should have been a festive farewell banquet. And Comus, in whose honour the feast was given, did not contribute much towards its success; though his spirits seemed strung up to a high pitch, his merriment was more the merriment of a cynical and amused onlooker than of one who responds to the gaiety of his companions. Sometimes he laughed quietly to himself at some chance remark of a scarcely mirth-provoking nature, and Lady Veula, watching him narrowly, came to the conclusion that an element of fear was blended with his seemingly buoyant spirits. Once or twice he caught her eye across the table, and a certain sympathy seemed to grow up between them, as though they were both consciously watching some lugubrious comedy that was being played out before them.

An untoward little incident had marked the commencement of the meal. A small still-life picture that hung over the sideboard had snapped its cord and slid down with an alarming clatter on to the crowded board beneath it. The picture itself was scarcely damaged, but its fall had been accompanied by a tinkle of broken glass, and it was found that a liqueur glass, one out of a set of seven that would be impossible to match, had been shivered into fragments. Francesca's almost motherly love for her pos-

sessions made her peculiarly sensible to a feeling of annoyance and depression at the accident, but she turned politely
to listen to Mrs Greech's account of a misfortune in which
four soup-plates were involved. Mrs Henry was not a
brilliant conversationalist, and her flank was speedily
turned by Stephen Thorle, who recounted a slum experience in which two entire families did all their feeding out
of one damaged soup-plate.

'The gratitude of those poor creatures when I presented
them with a set of table crockery apiece, the tears in their
eyes and in their voices when they thanked me, would
be impossible to describe.'

'Thank you all the same for describing it,' said Comus.

The listening eyes went swiftly round the table to gather
evidence as to how this rather disconcerting remark had
been received, but Thorle's voice continued uninter-
ruptedly to retail stories of East End gratitude, never failing to mention the particular deeds of disinterested
charity on his part which had evoked and justified the
gratitude. Mrs Greech had to suppress the interesting
sequel to her broken crockery narrative, to wit, how she
subsequently matched the shattered soup-plates at Har-
rod's. Like an imported plant species that sometimes
flourishes exceedingly, and makes itself at home to the
dwarfing and overshadowing of all native species, Thorle
dominated the dinner-party and thrust its original purport
somewhat into the background. Serena began to look
helplessly apologetic. It was altogether rather a relief when
the filling of champagne glasses gave Francesca an excuse
for bringing matters back to their intended footing.

'We must all drink a health,' she said. 'Comus, my own
dear boy, a safe and happy voyage to you, much prosperity
in the life you are going out to, and in due time a safe and
happy return——'

Her hand gave an involuntary jerk in the act of raising
the glass, and the wine went streaming across the table-
cloth in a froth of yellow bubbles. It certainly was not
turning out a comfortable or auspicious dinner-party.

'My dear mother,' cried Comus, 'you must have been drinking healths all the afternoon to make your hand so unsteady.'

He laughed gaily and with apparent carelessness, but again Lady Veula caught the frightened note in his laughter. Mrs Henry, with practical sympathy, was telling Francesca two good ways for getting wine-stains out of tablecloths. The smaller economies of life were an unnecessary branch of learning for Mrs Greech, but she studied them as carefully and conscientiously as a stay-at-home plain-dwelling English child commits to memory the measurements and altitudes of the world's principal peaks. Some women of her temperament and mentality know by heart the favourite colours, flowers, and hymn-tunes of all the members of the Royal Family; Mrs Greech would possibly have failed in an examination of that nature, but she knew what to do with carrots that have been over-long in storage.

Francesca did not renew her speech-making; a chill seemed to have fallen over all efforts at festivity, and she contented herself with refilling her glass and simply drinking to her boy's good health. The others followed her example, and Comus drained his glass with a brief 'Thank you all very much.' The sense of constraint which hung over the company was not, however, marked by any uncomfortable pause in the conversation. Henry Greech was a fluent thinker, of the kind that prefer to do their thinking aloud; the silence that descended on him as a mantle in the House of Commons was an official livery of which he divested himself as thoroughly as possible in private life. He did not propose to sit through dinner as a mere listener to Mr Thorle's personal narrative of philanthropic movements and experiences, and took the first opportunity of launching himself into a flow of satirical observations on current political affairs. Lady Veula was inured to this sort of thing in her own home circle; and sat listening with the stoical indifference with which an Eskimo might accept the occurrence of one snowstorm the more, in the course of an Arctic winter. Serena Golackly felt a certain relief at the fact that her imported guest was not, after all, monopolizing the conversation. But the latter was too determined a personality to allow himself to be thrust aside for many minutes by the talkative M.P. Henry Greech paused for an instant to chuckle at one of his own shafts of satire, and immediately Thorle's penetrating voice swept across the table.

'Oh, you politicians!' he exclaimed, with pleasant superiority; 'you are always fighting about how things should be done, and the consequence is you are never able to do anything. Would you like me to tell you what a Unitarian horse-dealer said to me at Brindisi about politicians?'

A Unitarian horse-dealer at Brindisi had all the allurement of the unexpected. Henry Greech's witticisms at the expense of the Front Opposition bench were destined to remain as unfinished as his wife's history of the broken soup-plates. Thorle was primed with an ample succession of stories and themes, chiefly concerning poverty, thriftlessness, reclamation, reformed characters, and so forth, which carried him in an almost uninterrupted sequence through the remainder of the dinner.

'What I want to do is to make people think,' he said, turning his prominent eyes on to his hostess; 'it's so hard to make people think.'

'At any rate you give them the opportunity,' said Comus cryptically.

As the ladies rose to leave the table Comus crossed over to pick up one of Lady Veula's gloves that had fallen to the floor.

'I did not know you kept a dog,' said Lady Veula.

'We don't,' said Comus, 'there isn't one in the house.'

'I could have sworn I saw one follow you across the hall this evening,' she said.

'A small black dog, something like a schipperke?' asked Comus in a low voice.

'Yes, that was it.'

'I saw it myself tonight; it ran from behind my chair just as I was sitting down. Don't say anything to the others about it; it would frighten my mother.'

'Have you ever seen it before?' Lady Veula asked quickly.

'Once, when I was six years old. It followed my father downstairs.'

Lady Veula said nothing. She knew that Comus had lost his father at the age of six.

In the drawing-room Serena made nervous excuses for her talkative friend.

'Really, rather an interesting man, you know, and up to the eyes in all sorts of movements. Just the sort of person to turn loose at a drawing-room meeting, or to send down to a mission-hall in some unheard-of neighbourhood. Given a sounding-board and a harmonium, and a titled woman of some sort in the chair, and he'll be perfectly happy; I must say I hadn't realized how overpowering he might be at a small dinner-party.'

'I should say he was a very good man,' said Mrs Greech; she had forgiven the mutilation of her soup-plate story.

The party broke up early, as most of the guests had other engagements to keep. With a belated recognition of the farewell nature of the occasion they made pleasant little good-bye remarks to Comus, with the usual predictions of prosperity and anticipations of an ultimate auspicious return. Even Henry Greech sank his personal dislike of the boy for the moment, and made hearty jocular allusions to a home-coming, which, in the elder man's eyes, seemed possibly pleasantly remote. Lady Veula alone made no reference to the future; she simply said, 'Good-bye, Comus,' but her voice was the kindest of all, and he responded with a look of gratitude. The weariness in her eyes was more marked than ever as she lay back against the cushions of her carriage.

'What a tragedy life is!' she said aloud to herself.

Serena and Stephen Thorle were the last to leave, and Francesca stood alone for a moment at the head of the

stairway watching Comus laughing and chatting as he
escorted the departing guests to the door. The ice-wall was
melting under the influence of coming separation, and
never had he looked more adorably handsome in her eyes,
never had his merry laugh and mischief-loving gaiety
seemed more infectious than on this night of his farewell
banquet. She was glad enough that he was going away
from a life of idleness and extravagance and temptation,
but she began to suspect that she would miss, for a little
while at any rate, the high-spirited boy who could be so
attractive in his better moods. Her impulse, after the guests
had gone, was to call him to her and hold him once more
in her arms, and repeat her wishes for his happiness and
good-luck in the land he was going to, and her promise
of his welcome back, some not too distant day, to the land
he was leaving. She wanted to forget, and to make him
forget, the months of irritable jangling and sharp discus-
sions, the months of cold aloofness and indifference, and
to remember only that he was her own dear Comus as in
the days of yore, before he had grown from an unmanage-
able pickle into a weariful problem. But she feared lest
she should break down, and she did not wish to cloud his
light-hearted gaiety on the very eve of his departure. She
watched him for a moment as he stood in the hall, settling
his tie before a mirror, and then went quietly back to her
drawing-room. It had not been a very successful dinner-
party, and the general effect it had left on her was one of
depression.

Comus, with a lively musical-comedy air on his lips, and
a look of wretchedness in his eyes, went out to visit the
haunts that he was leaving so soon.

CHAPTER XV

Elaine Youghal sat at lunch in the Speise Saal of one
of Vienna's costlier hotels. The double-headed eagle, with
its 'K.u.K.' legend, everywhere met the eye and announced

the imperial favour in which the establishment basked. Some several square yards of yellow bunting, charged with the image of another double-headed eagle, floating from the highest flagstaff above the building, betrayed to the initiated the fact that a Russian Grand Duke was concealed somewhere on the premises. Unannounced by heraldic symbolism, but unconcealable by reason of nature's own blazonry, were several citizens and citizenesses of the great republic of the Western world. One or two Cobdenite members of the British Parliament, engaged in the useful task of proving that the cost of living in Vienna was on an exorbitant scale, flitted with restrained importance through a land whose fatness they had come to spy out; every fancied overcharge in their bills was welcome as providing another nail in the coffin of their fiscal opponents. It is the glory of democracies that they may be misled, but never driven. Here and there, like brave deeds in a dust-patterned world, flashed and glittered the sumptuous-uniforms of representatives of the Austrian military caste. Also in evidence, at discreet intervals, were stray units of the Semitic tribe that nineteen centuries of European neglect had been unable to mislay.

Elaine, sitting with Courtenay at an elaborately appointed luncheon table, gay with high goblets of Bohemian glassware, was mistress of three discoveries. First, to her disappointment, that if you frequent the more expensive hotels of Europe you must be prepared to find, in whatever country you may chance to be staying, a depressing international likeness between them all. Secondly, to her relief, that one is not expected to be sentimentally amorous during a modern honeymoon. Thirdly, rather to her dismay, that Courtenay Youghal did not necessarily expect her to be markedly affectionate in private. Some one had described him, after their marriage, as one of Nature's bachelors, and she began to see how aptly the description fitted him.

'Will those Germans on our left never stop talking?' she asked, as an undying flow of Teutonic small-talk rattled and jangled across the intervening stretch of carpet. 'Not one of those three women has ceased talking for an instant since we've been sitting here.'

'They will presently, if only for a moment,' said Courtenay; 'when the dish you have ordered comes in there will be a deathly silence at the next table. No German can see a *plat* brought in for some one else without being possessed with a great fear that it represents a more toothsome morsel or a better money's worth than what he has ordered for himself.'

The exuberant Teutonic chatter was balanced on the other side of the room by an even more penetrating conversation unflaggingly maintained by a party of Americans, who were sitting in judgment on the cuisine of the country they were passing through, and finding few extenuating circumstances.

'What Mr Lonkins wants is a real *deep* cherry pie,' announced a lady in a tone of dramatic and honest conviction.

'Why, yes, that is so,' corroborated a gentleman who was apparently the Mr Lonkins in question; 'a real *deep* cherry pie.'

'We had the same trouble way back in Paris,' proclaimed another lady; 'little Jerome and the girls don't want to eat any more *crème renversée*. I'd give anything if they could get some real cherry pie.'

'Real *deep* cherry pie,' assented Mr Lonkins.

'Way down in Ohio we used to have peach pie that was real good,' said Mrs Lonkins, turning on a tap of reminiscence that presently flowed to a cascade. The subject of pies seemed to lend itself to indefinite expansion.

'So those people think of nothing but their food?' asked Elaine, as the virtues of roasted mutton suddenly came to the fore and received emphatic recognition, even the absent and youthful Jerome being quoted in its favour.

'On the contrary,' said Courtenay, 'they are a widely-travelled set, and the man has had a notably interesting career. It is a form of homesickness with them to discuss and lament the cookery and foods that they've never had the leisure to stay at home and digest. The Wandering Jew probably babbled unremittingly about some breakfast dish that took so long to prepare that he had never time to eat it.'

A waiter deposited a dish of Wiener Nierenbraten in front of Elaine. At the same moment a magic hush fell upon the three German ladies at the adjoining table, and the flicker of a great fear passed across their eyes. Then they burst forth again into tumultuous chatter. Courtenay had proved a reliable prophet.

Almost at the same moment as the luncheon-dish appeared on the scene, two ladies arrived at a neighbouring table, and bowed with dignified cordiality to Elaine and Courtenay. They were two of the more worldly and travelled of Elaine's extensive stock of aunts, and they happened to be making a short stay at the same hotel as the young couple. They were far too correct and rationally minded to intrude themselves on their niece, but it was significant of Elaine's altered view as to the sanctity of honeymoon life that she secretly rather welcomed the presence of her two relatives in the hotel, and had found time and occasion to give them more of her society than she would have considered necessary or desirable a few weeks ago. The younger of the two she rather liked, in a restrained fashion, as one likes an unpretentious watering-place or a restaurant that does not try to give one a musical education in addition to one's dinner. One felt instinctively about her that she would never wear rather more valuable diamonds than any other woman in the room, and would never be the only person to be saved in a steamboat disaster or hotel fire. As a child she might have been perfectly well able to recite 'On Linden when the sun was low,' but one felt certain that nothing ever induced her to do so. The elder aunt, Mrs Goldbrook, did not share her sister's character as a human rest-cure; most people found her rather disturbing, chiefly, perhaps, from her habit of asking unimportant questions with enormous solemnity. Her manner of inquiring after a trifling ailment gave one the impression that she was more concerned with the fortunes of the malady than with oneself, and when one got rid of a cold one felt that she almost expected to be given its postal address. Probably her manner was merely the defensive outwork of an innate shyness, but she was not a woman who commanded confidences.

'A telephone call for Courtenay,' commented the younger of the two women as Youghal hurriedly flashed through the room; 'the telephone system seems to enter very largely into the young man's life.'

'The telephone has robbed matrimony of most of its sting,' said the elder; 'so much more discreet than pen and ink communications which get read by the wrong people.'

Elaine's aunts were conscientiously worldly; they were the natural outcome of a stock that had been conscientiously strait-laced for many generations.

Elaine had progressed to the pancake stage before Courtenay returned.

'Sorry to be away so long,' he said, 'but I've arranged something rather nice for tonight. There's rather a jolly masquerade ball on. I've 'phoned about getting a costume for you, and it's all right. It will suit you beautifully, and I've got my harlequin dress with me. Madame Kelnicort, excellent soul, is going to chaperon you, and she'll take you back any time you like; I'm quite unreliable when I get into fancy dress. I shall probably keep going till some unearthly hour of the morning.'

A masquerade ball in a strange city hardly represented Elaine's idea of enjoyment. Carefully to disguise one's identity in a neighbourhood where one was entirely unknown seemed to her rather meaningless. With Courtenay, of course, it was different; he seemed to have friends and acquaintances everywhere. However, the matter had progressed to a point which would have made a refusal to go seem rather ungracious. Elaine finished her pancake and began to take a polite interest in her costume.

'What is your character?' asked Madame Kelnicort that evening, as they uncloaked, preparatory to entering the already crowded ball-room.

'I believe I'm supposed to represent Marjolaine de Montfort, whoever she may have been,' said Elaine. 'Courtenay declares he only wanted to marry me because I'm his ideal of her.'

'But what a mistake to go as a character you know nothing about. To enjoy a masquerade ball you ought to throw away your own self and be the character you represent. Now Courtenay has been Harlequin since half-way through dinner; I could see it dancing in his eyes. At about six o'clock tomorrow morning he will fall asleep and wake up a member of the British House of Parliament on his honeymoon, but tonight he is unrestrainedly Harlequin.'

Elaine stood in the ball-room surrounded by a laughing, jostling throng of pierrots, jockeys, Dresden-china shepherdesses, Rumanian peasant-girls, and all the lively makebelieve creatures that form the ingredients of a fancy-dress ball. As she stood watching them she experienced a growing feeling of annoyance, chiefly with herself. She was assisting, as the French say, at one of the gayest scenes of Europe's gayest capital, and she was conscious of being absolutely unaffected by the gaiety around her. The costumes were certainly interesting to look at, and the music good to listen to, and to that extent she was amused, but the *abandon* of the scene made no appeal to her. It was like watching a game of which you did not know the rules, and in the issue of which you were not interested. Elaine began to wonder what was the earliest moment at which she could drag Madame Kelnicort away from the revel without being guilty of sheer cruelty. Then Courtenay wriggled out of the crush and came towards her, a joyous, laughing Courtenay, looking younger and handsomer than she had ever seen him. She could scarcely recognize in him tonight the rising young debater who made embarrassing onslaughts on the Government's foreign policy before a crowded House of Commons. He claimed her for the dance that was just starting, and steered her dexterously into the heart of the waltzing crowd.

'You look more like Marjolaine than I should have thought a mortal woman of these days could look,' he declared, 'only Marjolaine did smile sometimes. You have rather the air of wondering if you'd left out enough tea for the servants' breakfast. Don't mind my teasing; I love you to look like that, and besides, it makes a splendid foil to my Harlequin—my selfishness coming to the fore again, you see. But you really are to go home the moment you're bored; the excellent Kelnicort gets heaps of dances throughout the winter, so don't mind sacrificing her.'

A little later in the evening Elaine found herself standing out a dance with a grave young gentleman from the Russian Embassy.

'Monsieur Courtenay enjoys himself, doesn't he?' he observed, as the youthful-looking harlequin flashed past them, looking like some restless gorgeous-hued dragon-fly. 'Why is it that the good God has given your countrymen the boon of eternal youth? Some of your countrywomen, too, but all of the men.'

Elaine could think of many of her countrymen who were not and never could have been youthful, but as far as Courtenay was concerned she recognized the fitness of the remark. And the recognition carried with it a sense of depression. Would he always remain youthful and keen on gaiety and revelling, while she grew staid and retiring? She had thrust the lively intractable Comus out of her mind, as by his perverseness he had thrust himself out of her heart, and she had chosen the brilliant young man of affairs as her husband. He had honestly let her see the selfish side of his character while he was courting her, but she had been prepared to make due sacrifices to the selfishness of a public man who had his career to consider above all other things. Would she also have to make sacrifices to the harlequin spirit which was now revealing itself as an undercurrent in his nature? When one has inured oneself to the idea of a particular form of victimization it is disconcerting to be confronted with another. Many a man who would patiently undergo martyrdom for religion's sake would be furiously unwilling to be a martyr to neuralgia.

'I think that is why you English love animals so much,' pursued the young diplomat; 'you are such splendid animals yourselves. You are lively because you want to be lively, not because people are looking on at you. Monsieur Courtenay is certainly an animal. I mean it as a high compliment.'

'Am I an animal?' asked Elaine.

'I was going to say you are an angel,' said the Russian, in some embarrassment, 'but I do not think that would do; angels and animals would never get on together. To get on with animals you must have a sense of humour, and I don't suppose angels have any sense of humour; you see it would be no use to them as they never hear any jokes.'

'Perhaps,' said Elaine, with a tinge of bitterness in her voice, 'perhaps I am a vegetable.'

'I think you most remind me of a picture,' said the Russian.

It was not the first time Elaine had heard the simile.

'I know,' she said, 'the Narrow Gallery at the Louvre: attributed to Leonardo da Vinci.'

Evidently the impression she made on people was solely one of externals.

Was that how Courtenay regarded her? Was that to be her function and place in life, a painted background, a decorative setting to other people's triumphs and tragedies? Somehow tonight she had the feeling that a general might have who brought imposing forces into the field and could do nothing with them. She possessed youth and good looks, considerable wealth, and had just made what would be thought by most people a very satisfactory marriage. And already she seemed to be standing aside as an onlooker where she had expected herself to be taking a leading part.

'Does this sort of thing appeal to you?' she asked the young Russian, nodding towards the gay scrimmage of masqueraders and rather prepared to hear an amused negative.

'But yes, of course,' he answered; 'costume balls, fancy fairs, café chantant, casino, anything that is not real life appeals to us Russians. Real life with us is the sort of thing that Maxim Gorki deals in. It interests us immensely, but we like to get away from it sometimes.'

Madame Kelnicort came up with another prospective partner, and Elaine delivered her ukase: one more dance and then back to the hotel. Without any special regret she made her retreat from the revel which Courtenay was enjoying under the impression that it was life and the young Russian under the firm conviction that it was not.

Elaine breakfasted at her aunts' table the next morning at much her usual hour. Courtenay was sleeping the sleep of a happy tired animal. He had given instructions to be called at eleven o'clock, from which time onward the *Neue Freie Presse*, the *Zeit*, and his toilet would occupy his attention till he appeared at the luncheon table. There were not many people breakfasting when Elaine arrived on the scene, but the room seemed to be fuller than it really was by reason of a penetrating voice that was engaged in recounting how far the standard of Viennese breakfast fare fell below the expectations and desires of little Jerome and the girls.

'If ever little Jerome becomes President of the United States,' said Elaine, 'I shall be able to contribute quite an informing article on his gastronomic likes and dislikes to the papers.'

The aunts were discreetly inquisitive as to the previous evening's entertaintment.

'If Elaine would flirt mildly with somebody it would be such a good thing,' said Mrs Goldbrook; 'it would remind Courtenay that he's not the only attractive young man in the world.'

Elaine, however, did not gratify their hopes; she referred to the ball with the detachment she would have shown in describing a drawing-room show of cottage industries. It was not difficult to discern in her description of the affair the confession that she had been slightly bored. From Courtenay, later in the day, the aunts received a much livelier impression of the festivities, from which it was abundantly clear that he, at any rate, had managed to amuse himself. Neither did it appear that his good opinion of his own attractions had suffered any serious shock. He was distinctly in a very good temper.

'The secret of enjoying a honeymoon,' said Mrs Gold-brook afterwards to her sister, 'is not to attempt too much.'

'You mean——?'

'Courtenay is content to try and keep one person amused and happy, and he thoroughly succeeds.'

'I certainly don't think Elaine is going to be very happy,' said her sister, 'but at least Courtenay saved her from making the greatest mistake she could have made—marrying that young Bassington.'

'He has also,' said Mrs Goldbrook, 'helped her to make the next biggest mistake of her life—marrying Courtenay Youghal.'

CHAPTER XVI

It was late afternoon by the banks of a swiftly rushing river, a river that gave back a haze of heat from its waters as though it were some stagnant steaming lagoon, and yet seemed to be whirling onward with the determination of a living thing, perpetually eager and remorseless, leaping savagely at any obstacle that attempted to stay its course; an unfriendly river, to whose waters you committed yourself at your peril. Under the hot breathless shade of the trees on its shore arose that acrid all-pervading smell that seems to hang everywhere about the tropics, a smell as of some monstrous musty stillroom where herbs and spices have been crushed and distilled and stored for hundreds of years, and where the windows have seldom been opened. In the dazzling heat that still held undisputed sway over the scene, insects and birds seemed preposterously alive and active, flitting their gay colours through the sunbeams, and crawling over the baked dust in the full swing and pursuit of their several businesses; the flies engaged in Heaven knows what, and the fly-catchers busy with the flies. Beasts and humans showed no such indifference to the temperature; the sun would have to slant yet farther downward before the earth would become a fit arena for their revived activities. In the sheltered basement of a wayside rest-house a gang of native hammock-bearers slept or chattered drowsily through the last hours of the long midday halt; wide awake, yet almost motionless in the thrall of a heavy lassitude, their European master sat alone in an upper chamber, staring out through a narrow window-opening at the native village, spreading away in thick clusters of huts girt around with cultivated vegetation. It seemed a vast human ant-hill, which would presently be astir with its teeming human life, as though the Sun God in his last departing stride had roused it with a careless kick. Even as Comus watched he could see the beginnings of the evening's awakening. Women, squatting in front of their huts, began to pound away at the rice or maize that would form the evening meal, girls were collecting their water-pots preparatory to a walk down to the river, and enterprising goats made tentative forays through gaps in the ill-kept fences of neighbouring garden-plots; their hurried retreats showed that here at least some one was keeping alert and wakeful vigil. Behind a hut perched on a steep hill-side, just opposite to the rest-house, two boys were splitting wood with a certain languid industry; farther down the road a group of dogs were leisurely working themselves up to quarrelling pitch. Here and there, bands of evil-looking pigs roamed about, busy with foraging excursions that came unpleasantly athwart the borderline of scavenging. And from the trees that bounded and intersected the village rose the horrible, tireless, spiteful-sounding squawking of the iron-throated crows.

Comus sat and watched it all with a sense of growing aching depression. It was so utterly trivial to his eyes, so devoid of interest, and yet it was so real, so serious, so implacable in its continuity. The brain grew tired with the thought of its unceasing reproduction. It had all gone on, as it was going on now, by the side of the great rushing, swirling river, this tilling and planting and harvesting, marketing and store-keeping, feast-making and fetish-worship and love-making, burying and giving in marriage, child-bearing and child-rearing, all this had been going on, in the shimmering, blistering heat and the warm nights, while he had been a youngster at school, dimly recognizing Africa as a division of the earth's surface that it was advisable to have a certain nodding acquaintance with. It had been going on in all its trifling detail, all its serious intensity, when his father and his grandfather in their day had been little boys at school, it would go on just as intently as ever long after Comus and his generation had passed away, just as the shadows would lengthen and fade under the mulberry trees in that far-away English garden, round the old stone fountain where a leaden otter for ever preyed on a leaden salmon.

Comus rose impatiently from his seat, and walked wearily across the hut to another window-opening which commanded a broad view of the river. There was something which fascinated and then depressed one in its ceaseless hurrying onward sweep, its tons of water rushing on for all time, as long as the face of the earth should remain unchanged. On its farther shore could be seen spread out at intervals other teeming villages, with their cultivated plots and pasture clearings, their moving dots which meant cattle and goats and dogs and children. And far up its course, lost in the forest growth that fringed its banks, were hidden away yet more villages, human herding-grounds where men dwelt and worked and bartered, squabbled and worshipped, sickened and perished, while the river went by with its endless swirl and rush of gleaming waters. One could well understand primitive early races making propitiatory sacrifices to the spirit of a great river on whose shores they dwelt. Time and the river were the two great forces that seemed to matter here.

It was almost a relief to turn back to that other outlook and watch the village life that was now beginning to wake in earnest. The procession of water-fetchers had formed itself in a long chattering line that stretched riverwards. Comus wondered how many tens of thousands of times that procession had been formed since first the village came into existence. They had been doing it while he was playing in the cricket-fields at school, while he was spending Christmas holidays in Paris, while he was going his careless round of theatres, dances, suppers and card-parties, just as they were doing it now; they would be doing it when there was no one alive who remembered Comus Bassington. This thought recurred again and again with painful persistence, a morbid growth arising in part from his loneliness.

Staring dumbly out at the toiling, sweltering human ant-hill, Comus marvelled how missionary enthusiasts could labour hopefully at the work of transplanting their religion, with its home-grown accretions of fatherly parochial benevolence, in this heat-blistered, fever-scourged wilderness, where men lived like groundbait and died like flies. Demons one might believe in, if one did not hold one's imagination in healthy check, but a kindly all-managing God, never. Somewhere in the west country of England Comus had an uncle who lived in a rose-smothered rectory and taught a wholesome gentle-hearted creed that expressed itself in the spirit of 'Little lamb, Who made thee?' and faithfully reflected the beautiful homely Christ-child sentiment of Saxon Europe. What a far-away, unreal fairy-story it all seemed here in this West African land, where the bodies of men were of as little account as the bubbles that floated on the oily froth of the great flowing river, and where it required a stretch of wild profitless imagination to credit them with undying souls! In the life he had come from, Comus had been accustomed to think of individuals as definite masterful personalities, making their several marks on the circumstances that revolved around them; they did well or ill, or in most cases indifferently, and were criticized, praised, blamed, thwarted, or tolerated, or given way to. In any case, humdrum or outstanding, they had their spheres of importance, little or big. They dominated a breakfast table or harassed a Government, according to their capabilities or opportunities, or perhaps they merely had irritating mannerisms. At any rate it seemed highly probable that they had souls. Here a man simply made a unit in an unnumbered population, an inconsequent dot in a loosely-compiled death-roll. Even his own position as a white man exalted conspicuously above a horde of black natives did not save Comus from the depressing sense of nothingness which his first experience of fever had thrown over him. He was a lost, soulless body in this great uncaring land; if he died another would take his place, his few effects would be inventoried and sent down to the coast, some one else would finish off any tea or whisky that he left behind—that would be all.

It was nearly time to be starting towards the next halting-place where he would dine, or at any rate eat something. But the lassitude which the fever had bequeathed him made the tedium of travelling through interminable forest-tracks a weariness to be deferred as long as possible. The bearers were nothing loath to let another half-hour or so slip by, and Comus dragged a battered paper-covered novel from the pocket of his coat. It was a story dealing with the elaborately tangled love affairs of a surpassingly uninteresting couple, and even in his almost bookless state Comus had not been able to plough his way through more than two-thirds of its dull length; bound up with the cover, however, were some pages of advertisement, and these the exile scanned with a hungry intentness that the romance itself could never have commanded. The name of a shop, of a street, the address of a restaurant, came to him as a bitter reminder of the world he had lost, a world that ate and drank and flirted, gambled and made merry, a world that debated and intrigued and wire-pulled, fought or compromised political battles—and recked nothing of its outcasts wandering through forest paths and steamy swamps or lying in the grip of fever. Comus read and re-read those few lines of advertisement, just as he treasured a much-crumpled programme of a first-night performance at the Straw Exchange Theatre; they seemed to make a little more real the past that was already so shadowy and so utterly remote. For a moment he could almost capture the sensation of being once again in those haunts that he loved; then he looked round and pushed the book wearily from him. The steaming heat, the forest, the rushing river hemmed him in on all sides.

The two boys who had been splitting wood ceased from their labours and straightened their backs; suddenly the smaller of the two gave the other a resounding whack with a split lath that he still held in his hand, and flew up the hillside with a scream of laughter and simulated terror, the bigger lad following in hot pursuit. Up and down the steep bush-grown slope they raced and twisted and dodged, coming sometimes to close quarters in a hurricane of squeals and smacks, rolling over and over like fighting kittens, and breaking away again to start fresh provocation and fresh pursuit. Now and again they would lie for a time panting in what seemed the last stage of exhaustion, and then they would be off in another wild scamper, their dusky bodies flitting through the bushes, disappearing and reappearing with equal suddenness. Presently two girls of their own age, who had returned from the water-fetching, sprang out on them from ambush, and the four joined in one joyous gambol that lit up the hillside with shrill echoes and glimpses of flying limbs. Comus sat and watched, at first with an amused interest, then with a returning flood of depression and heartache. Those wild young human kittens represented the joy of life, he was the outsider, the lonely alien, watching something in which he could not join, a happiness in which he had no part or lot. He would pass presently out of the village and his bearers' feet would leave their indentations in the dust: that would be his most permanent memorial in this little oasis of teeming life. And that other life, in which he once moved with such confident sense of his own necessary participation in it, how completely he had passed out of it! Amid all its laughing throngs, its card-parties and race-meetings and country-house gatherings, he was just a mere name, remembered or forgotten, Comus Bassington, the boy who went away. He had loved himself very well and never troubled greatly whether any one else really loved him, and now he realized what he had made of his life. And at the same time he knew that if his chance were to come again he would throw it away just as surely, just as perversely. Fate played with him with loaded dice; he would lose always.

One person in the whole world had cared for him, for longer than he could remember, cared for him perhaps more than he knew, cared for him perhaps now. But a wall of ice had mounted up between him and her, and across it there blew that cold breath that chills or kills affection.

The words of a well-known old song, the wistful cry of a lost cause, rang with insistent mockery through his brain:

> Better loved you canna be,
> Will ye ne'er come back again?

If it was love that was to bring him back he must be an exile for ever. His epitaph in the mouths of those that remembered him would be: Comus Bassington, the boy who never came back.

And in his unutterable loneliness he bowed his head on his arms, that he might not see the joyous scrambling frolic on yonder hillside.

CHAPTER XVII

The bleak rawness of a grey December day held sway over St James's Park, that sanctuary of lawn and tree and pool, into which the bourgeois innovator has rushed ambitiously time and again, to find that he must take the patent leather from off his feet, for the ground on which he stands is hallowed ground.

In the lonely hour of early afternoon, when the workers had gone back to their work, and the loiterers were scarcely yet gathered again, Francesca Bassington made her way restlessly along the stretches of gravelled walk that bordered the ornamental water. The overmastering unhappiness that filled her heart and stifled her thinking powers found answering echo in her surroundings. There is a sorrow that lingers in old parks and gardens that the busy streets have no leisure to keep by them; the dead must bury their dead in Whitehall or the Place de la Concorde, but there are quieter spots where they may still keep tryst with the living and intrude the memory of their bygone selves on generations that have almost forgotten them. Even in tourist-trampled Versailles the desolation of a tragedy that cannot die haunts the terraces and fountains like a blood-stain that will not wash out; in the Saxon Garden at Warsaw there broods the memory of long-dead things, coeval with the stately trees that shade its walks, and with the carp that swim today in its ponds as they doubtless swam there when 'Lieber Augustin' was a living person and not as yet an immortal couplet. And St James's Park, with its lawns and walks and water-fowl, harbours still its associations with a bygone order of men and women, whose happiness and sadness are woven into its history, dim and grey as they were once bright and glowing, like the faded pattern worked into the fabric of an old tapestry. It was here that Francesca had made her way when the intolerable inaction of waiting had driven her forth from her home. She was waiting for that worst news of all, the news which does not kill hope, because there has been none to kill, but merely adds suspense. An early message had said that Comus was ill, which might have meant much or little; then there had come that morning a cablegram which only meant one thing; in a few hours she would get a final message, of which this was the preparatory forerunner. She already knew as much as that awaited message would tell her. She knew that she would never see Comus again, and she knew now that she loved him beyond all things that the world could hold for her. It was no sudden rush of pity or compunction that clouded her judgment or gilded her recollection of him; she saw him as he was, the beautiful wayward laughing boy, with his naughtiness, his exasperating selfishness, his insurmountable folly and perverseness, his cruelty that spared not even himself, and as he was, as he always had been, she knew that he was the one thing that the Fates had willed that she should love. She did not stop to accuse or excuse herself for having sent him forth to what was to prove his death. It was, doubtless, right and reasonable that he should have gone out there, as hundreds of other men went out, in pursuit of careers; the terrible thing was that he would never come back. The old cruel hopelessness that had always chequered her pride and pleasure in his good looks and high spirits and fitfully charming ways had dealt her a last crushing blow; he was dying somewhere thousands of miles away without hope of recovery, without a word of love to comfort him, and without hope or shred of consolation she was waiting to hear of the end. The end; that last dreadful piece of news which would write 'Nevermore' across his life and hers.

The lively bustle in the streets had been a torture that she could not bear. It wanted but two days to Christmas, and the gaiety of the season, forced or genuine, rang out everywhere. Christmas shopping, with its anxious solicitude or self-centred absorption, overspread the West End and made the pavements scarcely passable at certain favoured points. Proud parents, parcel-laden and sur-

rounded by escorts of their young people, compared notes
with one another on the looks and qualities of their offspring and exchanged loud hurried confidences on the
difficulty or success which each had experienced in
getting the right presents for one and all. Shouted directions where to find this or that article at its best mingled
with salvos of Christmas good wishes. To Francesca, making her way frantically through the carnival of happiness
with that lonely deathbed in her eyes, it had seemed a
callous mockery of her pain; could not people remember
that there were crucifixions as well as joyous birthdays in
the world? Every mother that she passed happy in the
company of a fresh-looking, clean-limbed schoolboy son
sent a fresh stab at her heart, and the very shops had
their bitter memories. There was the tea-shop where he
and she had often taken tea together, or, in the days of
their estrangement, sat with their separate friends at separate tables. There were other shops where extravagantly
incurred bills had furnished material for those frequently
recurring scenes of recrimination, and the Colonial out-
fitters, where, as he had phrased it in whimsical mockery,
he had bought grave-clothes for his burying-alive. The
'oubliette'! She remembered the bitter petulant name he
had flung at his destined exile. There at least he had been
harder on himself than the Fates were pleased to will;
never, as long as Francesca lived and had a brain that
served her, would she be able to forget. That narcotic
would never be given to her. Unrelenting, unsparing memory would be with her always to remind her of those last
days of tragedy. Already her mind was dwelling on the
details of that last ghastly farewell dinner-party and recalling one by one the incidents of ill-omen that had marked
it; how they had sat down seven to table and how one
liqueur glass in the set of seven had been shivered into
fragments; how her glass had slipped from her hand as
she raised it to her lips to wish Comus a safe return; and
the strange, quiet hopelessness of Lady Veula's 'Good-bye';

she remembered now how it had chilled and frightened her at the moment.

The park was filling again with its floating population of loiterers, and Francesca's footsteps began to take a homeward direction. Something seemed to tell her that the message for which she waited had arrived and was lying there on the hall table. Her brother, who had announced his intention of visiting her early in the afternoon, would have gone by now; he knew nothing of this morning's bad news—the instinct of a wounded animal to creep away by itself had prompted her to keep her sorrow from him as long as possible. His visit did not necessitate her presence; he was bringing an Austrian friend, who was compiling a work on the Franco-Flemish school of painting, to inspect the Van der Meulen, which Henry Greech hoped might perhaps figure as an illustration in the book. They were due to arrive shortly after lunch, and Francesca had left a note of apology, pleading an urgent engagement elsewhere. As she turned to make her way across the Mall into the Green Park a gentle voice hailed her from a carriage that was just drawing up by the side-walk. Lady Caroline Benaresq had been favouring the Victoria Memorial with a long unfriendly stare.

'In primitive days,' she remarked, 'I believe it was the fashion for great chiefs and rulers to have large numbers of their relatives and dependants killed and buried with them; in these more enlightened times we have invented quite another way of making a great sovereign universally regretted. My dear Francesca,' she broke off suddenly, catching the misery that had settled in the other's eyes, 'what is the matter? Have you had bad news from out there?'

'I am waiting for very bad news,' said Francesca, and Lady Caroline knew what had happened.

'I wish I could say something; I can't.' Lady Caroline spoke in a harsh, grunting voice that few people had ever heard her use.

Francesca crossed the Mall, and the carriage drove on.

'Heaven help that poor woman,' said Lady Caroline, which was, for her, startlingly like a prayer.

As Francesca entered the hall she gave a quick look at the table; several packages, evidently an early batch of Christmas presents, were there, and two or three letters. On a salver by itself was the cablegram for which she had waited. A maid, who had evidently been on the look-out for her, brought her the salver. The servants were well aware of the dreadful thing that was happening, and there was pity on the girl's face and in her voice.

'This came for you ten minutes ago, ma'am, and Mr Greech has been here, ma'am, with another gentleman, and was sorry you weren't at home. Mr Greech said he would call again in about half an hour.'

Francesca carried the cablegram unopened into the drawing-room and sat down for a moment to think. There was no need to read it yet, for she knew what she would find written there. For a few pitiful moments Comus would seem less hopelessly lost to her if she put off the reading of that last terrible message. She rose and crossed over to the windows and pulled down the blinds, shutting out the waning December day, and then re-seated herself. Perhaps in the shadowy half-light her boy would come and sit with her again for awhile and let her look her last upon his loved face; she could never touch him again or hear his laughing petulant voice, but surely she might look on her dead. And her starving eyes saw only the hateful soulless things of bronze and silver and porcelain that she had set up and worshipped as gods; look where she would they were there around her, the cold ruling deities of the home that held no place for her dead boy. He had moved in and out among them, the warm, living, breathing thing that had been hers to love, and she had turned her eyes from that youthful comely figure to adore a few feet of painted canvas, a musty relic of a long-departed craftsman. And now he was gone from her sight, from her touch, from her hearing for ever, without even a thought to flash between them for all the dreary years that she should live, and these things of canvas and pigment and wrought metal would stay with her. They were her soul. And what shall it profit a man if he save his soul and slay his heart in torment?

On a small table by her side was Mervyn Quentock's portrait of her—the prophetic symbol of her tragedy; the rich dead harvest of unreal things that had never known life, and the bleak thrall of black unending Winter, a Winter in which things died and knew no re-awakening.

Francesca turned to the small envelope lying in her lap; very slowly she opened it and read the short message. Then she sat numb and silent for a long, long time, or perhaps only for minutes. The voice of Henry Greech in the hall, inquiring for her, called her to herself. Hurriedly she crushed the piece of paper out of sight; he would have to be told, of course, but just yet her pain seemed too dreadful to be laid bare. 'Comus is dead' was a sentence beyond her power to speak.

'I have bad news for you, Francesca, I'm sorry to say,' Henry announced. Had he heard, too?

'Henneberg has been here and looked at the picture,' he continued, seating himself by her side, 'and though he admired it immensely as a work of art, he gave me a disagreeable surprise by assuring me that it's not a genuine Van der Meulen. It's a splendid copy, but still, unfortunately, only a copy.'

Henry paused and glanced at his sister to see how she had taken the unwelcome announcement. Even in the dim light he caught some of the anguish in her eyes.

'My dear Francesca,' he said soothingly, laying his hand affectionately on her arm, 'I know that this must be a great disappointment to you, you've always set such store by this picture, but you mustn't take it too much to heart. These disagreeable discoveries come at times to most picture fanciers and owners. Why, about twenty per cent. of the alleged Old Masters in the Louvre are supposed to be wrongly attributed. And there are heaps of similar cases in this country. Lady Dovecourt was telling me the other day that they simply daren't have an expert in to examine the Van Dykes at Columbey for fear of unwelcome disclosures. And, besides, your picture is such an excellent copy that it's by no means without a value of its own. You must get over the disappointment you naturally feel, and take a philosophical view of the matter. . . .'

Francesca sat in stricken silence, crushing the folded morsel of paper tightly in her hand and wondering if the thin, cheerful voice with its pitiless, ghastly mockery of consolation would never stop.